Also by David Lagercrantz

The Girl in the Spider's Web
I Am Zlatan Ibrahimović

Fall of Man in Wilmslow

Fall of Man in Wilmslow

DAVID LAGERCRANTZ

TRANSLATED FROM THE SWEDISH BY
GEORGE GOULDING

ALFRED A. KNOPF   NEW YORK   2016

Library of Congress Cataloging-in-Publication Data
Names: Lagercrantz, David, author.
Title: The fall of man in Wilmslow : the death and life of Alan Turing : a novel / David Lagercrantz.
Other titles: Syndafall i Wilmslow. English | Death and life of Alan Turing
Description: New York : Knopf, [2016]
Identifiers: LCCN 2015037014 | ISBN 9781101946695 (hardback) | ISBN 9781101946701 (ebook)
Subjects: LCSH: Turing, Alan Mathison, 1912–1954—Fiction. | Mathematicians—Fiction. | BISAC: FICTION / Literary. | FICTION / Historical. | FICTION / Gay. | GSAFD: Mystery fiction. | Biographical fiction. | Historical fiction. | Detective and mystery stories.
Classification: LCC PT9877.22.A44 S9613 2016 | DDC 839.73/8—dc23 LC record available at http://lccn.loc.gov/2015037014

Jacket photograph by John Shipes / Getty Images
Jacket design by Peter Mendelsund

Manufactured in the United States of America
First United States Edition

For Anne, Signe, Nelly and Hjalmar

Opinion is not worth a rush;
In this altar-piece the knight,
Who grips his long spear so to push
That dragon through the fading light

W. B. Yeats, "Michael Robartes
and the Dancer"

Fall of Man in Wilmslow

1

WHEN DID HE MAKE UP his mind?

Not even he knew. But once the doubts subsided and could only be heard as distant siren calls, the dull weight in his body turned into a throbbing anxiety which he realised he had actually been missing. Life became more vivid. Even the blue buckets in the hobby workshop took on a shining new lustre and his every perception contained an entire world, a whole chain of events and thoughts, and the mere idea of trying to summarise them would be pointless, or even dishonest.

His mind teemed with a mass of thoughts and images, and even if his breathing was already painfully quick, his body quivered with an intense sensation bordering on desire, as if his decision to die had given him back his life. In front of him on a grey table, covered with stains and small holes which in some cases were burn marks but also something else, something sticky, there were a hot-plate, a couple of bottles with black liquid and then a gilt teaspoon which was to play a certain part in the story. The rain could be heard outside. It fell and fell. Never before had the heavens opened like this over a Whit Sunday weekend in England, and maybe that affected his decision.

Maybe he was just influenced by smaller things, like his hay fever and the fact that his neighbours, Mr. and Mrs. Webb, had just moved to Styal and left behind them a feeling that life was going away or was even happening in some other place to which he had not been invited. It was not like him to get worked up about things like that. But neither was it unlike him. It is true that everyday things did not affect him in the same way as the rest of us. He had a particular gift for ignoring the chattering around him. But then again he could fall under dark spells for no reason at all. Small things could affect him in big ways. Insignificant events could lead to drastic decisions or the strangest ideas.

Now he was going to leave this world taking his cue from a children's film about some funny dwarfs, which is of course ironic. There was no shortage of irony and paradox in his life. He had shortened the course of a war and thought more deeply than most about the foundation stones of intelligence, but had been placed under a probation order and forced to take a repugnant medicine. Not long before, he had been scared out of his wits by a fortune teller in Blackpool, and he had been in a state about it for a whole day.

What was he to do now?

He plugged two wires from the ceiling into a transformer on the table and put a pan with some black sludge in it on the hotplate. Then he changed into some grey-blue pyjamas, and took a red apple from a blue fruit bowl by the bookshelf. He often had an apple at the end of his day. Apples were his favourite fruit, not just because of their taste. Apples were also . . . never mind. He cut the fruit in two and went back to the hobby workshop, and then he realised. His entire being understood, and with unseeing eyes he looked out towards the garden. Isn't it odd, he thought, without really knowing what he meant. Then he remembered Ethel.

Ethel was his mother. One day Ethel will write a book about him, without having the least understanding of what he had been doing, but to be fair one can say that it was not easy. The man's life consisted of too many numbers and secrets. He was different. Besides, he was young, at least in a mother's eyes, and although he had never been regarded as a beauty and had lost his fine runner's physique since a court decision in Knutsford, he was not bad looking. Ever since he was little and could not tell right from left and thought that Christmas came at pretty much any time of year, sometimes often and sometimes seldom, like other beautiful, enjoyable days, he had thought thoughts which were totally not of their time. He became a mathematician who dedicated himself to something as prosaic as the art of engineering, an unconventional thinker who got it into his head that our intelligence is mechanical, or even computable as a long, snaking series of numbers.

But above all, and this mothers find especially hard to understand, on this day in June he no longer had the strength to go on living, and he therefore continued with his preparations, which would later be seen as strangely complicated. It was just that his concentration was disturbed. He heard something, footsteps down by the front door he thought, the crunch of gravel, and an absurd thought struck him: someone is bringing good news, perhaps from far away, from India or from another time. He gave a laugh or sobbed, hard to tell which, and he started moving, and even if he heard nothing more, nothing more than the sound of dripping against the roof, his mind stuck with the thought: *There's someone out there. A friend, worth listening to,* and as he passed the desk he thought *want to, don't want to,* like a child pulling the petals off a flower. He perceived every detail in the corridor with a vibrant precision that would have fascinated him on a better day. With a sleepwalker's steps he went into the bedroom and saw the *Observer* lying on the bedside table and the wristwatch with the black leather strap, and right next to it he laid the half apple. He thought of the moon shining behind the school building at Sherborne, and he lay down on his back on the bed. He looked composed.

2

IT RAINED THE NEXT DAY as well and young Detective Constable Leonard Corell came walking along Adlington Road. When he drew level with Brown's Lane, he took off his trilby because he felt warm despite the rain, and he thought of his bed, not the miserable bed in his flat but the one waiting at his aunt's in Knutsford, and as he did so his head sank down to his shoulder, as if he were about to fall asleep.

He did not like his job. He did not like the salary, the walking, the paperwork, or godforsaken Wilmslow where nothing ever happened. It had got to the point where even now he felt nothing but emptiness. And yet the housekeeper who called had mentioned a white froth around the dead man's mouth and a smell of poison in the house, and in the past a report like this would definitely have sparked some life in Corell. Now he just plodded along the puddles of water and the garden hedges. Behind lay the field and the railway. It was Tuesday, June 8, 1954, and he glanced down, looking for the signs with the house names on them.

When he found the address "Hollymeade," he turned in to the left and was met by a large willow which looked like a big old broom, and without needing to he stopped and retied his shoelaces. A brick pathway stretched halfway across the yard and then came to an abrupt stop, and he wondered to himself what had happened here, although obviously he realised that, whatever it was, it had nothing to do with the brick footpath. Over by the left-hand entrance stood an elderly woman.

"Are you the housekeeper?" he said, and she nodded. She was a colourless little old lady with sad eyes, and when he was younger Corell would probably have given her a warm gentle smile and put a hand on her shoulder. Now he just looked down grimly and followed her in, up a steep staircase, and there was nothing pleasant about the walk, no excitement, no policeman's curiosity, hardly even a feeling of unease, only a "Why do I have to keep on with this?"

Already in the hallway he sensed a presence, a closeness in the air, and as he went into the room he closed his eyes and, to be honest, perhaps strange given the circumstances, one or two inappropriate thoughts of a sexual nature went through his mind which there's no need to elaborate on now, other than to say that they seemed absurd even to him. When he opened his eyes, the associations lingered over the room like a surreal membrane, but they dissolved into something else when he discovered the bed, the narrow bed, and on top of it a man, dead, lying on his back.

The man was dark-haired and perhaps a little over thirty. From the corner of his mouth, white froth had run down his cheek and dried into a white powder. The eyes were half open and were set deep down under a protruding, domed forehead. Although the face did not exactly radiate tranquillity, one could sense a certain resignation in the features, and Corell should have reacted with composure. He was no stranger to death and this was no gruesome end, but he felt sick and had still not realised that it was the smell, the stench of bitter almonds hovering over the room, and he looked out through the window towards the garden and tried to return to the inappropriate thoughts, but was not successful and instead noticed half an apple on the bedside table. Corell thought, which surprised him, that he hated fruit.

He had never had anything against apples. Who does not like apples? From his breast pocket, he took out his notebook.

The man is lying in a nearly normal position, he wrote, and wondered if that formulation was good, it probably wasn't really, but on the other hand it wasn't excessively bad either. Apart from the face, the man could just as well have been asleep, and after having scribbled down a few more lines—which he was not happy with either—he examined the body. The dead man was skinny, quite fit, but with an unusually soft, almost female chest, and even though Corell was not being too meticulous he found no signs of violence, no scratches or bruises, only a slight black colouration on the fingertips and then the white froth in the corner of his mouth. He sniffed at it and understood why he felt so sick. The stench of bitter almonds penetrated his consciousness and he turned back to the hall again.

At the far end of the corridor he found something odd. In an opening where a dormer window looked out over the garden, two wires hung from the ceiling and a pan was bubbling on a table, which he approached quite slowly. Could it be dangerous? Surely not! The room was some sort of experimental workshop. There was a transformer in there and clamps for the wires, and then bottles, jam jars and pots. Probably nothing to worry about. But the stench crept in under his skin and it was with reluctance that he leaned over the pan. A revolting soup was bubbling away at the bottom and suddenly, from out of the blue, he remembered a train racing through the night long ago in his childhood and he braced himself against the table, panting. Then he rushed out and opened a window in the next room. The rain was falling. It was insane the way it fell. But for once Corell did not curse at it. He was glad that the stench and the dark memories disappeared with the wind and the water and, reasonably calm again, he looked around the house.

There was a bohemian feel to the home. The furniture was good, but had been arranged without thought or care, and there was obviously no family in residence, certainly no children. Corell picked up a notebook from the windowsill. It contained mathematical equations, and once upon a time he might have understood some of them. Now he understood nothing, no doubt also because the handwriting was hard to read and covered with ink blots, and he became irritated, or possibly envious, and grumpily he searched through a glass-fronted cupboard to the right of the window and found wine glasses, silver cutlery, a small porcelain bird and then a bottle containing something black. It was similar to the jars in the experimental workshop, but unlike them it had a label on it with the words Potassium Cyanide.

"I should have realised," he muttered and hurried into the bedroom and sniffed at the apple. It smelled the same as the bottle and the pan.

"Excuse me," he shouted. "Excuse me!"

He got no answer. He called out again and then steps were heard and a pair of fat calves stepped in over the threshold. He directed a challenging stare at the grey face with the thin, almost vanishing, lips.

"What did you say your employer's name was?"

"Dr. Alan Turing."

Corell wrote down in his notebook both the fact that the apple had smelled of bitter almonds and also the name which seemed familiar or at least, like so much else in the house, awakened dim recollections in him.

"Did he leave anything behind?"

"What do you mean?"

"A letter or something which could explain."

"Do you mean that he might . . . ?"

"I don't mean anything. I was just asking a question," he said, far too severely, and when the poor woman shook her head in fright he tried to sound a little more friendly.

"Did you know the deceased well?"

"Yes, or rather no. He was always very kind to me."

"Had he been ill?"

"This spring he did suffer from hay fever."

"Did you know that he handled poisons?"

"No, no, goodness me. But he was a scientist. Don't they . . . ?"

"It all depends," he interrupted.

"My employer was interested in many things."

"Alan Turing," he continued, as if he were thinking out loud. "Was he known for anything in particular?"

"He worked at the university."

"What did he do there?"

"He studied mathematics."

"What sort of mathematics?"

"I wouldn't know."

"I see," he muttered, and turned out into the corridor.

Alan Turing. There was something about the name, he could not quite think what, except that the bells which it rang were not good ones. Presumably the man had done something stupid. The odds on that were quite high, if Corell had come across his name at work, and he walked around the house feeling increasingly nervous. Both absent-minded and angry he collected pieces of evidence, if you could call them that, although they were at least material: the bottle of poison from the glass cupboard and then glass jars from the experimental workshop, a couple of notebooks with calculations, and also three books with the handwritten title *Dreams*.

On the ground floor he plucked on the strings of an untuned violin, and read the opening lines of *Anna Karenina*, one of the few books in the house that he recognised, apart from some by Forster, Orville, Butler and Trollope, and as so often on other occasions his thoughts fled to landscapes were they had no business to be.

The doorbell rang. It was Alec Block, his colleague. He knew Alec remarkably little considering how closely they worked together and, had he been asked to describe him, he would not have been able to come up with much more than that he was shy and timid and that he was treated badly by most people at the station, but above all that he had freckles and red hair, incredibly red hair.

"The man appears to have cooked up poison in the pan over there and dipped an apple in the mess at the bottom of the pan and taken a couple of bites," Corell explained.

"Suicide?"

"Looks like it. This bloody stench is making me feel sick. Can you see if you can find a suicide note?"

When his colleague disappeared, Corell again thought about the train racing through the night and it did not make him feel any easier. When he ran into the housekeeper on the ground floor he said:

"I'll need to talk to you in more detail soon. But in the meantime I'd like you to wait outside. We're going to seal off the house," and in a rush of kindness he grabbed an umbrella in the hall and when she protested and said that it was Dr. Turing's he snorted discreetly, that was surely showing a little too much respect. Why shouldn't she be able to borrow an umbrella? Once she accepted and disappeared out into the garden, he wandered around the house again. Up by the dead man he found a copy of the *Observer* of June 7, which showed that he had been alive yesterday, and he noted down that and some other things. As he glanced through a new booklet of mathematical calculations, he was gripped by a strange desire to add some numbers which would supplement or complete the man's equations, and as so often before, he became a not particularly focused policeman. The same could not of course be said of Block.

He reappeared looking as if he had found something extremely interesting. He had not, or at any rate he had not found a suicide note, but he had found something which seemed to point in a different direction: a couple of theatre tickets for the coming week and an invitation to the Royal Society's meeting on June 24 for which the man had written an acceptance which he had never posted, and even though Block probably realised that it was not much of a discovery, he clearly hoped that he had opened up a new lead. They were not exactly spoiled with murders in Wilmslow, but Corell immediately put the thought out of his mind.

"That doesn't mean anything."

"Why not?"

"Because we're all complicated buggers," Corell said.

"What do you mean?"

"Even someone who wants to die can plan for a future. We're all torn this way and that. In any case, this idea could have occurred to him at the last moment."

"He appears to have been a very learned man."

"Quite possibly."

"I've never seen so many books."

"I have. But there's something else about him too," Corell said.

"What?"

"I can't quite put my finger on it. I just know that something isn't quite right. Did you turn off the hotplate up there?"

Block nodded. It looked as if he wanted to add a few words but was not sure if he dared to.

"Isn't there rather a lot of poison in the house?" he said.

"Yes, there is," Corell said.

There was enough to kill an entire army company, and they discussed that for a while, without getting anywhere.

"Feels a bit like he was trying to play the alchemist. Or at least the goldsmith," Block said.

"Why do you say that?"

Block told him that he had found a gilt spoon in the experimental workshop.

"It's quite a good piece of work. Although you can still tell that he did the gilding himself. You can see it upstairs."

"Really," Corell said, trying to sound enthusiastic, but he had almost stopped listening.

He was once again lost in thought.

3

EVER SINCE THE WAR YEARS, Corell had had an idea that you could sense insanity at a distance, like a tightening in the air or even like a smell, perhaps not exactly the stench of bitter almonds, but when he stepped out into the rain again he was convinced that what he had felt in there was encapsulated madness. He could not rid himself of the feeling that he had been tainted by something unwholesome, even when the medical orderlies carried out the body at twenty to seven. A warmer wind then blew in from the east and the rain eased, without of course stopping, and he looked towards the housekeeper who sat under the light from the lamppost with her borrowed umbrella and seemed so remarkably small, like a very old child, and he now gently began to interview her.

Her name was Eliza Clayton and she lived on Mount Pleasant, Lacey Green, not far away. She had helped Dr. Turing four days a week, and there had never been a problem, she said, it had only been a little difficult to know what to do with all the papers and books. This afternoon she had got into the house with her own key. At the time, the light had been on in the bedroom. Neither the milk bottles nor the newspaper had been brought in and there were the remains of a helping of lamb chops in the kitchen. Dr. Turing's shoes stood outside the toilet, which she thought strange, and she found him lying in the bedroom, "just as you saw him," with the blanket pulled up to his chest. She touched his hands. They were cold, and she must have screamed. "I got such a shock, such a terrible shock," and since Dr. Turing did not have a telephone she used her neighbour's one, at Mrs. Gibson's, "and then you came, that's all I know."

"I wouldn't be so sure about that."

"No?"

"It's what happened before that we're interested in," he said, and then she nodded and told him that Alan Turing had had a visit from his friend, Dr. Gandy, the previous weekend, and that they'd "had a very good time" and "done some nice things," and that on the Tuesday he had invited his neighbours Mr. and Mrs. Webb to dinner, that too was "a great success," and that Mr. and Mrs. Webb had then moved house on Wednesday or Thursday.

"My employer was in a very good mood. He was happy. He joked with me."

Corell did not contradict her, nor did he bother to ask in what way Turing had joked with her. He let her talk and made only occasional notes. It felt more like a speech for the defence than a statement of evidence, and he understood very well why. Suicide was a crime, and she was bound to feel a certain responsibility. She was the housekeeper. There seemed not to have been any other woman in the home and several times she mentioned his mother, Ethel.

"Dear God, whatever shall I tell her?"

"Nothing for the time being. We'll get in touch with the relatives. Do you have someone you can talk to?"

"I'm a widow, but I can manage," she said, and after a few more questions he took his leave and wandered off in the direction of the police station on Green Lane, past the leafy thickets of the gardens in the area, and shortly afterwards the rain stopped.

It was nice to have a dry spell. There had been more rain than he could ever remember before, day in and day out, and all the time he had been wading through puddles. Doris Day could be heard from a window: "So I told a friendly star / The way that dreamers often do." The song had been high up in the charts throughout the spring, and he hummed along—he had seen the film *Calamity Jane,* which the tune came from—but the music died away with his steps and he looked up at the sky. Grey streaks of cloud were passing overhead. He ran through what he had

seen in the house and wondered what might suggest that it was not suicide, apart from the absence of a note. He could not think of much. On
the other hand, he did not manage to stay concentrated for particularly
long. He kept going off on tangents, and soon all that was left of the
case in his thoughts was a vague feeling of unease. Although the investigation should have been making his work a little more stimulating,
it kept slipping away from him, into the depths of his melancholy, and
only the mathematical calculations emerged dancing into his consciousness, like troubled flashes from another, better world.

Leonard Corell was twenty-eight years old, young enough to have
just missed the war, already old enough to have a feeling that life was
passing him by. He had come off the beat unusually soon and been
transferred to criminal investigations in Wilmslow, rather a quick pro-
motion in the police, but it was not really what he had expected of the
world, not just because of the class into which he had been born, and
now no longer belonged to, but more because he had been good at
school. Also, he had been a boy with a head for numbers.

He was born in the West End of London. But his family already suffered its first fatal blow with the crash of the financial markets in 1929.
His father, an intellectual with some connections to the Bloomsbury
Set, managed to keep up appearances for a long time, which doubled
the amount of damage done. The family's money ran through his fingers even faster while he pretended that nothing had happened. Not
only that, but with his patter and his grand façade he managed to persuade his son that their family was chosen and special and that Leonard
could become whatever he wanted. But they were empty promises. The
world and the opportunities it offered shrank and in the end the only
thing that was left was a feeling that he had been cheated. Sometimes
Corell's early years seemed to him like a country that had been taken
away from him, bit by bit. At the time it felt as if his childhood had been
a journey into solitude: the servants had to go, one by one, and by the
time that the family moved to Southport only he and his parents were
left. But his father and mother were also to disappear, each in their own
way. Everything was snatched from him. It would of course be an over-
simplification to blame his whole situation on external circumstances.
That would be just the sort of romanticising which he often indulged

in, far too sentimental a view of a life where there had still been opportunities and in which he had all too often taken refuge in self-pity and resignation. But the world had dealt him his share of knocks and tragedies and it might well have been true, as he felt, that a part of his personality had been stifled or had shrunk with the years. When he looked at his life as if from a distance, as he sometimes did, he could not reconcile it with the image he still had of himself, and there were times when he could not quite fathom that the person walking down the streets of Wilmslow was really him.

He was surprised by the haste with which the investigation was being carried out. Someone high up in the police in Chester had decided that a preliminary autopsy was to be performed that same evening and that Corell should be present. Afterwards, he had only vague memories of it. He disliked autopsies intensely and for the most part he had looked away, but that did not help much. The sound of the knife, the twilight outside, and the stench of bitter almonds rising even from the dead man's intestines were obvious enough. Dear God, what awful work! When Dr. Charles Bird muttered, "poisoning, quite clearly poisoning," Corell's mind imagined colour, a beautiful blue, as if he wanted to paint over the naked fear inside, and for a long time he hardly listened to the pathologist's questions. He answered yes or no to those that called for more elaborate replies and that was perhaps why the doctor wanted to see the house with his own eyes. Corell was to be his guide, and at first Corell thought no, under no circumstances, I've seen enough of that place. Then he changed his mind. He did not like Bird. He was a conceited man. The doctor's conversation was amiable enough, but between the lines and with a little glance here and there he made it clear that it was he who stood for education and status. He looked repulsive. The pupils of his eyes were covered by a sort of cloudy film. Corell would have preferred any other company. On the other hand, he had no wish to go home either, and it might be good to see the place again, however many demons it might awaken. So it was that he once again found himself wandering along the narrow pavement towards the house on Adlington Road. The doctor talked non-stop, as if the chance to do yet another autopsy in his free time had cheered him up.

"Did I tell you that my son's going to medical school?"

"No."

"You're not very chatty today."

"Possibly not."

"But you're interested in astrological phenomena, are you not? You must have heard that there's going to be a total eclipse of the sun."

"I think so."

"That'll be rather exciting, won't it?"

"I'm not quite sure. Isn't it over rather quickly?"

"An orgasm is also over quickly, but mankind seems to enjoy it all the same," the doctor said and gave out a dreadful laugh, which Corell ignored; he kept his counsel while the doctor elaborated on some sort of theory about the solar eclipse and the human eye, ending up at last with the fact that rationing was to come to an end in the summer:

"Time to become a glutton again."

The mere thought of Charles Bird tucking into food disgusted Corell and he looked down wordlessly at the pavement, although he may still have muttered something because the doctor countered with an incomprehensible: "Time will tell!" The willow tree appeared in the distance. It served its purpose as a marker. The houses on Adlington Road had no numbers, only their names, and as Corell walked through the gate past the shabbily painted sign saying HOLLYMEADE he looked up in the direction of the unfinished brick path, as if he anticipated that by now it would have made further progress in its journey towards the door, but the path still lay there like a track which has disappeared in a puff of smoke. Pensively he unlocked the front door with the key which the housekeeper had given him. In the hall he sniffed, alert. Something had changed. At first he could not tell what it was, but then he sensed that something was very obviously missing, and realised that the stench was no longer quite so strong, although it was of course still apparent enough.

"Cyanide, definitely cyanide," the doctor muttered like a proud connoisseur as he climbed up the stairs with eager, lanky movements.

Corell remained standing down there and wanted nothing more than to leave. The house still made him feel uncomfortable, and he tried to escape to the same inappropriate thoughts as before but was not successful, and he could feel himself sweating under his shirt. He did go upstairs, of course, and when he got into the bedroom he managed to relax. The room seemed transformed and looked almost innocent in its bohemian mess. The sheets and blankets lay crumpled over the mattress, as if someone had got up without making the bed, nothing more than that.

"And this is the apple that you were talking about?"

The doctor stood bent over the fruit, poking with a matchstick into one of the brown bite marks.

"The apple was meant to take away the bitter taste, perhaps," he said.

"I imagine that Mr. Turing wasn't exactly looking for a taste experience," said Corell.

"Man always tries to limit his suffering."

"But why an apple, in that case?"

Corell was not quite sure what he was trying to say, he just felt an irresistible urge to answer back.

"What do you mean?"

"That the apple may have some significance."

"In other words a symbolic meaning?"

"Maybe even that."

"Like something biblical? Some sort of Fall, even."

Corell muttered, without really knowing what he meant:

"Paradise Lost."

"Ah, you're referring to Milton," the doctor exclaimed in his unmistakably supercilious way, and Corell thought "Go to hell," but he said nothing.

Knowing the title of Milton's masterpiece was not much to feel proud about and the mere suspicion that he had tried to compensate for his sense of inferiority with an attempt at intellectual snobbery made him feel ashamed. He went out into the corridor and turned left into the room where he had found the bottle of potassium cyanide. A mahogany desk with green velvet over its surface stood by the window. It was a handsome piece of furniture. Ornate desks always aroused a sense of longing in him and he ran his hand over the gold-coloured keyholes. When he picked up the notebook which he had looked in earlier, and let his index finger follow an equation from left to right, the numbers seemed to whisper "come and work us out" and he remembered what a teacher at Marlborough College had once said to him:

"You're quick to understand, Leonard. Do you even count?"

"No sir, I see."

Before, he used to be able to see. Now he could only follow the first part of the equation and that annoyed him and with a puzzled expression he looked out over the room. In actual fact there was probably nothing strange or different about it, but just then the house itself seemed to him like a riddle waiting to be solved and even though he realised that most of it was a series of dead ends, of interest to a biographer or a psychologist but unimportant for the police investigation, there was something intriguing about the story as a whole.

Things appeared to have been going on everywhere, experiments, jottings, calculations, it was as if life had been cut off in mid-step. Whoever lived here may perhaps have been tired of life, but he had been deeply involved in it, and that was maybe not so strange either: we all have to live until we die. But if it was suicide, was the way in which he went about it not rather complicated? If the man had wanted to take his own life, why had he not just drunk from the bottle of poison and dropped down dead? Instead, he had set in motion an entire process with a bubbling pan, wires from the ceiling and half an apple. He may well have been trying to say something with it. Bloody Bird could take a running jump and, his curiosity awakened, Corell looked through the desk drawers.

It was of course part of his job, but he did not feel comfortable doing it, especially when he heard the doctor's footsteps out there, and when he found something in the bottom left-hand drawer which the owner seemed to have wanted to keep hidden. It was a medal, a silver cross with a red enamel ring in the middle, resting on a bed of velvet. The motto read, "For God and the Empire." What had Turing done to earn it? It was not an athletics prize, nothing of that sort. It was more distinguished, perhaps a decoration from the war, and for a moment Corell weighed the medal in his hand, and fantasised that he was the one who had been awarded it for some extraordinary achievement, but although he had often invented heroic deeds of his own in no time at all, he could not think of anything specific and, embarrassed, he put the medal back in its place. He kept on looking. Documents and objects were lying everywhere in the drawers, a pair of sand-coloured stones, a protractor, slide rules and a brown pocketknife. In the top right-hand drawer, under an envelope from the Walton Athletic Club, he found two handwritten sheets of paper, a letter to someone called Robin, and—without understanding why—he slipped them into his inside pocket and went out into the hall. He met Dr. Bird there, who was looking both unwell and solemn. The doctor was holding a small bottle of poison.

"Poisoning by deliberate ingestion of cyanide. That's my preliminary conclusion, but I expect you already worked that out," he said.

"I haven't worked anything out. I try not to reach such hasty conclusions," Corell said.

"That does, of course, do you credit. But being slow is not always a virtue. Let's leave now, I'm dying for a glass of sherry," the doctor said, and then they trooped down the stairs and out into the weak light from the street lamp.

By the gate, next to the ferns and the blackberry bushes, they parted, and Corell wandered off, hoping to run into Block, whom he had sent to knock on doors in the neighbourhood. But it was much too late. No-one was out. Only the rain could be heard, and a whimpering dog, and so he walked faster and faster, and up by Wilmslow Park he started to run, as if he could not get home fast enough.

4

CORELL DID NOT SLEEP MUCH. He was used to lying awake, but even dire nights have their degrees of hellishness and this night was among the worst, not because he lay awake but because his thoughts turned evil, and because he sat up in bed at five in the morning gasping for breath in panic, exactly as if the cyanide had penetrated his flat. But the window was open and there was nothing there but a faint smell of rain and lilac.

When he got up and saw that the sun was shining, his spirits lightened somewhat, but without becoming bright. His home was untidy, and impersonal, without a single picture on the walls, except for a murky reproduction of Gauguin's *Te Rerioa*. The only things which gave the flat any character at all were a brown leather sofa in the middle of the room and a white repaired Queen Anne chair. On the bedside table stood a new radio, a Philips Sirius. He usually listened to the B.B.C. news at seven or eight, while making tea and frying bread, tomatoes and black pudding. Today, though, he did not bother with breakfast and headed out immediately. There were puddles of water on the pavements and in the streets. The trees and bushes seemed heavy with the rain, and for a long time he walked the wrong way up towards the River Bollin, as far as Hollies Farm where Gregory, the retarded labourer, waved to him, and he arrived late at the police station, still gloomy, but nevertheless with a feeling that things would probably be all right.

The police station was in a red-brick house on Green Lane with a dreary yard, and even though it was well situated right next to the main street, Manchester airport was only a few miles away, and they all suffered from its noise. Corell stepped in and walked past the reception with its jumble of forms and the telephone operator sitting by the old Dover switchboard. He exchanged a quick greeting with the station police sergeant and climbed the stairs to the small criminal section, where Sandford was the boss and Corell and three other detective constables worked. There were a number of posters of wanted and missing persons on the walls and then a lot of unnecessary information about illnesses and parasites, among other things some new rubbish about a beetle which spread disease in potatoes. Kenny Anderson was sitting by his desk, partly hidden by the coat-stand, and he imagined Gladwin smoking his pipe over by the archive room.

"At last the bloody rain has stopped."

"I'll believe it when I see it," Corell said, with a look that was intended to mark the end of the conversation.

Kenny Anderson was about fifteen years older than Corell and looked pretty ill-used by life and, although most of the time he behaved well enough, he had a tendency to act unreasonably which irked Corell, so that from time to time he needed space for himself, especially in the mornings. For some time now Corell had been suffering from a certain sluggishness, a difficulty in getting to grips with things, and he always sat for a while with the *Manchester Guardian* and the *Wilmslow Express* before he got down to some real work.

There was not a single word about the death, which was perhaps to be expected. The journalists would hardly yet have had time to get the news in. But there was a lot about the rain, including floods in Hammersmith and Stapenhill, and then about a cricket match in Leeds which 42,000 people had paid to watch and the organisers had been forced to cancel. On the next page he read about the end of rationing, which the pathologist had talked about. From July 4, the English were to be allowed to buy even meat and butter without limit, not that it would make much of a difference to him. With his £670 a year he could not afford to splash out money anyway, and almost angrily he flicked through to the sports pages. An Australian called Landy had tried to beat Bannister's fantastic new record for the mile in Stockholm the day before, and Corell drifted off into daydreams. He became vaguely aware that Kenny Anderson was saying something, and made a real effort not to listen.

"Anderson calling Corell."

"What do you want?"

He turned around reluctantly and was hit by a wave of alcohol, tobacco and peppermint-laden breath.

"I heard that bum bandit died."

"Who?"

"Didn't you go to his house yesterday?"

"What are you talking about?"

"The man on Adlington Road."

"Yes, that's right," Corell said. "I was there." A whole stream of loose associations and thoughts ran through his mind.

"Suicide?"

"Looks like it."

"How did he do it?"

"He'd cooked up a whole pan full of potassium cyanide. It smelled awful."

"He probably couldn't stand the shame. After all, it was a pretty awkward story, wasn't it?"

"Yes," Corell said, as if he knew what he was talking about. "Pretty awkward all right!"

"Can you believe that he just admitted everything?"

"I haven't read up on it much yet. What do you know?" he said, and still had only a rather vague idea of what Kenny was talking about, but he did now understand why the dead man's name had seemed familiar.

He was a convicted homosexual, one of quite a few recent cases. When Corell first started working in the B division in Manchester immediately after the war, no-one had bothered much about them, and only after the spy scandal in 1951 when Burgess, that hopeless queer, and the other one—Corell could not remember his name—had escaped to the Soviet Union did they start to pursue homosexuals more systematically. It had suddenly become important, maybe for patriotic reasons.

"There's not an awful lot to read," Kenny said.

"What do you mean?"

"Just a pederast who messed things up. A pretty typical story. Doesn't seem to have been particularly bright."

"He was a mathematician."

"Well that doesn't mean a damn thing."

"He seems to have got some kind of medal for what he did in the war."

"Nearly everyone got a bloody medal."

"Did you?"

"Get lost!"

"Do you know the story?"

"Not in any detail," Kenny said in his bleating Midlands accent, a bit put out. But he still pulled up his chair right next to Corell, his face eager. His chapped lips parted as they always did when he thought that he had something entertaining to say and Corell discreetly turned his head away to avoid the breath.

"It started when someone broke into the house on Adlington Road," Anderson said. "A pretty bloody unsuccessful effort. All they took was a load of rubbish, some fishing knife and a half-empty bottle, that sort of stuff. Not much to talk about. But the bum bandit thought that laws were laws and so he came to us."

"Who fielded the report?"

"Brown, I think, according to the roster. The queer seemed to think that he knew who the burglar was. He suspected that his lover was involved, some penniless young chap he'd picked up on the Oxford Road."

"A criminal type?"

"A chancer selling himself under the bridge. But the bum bandit, whatever his name was—"

"Alan Turing," Corell interjected.

"Turing was dim enough to tell us what he suspected. Well, of course he didn't say everything. He didn't say that the young man was his little queer friend. Instead he concocted some story which was so transparent that our colleagues in Manchester saw straight through it."

"What happened?"

"Our colleagues ignored the burglary of course. They concentrated on getting Turing and like the bloody fool that he was he confessed at once. Must have been a bit disappointing," Kenny said with a lopsided smile.

"What do you mean?"

"To come to us thinking he was going to get help in catching some burglars and then ending up in jail himself."

"Did he go to jail?"

"Well they certainly nailed him good and proper, and since then he hasn't been heard of much, not until now that is. He probably went into hiding up at Dean Row, in shame."

"Yesterday I got the feeling that he'd been crazy in some way."

"Doesn't surprise me. Certainly bloody sick."

"I wonder," Corell said slowly.

"You just said that he was crazy."

"Well . . ."

He realised that he was contradicting himself. Ever since his years at Marlborough College he had avoided any thought of homosexuals, and might well have described the dead man as sick himself, but he had such a low opinion of Anderson that he simply did not like agreeing with him, and perhaps he was also offended. He did not think that his colleague had any right to express an opinion on Turing's state of mind. Kenny had not been up there in the house and seen the mathematician lying on his back in his pyjamas and felt the sharp stench of bitter almonds in his nose. Besides, he was hopelessly simplistic when it came to defining someone's character. He made everything sound coarse and basic, and whatever you might say about the dead man, his equations went far beyond Kenny's level of comprehension.

"Are you saying that a good criminal investigator shouldn't jump to conclusions?"

"Something like that."

"I thought we were just chatting."

"Indeed we were," Corell admitted. "So this Turing had dealings with criminals?"

"Isn't that sort of a prerequisite for being a practising homosexual?"

"Obviously. I was just thinking . . ."

"What?"

"That it could be something to look into."

"Absolutely. No-one will be happier than me if this turns out to be an exciting murder, with a contract put out by the underworld, but there's no doubt that the man had reason to end his life. There probably wasn't a single person around him who didn't know what he'd done. People must have been gossiping away behind his back all day long."

"I'll bet."

"Did I say that Ross needs to talk to you?"

"What does he want?"

"What does he usually want? To mess you about in one way or another!"

"He's such an idiot," Corell said quietly.

"A bit the worse for wear, are we?"

Corell did not answer, and not just because he was sick and tired of all the banter and of the conversation itself. He had no idea. He was so tired that he did not even know what was wrong with him, and it took him a while to realise that he had not drunk a drop yesterday, and with a show of resolve he put the morning papers to one side and got to his feet to go and fetch what they had on Turing. He did not get very far. Alec Block came through the door, although it was not exactly an energetic entrance. Anderson sighed deeply, not necessarily at Block. It might have been aimed at life in general, but it deflated Alec and made him look hurt, and Corell felt the need to say a few kind words. But he simply could not manage it and without even wishing Alec good morning he said:

"What did you get hold of yesterday?"

"There's a report on your desk. You weren't here this morning."

"Very good. I haven't seen it, what does it say?"

Block started to tell him and it was clear from his movements and his eyes that he had something which he thought was exciting. Although Block did have a tendency to get worked up about very little, this time he had made Corell curious to hear more and it therefore irritated him that he began with a lot of irrelevant information, such as the fact that Mr. Turing had not had contact with any of his neighbours other than Mr. and Mrs. Webb from the semi-detached house next door, and that the Webbs had just moved and that it had not been possible to contact them, and that Mr. Turing seemingly could not have cared less about his appearance. The neighbours described him as slovenly and unkempt, and as a man who disliked small talk. Somebody said that he was liable to walk off in the middle of a sentence if he found the conversation boring, another mentioned that he had recently exchanged his motorised bicycle for a lady's one, which prompted Alec—who must also have heard about the dead man's inclinations—to venture a quip about old pansies, but Corell ignored the joke, and Block seemed almost grateful for that.

"Mr. Turing was working on a new machine at Manchester University. But I'm sure you already knew that."

"Yes, I did," Corell lied. "Anything else?"

"I asked if he had any enemies."

"And what did people say?"

"That he did not, so far as they knew, even though one woman, a Mrs. Rendell, suggested that his talk about machines had perhaps annoyed someone."

"What had he said about machines?"

Block was not entirely sure about that. Something about their eventually being able to think, something which the woman said was at odds with the Christian view of things, just like his sexual inclinations.

"Christians after all think that only man has a soul," Block said, by way of clarification.

"So Turing thought that machines would be able to think?"

"That's what the woman said. But perhaps Mr. Turing only meant it figuratively speaking."

"Or else he really was crazy," Corell said.

"He could have been that. But he was apparently a university professor and had a doctorate from the U.S.A."

"That doesn't stop you from going mad though."

"I suppose so," Block said, fidgeting.

"You seem to have something more."

He did. But he did not want to make too much of it. Or maybe he did. There was a Mrs. Hanna Goldman, who lived across the street from Turing, he said. For what it was worth, Hanna Goldman looked rather like a heavily made-up scarecrow. She smelled of perfume and alcohol and what she said was somewhat muddled, Alec told him honestly, even though it obviously weakened what he was trying to say. The neighbours thought that she was dotty, but Block was not quite so sure. Mrs. Goldman had told him quite categorically about a visit a few years earlier from a "real gentleman" with a Scottish accent who worked for the government.

"For the government?"

"Well, something like that, and this man wanted to have the use of her house to keep watch over Turing."

"Why?"

"If I understood correctly, to stop Mr. Turing from having any more homosexual relationships."

"Why should the government care about that?"

"I think that Mr. Turing was someone important."

"Did she let the visitor use her house?"

"No. She didn't co-operate with the authorities, she said."

"For someone who doesn't co-operate, she seems rather chatty."

"I suppose so."

"There's quite a lot of *I suppose so* about this story, Alec."

"I thought that I should tell you, even so."

"Of course! One never knows. Have you got hold of the family?"

Block had talked to a brother, a lawyer from Guildford who was on his way here. They had not got hold of the mother, Sara Ethel. She was travelling in Italy. The brother was going to try to reach her, and Corell thought that sounded like good news. He did not like talking to mothers who had lost their sons, and after that he asked Block, even though it was of course cheeky to do so—he and Block had the same rank—to fetch everything they had on Turing, insofar as the material was not now in Manchester.

"I have to make a few calls," he explained.

There was in fact no-one for him to call, or if there was then he could not be bothered to do so, and instead he sat down again and looked at his heaps of paper. He remembered his father's desk from long ago during his childhood and all the wonderful things which used to lie on it, leather-bound books, postcards from faraway places, leather diaries and then the tarnished iron keys to the mahogany drawers with their engraved laurel wreaths. Often Leonard had hammered away rhythmically and randomly at the typewriter on the desk, as if it were a musical instrument rather than some working tool, and he had run his hands over the table and the books and smelled a scent of the future and of all the knowledge that he was going to acquire.

Here at the police station there was nothing of that. Here everything was cheap, sad and badly written, and you were not tempted to read anything. It was just rubbish, glimpses of unhappy lives. There was a littering case to which Inspector Richard Ross was giving particular priority and Corell could not understand why the C.I.D. should have to deal with it. Someone had thrown a number of empty bottles into the yard outside, a matter of singular unimportance, but because it had happened right next to the police station Ross saw it as a "challenge to the forces of law and order" and had drawn some Sherlock Holmes–like conclusions about the perpetrator not being a down-and-out since the rubbish included Haig whisky bottles, the ones with the advertising slogan "Don't be vague, ask for Haig," and no normal drunk would be able to afford that, according to Ross. Corell could not give a tuppenny damn about the littering, regardless of the vandal's standing, and he did not intend to lift a finger to help in the case, other than to turn over some papers for appearances' sake. He was good at pretending to work while his mind was exploring secret realms, which branched out into a myriad of parallel dream worlds. Alec emerged again.

"Turns out we have a whole lot on Turing."

"Excellent! Thank you!"

Corell took the material, irritated at first to have been disturbed, then curious in spite of himself; there was something titillating about these contacts with criminals in Manchester. Even so, he did not start work at once. He needed to take a run-up at it and he looked up at Block, who seemed very tired and whose freckles appeared to have paled, but probably it was an optical illusion, an effect of the sharp and unhealthy light over the desk, and to be on the safe side, and also to make sure that Alec would leave him in peace, he thanked Block once more.

Then he looked through the window towards the yard and the fire station and only after that did he start to read. For a long time his eyes strayed up and down and he let Kenny's occasional comments and stupid remarks distract him, but gradually he was caught up by the story.

Not so much for the sake of the story itself, but because it seemed to point towards Corell's own life, and therefore typically enough he was fascinated most of all by something which had nothing to do with his investigation—a few lines about a paradox which was said to have caused a crisis in the world of mathematics—and he sank into profound concentration.

5

HE STARTED WITH FRIGHT in his chair.

Inspector Richard Ross's grey and disapproving look darted back and forth over him and whatever he saw was not to Corell's advantage. Ross was almost bald and though he was neither tall nor large he gave off a bearlike impression. It seemed odd to think that he was an avid butterfly collector, and that he had been seen to hug his fourteen-year-old daughter with no little tenderness on a couple of occasions. Moreover, something in Ross's appearance gave the observer the unavoidable impression that he had suffered a great injustice, and it was said that he had once kicked to death a dog which bit him in the leg, and while that was perhaps not altogether true, it was telling that the story had spread. In addition, Ross had a fondness for hats which were too small for him and he was known for being malicious.

"Where've you been?" he snapped.

"I've been working."

"Is that so? Homework in that case, I suppose. Some people do take liberties. You're about to have a distinguished visitor."

"Who's that?"

"Chief Superintendent Hamersley. Since Sandford is on holiday, you'll have to see him. So I hope you'll be on your best behaviour. He's come all this way to talk to you."

"How come?"

"You may well ask. But it's about this dead chap. The case is apparently sensitive. I hope to God that you've already read up on it. And see to it that you tidy up your desk. How on earth can you put up with it like that? And for God's sake make it quick. The Chief Superintendent will be here any moment."

"Yes, of course, I'll do it right away," Corell answered in a servile tone which offended him as much as Ross's rebuke.

The news that Hamersley was on his way had knocked him off balance, and he realised how much he would have liked to have continued reading. He had found peace and refuge in the old investigation, and even if he had not understood much more than that the dead man was a convicted homosexual, and an unusually inept criminal, he longed to be able to turn over in his mind those sentences about the paradox and the crisis in mathematics, which admittedly sounded irrational but which had fired his imagination and left him with a feeling of something unexplored and obscure. What he least of all wanted was to meet Hamersley.

Charles Hamersley was not just a superior. He was a big beast. He was one of the most senior bosses of the Cheshire district and was stationed at the headquarters on Foregate Street in Chester. Corell had met him two or three times before and always come to feel ill at ease. Charles Hamersley was not malicious like Ross. He had a gentle, fatherly smile and no-one would have been surprised if he had lavished affection on his daughters, but he upset Corell simply through his benevolence, which was neither pitiful nor contemptuous, but which left Corell feeling belittled and cast him back in time. In Hamersley's presence he became again a schoolboy, and never managed to utter any of the clever remarks that came to him and that he so wanted to voice.

"So young sir is to have the honour of speaking to the Chief Superintendent," Anderson said, and Corell sighed as if he found it tiresome, but in the next moment he stood to attention.

A familiar voice was heard out there, and now Charles Hamersley stepped in and said his greetings right and left. There was something different about him and it took Corell a while to work out what it was. The beard had gone and the spectacles were new and extravagant and represented a complete change of style from the old Hamersley. The Chief Superintendent was over sixty, lean and tall with thin lips and a distinguished appearance, and seemed to have sprung from another century than his new glasses, which were probably imported from the U.S.A. The Chief Superintendent admired the Americans. He was an old-fashioned man who wanted to be modern, but the new simply looked ridiculous on him. Modern times suited him as badly as his spectacles.

"How are things here, then?"

"Very well, sir," Corell lied. "And you, sir?"

"I'm extremely well, thank you! But these are busy times. We've got a delicate matter on our hands."

"So I understand, sir."

Corell thought of Mrs. Goldman and the haste with which the autopsy had been ordered last night.

"Dr. Turing worked for the Foreign Office," Hamersley continued.

"On what?"

"I don't honestly know. Those buggers are so secretive. But we've got orders to speed up the investigation. People from the Foreign Office will search the house. They're bound to get in touch with you."

"People from the Secret Service?"

"Again, I don't know," said Hamersley, looking pleased with himself, as if he knew perfectly well whether they were from the Secret Service or not, and this annoyed Corell.

He tried to think of something clever to say. He could not come up with anything.

"I assume that you know about his background?"

"He was a homosexual," Corell said without really knowing what he was expecting, perhaps a nod, a short confirmation, or a brusque dismissal that this was not at all what Hamersley had been driving at, but the Chief Superintendent broke into an engaging smile. He even pulled up a chair and sat down with a soft movement which, given his age, seemed surprisingly graceful, almost feminine.

"Exactly, exactly," he said, and then started to speak, or rather preach, and oddly enough—as an altogether too dramatic introduction to a rather banal story—he took as his starting point the Soviet atom bombs, the first one had been tested five years earlier, in 1949, and as recently as August the previous year the Russians had detonated something even worse, a hydrogen bomb, and "many had of course wondered how the Russians had managed to produce the bomb so quickly. Now we know," Charles Hamersley said.

"We do?"

"Through espionage! The Soviets have spies everywhere, both among their own people and among ours."

"They had that man Fuchs."

"He wasn't the only one. Don't forget the Rosenbergs. People think there may be hundreds. Hundreds, Corell."

"Is that so, sir?"

"And in that kind of situation it's of course of the utmost importance to find out which sort of person is capable of betraying his country. Who do you think that is most likely to be?"

"The communists?" Corell ventured.

"You're right, of course. The communists are the big threat, not just those who are already convinced, but also those who are flirting with these doctrines or who mix in those circles, like Oppenheimer himself, who learnt his lesson only the other week. In the U.S.A. there's an enterprising senator, I'm sure you've heard of him, you do like to keep up with what's going on, don't you? I'm talking about Joseph McCarthy, of course . . . yes, I know that he too now has his critics, but believe me, he's a force who's needed, and what not many know, maybe not you either, Corell, is that McCarthy and his allies are keeping an eye not only on the communists but also on the homosexuals, especially those who work in the civil service or who have had access to government secrets. Do you know why?"

Corell would have preferred not to answer, and not only because he was afraid of making a fool of himself. Secretly, and much against his will, he had been flattered by Hamersley's compliments and wanted to stay in his good books. He said:

"Because of the risk of blackmail."

"Absolutely, of course, you're right again, you have a quick mind. Homosexuals are ideal blackmail victims. They'll do almost anything to stop their leanings from being exposed. Our friends at the F.B.I. have also noticed that the Russians specifically try to recruit queers. But that's not the whole truth, or even the main explanation. Not at all, no, the important point is that those who get themselves involved in perverted activities lack character. They don't have enough moral fibre to be able to occupy a responsible position. I'm not saying this just like that or guessing at it, there's an abundance of evidence. You know, the Americans have a new, very professional organisation . . . you've perhaps heard of it. It was created to avoid a new Pearl Harbor. It's called the C.I.A. and they have carefully analysed perverts, and come to the conclusion that they can't be trusted. In government service they represent a security risk and actually, between us, Corell, the logic is very simple. When our characters are undermined, then we're vulnerable, isn't that the case? Then the temptations pile up. If one has sunk so low as to sleep with another man, then one can do other awful things as well. A man who can make love with another man can also make love with the enemy, as someone has apparently rather cleverly put it."

"I understand," Corell said.

"Of course you do. You're one of our talents, even if I've heard that you've been a bit down recently. But I'm sure we'll get that out of you. There's far too much important stuff to be done to be going round with a hangdog face, not least cleaning up that dreadful swamp of buggery. You understand, only in recent years have people realised how serious the situation is. The Americans were ahead of us, even there, yes, it's sad about old England. Egypt, Iran, India, we're losing everything and maybe it's because—well, what do I know—because we've lost control, not just of the world but also of our own morals. But in the U.S.A. people are prepared to look the truth in the eye. They have a zoologist, a man by the name of Kinsey or Kensey, I can't really remember which. He's done research into mankind's perversions and come to the conclusion that homosexuality is incredibly common, this is simple science, his data can't be ignored and still . . . many here have tried to reject it all. Dismissed homosexuality as an American vulgarity. But you and I, Corell, we've both of us been to boarding school, haven't we?"

Corell nodded reluctantly, it was a long time since he had taken pride in his background, or even referred to it in conversation. His past remained mostly an embarrassment, a distant landscape which shone in his memory as a broken promise.

"So you and I have known about this filth," Hamersley continued. "But our leaders needed a real alarm call. You know what I'm referring to, the scandal with Burgess and Maclean. It actually defies belief that they were able to escape! They had been under suspicion for a long time, after all. The cheeky buggers are probably eating caviar and drinking vodka in Moscow right now and even if the Russians are insisting that they only defected for ideological reasons there's no doubt that they're traitors of the worst sort and of course we know who's the most guilty of the two!"

"Do we?"

"Burgess, of course, an appalling libertine, boozer, incurable bum boy, it's obvious that he seduced and ruined Maclean and this is something that we have to think about, Corell. Homosexuals affect everything around them. They bring about the downfall of others. But the whole story did have the advantage of opening our eyes and in the government there is at least one strong figure, the Home Secretary Sir David Maxwell Fyfe . . . Well, I'll not hear an ill word said about Churchill, but between you and me, he's starting to get old. Sir David on the other hand . . . I've never had the pleasure of meeting him, but he gets things done. He's been influenced by the Americans and got us going in the police force, and to be honest I've played a modest part in that myself. If you look at the statistics, Corell, not least here in Cheshire, you'll see . . . I've actually got the figures here . . . let's see now . . . in 1951, the year when Burgess and Maclean disappeared, we convicted thirteen men for homosexual offences. Before then it was even fewer. Last year, the number was fifty-nine. Not bad, don't you think?"

"Not bad at all!"

"Not since the days of Oscar Wilde have we got to grips with the problem with such force and you shouldn't think that the privileged classes are left out of this, or protected. Quite the opposite, perversion is probably especially common among the upper classes. At Cambridge and Oxford people say it's the height of fashion. Can you imagine what that means for the future of England?"

Corell threw up his arms.

"It means that we have to do something about it before it's too late. You presumably read about Lord Montagu?"

"Of course," Corell lied.

"He was even arrested twice for the crime, and that's an important signal. Old offences can be brought up as well. No practising homosexual should feel safe. Actually even the press have woken up. *Sunday Pictorial*—not a paper I normally read—but they've investigated this.

'Evil Men,' they called their series, perhaps a little bit exaggerated, but still . . . the subject can now be openly discussed. A Methodist minister wrote that the problem is worse in Manchester than anywhere else. The conspiracy of silence has been broken."

"The conspiracy . . . ?"

"Many people have known, of course, but stuck their heads in the sand. Pretended that the filth doesn't exist. But that won't do anymore. These are dangerous times, Corell. The world can be blown to pieces. We must be able to rely on our own people."

"Is anyone suggesting that Mr. Turing was also co-operating with the Russians?"

Corell bit his tongue, he did not want to come across as naive.

"I don't judge anyone without hearing them," Hamersley said. "But I have my antennae, and the Foreign Office is worried, I could hear that over the telephone this morning. A suicide . . . because that's presumably what it is?"

"There's a lot to suggest that."

"A suicide always raises suspicions, doesn't it? Was he trying to escape from something? Were there secrets he couldn't live with? All that sort of stuff."

"I understand."

"And then there's more, there's pure psychology, and also knowledge about how the Russians operate. They may be communists, but they're not stupid, not in the least bit. They know that someone who's developed a taste for one extreme will willingly try another. They certainly have no doubts about where to aim their blows. In the end it's all about character! Character, Corell!"

Corell did not feel that his own character was particularly strong or robust, but he could not help feeling inspired by the Chief Superintendent's words. They felt like a breath of fresh air from the big wide world, something he had not been spoiled with all that often, and even if he once again felt that his own role in it all was insignificant and awkward, there was a new eagerness in him which broke through his boredom. "Was Mr. Turing privy to any sensitive secrets?" he said.

"Well now, let's not rush ahead of ourselves," Hamersley answered. "The man has just departed our world, and you and I, Corell, our job is humbly to take care of our small part of the story, but of course, if one is an intelligent person, as I flatter myself to be, then one can put two and two together: people from the Foreign Office have got in touch and seem to be troubled, and this Turing, he was some sort of scientist, wasn't he?"

"He was a mathematician."

"I see, I see. I'm not especially gifted in that direction, myself. I've never understood any of it, to be honest. But isn't it precisely the mathematicians and physicists who are the key figures in the armaments industry these days? Perhaps Turing helped with producing our bomb? Not that I know. Well, it's perhaps wrong of me to speculate away like that. But you're probably right. He must have known something. And it isn't a nice thought that Mr. Turing's secrets, whatever they might have been, have got mixed up with Oxford Road, with all the riff-raff there. What wouldn't a man be capable of saying when under the influence of such shameful passions?"

"Who knows?"

"Incidentally, wasn't Turing subject to some sort of blackmail when he was had up a couple of years ago?"

"There was some of that. And it was certainly no coincidence that they broke into his house."

"Wasn't it?"

"The thieves knew about his inclinations, so they probably didn't think that he would dare to report the break-in. They were no doubt assuming that he would have no legal means to help him," Corell said, and for some reason Hamersley did not seem to like what he had said.

The Chief Superintendent pulled a face and then asked, in a more matter-of-fact, restrained tone, what they had seen in the house on Adlington Road. But when Corell told him, Hamersley did not really seem to be listening, and so Corell did not bother to mention the letter which he had found or even the medal. He did, however, rather timidly enquire about what Mrs. Goldman had told Block about someone "who worked for the government" having kept an eye on Turing.

"What . . . no," Hamersley muttered. "I haven't heard anything about that. But it wouldn't surprise me, not at all. These are serious matters, Corell."

"She didn't seem completely reliable."

"Did she not? Goldman, you said. Jewish, of course. Well, you never know. But wait . . . I wonder if it wasn't our colleagues from Manchester who went to see her, you could say that they also work for the government. They were in this neighbourhood a few years ago."

"What were they doing?"

"If I remember right, Dr. Turing was expecting a visit from a homosexual from some Nordic country. My guess is that they wanted to prevent any such encounter."

"Doesn't that sound a bit strange?" Corell ventured.

"What do you mean?"

"Surely we don't guard people who risk reoffending like that, do we?"

"Maybe not, Corell. Maybe not. But we ought to. Look on it as a moral lesson. We cannot be careful enough when it comes to the threat of homosexuality. Besides, you and I have reached the conclusion that our mathematician must have been sitting on secret information, haven't we, which makes it even more important to keep an eye on him. But where had we got to?"

"I'm not sure."

"Well, it doesn't matter. I hope that you'll take care of this tidily and discreetly and report directly to me. You see, some people, our friend Ross for one, think that you're too young to look after this matter, but me, I trust you, and to be honest, I'm glad I've got a man with your background on the case now that the Foreign Office is involved. I'm sure they'll get in touch with you and I need hardly emphasise how important it is that you co-operate in every way."

"Of course."

"Well then!"

They both got to their feet, and Corell should probably have said something edifying and saluted. Salutes were not uncommon in the force, not for big beasts like Hamersley. Even so, Corell just stood there, and though he was rather desperate to get rid of the Chief Superintendent and be left alone with his thoughts, he could not manage so much as a nod. In the end it was Hamersley who broke the silence.

"Again, it's been a pleasure talking to you," he said and disappeared off while Corell remained standing by his desk, looking down at his hands, his long fine hands which at that moment he felt did not belong here in the police station.

Dull thuds could be heard from down in the cells, as if someone were throwing themselves against the walls, and Corell looked up at the ceiling which had once been painted white but had long since turned grey or rather almost black from the cigarette smoke. *He must have been privy to some secret information.* Corell was not exactly pleased about the visit, but the case had without doubt become more interesting. Was there an opportunity here for him to put his best foot forward? He thought so, and with some enthusiasm he read on about the mathematician's past offences. Exactly as before he concluded that the report was written in rather conventional terms, but still with many digressions and dead ends which made it seem as if it were something more than just the usual bureaucracy, and although it did not exactly make Corell start to feel more positive about Alan Turing, it did trigger something in him. He was reminded of his own dreams from his school years, not just those about reading mathematics at university, which seemed reasonable at the time, but also the more extravagant ones that he would invent something revolutionary and big which would change the world, and for the first time in years he picked up his notebook and compiled a short sequence of numbers. It felt like a return to something long forgotten.

6

ALAN MATHISON TURING WAS BORN on June 23, 1912, in Paddington, London, which made him older than Corell had thought. He would have turned forty-two in two weeks' time. He had studied at King's College, Cambridge, and then in some form or other at Princeton, New Jersey, and had a doctorate, although it was not clear in which subject, and after the war he had ended up in Manchester where he became involved in a major project to design a new machine, exactly as Block had said. In purely biographical terms, that left many questions unanswered, but it was not for the sake of his career that Alan Turing had ended up in the police's records.

It was because of Oxford Road, or to be more exact because of the point under the railway bridge where it becomes Oxford Street, not far from the refugee centre with its clock tower and the two cinemas. This was the neighbourhood where the homosexuals gathered, Corell did not know why, but they presumably had to congregate somewhere, and with a bit of luck, good or bad, he and Turing might have bumped into each other before. During his early years in the force, when he was in B division in Manchester, Corell had often walked in the area, past the smell of piss under the bridge and the graffiti on the red–black brickwork.

For several of his colleagues, the queers represented a source of additional income, perhaps not altogether legal, but regarded as legitimate enough in the immediate post-war years when the force was seething with discontent, and Corell did not condemn anyone for it, even though he himself never accepted a penny, both for moral reasons and because of the timidity and lack of pushiness he had suffered from since his school years. Oxford Road was no place for Cambridge-educated people, or anyone else for that matter. It was a place where men went off into the shelter of the urinals to commit dreadful acts of indecency. The mere thought of it made Corell feel sick and the realisation that Alan Turing had been a regular visitor to the area certainly did not make him feel any better about it. In Corell's experience, investigations into homosexual offences almost always yielded scant information, and it was not easy to secure convictions. Those involved had every reason to keep quiet, and where witnesses could be found they were rarely inclined to talk, but in this case there was a surprising amount of material. Corell could therefore read that Alan Turing had stood staring at a film poster up by the arcade in the area, or rather had pretended to be doing so while looking out for men, one afternoon in December 1951. The queers probably used to engage in this type of introductory charade, Corell thought, but one does not usually get to hear about it. In this case, however, there was a five-page confession in which Turing spoke openly and did not seem in any way to see his homosexuality as a problem. If there were any moral or legal difficulties, they were on an altogether different plane, he felt, and this incensed Corell. Could not the man at least have the decency to feel ashamed? Brazenly matter-of-fact he described how, in the throng on Oxford Road, he had caught sight of a young man by the name of Arnold Murray.

"Where are you going?" Turing had asked.

"Nowhere."

"Me too."

They had gone to the station café over the road and, like so many others who met up in the area, they were an odd couple. Both the high and the low met on the Oxford Road, Corell had known that for a long time. It was presumably much the same as in any ordinary red-light district. Those with money paid. Those without took it. While Turing worked at the university and had diplomas and titles and maybe also a medal from the war, Murray was nineteen years old, poor and miserable. His father was a bricklayer and a drunk. According to the file, his best years were at the local catchment area school where he had ended up during the war, but there was no question of further education for a young man with his background. The result was crime and unemployment, and it was plain to Corell that the boy was longing for recognition from above. He wanted to be noticed and seemed to think, assuming that he was not playing the innocent or simply following his lawyer's instructions, that homosexuality was part of the world of the cultivated. "Isn't that what they do at Cambridge and Oxford?" he asked when he was being questioned.

It would have been easy for him to have been duped by a man like Alan Turing, especially since Murray had himself once dreamed of becoming a scientist, and since Turing had already claimed at an early stage that he was building "an electronic brain." *A brain.* Surely that could not be even the slightest bit true? No, the longer Corell thought about it, the cheekier he thought it was, but the words must have impressed a poor uneducated nobody from the slums, however much of a lie it was. Perhaps it was all part of the mathematician's line about machines which would be capable of thought. It could just have been loose talk or a figure of speech, or simply pure madness—Corell remembered the feeling of lunacy in the house—but more likely, he thought, it was bragging which was ill-intentioned and meant to seduce, and sure enough Turing invited the boy out to his house in Wilmslow the following weekend.

Murray never showed up, not on that occasion. Instead they saw each other the following month, in January 1952, again on Oxford Road, and this time Turing's invitation was more direct and the offence was committed for the first time, gross indecency as it was called under section 11 of the Criminal Law Amendment Act 1885, a famous section as Corell knew, not least because it had once brought down Oscar Wilde. You could probably call the whole thing an ordinary love story. Turing gave the boy presents and described him in his confession with a few tender words as "a lost sheep" and "a quick-witted man with a thirst for knowledge and a good sense of humour." But there were quite a few sordid aspects to it as well.

On January 12 the mathematician invited Murray to dinner, which was clearly a major event for him. Turing had a housekeeper. "Suddenly I found myself amongst the gentry and not with the staff," Murray said and it seemed to intoxicate him: "Our relationship was one of equals." After dinner they drank wine on the drawing room carpet and Murray recounted a nightmare which oddly enough was recorded in the minutes of the police interview. Although Corell had heard that dreams can reveal something of a person's personality and passions—he knew a little bit about Freud—he doubted that his colleagues in Manchester would attempt this sort of analysis. On the other hand, attention to detail can be a virtue, and no-one can know beforehand which particulars will prove to be relevant in the end, and this dream was certainly pretty awful. In it, Murray was lying on a completely featureless surface, in a totally empty space, with no reference in time or space. He was enveloped by a sound which grew louder and more unbearable, and when Turing asked about the noise, Murray could only say that it was a terrible sound which was on the verge of completely taking him over and perhaps everything else as well.

Turing appeared to find the dream interesting. Corell gathered that the mathematician had a special interest in dreams. He had after all recorded his own dreams in three notebooks, and this conversation also gave rise to a sense of intimacy, and the offence was committed once more. Corell did not want to know any of the details, neither did he get any, but he could not stop thinking about Turing's rather feminine chest and his own fingers unbuttoning the pyjama top at Adlington Road. He put the image out of his mind, as if the mere thought were dangerous, and it struck him that the comment "Our relationship was one of equals" probably spoke volumes. Before Murray did anything he needed to have a crumb of respect and recognition. He needed to be seen as a human being before he sullied himself. But something went wrong here and Corell could not help but be fascinated by it.

Murray did not want to accept the money which Turing offered him. He was no prostitute, he said. He had come as an equal and been invited to dinner, and that was all as it should be. Turing seemed to enjoy the idea that this was a flirtation like any other. The only problem was the original reason why Murray found his way to Oxford Road. He was poor. He lived in squalor. What was he to do? Instead of accepting the payment, he stole from Turing's wallet and that could have been the end of the story. When Turing discovered the theft he wrote him a letter to say that he wanted to break things off.

Yet a few days later Arnold was back, protesting his innocence, and he was forgiven. It was not easy to say why. The mathematician gave the impression of being very naive. Kenny Anderson had said that he "didn't seem to be particularly bright," and even if Corell was reluctant to acknowledge that his colleague might have a point, there was no doubting that Turing's behaviour had been astonishingly stupid. After their reconciliation, when Murray changed his approach and asked for money outright to buy a suit, he immediately got it. "Here you are," Turing said. "Take it. I'm sure the suit'll look very good on you." But by then the mathematician was already heading into a trap. How humiliating it must have been for him!

Certainly it was not easy to tell how artful Murray was. If Anderson—who was inclined towards categoric and damning character descriptions—had read up on the case, he would no doubt have asserted that the man was a typical criminal who was bent on cheating his way to as much as possible. Corell was not quite so sure. In any case Murray did not seem to be completely rotten. He suffered pangs of conscience. He was eager to learn and was always asking Turing about things. "We even discussed developments in physics." But all the same . . . in a milk bar on Oxford Street he gossiped about the mathematician's house. He had been there with a friend, one Harry Greene. The young men were bragging about their adventures and naturally Turing's name came up, the man who claimed that he was building an electronic brain.

Greene suggested a raid on the house. Murray said no—or so he claimed. But the idea was hatched. That much was certain. During these days in January 1952—which Turing described as anxious and restless—he was robbed at the university, although it was not clear what was taken. He felt "superstitious and frightened." On January 23 he took part in some sort of radio programme but without being particularly pleased with his contribution. That same evening he came home to Adlington Road and realised that he had been burgled. He had "a dark, ominous feeling of being threatened."

The break-in as such was not much to fuss about, just as Anderson had said. The only things which were missing were some fish knives, a pair of trousers, a tweed shirt, a compass and a half-finished bottle of sherry, but the uncomfortable part was knowing that someone had prowled around his home, and this was enough for Turing to make his fatal mistake. He reported the break-in. Of course, even criminals should be entitled to the protection of the law. But why the hell did he take such a risk? Corell could not understand it.

For the sake of an opened bottle of sherry the mathematician put his life on the line. For some bits of rubbish, he bared his throat and he was very determined in doing so. In other ways he remained as evasive and weak as before. Although he had resolved not to do so, he allowed Murray into his home again on February 2 and they did indeed have another argument. Apparently there was a terrible scene, and there was no doubt that the mathematician suspected Murray.

But there was a lull in the storm. They had a drink, and once again had an intimate conversation, and finally Murray felt like confessing, and ingratiating himself with Turing, as though he wanted both to take revenge on him and become friends: he shopped Greene. He told Turing what had happened at the milk bar, and soon after that the two of them committed their offence again. But that night the mathematician lay awake. He wrote in his confession that he "liked Arnold," but that he "didn't want to be dragged into something that looked like blackmail. Mr. Murray had threatened to report me to the police." For that reason the mathematician stole away like a thief in his own home and put aside a glass which Murray had drunk from, hoping that his fingerprints could be compared with those of the burglar.

The next day he went out with Murray and had him wait on a bench outside the police station while he himself slipped in and reported the new information to Constable Brown, a dear little man with a squint and a receding hairline whose reports were always full of spelling mistakes and oddities. Sure enough, there were two references to "she" in the report when Brown meant Turing, but the mistakes had the benefit of underlining how strange the story was.

In his report, Turing did not say a word about Murray. Still, he needed to come up with a plausible explanation for the new information he had about Greene, so he spun a tale about a door-to-door salesman who had been selling something or other, probably brushes, and this salesman— for whom Turing gave neither name nor any particular identifying features—had in passing mentioned that he knew who had carried out the burglary at Turing's house. Just how the salesman had got to know this was not made clear. The lie seemed pretty inept and inevitably one thing led to another, even if at first it looked as if matters were going to go Turing's way. Harry Greene was a real villain. He was in prison in Manchester on other offences and the police linked him to the break-in at Adlington Road, but what Turing should have been able to work out was that Greene held a trump card. He could negotiate with the police.

"My mate Arnold got up to bad things with that man," he said.

That in itself need not have mattered a great deal. Had Corell himself not listened to endless rubbish and loose accusations from criminals? None of that usually leads anywhere, especially if someone from a higher social class claims the opposite. But in this case, something did happen. Two colleagues in Manchester, Sergeants Willis and Rimmer, read Turing's report about the door-to-door salesman and suspected that it was untrue. They decided to go for him. On February 4, 1952, they went to the mathematician's house, officially to talk about the burglary, but right from the beginning their behaviour was threatening or at least hostile, and even if Corell himself was sceptical about the value of direct confrontations, it appears to have been the correct strategy in this case. After all, the suspect was no ordinary villain, he may even have been weaker than most. He probably had no idea that the police were after him. He had reported a break-in and come forward with valuable information. Why would the police not be on his side?

"We know the full story," Sergeant Willis said without being clear what he meant by the full story, and obviously that threw Turing off balance.

When he came to repeat what was in his report, he got himself into a muddle, and apparently it got worse the more that he was put under pressure. His account was rather vague and he still was not able to produce any convincing details. The door-to-door salesman remained a mysterious figure.

"We have reason to believe that your description of events is false," Willis told him, and presumably there were a few more exchanges, but the moment of truth was approaching. Corell imagined how Turing must have groped for a way out, a branch to hold on to, and how at last he gave in, presumably in the belief that a confession would bring relief, a release from all the straining to lie convincingly, but in reality he could not have been more mistaken. It may be a release to confess to friends. Policemen on the other hand are predators. While the guilty man dreams of sympathy, the police scent victory and are only interested in trapping him. For Corell's colleagues, that moment was a triumph; for Turing it seemed to have been nothing less than the beginning of the end. What do you mean by lies, he should have said. *I'm an important man.* No-one could have brought him down without a confession. But what did he do? He spat it all out.

"Arnold Murray and I had an affair!"

And as if that were not enough he grabbed hold of a pen and there and then, under the eyes of the waiting policemen, wrote out his five-page witness statement, which was marked by the most extraordinary lack of understanding of the seriousness and significance of the situation. He did not appear to have any idea that the break-in no longer mattered and he even thought that the police ought to be more interested in his mental struggle—his unwillingness to surrender to blackmail—than his sexual offence. It was as if he thought there was a significant moral issue which lay on a different level. "How far should one go to protect oneself and to what extent should one accept some injustices to avoid harming another person, that is in many respects an interesting moral and philosophical question. How much is it reasonable for us to suffer ourselves in order to help a weaker person?" he wrote in his confession, apparently wholly unaware that his own offence could get him two years in prison, and that everything else was no more than lofty theorising which had nothing to do with the police investigation.

Turing's position and social background were no longer of any use to him, that much was clear from the letter of the law. Once he had confessed, his background would merely be turned against him and reinforce his image as a devious character who seduced young and unsuspecting men from a lower social class, but it seems to have taken some time for any of this to sink in with the mathematician. After his admission he even seemed to relax and Sergeant Rimmer's objectivity as a policeman failed him on several occasions when he described Turing as a real convert, someone who was totally convinced that he had done the right thing, and in a peculiar marginal note he added "a man of honour," although it was not quite clear what Rimmer had meant by that.

Perhaps he was referring to Turing's open-heartedness. Or to his careless generosity. It was not possible to gain any particularly clear impression of Turing from the report. One moment he seemed to be worried, at other times it was as if he were above the mundane and free of cares and suffering. At one point he offered the policemen some wine, as if they were friends, and at another juncture he tried to explain a mathematical theory. At least Sergeant Rimmer had scribbled down those lines in the report which had so intrigued Corell, those strange words about the so-called liar's paradox. "I'm lying! If that sentence is true, then it's a lie, because the speaker is lying, but then he is of course telling the truth because he says that he's lying, and so on," Rimmer had written, and added something about contradictions like this one having caused a crisis in mathematical logic which in turn had prompted Turing to sketch out the concept for a new sort of machine. Hundreds of steps in the thought process seemed to have gone missing along the way, but Corell not only found it touching that Rimmer had gone to the trouble of understanding something which lay far beyond his own horizon, and which had nothing to do with the investigation. It also made him happy, because it was just the kind of problem that his recent life had been lacking. *I'm lying.* He tasted the words. *If it's true that I'm lying then I'm telling the truth* . . . The sentence was both true and false, it skipped between its two poles in a perpetual loop, and Corell realised that his father had told him something about it many years ago. He could not remember what, and as he continued to read he felt distracted, as if the sentence were continuing to contradict itself in his head, and his thoughts went back to the poisoned apple on the bedside table, as if it too were a part of the paradox.

7

CORELL HAD THE PARTICULAR QUALITIES required in order to explore the significance of an apple left behind. He had once stared at a black ribbed leather glove next to the railway line in Southport and read an entire life into it. It was just before the outbreak of war and two years after they had moved from London.

At the time they lived not far from the edge of the sea, in a small stone house whose main feature was the large windows on the ground floor. As Corell recalled it, one day his father stopped talking, perhaps not exactly at a given moment, but not far from it, and it was no small matter. James Corell had always been ebullience itself. His chuckling and his theatrical outbursts were the basic characteristics of the family. Leonard's and his mother's lives revolved around his stories and antics, which either gave them energy or sucked it from them, and it would not be wrong to say that James Corell made other fathers seem dull and lifeless in comparison. He was surrounded by a never-ending party. One could tell when he was approaching because, wherever he went, he jangled his keys in his trouser pockets and he usually made something grand of his entrances, even if it was only to shout out: "What a delightful gathering! May a simple man such as I join your company?"

It was generally known that Leonard's father had suffered a number of setbacks and that he had lost a lot of money. But so long as his father kept on talking, Leonard did not care. Their fortune had disappeared from both bank and wallet but remained in the gestures and the words, and Leonard's father was also larger than life. He knew famous people. At least he said that he knew famous people, and more than once he dismissed the great and good with regal contempt. Leonard of course knew relatively little at the time. He was aware that his father had been to Trinity College, Cambridge, and that he had written some novels and two non-fiction books, not exactly best-sellers, but important works with their own merits, it was said, even if a few embarrassing literary flourishes and fabrications had been pointed out in them. Keeping fact and fiction apart was not his father's greatest strength, he even said as much himself. One of the books was a biography of the painter Paul Gauguin, and the other was one of an American decathlete, an Indian by the name of Thorpe who won the pentathlon and the decathlon at the Olympic Games in Stockholm in 1912, but whose medals were later taken away for stated reasons, but in fact probably because of racism.

Corell's father said that he fought for the weak and for those who were persecuted because they were different from the normal and narrow-minded and that he loved to expose "the establishment and the pompous bourgeoisie." It was claimed, although this probably belonged to family lore, that he was feared for his articles in the *Manchester Guardian*, of which there could not in any case have been all that many, and among friends and "in broad-minded circles" his three novels, which Leonard's mother did not want him to read, were considered to be "underrated and worthy of a better fate." He was tall, straight-backed and elegant, with slanting brown eyes and curly hair which did not seem to want to thin or turn grey, and he spoke with more fire than anyone Leonard had ever met. And yet one of the worst insults that his father had heard directed at him was that he "should write with the same passion with which he spoke" and generally he wanted to be complimented on everything other than how he talked. Speech means nothing, he said, spitting on the only thing that he was actually good at, but these were insights which came to Leonard much later. At the time, he worshipped his father.

Corell's mother was twelve years younger, more reserved in comparison, and less striking, slightly stooped and with narrowed eyes which made people nervous and which from time to time stared at James with a hostility which for a long time remained incomprehensible to Leonard. He sometimes could not imagine how they had found each other; he was never, it is true, particularly close to his mother, not even during the good times, but before the summer when his father fell silent that was not necessary. He had James. His mother was more of a barred door, a closed face with something unfulfilled about it, but sometimes she roused herself out of her lethargy and argued with wit and passion, and at those times conversations at home became moments of intense enjoyment. Not one word was heard then about shopping, weather or gossip. The discussion crackled with the world's big and weighty issues and no-one was too famous or important to be called a dilettante or trickster. Lack of respect was a virtue, and all his life Corell would feel paralysed and gloomy when faced with the trivial. "I cannot stand the humdrum," he said, for as long as he still had some pride left in his body and before he was drowned in the normality of his job; and perhaps he ended up suffering from having to carry some ideological ballast. His parents had a tendency to romanticise. They revered artists and scientists, people who placed themselves outside their time, and that frightened Leonard because it strengthened his feeling that he would never be good enough. But just as often he was seized by a feeling that he was chosen, and he dreamed that he would one day come up with an idea, a great thought which would revolutionise the world. Exactly what it was going to be or in which discipline was never clear—it changed from day to day—but he fantasised about the consequences and the glory, and probably lived with high expectations generally. Not that he believed the dreams would come true, but he was convinced that he would become something important, especially when he put up any resistance to his father in their discussions at home, and often he heard: "My God, Leo, what a storyteller you are!" Up until those days in August and September 1939 when he was thirteen years old and about to be sent to Marlborough, a public school known for its strict discipline, he was prepared for nothing but a bright future. Worries were looming like clouds on the horizon, but so long as his father was in a good mood he did not notice them. In his father's presence, even the dwindling number of dinner guests, the reduced summer holidays, the feeling that the world and their circumstances were shrinking, seemed natural, part of a new order of things. The move from London to Southport too, which was said to have taken place because "the Sefton coast is the best there is in England," felt like a part of this new order, and sometimes when his father sat by the water's edge with a book on his knee, looking at the wading birds, at the lapwings, the herons and the plovers, and eagerly pointing when they were being attacked by the falcons, Leonard was convinced that life really was better now, and that the servants and too much money were only a nuisance. Generally he only saw what he wanted to see.

One evening he was lying in bed, looking up at his father's slanting eyes. The sea and the ospreys could be heard outside, and he very clearly did not want to go to sleep. These were his best times, when his father sat on the edge of the bed, and perhaps they had just been reading from one of the classics and had discussed it or Leonard had been allowed to say how he would like the book to continue, and probably he had been praised and felt a warm hand on his head. But that evening his father's features changed. There was a new, brighter light in his eyes.

"Are you sad, my boy?" he said, and there was something strange about it.

Leonard was not gloomy and he was about to answer "no, Father, not at all," but he felt drawn by the question. It reached out to him like two open arms and maybe, he thought, his father had seen something which he himself had missed. Perhaps Leonard really was sad. The question forced itself into his body like an exquisite pain.

"Yes, perhaps I do feel a little bit sad."

"I understand that, you're very sad," said his father, and he ran his coarse hand with the powerful blue veins over the boy's hair and it felt wonderful, so immensely caring.

It was like being seen with new, sharp eyes. Nothing that he had said or done before had touched his father so deeply. Leo was used to generous reactions from his father, to applause and congratulations, with all the theatricals, but never before had he been met with such emotion. There were tears in his father's eyes, and the large hand held the back of his neck and Leonard wanted to nestle into his sorrow, his affected sorrow, and he felt happy, happy in his suffering, and it never occurred to him that his father was not crying over him but over his own life. What he perceived as love was nothing other than his father's own pain, because it was not true, as he believed at the time, that they could talk about anything in the family.

They were not allowed to speak about his father's own shortcomings and sorrows. That was the most important rule in the household. But Leonard had not noticed it for the simple reason that he just could not imagine his father as being afflicted by any form of darkness, and only much later did he realise that his father must have been suffering from some kind of emotional block, something not entirely unusual in English men, but certainly unusual in a man who always seemed willing to give of himself, and who at least in general terms never had difficulty in dealing with any of the heart's complications and sorrows.

Their house in Southport was simply furnished with few pictures on the walls. They had not brought many things with them from London, just James's large desk with the engraved laurel wreaths and three walnut Queen Anne chairs. They had white cushions embroidered with red roses. Two of the chairs stood in the living room next to the chest table, and James used to sit on the third one during dinner. This was no particular extravagance, nor was it something the family joked about. He quite simply sat on the Queen Anne chair, and if Leonard had thought about it before he would just have regarded it as a sign of his father's standing in the family and in life. That summer, though, James often missed meals and at those times something happened to the chair. It took on the weight of his worrying absence and an entirely new diffidence crept into their conversation. Even trivial remarks such as "pass the salt" or "look how strong the wind is out at sea" became charged with an underlying tension. Sometimes when Leonard's father was there he would stumble over subjects which were more sensitive than all the horrors on the continent: a rash comment about a fellow author who had done rather well; a sentence to the effect that "someone had hidden himself away on his estate with all his money"; and then his face froze, and he sucked in the air through clenched teeth making a sibilant, unpleasant sound.

"What is it, Father?"

"Nothing, nothing!"

It was never anything, nothing to talk about. If one was allowed to do anything at all it was to clatter one's cutlery or push back one's hair and say something like: "What a lovely evening. Can't Richardson keep his cows under control?" and often his father would regain his composure, especially if they managed to pretend that nothing had happened, or else he did not and then he usually left and let the Queen Anne chair turn into a symbol of everything that was kept hidden. Leonard did not know how much of this he realised that summer and how much he reconstructed later. But there were signs. Even something so simple as the way his father breathed when he slept during the day. He wheezed too heavily, too whiningly. "It's the sherry," his mother said. "He drinks too much sherry." And then there was his reading. He was always reading. But that summer there was curiously little turning of pages, as if he were always staring at the same words. His walk seemed different. One could sense a shuffling indifference in his steps. The regular, military walk had gone, there was hardly even the jangling of keys in the trouser pocket. There was also the mail, which he always used to open with zest or with worry, hard to determine which, and which was now left to lie on the hall table, and it did not even seem to frighten him any longer.

At the end of August, when the holidaymakers started to leave and round about the time when the first geese and ducks arrived, something happened to his shoulders. They were pushed up so that his neck completely disappeared, but none of them ever found out what caused this. They did not even know when he left the house. August 30 was the same day that two sheds in Southport burned to the ground. They could be seen from far away, like two shining torches. It had been a beautiful clear day, but towards evening dark clouds rolled in and there were huge waves out at sea.

For dinner they had something which included Yorkshire pudding and they must have started talking about the weather because he remembered his mother saying, "I think the snow is going to come early this year." Soon afterwards she dropped a glass on the floor and burst out with *"Merde!"* in French. They talked about Marlborough. "You're lucky to be going there. It's costing us a lot of money." But they said nothing about the father's absence, or rather, they must have mentioned it in some way because after they had finished eating they set out to look for him. By then the sun had set and a faint smell of seaweed and salt drifted in from the sea. They walked along the beach, past mossy sand-dunes, all the way to the pier. At one point they saw a red squirrel, and his mother reached for his hand, but he felt that he was too old for that sort of thing and stuffed his hands into his pockets and soon it was ten and then eleven at night and it started to get cold. The wind blew straight through his tartan pullover.

"I'm sure he's sitting somewhere drinking," his mother said.

Not long afterwards he saw a shape down by the water's edge, something stretched out which could have been his father, and he looked at his mother and when she did not seem to know he ran towards the water shouting, "Daddy, Daddy." But it was only a couple of boxes, with Dublin 731 stencilled on them, and at midnight they returned home.

8

THE PAPERS FROM THE court proceedings were in an indescribable mess, yet Corell soon managed to get a reasonable picture of what had happened. Alan Turing had been arrested and his photograph and fingerprints had been taken and sent on to Scotland Yard, which must have meant that the whole of Turing's life was open to scrutiny, exactly as Hamersley had said, and that can hardly have been easy for him to cope with. Not that Corell knew anything about Turing's circle of acquaintance or state of mind, but one might have expected his friends and work colleagues to have withdrawn somewhat. Someone exposed as a homosexual was no doubt treated rather like a leper, he supposed, and that eats into you, Corell knew as much from his own experience. But that was now Turing's business and he evidently more than deserved it.

According to the report, the mathematician had behaved "brazenly and without remorse" during the trial, which can hardly have helped his cause. Arnold Murray was presented as young and naive, but not without future prospects, and it was said that he had been seduced by the older and more educated Turing, and that was obviously not exactly helpful either. Naturally Turing's counsel mentioned all the good things that he knew about his client, for example—and Corell noted this in particular—that the mathematician had been awarded the O.B.E., the Order of the British Empire, for his work during the war. On the other hand there was no mention at all of where the mathematician had served, but it was unlikely to have been at the front. He did not appear to have been any sort of a hard man, and apart from two character witnesses who appeared in his defence, including a Hugh Alexander—

a name which Corell vaguely recognised—he did not seem to have enjoyed a great deal of support.

One of the receptionists put her head around the door to say that he had another visitor. He swore under his breath, making a brave attempt to tidy up his desk, but did not get far. A man with a bright red face stormed in. He seemed to be impelled by some pent-up fury and for a brief moment Corell expected a reprimand or, worse, a slap in the face, but when the man took off his hat and reached out his hand Corell wondered if it really was anger that he had seen. The man was around forty-five or fifty years old with dark hair parted at the side and a small pot belly. To judge from his shoes and suit, he was a person of consequence, perhaps even from the Foreign Office. Corell had already started to daydream about receiving privileged information in his capacity as police investigator and in his fantasies he had already imagined a few scenarios. But there was also something about the visitor that he could not quite put his finger on. He seemed troublingly familiar, as if they had met before and had an unpleasant scene, and for a moment Corell remained sitting at his desk, unsure what to do.

"Is it me you're looking for?"

"I think so. You're Detective Constable Corell, aren't you? My name is John Turing. I came as soon as I heard," and even though Corell of course immediately recognised the name, it took a while before he realised that this was the brother and that his sense of déjà vu was presumably only due to the man's resemblance to the deceased.

"My sincere condolences," he said once he had gathered his wits, and he got to his feet and reached out his hand. "Have you come up from London?"

"From Guildford," Turing said, his answer short and rough, conveying the feeling that he would stand firmly on his dignity and behave with formality and reserve.

"Would you like to sit down?"

"I'd rather not."

"In that case, may I suggest that we go outside? The weather seems to have improved. I assume that you would like to see your brother. I could call . . ."

"Is that necessary?"

"I'm afraid we do need a reliable identification."

"But hasn't the housekeeper already . . . ?"

"It's supposed to be a good thing to say one's last goodbyes."

"I assume that it's better for me to do it rather than our mother."

"Is she on her way here?"

"Yes, but it'll probably take a day or so. She's in Italy. Can you tell me a little about what you know?"

"I'll give you the whole background. I've just got to arrange for someone to meet us at the morgue," he said and closed his eyes as if to steel himself for yet another trial.

The sun was shining outside. It was almost hot and quite a few bits of broken glass and some rubbish were still lying in the yard. In the distance could be seen the white stone house which provided such a painfully beautiful contrast to the police station, and the trail of an aeroplane could be seen in the sky. Corell spoke about the apple, the poison, the electric wires, the bubbling pan, the feeling of "calm and resignation" in Alan Turing's face, and the brother asked surprisingly few questions considering how peculiar it all was.

"Were you close?" Corell said.

"We were brothers."

"Not all brothers keep in touch."

"True."

"And you?"

"We didn't see each other very often. So you're right. But when we were small . . ."

John Turing hesitated, as if he were wondering whether it was worth saying anything at all.

"What about then?"

"We were very close at that time. To a large extent we grew up without our parents. Our father was in India and I suspect they didn't want to expose us to the climate there. Amongst others we lived with an old colonel and his wife in St. Leonards-on-Sea. It wasn't entirely straightforward."

"You were the older brother."

"By four years. So I felt a great sense of responsibility."

"What was he like?"

"As a child, do you mean?"

"As whatever you like."

John Turing started, as if the question had been strange or painfully intrusive. But then he started to speak, not with any particular feeling, not at all. At times it was as if he were doing so out of duty, as if he felt remote from it all, but at other points he seemed to get carried away and to forget to whom he was talking.

"Already as a small boy," he said, "Alan thought that numbers seemed to be much more fun than letters, and he saw them everywhere, on lamps, letters, packages. Long before he could read he was putting together double-digit numbers, and once he had learned to write his handwriting was all over the place. Hardly anyone could read it."

Hardly anyone even now, Corell thought, recalling Turing's notebook. It disturbed him that the man who had stared out at him with his rigid face and who had turned out to be a pervert had once been a boy who for many years put his shoes on the wrong way round; neither did he like to hear that Alan Turing had been clumsy from a young age, and an outsider, and that he had difficulty making friends and had not even been particularly popular with the teachers. One of them had said that he reeked of mathematics. Someone had written a verse about him: *Turing's fond of the football field / For geometric problems the touchlines yield.*

"Were you at the same school?"

"To begin with. We went to Hazelhurst, but then I started at Marlborough, and then . . ."

"At Marlborough," Corell interrupted, and was just about to reel off a long diatribe when he realised that this would force him to explain why he was just an ordinary police officer in a small town, and he did not think that his self-esteem could cope with that.

"Personally I thought it was O.K.," Turing said. "I was, after all, more sporty. But there was also something inhuman about the school and I realised that Alan would be miserable there. So I advised strongly against it."

"So he wasn't made to go to Marlborough."

"He ended up at Sherborne instead and that probably wasn't perfect either, but it was better."

"I'm sure," Corell said tonelessly.

They turned into Grove Street and passed a pub called The Zest and the low red-brick houses and then the row of shops and hairdressers. Quite a few people were out and about. The sun was still shining, but there were dark, brooding clouds, and in a rapid flashback Corell remembered a damp, unpleasant night at school. *So he didn't have to go to Marlborough.* It took a huge effort to concentrate on his companion.

"When did you last see each other?" he said.

"At Christmas, at our home in Guildford."

"How was he?"

"Well, I thought. Much better."

"Better than when?"

"Than during the whole trial."

"Was he depressed then?"

"I would say that he was. Or maybe I don't really know, to be honest. We didn't quite see eye to eye after that business. I never really understood."

"Did you distance yourself from him?"

John Turing stopped in mid-step and looked down at his hands. There was a hint of a grimace on his face, but it quickly disappeared.

"Not at all," he said. "I helped him as best I could, with legal advice, with all sorts of things. I put him in touch with people."

"You're a solicitor, are you not?"

"Yes. But Alan wasn't easy to discuss things with. He never had been. I advised him to confess during the trial as well and to bloody well avoid trying to explain everything. But he didn't really want to do either the one or the other."

"How do you mean?"

"On the one hand he naturally wanted to say things exactly as they were. He loathed lies and hypocrisy, and of course that does him credit. But nothing was simple for Alan. He turned everything around, and while that must have been an advantage in his own work, in court . . . my God . . . there he was a fish out of water. He said that it would be just as wrong to declare himself guilty as to deny what had happened."

"I'm not sure that I understand."

"He meant that if he admitted his guilt he would of course be telling the truth in the sense that he had in fact slept with that man, but at the same time he would be conceding that what he had done was a crime and that he refused to accept. He was only being true to his nature, he said."

"And you didn't agree with him?"

"No!"

"In what sense?"

"I honestly don't want to talk about it."

"I understand."

"But if that's what you're after, I can tell you right away that I did not like what he called his inclinations one little bit," John Turing snapped with unexpected venom. "I was absolutely shocked when he wrote and told me about it. I didn't have the slightest idea."

"Did you fall out?"

"Is this an interrogation?"

"I wouldn't say so."

"Alan would have loved that reply."

Corell jumped. He was so sensitive that he thought he was being made fun of.

"Or else Alan would have taken the question very seriously and wondered what the boundary was between 'yes' and 'no' and whether 'I wouldn't say so' belonged to one or the other or whether the sentence was simply some logical nonsense," the brother continued, in a more friendly tone.

"I just wanted . . ."

"But I've got nothing against talking, 'I wouldn't say so.' What was your question?"

"Whether you fell out."

"No more than that he reproached me for certain things. Like the fact that I didn't understand how hard things were for homosexuals."

"So he thought . . ."

"That his kind were an exposed and persecuted group. He gave me a whole lecture, but my God, I really had other things to worry about. I had him of course, my brother. But he didn't understand that. 'You're only thinking about your own reputation,' he said, which wasn't true. I was thinking about nothing other than his reputation, and I did what I could to stop it from being damaged too much, but if you had even the slightest idea . . . it's enough to drive one mad."

"What is?"

"That outside his intellectual world Alan was so incredibly naive."

"He messed up the police investigation pretty badly," Corell conceded, very conscious of the fact that it was hardly his role to agree.

"He certainly did."

"The sentence itself or the treatment, how did he take that?"

"I don't really know. But it sounded pretty awful, didn't it?"

"In what sense?"

"To force oestrogen into a man, could anything be more humiliating?" said John Turing, and Corell thought: Oestrogen, what the hell is that? But he kept quiet because he did not want to betray his ignorance.

"Did it have any effect?" he said instead.

"In the short term perhaps, but in the longer term I think it was just bad for him. I suspect that they used him as a guinea pig. There were probably a number of studies, but a lot was still unclear. Not that I'm much of a medic. On the other hand I know that they had not been using it for very long. It was all based on new findings. He was their bloody lab rat, and it beggars belief that the world of science should have cast him of all people in that role. Later I even heard that oestrogen treatment was something they had picked up from the Nazis. Those bastards carried out similar experiments in the concentration camps. Forgive me, it makes me furious just to think about it. I'm not sure that I can bear to see him right now."

Corell did not say anything. They were already close to the morgue, and for a moment—he was not sure why—he was about to say that he too had been to Marlborough. Instead he said:

"Do you know where Alan was during the war?"

"Why do you ask?"

"I've got the impression that he worked on sensitive assignments."

"That may be so. All I really know is that he was somewhere between Cambridge and Oxford. He and a lot of other boffins."

"What do you mean?"

"That the military gathered Alan and a gang of other clever boys in one and the same place."

"To do what?"

"I have my ideas. But since Alan never said a word about it I'll probably have to keep my mouth shut. But I do know that he went back there the other year."

"Was he called up again?"

"No, no, it was one of those typical Alan things. He wanted to fetch some silver ingots that he had hidden during the war. You understand, he thought it was a splendid idea to buy silver and bury it in some obscure place instead of letting one of the established banks look after it."

"Did he find the silver?"

"Of course not, and perhaps he couldn't have cared less. He was not particularly interested in money. He was a treasure hunter who never really cared much about the treasure."

"Here we are," Corell said.

He stopped.

"What?"

"The morgue."

John Turing started, and seemed both fearful and surprised, and it was true, the building did not look like a morgue. It was white limestone with a black metal roof and a light-blue door and it was hard to associate it with death and decay. There was also a neat flower bed and two cypresses grew in front of the building, as well as a young holly tree, but since Corell knew what was hidden away in there he saw nothing pleasant even about the flowers. Feeling tense, he opened the front door and was surprised to encounter two men in tweed suits, who politely raised their hats. One of them was unusually tall and probably also unusually elegant, at least for his age, with clear-cut features and dark, intense eyes. He appeared to be genuinely interested in John Turing and Corell, but what really marked him out was the fact that his neck was crooked, which gave him a somewhat frail air. He would have found a walking stick useful. The other man was more robust, with the build of a wrestler, although even he was of a certain age. He waddled forward, his cheeks ruddy and his nose shapelessly large, but he too radiated a strong sense of authority, and Corell had just time to wonder what they were doing there when a nurse came up and informed them that Dr. Bird was waiting for them.

Charles Bird was the same as ever. His skin was yellow. He had the aura of death itself and as usual he wanted to impress with his knowledge. He showed greater deference towards John Turing, of course, and used more Latin terms, and obviously he tiptoed respectfully around the lawyer's bereavement, but in the end he became too detailed in his medical descriptions, and extremely tactless—who wants to hear about his dead brother's entrails?—and John Turing brusquely interrupted him.

"That's enough!"

"I didn't mean . . ." Bird muttered, and they both stood silent, the doctor embarrassed, and the brother deeply moved, with moist eyes and trembling lower lip. It was the kind of situation where one person's daily routine meets the other's tragedy, a scene of the sort which used to make Corell feel melancholy but which now gave him satisfaction because he had so desperately wanted to see the pathologist get his comeuppance. "Let's go," he said, and for a long time they walked without saying a word. The morgue was not far from the railway station, and in the distance a goods train could be heard. On Hawthorne Lane a Rolls Royce went by like a spiteful greeting from a better, finer world, but Corell felt reasonably at peace, despite everything. He had said a frosty goodbye to the pathologist, and taken pleasure in it. He should now have gone back to the police station. Yet he remained undecided, and did not really know where they were heading.

"There is one thing," John Turing said, in a voice which seemed to promise something important.

"Yes?"

"Are you sure it was suicide?"

Corell looked out towards the red-brown viaduct over the River Bollin and wondered if he was going to hear a murder theory, or in any event something which was consistent with Hamersley's speech about state secrets.

"Couldn't it have been an accident?"

"In what way an accident?"

"For years our mother has been saying that something would happen to Alan, the last time was at our place at Christmas. She went on at him as if he were a little boy. 'Wash your hands,' she said. 'Make sure that you really rub them!'"

"To get rid of what?"

"Of the poisons and chemicals. Alan messed about with all kinds of things, and she knew better than anyone how clumsy and forgetful he was, and she also knew that he handled potassium cyanide. She had warned him a thousand times."

"What did he have the poison for?"

"He gilded cutlery with it. I think you need it to separate the gold in some way. No, don't ask me why he was doing it. That's just the way he was. Had all sorts of ideas. Took gold from grandfather's old watch and transferred it to a spoon, completely crazy, don't you think? Just to stand there and mess about with potassium cyanide! It drove our mother mad. 'You'll make us all unhappy,' she said."

"We did in fact find a gilt teaspoon," Corell said, remembering Alec Block's discovery in the house.

"You see, you see."

The brother seemed agitated, and Corell regretted having mentioned the spoon at all.

"But what about the apple?" he said. "It was drenched in cyanide."

"Alan could just as easily have got the cyanide on it by mistake."

"I'm afraid the apple smelled too strongly for that. There was too much potassium cyanide on it to have got there by chance. He must have more or less dipped it in poison," Corell said, without being altogether sure about what he was saying, and without knowing if it had been right to have contradicted him.

If the mother and brother wanted to believe that it was an accident, they should be allowed to do so, and at that moment he was struck by a thought, a good one, he felt, and if he had wanted to trace its origin then he should have looked into his complicated relationship with his own mother and his constant and meaningless efforts during school holidays to be considerate to others by describing horrible events in a brighter, better light. It was a thought about how the dead man might have reasoned, but he did not say anything about it.

"I really appreciate the fact that you took the time to talk to me. But I'm afraid I need to get back to the police station," he said.

"Dipped it in poison," the brother said again, as if he had not been listening.

"I'm sorry?"

"There's something about that phrase," he said.

"In what way?"

"It reminds me of something."

"Of what?"

"Of something Alan said a long time ago, before the war. Isn't there a nursery rhyme about it?"

A nursery rhyme? There might very well be. An apple dipped in poison, that sounded like something of an archetype, but it did not ring any bells with Corell, and yet he was quite interested in nursery rhymes and nonsense verses. "Not so far as I know," he said, and then he took John Turing's details and address and promised to send him the books with Alan Turing's dreams which "definitely should not fall into the wrong hands." After that they said goodbye and if the brother had been showing some signs of openness, he now resumed his official persona and walked away. Only once his back could be seen as no more than a line far off in the distance did Corell realise that he had forgotten to ask about Alan Turing's work with paradoxes and machines, and for a moment he was seized by the usual regret that he had come across as only a pale reflection of his true self. *I'm more than that. I'm more than that*, he wanted to shout, *I was only a shadow of myself.* But he pulled himself together, and smiled with an air of strained dignity at two young women who were walking in the other direction.

Although he was feeling some stress, he did not go back to the police station but instead turned into Station Road in the direction of the library. The library was a place of refuge. Nowadays he would rather go there than to the pub. In the evenings he often sat there reading for hours in pursuit of an open-ended plan which he had to broaden his mind, but he never, or in principle never, used to go there during working hours. Now he did have work-related business to attend to, perhaps not directly linked to the investigation, and certainly not a matter of priority, but still not unimportant, and therefore he felt only a little guilty as he hurried past George Bramwell Evens's garden, into the building and up the curved staircase. A soft murmur could be heard, and he breathed deeply, drinking in the special atmosphere which, apart from the gentle smell of something sweet, contained such a pleasant combination of the mundane and the solemn, as in a house where one feels at home but nevertheless also senses the venerable presence of an educated and very wise person. *Books, books!* Perhaps he liked them best at a distance, as promises, or as starting points for his dreams, and unhurriedly he approached the information counter and the young woman there who he knew was called Ellen. He asked for a medical reference book.

"I hope you're not ill, sir."

"No, no," he said, a little disturbed, and walked off towards his usual place by the window.

9

THE MORNING AFTER HIS FATHER had disappeared in Southport, Leonard got up feeling that everything would still be all right, and that they had passed a low point the previous evening from which life would take an upwards turn. So full of hope was he that he even failed to recognise the man walking down by the beach and the red toolsheds. He thought that it was one of the local wags, who had come in a funny hat to ask after his father. But his mind was playing tricks on him. When he went into the kitchen and expected to hear that "Daddy was out misbehaving last night" he noticed that his mother was wearing the same clothes as the day before and that the man out there was not at all some joker but a policeman, a large bearded figure of authority, whose funny hat was in fact a helmet.

"Go to your room!"

He went no further than just out of sight, and did his best to eavesdrop. All he could hear were occasional snatches of conversation, and for a long time he glared out at the sea, and the black rowing boat down there, but in the end he could stand it no longer.

"What are you talking about? Where's Daddy?" he shouted.

"Calm down, Leonard!" his mother hissed with such tension in her voice that he immediately understood that the worst sort of accident had invaded their home, and even if it took a while before the details became clear, it emerged that a man had been hit by a goods train from Birmingham, and that it might be his father. His mother had therefore to go to see if she could identify the body, and if ever there had been a time to pray it was probably then, but as he remembered it, his hopes vanished immediately. I'm an orphan, I'm an orphan, he muttered as if both of them had gone, and so the shock was not that much greater when his mother came back, having identified the body. Standing on the threshold with her mouth painted strangely red and her eyes so small and squinting that it seemed remarkable that she could see at all, she declared: "Father is dead, he's no longer with us," as if that last bit were absolutely necessary.

He must have reacted in some way, by crying or breaking down, but all he could remember was that he smashed the white Queen Anne chair and that it had given him some satisfaction, especially since he had not done it in a rage, but methodically and calmly until three of the legs had been broken and the back had splintered. His mother, who as mothers go never did much right, at least had the good taste to dismiss his effort with the words, "I've never liked that chair anyway." Apart from that she began to stiffen, or perhaps he should say rather to assume a mask, remarkably quickly—as if her grief did not need to go through any stages—which to an outsider may have made her appear serene or maybe even at peace with herself, especially when she played her games of patience in the evenings to the sound of gay music or when she combed her hair with a sort of sensuous care. But she never fooled Leonard, and before long he was able to tell, even at a distance, how she was feeling, as if her pain spread like vibrations through the air.

When things were at their worst a strange, sour smell seeped through the cracks around the bedroom door, and he could probably have coped with that if his mother had only sung out a little of her despair or seen to it that there was some connection between her words and her body language. She could be smiling and talking about the weather, but look as if she were going through hell, and often he wanted to shout: "For God's sake cry!" but all he got by way of a response was that she disappeared increasingly behind her emotional shutters, and instead of trying to prise them open he fled into himself. He hardly said a word and often he walked for hours along the beach or up towards the railway line, where he laid out his own special graveyard.

It had taken him days to find the spot. No-one was exactly generous with information and he would probably never have found it if he had not made a discovery one day next to a rusty silo and two straggling bushes. In the grass next to the tracks lay his father's black ribbed leather glove, and even if later he could not recall his thoughts at the time, he immediately sensed that it was something momentous. It was as if he had opened up a crucial trail, as if his father's death, instead of just being a tragedy, had now become a mystery, in which it would be possible to reach some kind of solution provided he studied the evidence and drew the correct conclusions. Time and again he asked himself if the glove had fallen out of his father's pocket, or if it had been thrown there in anger, or had maybe even been laid beside the tracks as a secret message.

For many years Leonard would search through literature for references to black gloves, hoping to find some hidden meaning, and he would become obsessed with his father's last steps and wonder if it were true, as he had read, that one's eyesight sharpens during the last minutes and becomes so intense as to register every detail in the surroundings, and if life really does pass before one, and whether in that case he had himself featured in the stream of memories, and if so what he had been doing—and whether he had appeared in a good or bad light.

He persisted hour after hour, day after day, but the glove led him nowhere except back to himself and he learned nothing more significant that autumn than that his father really had driven the family to the brink of ruin. The poor man had got caught up in a circle of harebrained schemes and idiotic ideas to rescue the situation and it was perfectly clear that there was no longer any money to send the boy to Marlborough College.

Leonard made it there anyway, just a little bit later, thanks to Aunt Vicky and a scholarship to study English and mathematics. He was pleased about it at first. He saw it as a means of getting away from home. But nothing was straightforward. It was October 1939. A war had broken out, and he stood at the station with his brown suitcases, and had the feeling that the whole world had gone to pieces. There were soldiers everywhere. A small child screamed, and his mother, who had a shiny pin in her hat, stroked his hair. From a distance it must have looked perfect if, that is, someone were looking at them in the same way that he observed others. His mother said all the right things:

"You'll be fine, Leonard. Write to me all the time," but everything that she said sounded hollow.

It was as if she were only acting the part of the loving mother, and while she pressed her lips against his cheek he imagined her eyes being completely vacant or even looking out for the men on the platform. Because it had got to the point where he thought that she only lit up when she met men who exuded worldliness and money. Probably it was unfair of him, but he was convinced that he was no longer any concern of hers and that she had turned towards a distant landscape where there was now no place for him, and he wanted to challenge her: *Why don't you see me? Why don't you love me anymore?*

But her offence was too subtle, too understated. There was no smoking gun, nothing to get hold of, and of course he hoped that he had been mistaken and that nothing had happened to his mother's love and presence, and that it was only her grief for his father which had stolen her away from him. But something within her really had hardened and if she had slapped him or punched him right there on the platform it could not have been more painful than the frostiness with which she delivered the edifying words: "You'll make me proud of you at school." "You're such a clever boy." "Keep away from the troublemakers!"

As the train pulled out of the station and he sat in his seat, which smelled of carbolic soap and alcohol from the soldiers, his mother did, it's true, look so small and sad there on the platform that for one moment he regretted not having thought more kindly of her, but in the next second a wave of pain washed through him, and in a quick entry in his diary which under other circumstances could have been the start of something better and represented some sort of low point, he wrote: "Be strong, be strong!"

The only problem was that Marlborough College didn't give him any opportunities to rebuild his strength. Instead the school confirmed the alarming feeling of homelessness which had appeared after his father's death and he came to loathe the place with a passion. Not only for the usual reasons: the dreadful food, the strict and unimaginative teachers and the vile system of fagging and punishment which condoned bullying by the older pupils. Nor was it because he lived in "A" House, which was known as "the prison," nor that the only things which really counted were rugby, cricket and athletics, all kinds of boring rubbish which he could not stand, and that it was no advantage at all to be the star pupil that he was. The real reason was entirely other.

10

HE HAD HELD THE medical reference book in his hands before, not only on occasions when he thought that he was ill but when he had wanted to read up on human biology. The book was brown and well-thumbed and not altogether up to date. Reading it gave him a feeling of travelling through his own body and sometimes he had felt the symptoms of the illnesses he was reading about, as if he had been infected by the words or simply that only through reading it did he understand how he felt. But this time, as he leafed through the book, he did not get stuck in any one place, and he quickly found what he was looking for: "Oestrogen, a steroid hormone . . . present in both men and women, but to a greater extent in women . . . diffuses across the cell membrane . . . affects secondary sexual characteristics such as the development of breasts and . . . is believed to govern the menstrual cycle . . . therefore known as the female sexual hormone."

He did not understand. "Known as the female sexual hormone"? Why in that case had they given it to Turing? He must have misheard. Not been paying attention. But no, he had repeated the word several times in his mind in order to remember it, and the brother had been certain. Alan Turing must have been given oestrogen. But it sounded so twisted, so sick. Corell did not know much about medical things, but *female hormone*, that was simply sickening, and shouldn't it rather have been the other way round?

He raised his eyes from the book and tried to consider this more soberly. *Female sexual hormone, female.* He did not have any idea what it was that caused homosexuality, but if it was anything, surely it wasn't lack of femininity! Pansies, they called them. His aunt had talked about a street in the West End of London where so-called Mollies, men dressed as women, offered themselves to other men. If homosexuals were missing anything at all, then surely it was manliness. Why not give them more of the male sexual hormone instead? Let them get a bit more of a beard and put some hair on their chests, become a little bit more manly. He did not understand. Why give Turing that stuff? It could not have been to mess him about. They had written "treatment," "medical treatment." There must have been a reason for it. You would not do something like that without extensive studies. There must be a scientific explanation. It was just that he did not have the whole picture. Scepticism, my boy, scepticism, the scholars are seldom as bright as they seem, his father used to say, and that could well be right, but surely they are not totally stupid? They would hardly force a university professor to take female hormones without good reason, would they?

Corell sat and looked out of the window for several minutes, feeling ill at ease, and he remembered the moment when he unbuttoned Turing's pyjamas and discovered the rather feminine breast and let his hands examine the body. There was something pretty threatening about that memory, wasn't there? He stood up. He went to the bundles of newspaper back copies, and looked feverishly for two things, the series about homosexuality in the *Sunday Pictorial* which Hamersley had spoken about and then what was written about Turing's trial. Neither was easy to find. He went back two, three years and leafed through the papers so eagerly that he tore several pages, and he was on the point of giving up. He looked nervously at his watch, he should have been back by now, but here . . . he saw some text about hormone treatment against homosexuality in the *Sunday Pictorial*. The article was lofty and without real substance, but he understood enough to realise that opinions were divided about homosexuality.

Many saw it as moral decay which could affect anybody who did not look after themselves, degeneracy in a word, a consequence of loose living. It was probably especially common among intellectuals, the article said, partly as a result of the mentality at private schools, and that was probably true. But it was also thought to be a sign of the times. To question established values, everything from the political system to sexual morality in general, was the fashion in artistic circles, the author wrote. Guy Burgess the spy and the Bloomsbury Set were cited, and so were certain groups at King's and Trinity, Cambridge, and the article went on to mention similarities between homosexuals and communists. Both organised themselves in underground cells, and both turned their backs on fundamental values. It was therefore not surprising that there were many bum boys amongst the reds, and what was needed, according to a succession of important people, was tougher punishments, no more nor less, in addition to unanimous condemnation.

Others, more "scientifically minded," defined homosexuality as an illness and prescribed treatment, which annoyed the conservatives who thought that this attitude relieved those who were guilty from all responsibility. Attempts had been made with lobotomy and chemical castration, but the results were unsatisfactory. Hormone treatment was seen as a more promising method. A Dr. Glass in Los Angeles had carried out some studies and come to the conclusion that homosexuals had more oestrogen in their bodies than other men, and this of course corresponded with Corell's assumption. In 1944 Dr. Glass had injected male sexual hormones into a number of bum boys and he apparently had high hopes of the experiment. He would be disappointed. At least five of the test cases became randier than ever, or "more homosexually inclined," as the article put it.

The failed experiment suggested that one should be doing the opposite. Give oestrogen instead. It seemed like a rather simplistic approach, Corell thought; if black doesn't work then try white. But a British doctor by the name of F. L. Golla, the head of the Burden Neurological Institute in Bristol, became a pioneer in the field and his studies suggested that oestrogen was indeed very effective. Provided the doses were sufficiently high, sexual desire disappeared within one month. There were minor side effects, of course, but they were considered negligible, temporary impotence for example, and also the development of breasts.

Turing was not mentioned in the article, and Corell leafed through the *Wilmslow Express* and the *Manchester Guardian*. He found very little about the trial, suggesting that Turing was not a prominent person. No reporter seemed to have found it worth the trouble to dig around in his dirty linen. Corell found a single short article under the headline: "University professor given probation order. To undergo organotherapeutic treatment."

Apart from recording the crime itself, the article said that the court had taken into account the fact that this was Turing's first offence. Neither were the courts as strict as they had been in Oscar Wilde's days, it stated. Only 176 of the 746 men who had been found guilty of gross indecency in 1951 had ended up in prison, and many, like Turing, had been given the choice between treatment and jail, between clink and female sexual hormones. Some choice, Corell thought, wondering if he would not himself have preferred to end up behind bars. In prison he could at least be himself. He could remain a man.

According to the *Sunday Pictorial* article, the oestrogen could conceivably—even if it was not considered likely—affect the nervous system. Experiments had been carried out on rats and some of them had shown signs of depression, although heaven knows how one can tell if a rat is depressed. Because its tail droops? Total nonsense! But to take a pill, have an injection, which gets into your bloodstream where it works away unseen and not only makes your bum look like a girl's but your breasts as well! Appalling. Without thinking, he touched his own breast, as if he were worried that it too had softened. He felt an inexplicable fear. To be wrenched out of your sexual identity, to wake up in the mornings and find yourself looking for fresh signs of change! He would not have been able to stand it for one day. He too would have wandered along that corridor on the upper floor and dipped the apple in the evil brew. What is there left once you lose your manliness? But actually . . . it was none of his business. *Be thankful that you never . . .* he could not stand it. He tried to think of something else. He tried to focus on his series of numbers again, but then . . . He was struck by a thought which could probably be said to be entirely professional. According to the article, the treatment was only to last for one year, which should mean that Turing stopped taking oestrogen in 1953, at least a year before his death, and that he started living normally after that. Not that Corell knew all that much about him, but at least it had not broken him. He had felt better, according to his brother, and bought tickets to the theatre, which of course meant nothing, but it was in any case not impossible that there were other reasons for his death than the trial. He had been watched. He had had his secrets. All sorts of things could have happened. On the other hand . . . Corell would never know, would he? Turing had taken his reasons with him to the grave. He should forget all about it. Anyway, he really needed to leave. Ross was probably already furious. Corell decided to hurry up and still—which surprised him— did not go straight back to the police station. He turned to the right, towards Alderley Road, as if the wind and the summer drew him away or as if his thoughts about the oestrogen and the suicide had awakened an urge in him to prove his manliness, and he walked to Harrington & Sons gentlemen's outfitters, not to buy clothes, God forbid. Without his aunt's allowance he could hardly afford a neckerchief in the shop. His intentions concerned a girl.

Her name was Julie. He did not know her surname. She was an assistant in the shop and when he had been in there to be measured for the tweed suit his aunt had given him for his birthday she had stuck pins into his trouser legs, measured his shoulders and waist, and it had felt good. It was care and attention he did not usually get, and he had stood tall, as if he really were someone to be reckoned with. Yet it had taken a while for him to notice her. She was neither beautiful nor striking, if anything shy to the point where she became invisible, but one incident was to change this very significantly. Leonard Corell was no ladies' man. He was often surprised at how solitary he had become, surprised by how few women he had had—the more so if one disregards the unsuccessful experiences with prostitutes in Manchester—and even though there were many reasons for this, his self-esteem was a decisive factor. He wanted to be more than he was today, one size larger as it were, an extension of Detective Constable Corell, the same person but with a few additional qualifications and qualities, perhaps the very man he had pretended to be when Julie was pinning up his trouser legs, and while waiting for that to happen he did very little about it. He became an expert at putting off his initiatives and approaches. It was no conscious strategy, certainly not. He was just held back by the thought that he was not ready yet, not that he was sure he would ever become much more than he was, but if there was indeed a myth inside him it would have resembled the story of the ugly duckling, and instead of doing something, he dreamed.

One day about a month ago he had seen a figure with soft lines who was dressing one of the Clark Gable–like dummies in the shop window. As he came closer he saw that it was Julie. She wore her hair up. She was dressed in a sober, green-checked jacket and skirt, and a blouse in an eye-catching colour which he had learned was called celadon, but even then he did not find her beautiful, and only when she wrapped a red scarf around Clark Gable did something happen. She started to shine and he remembered that he thought she radiated tranquillity, and he followed with his eyes the troubling contours of her hips and breasts, but when she bent down and straightened the dummy's trouser legs he saw that tears were running from her eyes, and he was filled with an intense desire to liberate her from the shop and the display window, from whatever it was that was tormenting her.

After that evening he often passed the shop and secretly it was enough for him to catch a glimpse of her to experience a mixture of terror and joy. Once or twice—depending on how he counted—a look had come in his direction, a look which stayed with him during the desolate days, no seductive or inviting look, rather a shy glance, full of something subdued and restrained, and he came to fantasise about how he would take her by the hand and lead her out of the shop, to something better and richer, where she would never again need to cry.

Now, as once again he walked in the direction of the shop, he had no expectations, but as so often before he wondered if he would not venture in and pretend to be interested in some fabrics for a summer suit, choosing perhaps between one or another, and think up a few witty things to say, even say something clever just on the borderline of what was acceptable, something which Harrington and his son would not understand but she would, with a secret smile, and that could be a start. Not that he would invite her out right away, no, no, he would be careful and dignified, but it would break the ice and the next time that they met by chance on a free Sunday, then it would become serious, all this he thought, but as he approached his courage failed him, and a few paces from the shop window he noticed with relief that she did not seem to be there.

All he saw were the Clark Gable dummies and Harrington himself.

But she appeared as if from nowhere and by sheer bad luck she turned straight towards Corell. He could not have been less prepared. He gave her a glued-on smile which he would come to analyse to the point of desperation, and he raised his right hand to his trilby in something which must have looked like a half greeting, a terrible sign of indecision, but the fact was that Julie smiled back.

Their eyes met for an instant, which was not much, but something at least, and he managed to hold the look for a little while before he glanced down and felt how his body became twitchy and awkward, and as he went on his way—what else was he to do?—he imagined how the whole street stared at his ungainly steps, but after a minute or so he felt a certain confidence despite everything and thought, *one day, one day,* without really knowing what that might mean.

11

NO-ONE SEEMED TO HAVE noticed his absence, and for a long while he just sat at his desk, unable to work. Then he asked to be put through to Sergeant Eddie Rimmer in Manchester. Rimmer answered immediately and at once made it clear that he was happy to talk with a colleague from Wilmslow, regardless of whether the conversation was important or not, and sometimes he was just plain crazy with his hacking, shrill laugh, and he did not really leave Corell any the wiser, but the conversation kept him amused and they spoke for a long time, longer than they needed to. Rimmer liked Turing:

"Quite simply a nice chap, and yet he should have been really cross with us. We broke him, like nobody's business. Just like that!"—there was a clicking sound over the telephone—"He just spat everything out. I didn't even have time to roll up my sleeves. Ha, ha. An odd fellow, I have to say. He had his degrees and all that stuff, but he never got on his high horse."

"Wasn't he in the least bit arrogant?"

"He had his sides, naturally. Sometimes you simply couldn't understand him—and then he was homosexual, of course, completely incorrigibly so, I think. But he meant no harm, not really. He was just made the wrong way."

Rimmer too had understood that the Foreign Office was interested in Turing. It was something to do with the atom bomb, he believed.

"The atom bomb?" Corell said.

"Everything to do with the bomb is so sensitive, you see," Rimmer said. "And that machine he was working on, it was used when the British bomb was developed. To work out how the atoms whizzed around, something like that." That at least was what Rimmer had heard. Not that he knew for certain, and maybe, he thought, Turing had been dealing with something similar during the war, a secret weapon or some such. He had been given a medal—nothing special, it's true, according to Rimmer, an O.B.E., just a basic O.B.E., but still . . . more to it than met the eye. Rimmer had noticed. There had been a lot of talk, and "my God what a to-do there was on account of some Norwegian boyfriend coming to see him."

"How do you mean?"

"Nobody said as much, but it was clear that he was a special case. He made our bosses half hysterical."

"Ours too," Corell said.

"You see. There's something fishy about it."

"Could he have been murdered?"

No, no, Rimmer would not go that far. He did not want to speculate either, he said, oblivious that he had been speculating away pretty well just then, and Corell dropped the subject and told him a little bit generally about the apple, the pan and the electric wires. Then he got to the real reason for the call.

"That man Arnold Murray and the Harry who carried out the burglary, do you know where one can get hold of them?"

Rimmer did not. They did not exactly sit and wait by the telephone and were not helpful enough to live in the same place. But he could ask around, he said, send off a few telexes if it was important, and Corell could not very well claim that it was but he would still be grateful, and then they talked about the goings-on on the Oxford Road, which had apparently slowed down lately, "no doubt because the queers have moved on to new hunting grounds. Because that's how it is, of course. We just shift the problem on to a new place."

"Sad but true."

"Wilmslow must be a quiet and pleasant place to work in crime. Many rich people there, aren't there?" Rimmer went on, and Corell answered that that was pretty much how it was, but unfortunately there were no policemen in that category, least of all he himself.

"Ha, ha," Rimmer chuckled.

"There's another thing I've been wondering. It maybe sounds a bit stupid," Corell said, and even if he felt too proud to do so he could not help asking.

"I like stupid questions," Rimmer said. "They allow one to feel intelligent for once."

Corell reminded his colleague of the strange marginal jotting about the liar's paradox in the interview notes.

"What did you mean by that?"

Rimmer was not sure. It was one of those things that he had understood at first but then later had muddled up: "Hardly something you go around thinking about, is it?" Still, Corell wanted to be told what he remembered, and Rimmer said that Turing had told him something along the lines of there being oddities in mathematics, in other words not in any particular numbers or calculations, but in the whole system behind it. The "I am lying" sentence was an example. Somehow it could be converted into numbers, and perhaps it looks simple. But it is neither true nor false. "It makes you dizzy just thinking about it," Rimmer said, and pointed out that it was not just a play on words but something serious, something which had got the boffins to scratch their heads about both this and that, and in an attempt to sort it all out Turing had invented a machine.

"What kind of machine?"

"Broadly speaking the same sort of machine that he was working on here in Manchester, I think."

"Are you sure about that?"

Rimmer was not sure. It was all beyond him, but whatever it was that Turing had invented was frightfully clever.

"Dr. Turing said that it was the mathematicians who won the war."

"What did he mean by that?"

"Don't ask me. He said many strange things. He claimed that one day that machine would be able to think like you and me."

"I've heard something similar," Corell said. "But surely that can't be true?"

"In any case it's not easy to understand it."

"From what I gather he wasn't an especially prominent mathematician," Corell said without really knowing why.

It just slipped out of him, but perhaps he was thinking about the limited coverage which Turing had got in the newspapers and maybe he wanted to show authority. He disliked the affected way in which Rimmer displayed his inability to follow Turing's reasoning.

"Perhaps he was pulling the wool over my eyes just a bit," Rimmer said. "But he was a nice chap. Gave us wine and played 'Cockles and Mussels' on his violin, you know." Rimmer hummed a few notes. Tee tum tum, tee tum tum.

"A sad end, I have to say," he said.

Corell muttered something to the effect that "it was hardly surprising that he took his own life, given the circumstances," and his colleague could have answered both this and that, but he replied by talking about a woman on Alton Road in Wilmslow called Eliza, and he wondered if Corell knew her because she was apparently a bit of all right, maybe a little old, but well-rounded and nice and "with as wonderful an arse as you could wish for." Rimmer was wondering whether to call her, he thought that they might have something going, but Corell said, "Sorry, I don't know her. But I'd like to thank you for the useful conversation."

"Good luck with the investigation," Rimmer said, clearly put out by the abrupt end to the call—he had only just started to talk about important things like Eliza's bum—but Corell couldn't be bothered to listen any longer. Very different thoughts had taken over his consciousness.

It was as if he were being led away to a secret place which was constantly eluding him, and subconsciously he dug his fingernails into the palms of his hands. Could it be simply that Alan Turing had been working on the big bomb, and that that was why he had caused such hysteria? The mathematicians won the war, Turing had told Rimmer. What else could he have meant except that people like him had worked out how to trigger those terrible monstrosities and make them explode. "The military had put him and a whole lot of other eggheads together to work in one place."

He saw the brother's face before him. "I have my ideas. But since Alan never said a word about it I'll probably have to keep my mouth shut." Corell decided to forget about it. What else could he do?

Pigeons were pecking away in the yard, and Alec Block was sitting a little further along, bent over some papers. It was a sorry sight. Everything about Block radiated gloom and want of self-confidence, and Corell thought, not unaware of the relevance to himself, that his colleague might have appeared in another light altogether if circumstances had been different and he wanted to ask, "Are you worried?" or even, "Can you understand that a person might want to take his own life?" but he stopped himself.

"Have you managed to find anything new?" he said.

He had not much but still something that seemed to suggest that Turing was planning his life as normal—for what that was worth. Turing had booked time on the machine at the university for today, Wednesday.

"Booked time on the machine?" Corell said.

Apparently you had to do that to have access to the machine, Block said. There was a queue for it.

"What sort of a machine is that?"

"Some kind of mathematics machine. It can calculate things very quickly."

"Do people call it an electronic brain?"

Block seemed puzzled by the question.

"I don't think so," he said. "I haven't heard that."

"What was Turing going to calculate?"

Block had no idea. Turing clearly kept himself to himself up there. He was a bit of a rum fellow at the university, someone with a grand title who came and went as he pleased. In recent years he had for the most part taken care of his own business, among other things the mathematical formulae behind biological growth.

"It sounds frightfully clever, I know," Block said, a bit like Rimmer. "But apparently everything grows according to special patterns, there are mathematical theories about how a flower develops its petals. Someone said that he had even studied how the spots grow on a leopard."

"Spots on a leopard," Corell muttered and lost his concentration.

The numbers in Turing's notebooks danced out in his thoughts again, and he remembered his old mathematics teacher, and some other distant memories, and he closed his eyes.

He was woken from his reverie by a telephone ringing. A Franz Greenbaum was calling. Corell could not at first place him. But he had been looking for him earlier in the day. Greenbaum was a psychoanalyst and his name had been written at the top of a page in Turing's books of dreams. Once Corell had given the reason for his call and explained what had happened, Greenbaum fell silent, very clearly shaken, and when Corell insensitively showed signs of impatience Greenbaum said that he and Alan had been more than analyst and patient, even to the point of being close friends. Corell muttered an "I understand." Sensing criticism in Corell's words, Greenbaum answered stiffly that he worked according to Jung's principles and that, unlike Freud, Jung thought that one could well have a personal relationship with one's patients.

"Was there anything you knew of to suggest that he was thinking of taking his own life?"

Greenbaum did not think so. Turing had come to terms with himself. He had become closer to his mother. He had thought deeply and clearly and even though he was a complicated character he was for the most part not inclined to be pessimistic, although there was a limit of course to what Greenbaum could say. He was bound by professional confidentiality.

"Perhaps you can tell me for how long he was your patient."

"For two years."

"Was the intention to cure him?"

"Of what?"

"Of his homosexuality."

"Not at all. I don't believe in that sort of thing."

"You mean you don't think that it can be cured?"

"If indeed there's anything there to cure."

"What do you mean by that?"

"Nothing really."

"I've just been reading that people are trying out different scientific methods."

"That's rubbish!" Greenbaum snorted.

He didn't seem to want to continue the conversation, and Corell should certainly have dropped the subject. The psychoanalyst showed signs of irritation, even contempt, but Corell wanted an answer to his question:

"Why wouldn't there be anything to cure? Homosexuality makes people unhappy and leads young people to ruin."

"May I tell you a little story?"

"Well, yes . . . of course," Corell answered hesitantly.

"A man who's been dreadfully neurotic and full of strange thoughts appears at his analyst's and says: 'Thank you, dear doctor, for curing me of my delusions. But what do you have to offer me instead?'"

"What are you trying to say?"

"That our enthusiasms and passions are an important part of our personality and if you take them away you remove something very fundamental. Alan was Alan and I don't think that he wanted to be cured of that."

"But he still took the female sexual hormone."

"He had no choice."

"Did he suffer from it?"

"What do you think? Would you have enjoyed it? "

Corell dropped the subject, and asked about the dream books. Nothing remarkable about them, Greenbaum said. He had asked Alan Turing to write down his dreams. Dreams can tell you a lot about yourself, he pointed out, and since Corell's recent patchy and disturbed sleep had given him closer experience of his own dreams than for some time, he asked Greenbaum if he believed that dreams could be deciphered.

"Deciphered. Funny that you should use that word," the psychoanalyst said. "But no, I don't think that they can be solved like a riddle, like a mathematical equation. But they do allow us to understand some important things about ourselves, for example what we suppress. May I ask you something very important? "

"That depends."

"I would like you not to read what Turing wrote in his dream books. They were not meant for outsiders, least of all for the authorities," he said, with a lecturing tone in his voice. This annoyed Corell and therefore—or at least partly therefore—he answered sharply that whereas he of course respected other people's integrity, as a policeman he occasionally had to weigh one interest against another and if Greenbaum knew something which could help the police to work out if it was suicide or not, it was his duty to say so. At first Corell was convinced that this would be the end of the exchange. But Greenbaum clearly felt the rebuke, and nervously or at least tentatively he said:

"Well no, not that I can think of . . . or maybe there is one thing, for what it's worth."

It was something that had happened in Blackpool. Greenbaum, his wife Hilla and Alan had been there in May, a glorious day. They had walked along the Golden Mile, past the attractions, and eaten ice cream. On an old caravan not far away from them there was a red sign: YOUR FORTUNE TOLD, and when he saw it Alan told them about a gypsy woman who had foretold his talent, or even his genius, when he was ten years old. Hilla encouraged him to have it done again now, "you're bound to hear more good news," and eventually Alan gave in and climbed into the caravan, and there sat an older woman in a full skirt with some sort of scar on her forehead. Greenbaum thought that Alan would come out again quite quickly. But it took some time. The minutes went by and when Alan finally emerged he was a changed man. He was pale. "What's happened?" Greenbaum asked. Turing did not answer. He did not want to talk about it. He said hardly a word during the whole bus journey back home to Manchester. He was in a terrible state and "the truth is," the psychoanalyst said now, "it was the last time that we saw each other, although we know that he was looking for us on Saturday. It hurts to think about it."

"So you have no idea what the fortune-teller can have said?"

"Only that it must have been something unpleasant."

"I thought their job was to paint the future in rosy colours. "

"Yes, what an old bag," Greenbaum hissed unexpectedly, and Corell remembered all the fortune-tellers in Southport in the summers, particularly one old woman with brown sticky lips and deep wrinkles on her hands and forehead who had dragged her long red nails over his hand and made him feel very ill at ease, even though she said that he would find happiness with a dark, mysterious girl and achieve fame and glory in a scholarly career, but even then, when the future had seemed bright, he did not believe it for a single moment.

He had never liked fortune-tellers, never even read novels about them and he did not like the idea that a man of science had allowed himself to be influenced by one, and in his thoughts he assembled a picture of gypsy women, thinking machines, experiments with cyanide and gold and pans full of bubbling poison. It all seemed like alchemy and hocus-pocus. Perhaps Alan Turing was mad after all.

"So he seemed highly strung?"

"That's my judgement, at least he was at that time, but if you take a longer-term view he had become much better," Greenbaum said, and before long Corell said "thank you" and hung up.

That conversation had not made him any wiser either and he thought that he probably would not make much more progress. There always seemed to be a wall in the way, and even if he could certainly find cracks in it after a while, he did not have much time at his disposal. The order had been given for a speedy investigation. An inquest into the cause of death led by the coroner James Ferns was already to be held the following evening, and that was shamefully soon, he thought, given all the uncertainty, and he really ought to concentrate on essentials, but instead of doing something sensible he ran his index finger over one of the three dream books which were lying on his desk.

The book was bound in reddish-brown leather with "Harrods" in small letters in the top left-hand corner. "I would like you not to read what Turing wrote in his dream books." Greenbaum's words irritated him and made the book shine with a new lustre. He opened it. On the inside there was the heading "Dreams," written in blue letters which themselves seemed dreamlike. The semicircle of the "D" formed the back of the "R" and created a spider-like sign which looked as if it could have walked off the page on its own. Generally the handwriting seemed nervous, even occult—as if the letters were conscious of the fact that they were carrying a dark secret—but his learning of the incident with the fortune-teller was probably affecting his perception of it. Perhaps the fact that it was hard to read also heightened the sense of mystery. What might the fortune-teller have said? He could not care less. He had no time for superstition and similar nonsense, but still . . . what words from an unknown woman could have the power to throw a person completely off balance?

Of course it depends on all sorts of things—on a person's state of mind and his life. It isn't the content in itself, but rather which chords it strikes. One can be driven to despair simply because someone says bicycle pump or tractor and it was pointless to speculate about what could have been said. Two words did, however, occur to him, the words "damned" and "rejected." *You've been rejected, Leonard. You're damned . . .* that's the kind of thing you hear in a nightmare, the kind of thing you don't understand, but which can scare you witless, and that is why he has got to read these dream books. It was his damned duty, wasn't it? Perhaps there was something important in them, something which explained what had happened—Greenbaum could go to hell!—and feeling strained he read a little bit here and there in what seemed to be the most recent passages. It wasn't easy. The sentences were hard to decipher and he skipped back and forth. He came across the name Christopher several times, *darling Christopher, dear beautiful Christopher.* Who was that? Corell did not find any clues; he read about a night when Turing lay sleeping in an oblong hall and suddenly woke up and "heard the abbey bell ring." It wasn't clear where this was, it was perhaps in the dream that he woke up, in any case it was dark and quiet, and Turing walked up to a "four-paned window" and gazed at the sky through a pair of binoculars. "Above the Ross house" the moon was shining. It could have "become a beautiful night," but something happened. "Stars fell." A beam of light swept across the sky and "the world became smaller and colder" and Turing realised that "he would be left alone." The date February 6, 1930, was noted down. "His thoughts flew alone through the darkness." A great sorrow seemed to have struck him. Had Christopher died?

Corell read on, to find out more, but it was a book of dreams, nothing more. There was no single theme running through it. As soon as the words were clear they drifted away and Corell skimmed his way forward to a story in which a young man in shorts lay on the floor and listened to "clicking and clattering sounds just as at Bletchley," and where a hand was stretched out, a fine, long hand which passed over the body . . . Corell pushed the book aside. He would never think of reading something like that!

But still he did read on. The text drew him in, but no, he refused, he did not want to know, it was dreadful filth, and for a moment he felt transported back to the cold rooms at Marlborough College, and that was just too much. He jumped up and went out to fetch three envelopes. He put the dream books into them. Then he wrote John Turing's address in Guildford three times and sealed the envelopes, which he would come to regret, and he was clearly looking pained because Kenny Anderson asked:

"Are you having a stroke?"

"No, no. It's nothing."

"Are you sure?"

"Absolutely. I was just wondering. Do you know what Bletchley is?"

"What?"

"Bletchley," he repeated.

"Sounds like a make of car."

"You must be thinking of Bentley. This appears to be the name of a place."

"In that case I don't know."

"Have you seen Gladwin, by the way?"

"I think he's got the day off."

Corell mumbled something and walked with quick steps into the archive room, and started to leaf through the reference books.

12

AT MARLBOROUGH THERE WERE two boys called Abbott and Pickens. They were a year older than Corell and both the sons of bishops, and even though they both were very different, each had been endowed with a refined sadism. That Corell was the one who became their main target was probably only the result of an unfortunate whim on their part, but Leonard was a gratifying victim. He had no friends and nowhere to escape to, and he immediately repaid Abbott and Pickens in the currency which they most appreciated: in a visible and substantial suffering. During these years—the war years—the school was a cramped and messy place. More than four hundred boys from the City School in London had been evacuated to Marlborough to escape the Blitz, and even though Leonard, with his lack of pushiness, tended to be invisible, it was hard for him to escape. As he was walking up the stone steps of "A" House one winter morning he was stopped.

"We want to talk to you, boy."

Abbott was tall, fair and stooped and however unlikely it might have sounded for a boy of his age it looked as if he were going bald. A bare patch decorated the crown of his head. Pickens was dark, smaller and stockier. You did not need to be too sharp-witted to work out that he was good at rugby but had a difficult time keeping up at school. His eyes shone with an exquisite blend of brutality and dullness, but even though he was usually ingenious in his meanness, he could not find any fault with Corell that day. That was not necessarily to Corell's advantage. His inability to come up with something to pick on only made Pickens angrier, and in the end he was helped out by the school rules. According to them, school books should be carried under one's left arm and should only stick out a little at the front, and this rule was perhaps introduced to stop the pupils from hurting each other with their books, but the main objective was probably to give the older ones an opportunity to make life difficult for the younger ones:

"Your books are sticking out."

"Really?" Leonard said.

"What do you think it would look like if everybody carried their books like that?"

"What would it look like if everybody stopped each other on the stairs and made idiotic remarks?" Bearing in mind Corell's earlier behaviour in school, this was bafflingly outspoken, but since there was nobody else around, no-one who would be impressed by his cheek, he had little to show for it.

Pickens did not like wisecracks and replied by pushing Leonard in the chest and ordering him to run up and down the stone steps twenty times. Tearing back and forth on the stairs like this was a normal punishment in "A" House and while Leonard got going Abbott and Pickens stood down on the landing and supervised him. Until then Corell had not had a particularly complicated relationship with his own body. He had never devoted a thought to whether it was beautiful or ugly. Now he learned that he had a girl's bottom.

"Look at that girl's bum," Pickens said, and then they both laughed, and whether that meant that his behind was large or small Leonard did not know, but he understood enough to realise that it was far worse than being known as an idiot or a wimp.

It was something which stuck to him and sullied him, and he felt naked, even though he was properly dressed under his school uniform. Not long afterwards they began to call him "the Girl," and as always in those situations others joined in, not everybody, not at all, but enough for the name to spread and become his nickname. "He's a bum boy," Abbott told everybody. "I'm not," Leonard hissed, but it was not long before he started to examine his own body with a new suspicion, as if the assertion really might be true, and every day he thought that he had found worrying fresh signs. His chest was too weak and sunken, his legs too spindly for his hips, and the long eyelashes much too feminine, and sometimes he could not understand that the person looking out from the bathroom mirror was really him. Was there not some other representation of him somewhere, something which was closer to the image he had of himself?

It felt as if his own personality were falling away bit by bit, and as if he could no longer bring himself to occupy the present moment. His thoughts were sucked in on themselves, as if poisoned by their own reflecting, and, while he hated his tormentors and was furious about the accusations, most of all he was ashamed, and he despised himself, and in the end he had nowhere to escape to, neither inwards nor outwards.

He still did well at school, especially in English and mathematics, but he no longer came top. He lost his eagerness to learn and his positive spirit. Often he did not even dare to put his hand up and he became less and less visible. There was not a single area in which he was able to show what he was capable of, and it became an obsession, a constant feeling that he was letting down the person he had once been and was intended to become. It got to the point that he prayed to God that force of will or a stroke of magic would give him back his old self.

He became increasingly possessed by the thought that somebody, a teacher, a girl, or even a new idea would help him to bring out his real personality, and that he would one day be transformed into something bigger and richer than the inhibited boy his boarding school had made him. But nothing happened, nothing but new troubles, and even though he learned with time to look at life more objectively, the thought never entirely left him. After periods of listlessness it would flare up again and he could be galvanised for a while and think that he saw an opening, a crack in the door, but he had always been disappointed and it was almost against his will that he now allowed the investigation into Alan Turing to bring his old dreams back to life.

13

CORELL LOOKED UP the liar's paradox in the *Encyclopaedia Britannica*. He was not expecting to find an explanation of Rimmer's extract in the interview notes, still less to learn anything about the dead man's work, but he did hope that it would help him to understand a little better what he found appealing in the paradox.

It was described as a statement claiming to be false and therefore true precisely when it is false and whose inherent contradiction causes our concept of the truth to break down or, so to say, to be temporarily suspended.

It had been invented by a Cretan philosopher, Epimenides, many hundreds of years before Christ. In its original version it read: *The Cretans are always liars, as a Cretan poet said to me*, but it could be expressed in other ways, for example in the simpler form: *This statement is false.* Corell did not know why, but the statement seemed to him to have a kind of elusive quality. Not that he really believed Rimmer when he claimed that it had caused a crisis in mathematics and given rise to a revolutionary machine, but he liked to ponder it—the statement got his thought processes working—and he tried to find variations of it. Among other things he muttered, "I don't exist," but it immediately struck him that this was another type of contradiction; something which could not be said without telling a lie, because of the very circumstances of life; and it took him a while before he managed to dismiss the topic. The paradox stuck with him like an old popular song that he could not get out of his head.

He only started to think about other things once he was on the bus going to see his aunt in Knutsford, and when he got off at Bexton Road and a cool breeze blew in his face he wondered if he should have brought a present with him, some flowers or something for pudding. But the shops were closing and as he passed the half-timbered houses he decided not to bother, and just to let himself be carried away by the evening and this momentary breathing space. Knutsford at dusk meant freedom for him. In a little while he would be sitting down with a glass of sherry, complaining about his day until the discussion slid over into something more agreeable. With his aunt he spoke more or less openly and without watching his tongue or concealing his background. He could be undisguisedly intellectual and refer to whichever books he wanted without annoying anybody, and even if there was something embarrassing about having an aged relative as his best friend, he always hurried through the streets of Knutsford as if setting out on some splendid adventure.

His aunt had never married. She was sixty-eight and had been a suffragette in her youth and had been arrested for throwing a stone at the window of a Member of Parliament. Her name was Victoria, but everybody knew her as Vicky, and she had gone to Girton College in Cambridge. Just like Leonard's mother, she had not finished her studies, but had instead taken a job as an editor at the publishers Bodley Head in London and reviewed books in the *Manchester Guardian* under the pseudonym Victor Carson. Her hair was always cut short and she insisted on wearing trousers whatever twists and turns fashion was currently taking. Ever since she was young, people had called her shrewish and masculine, and she could certainly flare up in conversation, but Corell never saw her as unfeminine or hot-tempered. She was the nearest thing he had ever known to a caring mother, and she always saw to it that he had enough to eat and plenty to drink, if only because she herself always got drunk. In fact, she drank like a fish. Yet she always moved with grace, despite her years and her rheumatism. You could not really say she was rich. But she was the only one in the family who had anything left, and since she had neither children nor expensive habits, apart from her drinking and her buying of books, she lavished a great deal on Leonard. She gave him an allowance and presents, most recently a radio and the made-to-measure tweed suit which he had owned for several months but not yet worn for the simple reason that he had not found a suitable occasion.

Surprisingly enough, given her social skills, she hardly saw anyone other than Rose, who was fifteen years her junior and sometimes came up from London and stayed for a few days.

As Corell turned in to Legh Road, with its many magnificent houses, and approached Vicky's unmown lawn and unweeded flower beds, and he saw the tower-like red-brick house which was also handsome but more run-down than those of the neighbours, he felt a sudden pang, and began to worry that he would not be received as warmly as before. But then he saw her wave and it felt as if he had come home.

Vicky was wearing a lilac jumper, a tight leather waistcoat and a pair of dark, flowing trousers, and she was leaning on a black silver-tipped cane which she would sometimes get out when she was feeling stiff.

"How are you feeling?" he said.

"I'm an old bag. But it's a beautiful evening, and now you're here, so I'll probably survive. What happened to my little boy? What a handsome man you are."

He said nothing. He thought that the compliment was silly. Still, he was happy to hear it, and he went into the house and took a deep breath. Dinner was ready. From the window he saw that the table had been laid in the back garden and without asking he carried out the pans and shooed away some pigeons which had been drawn to the butter and bread there. They were having shepherd's pie with beans and potatoes and decided to start with mild ale before going on to sherry and for safety's sake they wrapped grey blankets around themselves. It was a beautiful evening, but there was a breeze, and Vicky curled up on her chair and started to talk about politics. She laid into Eisenhower and his talk about the domino theory, and Corell started to think about other things—above all about Julie—but as they refilled their glasses the mood lightened.

"Do you remember that Daddy used to tell us some funny story about the liar's paradox?"

"Remind me, what was the liar's paradox."

Corell told her.

"Yes . . . yes . . . I think I know what you mean. What was it again? Something about a dragon's head, wasn't it? A statue?"

"He'd been somewhere in Rome."

"That's right, and there was this dragon's head and according to some legend whoever put his hand in the dragon's mouth and told a lie would never be able to pull it out again, wasn't that it?"

"Exactly!"

"But your father put his hand in and said . . . Or rather, he claimed to have said—I'm pretty sure that he pinched the story from someone else."

"Me too."

"It's too good to be his own. But he claims that he said . . . help me here, Leo . . . I can't remember, what could he have said?"

"I think it was something like: 'I will never again be able to take my hand out.'"

"That's right, which was supposedly very clever."

"Very."

"Now, why was that? This sort of stuff makes my head spin."

"Because the poor dragon must have been completely confused," he said. "What was it meant to do? If it allowed the hand to remain there, then the words were true and Daddy should have been able to pull out his hand. But if the statue let him pull it out, then the legend would be wrong. So it was possible to lie and keep one's fingers. The way in which he said it defeated the dragon."

"Poor dragon. What made you think of it?" she said, and downed yet another glass of sherry.

"Well, I don't know . . ."

He wasn't really sure what to say.

". . . perhaps because I always thought that the liar's paradox was only an amusing riddle, a little flourish, but now I've heard that contradictions like that one have posed problems for mathematics as a science," he said.

"I see," she said, and suddenly seemed tired.

The hand holding the sherry glass shook slightly, and she had unusually dark rings under her eyes.

"I hope you're looking after yourself," he said.

"I'm one big health farm. What's going on at the station? Let's have some gossip! Tell me what idiots your bosses are!"

"You can't imagine how daft they are!"

"Especially that man Ross."

"Especially him! Right now he thinks that the most important thing in the world is to nail someone who's been dropping litter."

"But aren't you doing anything exciting? Can't you tell me a little bit about the underworld?"

She gave an encouraging smile.

"I'm investigating the death of a homosexual."

"A homosexual? Thank goodness it wasn't a heterosexual," she answered with unexpected sarcasm.

Corell was startled.

"I didn't mean it like that," he said, wounded.

"Didn't you?" she answered. "You're not usually so precise about the sexual leanings of the victims you deal with."

"I only said it because it is relevant to the case. The victim was convicted of gross indecency and we think that his despair over that drove him to suicide."

"I see. Did he do anything else apart from being a homosexual?"

"Yes," he said sulkily.

"So he wasn't a full-time queer. How vexing for him. There's never any time for pleasure nowadays."

Why this sudden acid tone?

"He was a mathematician," he muttered.

"Was he, now? An intellectual, in other words. Where did he study?"

"At King's, Cambridge."

"You used to be pretty clever yourself, once," she said in an obvious effort to repair the mood.

"I was," he answered and knew very well that he sounded like a hurt child.

"Can you tell me about this man's trial? It would interest me, and forgive me, dear boy, if I sounded touchy just then. I've been feeling a bit poorly today, as you've noticed."

"Don't worry," he said. "Don't think of it."

But he was still sullen. At work he had learned to cope with every conceivable tone of voice, but he was far more sensitive at his aunt's house and it took a while before he regained his composure and only once he had told her about the oestrogen did a tiny bit of intensity creep into his words.

"How awful," she said when he had finished his account. "How awful."

"Yes."

"May I ask you something, Leo? And don't take it unkindly. Do you think they were right to convict this man?"

"Yes, I think so . . ." he began, but stopped in the middle of the sentence.

He thought that he could see his aunt's lips forming into a new sarcastic expression.

Was she going to start all over again?

"It was dreadful to give him that female hormone," he said. "He seems to have become something of a guinea pig, but apart from that, yes, I think it was right, I do. He broke the law and society has to react to that. Otherwise the whole thing could spread."

"And what's so dangerous about that?"

"First of all, because it makes people deeply unhappy and alienates them from society."

"But that's hardly the fault of the homosexuals."

"Well whose fault is it then?"

"Ours, of course. We're the ones who marginalise them."

"But my God, Vicky . . ." He felt a sudden indignation. "They've chosen their own path and, say what you will, it can hardly be regarded as especially natural."

"In what way?"

"Surely it's obvious?"

"Is it? And since when has nature been our reference point? Some pretty strange things happen out there. Have you not noticed? Do we have to imitate all of it? Eat our spouses, the way those spiders do?"

"Don't be silly. But man and woman, that's the very basis for our continued survival, isn't it? If we were all queer, the human race would die out."

"So far as I know, not everybody *is* queer."

"Well it seems as if more and more are."

"Does it indeed?"

"That's what all the research seems to suggest."

"Some research!"

"What do you know about it? I was just talking to our chief, whom I happen to know quite well," he began and felt a bit boastful.

"I can see that you're hurt," his aunt interrupted. "But I can't help being surprised."

"About what?"

"To hear the son of James Corell, who preached tolerance and respect all his life, speak like that."

"Don't drag that old failure up again. I don't want to hear about him," he said with unexpected venom.

"Now you're just being silly," she snapped back.

"I'm not."

"Yes, you are, you're being unfair and touchy."

"Hasn't that idiot done me enough harm? Do you have to beat me over the head with him too?"

"James was a gasbag and a liar and a disaster at managing the family's money, but he was still a good person in many ways, you know that, Leo. Above all he showed political courage, and it wouldn't hurt . . ."

"If I did as well, is that what you're saying? That I'm a cowardly weakling and a failure?"

"For God's sake, Leo, what are you talking about? I think you're a wonderful person, you know that. I only mean—"

"What the hell do you mean?"

He could not understand why he was so upset.

"That you could stick up for this poor man. I assume your colleagues are also sneering at him."

"I'm not sneering at him. He's dead. I have the greatest respect . . ."

"O.K., O.K. Tell me instead, Leo, why do you have such a problem with homosexuals?"

"I don't have a problem with them."

"Did something happen to you? I know that you had some unpleasant experiences at Marlborough?"

"Nothing happened to me. I just think that homosexuals are harmful to society and sap our morals."

"How very like a priest you've suddenly become. May I tell you something?"

"Of course."

"You talked about nature. Christians also tend to do that. We're supposed to live in accordance with nature, they say, but certainly not like pigs, dogs and flies. But Leo, what if nature has given us homosexuals specifically to allow us to survive and see new perspectives. Have you ever considered how many new ideas have come to us from people with those inclinations?"

"I'm not so sure."

"Just look at the world which I know best, the world of literature. There's any number of homosexuals there. Proust, Auden, Forster, to name but a few, Isherwood, Wilde, Gide, Spender, Evelyn Waugh, well, I'm not entirely sure about him, and then Virginia Woolf, of blessed memory."

"She was married, surely."

"But she loved Vita Sackville-West, and has it occurred to you that it may not be a coincidence that there are so many of them?"

"What are you talking about?"

"Those who are different, also have a tendency to think differently."

"Just because it's different, doesn't necessarily mean that it's good."

"True. Sometimes what's conventional is right. It happens, but it isn't usual. This man who died, what did he actually do, do you know anything about that?"

"I've just started working on it. But I think he was doing something with machines," he said, happy that she had changed subject.

"Machines," she said in surprise. "Doesn't sound like something for a mathematician."

"Why not?"

"They usually consider themselves too good for engineering work.

How does that saying go? Mathematics is the art of the useless, a little bit like art for art's sake."

"I don't think he was a particularly good mathematician," he said, and repeated what he had said to Eddie Rimmer.

"Yes, well, it doesn't matter now. Poor devil!"

"Yes, I suppose so."

"Just think about it . . . he does no-one any harm, he just follows his natural inclinations, like all of us he looks for passion and love, 'the love that dare not speak its name' as Oscar Wilde put it, and for that he is disgraced and persecuted and hounded to his death. Can that be right?"

"Not exactly."

"But apparently almost so?"

"Do stop it!"

What was the matter with her?

"He picked up criminals on the Oxford Road," he said, "and do you know what sort of an area that is, the most disgusting place I've ever seen, full of—"

"Of what?" she interrupted.

"Of criminals and dirty old men."

"Of unfortunates, as Dostoyevsky would have put it."

"Spare me your bloody novels!"

"My, my, Leo. Surely you're the one who's so fond of literary references? But what was this man supposed to do? He couldn't very well ask men out to dance. Didn't you say that he was at King's?"

"That doesn't exactly make things better," Corell snorted.

"Pretty well everyone at King's is said to be homosexual."

"I wonder."

"Definitely," she said. "Or at least in my opinion pretty well everyone. There are perhaps no more there than anywhere else. But they're noticeable, and one can of course wonder why. But one reason must be the Apostles."

"What's that?"

"A select little society at King's and Trinity which your father so eagerly and vainly wanted to get into. Keynes, the economist, was a driving force then. I wonder if Wittgenstein wasn't also a member?

Forster definitely was. The Apostles idealised homosexuality. Lytton Strachey even referred to it as the higher sodomy—as something which was better than the good old biblical union."

"That's dreadful."

"Do you really think so? In my opinion homosexuals could do with some encouragement. They don't usually get much in the way of applause."

"That's not funny, Vicky."

"I'm not trying to be funny. I'm only trying to say that homosexuals are treated badly, even worse than us women, which is saying quite a lot. Our dead friend must have been snatched away from Cambridge's secure embrace to a bigoted and cold Manchester. I can't understand why we moved to the area, Leo. Incomprehensible! Have you ever seen an uglier city? Why didn't we choose a nicer part of the country?"

He did not answer. He felt misunderstood and thought that she was teasing him and normally there would not have been anything wrong with that. It was a joy when she heckled the world, but now her sallies were directed at him and they hurt. She was his refuge. She of all people should stand by his side. Now she accused him of being intolerant and it was unfair. Had he not always supported her when it came to women's rights? Had he not agreed that Indians and Pakistanis in London were being treated disgracefully? There was a limit to his tolerance and, quite honestly, his aunt ought to see that it would be doing homosexuals a disservice to let them carry on. For heaven's sake, these were people who knowingly and willingly had chosen the unnatural and perverse, and even though she would certainly have dismissed this as dreary moralising it was simply a fact that one lapse so easily leads to another. He knew that from his own experience. The sum of all vices does not remain constant. Each one breeds another. But he could not be bothered to argue any longer. He wanted his good old Vicky back and therefore reached out a conciliatory hand, opening himself up a bit, although reluctantly, but it was usually guaranteed to get his aunt to soften:

"This man . . ." he began.

"Yes."

"He was probably a decent enough chap. Maybe a bit naive, and inclined to exaggerate, but affable and never arrogant it seems and sometimes . . . I don't know . . . I think that I envy him his life and what he got to learn. I'd even say that the mere fact of thinking about that paradox has livened me up a little and sometimes I wish . . ."

"What do you wish, my dear?"

"That I could have worked on it."

"What do you mean?"

He did not really know what to answer.

"They didn't send him to Marlborough," was all he said, and he heard how bitter he sounded. "He was meant to go there, but his brother advised against it and then he was up at Cambridge."

"And you would have liked that too."

"There wasn't the money."

"That could have been arranged, as you know. But you didn't want it, you wanted to get away from everything, and my guess is, that's exactly what you needed. Who knows, in the end that might turn out to have been the right decision?"

To become a policeman? That was nonsense, but she meant well, he knew that. It was just that certain things were better left unsaid, and he looked away with resignation at the ivy on the stone wall. Then he felt her hand against his cheek. Her fingers were rough against the stubble. They smelled of tobacco.

"Don't worry," she said.

"Please!"

He withdrew her hand.

"People are so unnecessarily negative about envy. It really ought to be struck off the list of deadly sins."

"My dear Vicky," he said. "You're talking an unusual amount of rubbish this evening."

"Envy," she said, "is nothing to be ashamed of, not if one's aware of it. It can even be constructive."

"That's utter balderdash."

"Unfortunately it's rather common for people to mistake their envy for some kind of righteous indignation at other people's faults, and that's when it can become unpleasant or even dangerous, but otherwise . . ."

"What?"

"It can lend a little clarity. Nothing much happens in the world without envy. I think it's a good thing that you envy this man his knowledge."

He said nothing. He emptied his glass and looked down at the white, flaking table. Vicky lit a cigarette and put it into a dark, long cigarette-holder and started to talk about other things, but their conversation had awakened such a feeling of unease in him that he just answered "yes" and "that would be nice," without really listening to the questions, until he realised that his aunt was talking about the imminent solar eclipse.

"Why don't we sit here in the garden and sip our drinks while the world grows dark?" she was saying.

"I doubt if I'll be able to take time off," he said. "It's presumably happening in the middle of the day?"

"Well, at night you don't really get much of a solar eclipse, do you?"

Later on, lying in the bed on the top floor which he had so longed for, the unpleasant thoughts returned again and true to their grim logic they grew stronger as he tried to keep them at bay, and he twisted and turned on the mattress until his aunt's wall clock in the hall struck three and he shuffled down the stairs and stopped the pendulum. It felt like an egg in his hand, and he looked down at his feet, and felt as if he were being carried back in time. He still had in him a lingering darkness from Marlborough. It was not just the memory of the insults *girl* and *queen*, or his recollections of being hit and mockingly fondled in the showers and the dormitories.

It was that he had allowed it to happen. His father had once said that a person can respond to a crisis either by fighting or fleeing, and that had immediately rung true, but his father had forgotten the third way. Corell read about it much later. A person can also play dead, like the Siberian raccoon dog, and looking back at the years at Marlborough, Corell realised that that is precisely what he had done. He had wandered around as if paralysed, and even though he promised himself time and again that he would fight and protest and grow as a human being, he did nothing, not the slightest thing, and sometimes when he was feeling especially pessimistic he thought that his life now in Wilmslow was continuing in exactly the same way.

Over and over again he had made the decision to escape from the police force and find something better and worthier to do. Take off, he had commanded himself, but he hadn't budged. He didn't have the strength to tear himself away, but one day, he thought, one day, and with that vague promise singing in his thoughts, he finally managed to fall asleep.

At the same time a tall man by the name of Oscar Farley climbed out of his hotel bed in Manchester with an aching body and looked out through the smog at the city. Unlike Corell he had had a good night's sleep, but that was only thanks to the sleeping pills and painkillers which he had taken the evening before and which, considering how he felt, must have come close to an overdose. He felt very sick and the lumbago which he had been suffering from for four days seemed worse than ever. "My God," he muttered, and stood still, leaning against the white wash-basin with a grimace which made his handsome face look old, or even like that of a dying man. Yet it was not the pain which affected Oscar Farley the most. He thought of Alan Turing: Alan on the autopsy slab in Wilmslow and Alan looking down into a pit by the side of an old pagoda tree in Shenley, and he felt guilty, not the sort of guilt you feel immediately after committing a crime or a sin but a more uncertain and worrying feeling that he had been a bad person. *Have we killed him?*

Farley himself had admittedly tried to stand up for Turing, and everything seemed to have been done in accordance with the rules, but there were still uncomfortable aspects to the story. The longer Farley thought about it and the more he analysed what had happened, the more it felt as if something important were eluding him, something which could blow up in their faces at any moment. It was not only the knowledge of all the information which Alan held, or even his trips abroad, and the heated atmosphere at Cheltenham. It was the feeling itself that he had left behind him.

Was there really no letter, no note anywhere which would explain things?

Farley looked around the hotel room, as if that letter might have turned up there, and he wondered if they had perhaps been in too much of a frenzy when they searched through the house. Could they have missed something obvious, like someone who looks everywhere for his spectacles except on the end of his nose? Or did the policemen who were first on the scene find something after all, a few lines which with their limited knowledge they were unable to interpret, or whose significance they did not understand? It would not of course have been like Alan to put his feelings into a letter, but he could at least have given them a clue, a message telling them that England did not need to worry. However headstrong he had been, had there not after all also been a considerate side to him? Farley looked at his watch. Was it in order for him to go in and see his colleague? They needed to discuss their strategy for all the meetings that day. No, it was still too early, and actually he did not really feel like it.

Robert Somerset was one of his friends at the firm, but something had happened these last few days. It was as if the death had driven them apart, and Farley had begun to observe the same signs of unhealthy suspicion of everything that was different and strange—or which could even remotely be connected with Burgess and Maclean—in Robert as in so many others, and Farley guessed that this was exactly how hysteria develops, that the first to be affected were those who were already overexcited, but that it then spread even to those who were more sensible. Was he becoming paranoid himself? While Oscar struggled to get dressed and tried to put a healthier colour on his face by giving himself a few small slaps, he remembered the only time when he had seen Alan cry, but at the time they had not been real tears, and when he thought about it he smiled and felt it was doing him good.

It was going to be a long day.

14

THE SUN WAS SHINING OVER Knutsford the morning of June 10, 1954. Leonard Corell was sitting in the paved back garden in a frayed blue dressing gown drinking Earl Grey tea while the radio played Cole Porter and his aunt, somewhat unsteady, emerged from the house carrying the breakfast tray.

"The full monty!"

"Wow!" he exclaimed, with genuine enthusiasm, and the plate really was piled high: there was fried bread, black pudding, tomatoes, baked beans, potato croquettes, mushrooms, bacon and eggs, and orange juice too.

He would not need to eat again until the evening and he gave a big grin, and said something about how he had stopped the pendulum. She replied that she could tell exactly at what time the crime had been committed and wondered if he had got any sleep at all. He said he had, and that he felt rested, which was not simply a lie. He had found a kind of rest in his tiredness, a pleasant exhaustion which killed off his unease, and reasonably content he started to read the *Manchester Guardian*, which lay neatly folded next to the tray. Nothing caught his attention. He would have preferred to lose himself in a book, like his aunt, who was browsing through Yeats's *The Hour Glass*, but he could not be bothered to get up and fetch one. He had to make do with one or another of the stories in the newspaper, for example that the B.B.C. was going to start broadcasting the news on television as well and that the House of Lords was debating why it was that policewomen in Scotland had to resign when they got married, or that a fellow officer in Douglas, Dundee, had stolen

£120 out of the police safe and that his lawyer had defended the theft on the basis that the man had been mixing with people from a higher social class than his own, and Corell sniggered a little at that, although he could not care less about it. Then he suddenly froze.

In the left-hand column on page eleven there was an article about Alan Turing. It was not much. Only an extended notice. But it concerned Corell's assignment, and when newspaper material was relevant to him, especially on the rare occasions when he was mentioned, the world came to a standstill for a moment and he became frightened. Still, he was pleased whenever his name was included. Whenever there was anything about him in the press he began to daydream, but even before he had fully understood what had been written he was always worrying that it would be something that humiliated or ridiculed him, and now he scanned the piece anxiously and realised to his disappointment that there was no reference to him, and that somebody else at the station, presumably Block, had provided the information. The article appeared under the heading "Obituary" and was very well-intentioned. It began:

> An inquest will be held today concerning Dr. Alan Mathison Turing, reader in the theory of computing at Manchester University since 1948, who was found dead in bed at his home in Adlington Road, Wilmslow, on Tuesday morning.

After a short and reasonably accurate account of the circumstances surrounding Turing's death, it continued:

> Dr. Turing was one of the pioneers behind the electronic calculating machine in this country. He is regarded as being the author of the theoretical basis for the digital data machine. While at Manchester he was one of the scientists responsible for the "mechanical brain," known as Madam (Manchester Automatic Digital Machine) and "A.C.E."
>
> One of his machines, he claimed, had solved in a few weeks a problem in higher mathematics which mathematicians had been working on since the nineteenth century. Together with Professor F. C. Williams, also at Manchester University, he invented two features for the

calculating machines which made a significant contribution towards improving their "memory" and range.

In an article in the magazine *Mind*, Dr. Turing seemed to have come to the conclusion that digital data machines will be capable of something akin to "thinking." He has also discussed the possibilities of educating a machine in the same way that one would a child.

Corell looked up from the newspaper. He did not like the article. It felt like a mixture of speculation and embellishment and it certainly did not make him any the wiser. To educate a machine like a child? What was that? Obviously a statement designed to appeal to the public—whether it came from the journalist or Turing himself—but there was not a single word to explain what it might actually mean. It must have been complete nonsense, or pure fantasy. The author of the article probably did not know what he was talking about either. Corell remembered the sentence from the minutes of the police interview when Turing told Arnold Murray that he was building an "electronic brain" and Corell had taken that for a lie, the sort of thing educated people scatter around them either to seduce or to oppress. But this article referred not to an electronic brain but to a *mechanical* one, and even though that too was a bit of jargon, something which was meant to sound spectacular, it was nevertheless an expression that was in use, clearly one among many, which stood for something. For what? A series of terms had been used, the last one being "digital machine." Digit meaning number, *digitus* finger, counting on one's fingers. He could still remember a bit of Latin from school.

"Do you know what a digital data machine is?" he asked Vicky.

"I'm sorry?"

"Forget it."

He ate some bacon and potato croquettes and gulped his tea, which had grown cold, and went on to read that Turing had worked at the Foreign Office during the war and was a member of the Royal Society. His leisure interests were long-distance running, chess and gardening. At the end of the article it said: "He ran for Walton Athletic Club." Corell snorted. Just like Marlborough. If you wanted to show that someone was a good chap, the essence of a good and clean Englishman, you would say that he was an athlete. All good boys were athletes. Turing was a good boy. He was also dead and in the newspapers the dead are always good chaps. One must not speak ill of the dead. *De mortuis nihil nisi bene!*

"Hypocrisy," he said.

"What?"

Hypocrisy was one of his aunt's favourite topics.

"Nothing. May I tear out an article?"

"You can crumple up the whole newspaper and stick it in your pocket, dear boy, but I'd be grateful if you would stop being so cryptic. Why are you so fascinated by this particular article?"

"It's to do with the case I'm working on."

"Oh, I understand. In that case I insist on reading it," she said, and instinctively he wanted to say no.

He had no desire to reopen yesterday's wounds and he wanted to keep his mathematician to himself, particularly now that he was not going to be able to answer her questions, but naturally he pushed over the newspaper and she eagerly started to read. Afterwards she seemed to be in unusually high spirits.

"It sounds like a novel by Edgar Allan Poe," she said. "To educate a machine, or what did they say? Delightfully crazy."

"Frightening, more likely."

"Well, it certainly gets you thinking. Seems to be an open-minded man, not at all some dreary engineer as you seemed to suggest yesterday."

"I didn't really do that, did I?"

"Perhaps I'm mixing things up."

"I will say though that I don't think he was completely right in the head," he said.

"Aren't you being a little hard on him, now?"

"But I know that he fooled—"

"In any case they seem to speak of him with great respect," she interrupted.

"As with all dead people."

"The article says that he was the author of the theoretical basis for something, and that his machine solved some difficult problem. Doesn't seem to have been any sort of dunce."

"I'm guessing that the author of the article didn't know what he was writing about."

"You tell me about it then."

"I haven't learnt much about it either."

"Wouldn't you like to get to know a little bit more, now that you're dealing with it anyway?"

"That's not my job!"

"Isn't it?"

"The machines were unlikely to have had anything to do with his death," he said in a funk, and he took back the newspaper and tore out the article, but at the same time he felt uncomfortable, or even as if he'd been found out, and since he was about to catch the bus to Wilmslow and did not want to part on bad terms from his aunt he ventured a light-hearted sally. In the tone of a soldier to his superior he said:

"I promise to find out everything about the machines and to report back to you!"

"I look forward to that."

15

LEONARD WAS DELIBERATELY a little late arriving at the police station, he knew that he was going to have to work overtime; but although he felt reasonably all right as he went up the stairs his despondency returned to him once he was in the criminal department. The room was stuffy. It smelled of cigarette smoke and bad breath. Kenny Anderson took a few sips of whisky without even trying to hide what he was doing. Corell opened the window. *Why had Vicky been such an idiot?* The row with her yesterday, the moments of irritation, were of course no big thing—indeed they were nothing at all—but he could not let it go. That was part of the problem with his aunt. Whenever there was the slightest strain between them, he would blow it up to ridiculous proportions. How could she defend . . . ?

"Today I just want to get pissed," he complained loudly, finding himself touchingly in harmony with Kenny, but when his colleague suggested that they hit the pub together after work, horror of horrors, he pretended not to hear and started to do some real work. It was slow going. He felt the lack of sleep and was genuinely glad when Alec Block came up to him.

"You should take a look at this," Block said.

"What is it?"

It was some papers from Chester & Gold, a firm of solicitors in Manchester, enclosed in a sober black folder, and when Corell looked through them one could see that he was disappointed—it was not entirely easy to say why, but he had been asked to write a report on the circumstances surrounding Alan Turing's death in anticipation of the inquest that evening, and these papers were not going to make his work any easier. If its conclusion had not been obvious before, it certainly was now. At the age of only forty-one and in full health, Turing had made a will on February 1 that year. The document was not a detailed one, nor did it contain any poetic words or dramatic statements to the effect that life was a torment. It listed only some dry pieces of information, for example that an author called Nick Furbank was to be the executor, and that the money, books and valuables were to be divided in this way and that. But it could hardly have been a coincidence that it had been made so recently.

Surely a forty-one-year-old who seems to have half his life before him does not sit down and write his will without having a reason to do so? Although Corell could imagine that there was some sort of bittersweet satisfaction to be had from setting out one's last will and testament; it's a bit like fantasising about one's own funeral. But no, he thought, it could not be a coincidence, an emotional whim. If you put the pieces together, the trial, its consequences, the social humiliation and the poisoned apple, there was too much to ignore. It made the scales tip. Assuredly Alan Turing had committed suicide!

The will stated that the housekeeper, Mrs. Taylor, was to have £30 and the members of his brother John's family £50 each, which must have come as a disappointment to them, and perhaps Turing was also making a point. The residue of his estate—which must have come to several thousand pounds just with the sale of the house—was to be divided between his mother and four friends: Nick Furbank, David Champernowne, Neville Johnson and Robin Gandy . . . Robin. *Dear Robin* . . . Corell suddenly remembered the letter which he had picked up at Adlington Road. How could he have forgotten it? According to the will, Robin Gandy was to inherit Turing's mathematics books. He seemed to have been the favourite. He must have been the one to whom Turing wrote personal letters, and in a hurried movement Corell stuck his hand into his inside pocket and was just about to take out the letter and start reading it when Richard Ross stepped into the room. Now what? Ross looked flushed and disgruntled as usual, but also in some way disarmed, as if something embarrassing had happened to him.

"You seem to have come up in the world," he said.

"How so?"

"Some important visitors are on their way."

"Again?"

"Don't look so bloody pleased about it," Ross said. Corell did not look in the least bit glad. "I asked if I could sit in on the meeting," the inspector said. "But they want to talk to you alone. You've probably dropped the ball in some way."

"Whom do I have the honour of meeting?"

"Not in that tone, you moron. It's very important that you co-operate."

"Of course. But with whom?"

"It's probably best if they introduce themselves," Ross said, sounding peevish, and Corell felt an irresistible urge to be disrespectful. *I don't feel like it. I've got some dirty magazines to read*, he wanted to say, but all he could think of was to sit with his arms crossed while his body language conveyed the message that he would co-operate only as far as he could be bothered.

"Pull yourself together for Christ's sake. They'll be here any moment," Ross hissed, and Corell nodded reluctantly.

Ross's ingratiating manner towards the approaching powers made him feel sick. At the same time he himself became nervous and longed to take a look in the mirror. He had to make do with straightening his tie and pushing his fingers through his hair.

Two gentlemen in their sixties came through the door. He recognised them immediately. They're famous, he thought. He wasn't just being silly, it was also wishful thinking. The truth was simply that he had met them in the entrance to the morgue. But he still had a point in that the taller man really did look like a film star. It's true that the long back gave the impression of being very stiff, but the face had such an exquisite dignity and harmony about it that Corell felt an immediate admiration. Ever since his father's death he had had a tendency to seek out distinguished men and subconsciously look for similarities between himself and them, as if he had been hoping to find his own future in their faces. Or, even worse, as if he were looking for a father figure. As he greeted the man—whose name was Oscar Farley and who exuded a certain melancholy—Corell thought that he detected curiosity in his eyes.

The other man was stocky with sparse, dishevelled hair and a thin nose which broadened out towards the tip. He introduced himself as Robert Somerset, and compared to his colleague he was rather ugly. Yet he had a certain good-natured look to him.

"Are you from the Foreign Office?"

"In a way," Somerset said. "We belong to a small group at Cheltenham which works on a couple of modest projects. Among other things we've been looking into the circumstances surrounding Alan Turing's death. Is there anywhere nearby where we can have some privacy?"

On the third floor, across the passage from the station police sergeant, there was a freshly painted meeting room with a couple of hideous paintings on the walls, where Corell had conducted the occasional sensitive questioning, to the extent that these were ever particularly sensitive in Wilmslow. He suggested that they go there. It was a place where things had gone well for him and he was glad of the scrap of reassurance which this offered. Should he give them tea? He decided not to. As they walked into the room, his nervousness grew, and Somerset's urbane but faintly ironic smile certainly did not make him feel any calmer since it seemed to Corell to be a warning that he could turn venomous. Nervously, Leonard looked at Farley. Farley rubbed his neck.

"I'm afraid we don't have any better chairs. We're usually aching all over after a day's work," Corell said.

"Thank you for being so considerate, but don't worry about me. I get like this from time to time, completely bent and crooked. I'm too tall for my own good. Should really lop off ten or twenty centimetres. I knew your father by the way."

Corell froze.

"Did you?"

"Not all that well, perhaps," Farley said. "We only met a couple of times, but we had a friend in common, Anthony Blunt, if the name means anything to you. Not? Well, they were both art experts, although completely different. James was more unconventional, more my type, to be honest. I liked his book about Gauguin and the one about the

Indian too in a way, an extremely unusual story. He was quite a character, wasn't he? Goodness how he could talk!"

"Occasionally he even managed to say something that was true," Corell added in a light tone of which he immediately felt proud.

"So he sometimes embellished a bit. Don't all good raconteurs do that? To elevate what is beautiful above what is true is their duty, so to speak. A noble virtue in a way."

"Unfortunately not entirely appropriate in our work," Somerset added.

"Sadly not," Corell said, disappointed that the conversation had already moved away from his father.

"The truth is of course a difficult discipline for us. Not only do we have to discover it. We've also got to handle it in the right way. It's enough to wear you down, isn't it?" Somerset said.

"Indeed."

"Certain truths almost cry out to be set free . . ."

"While others want to be suppressed at any price," Corell ventured.

"Exactly. You've got the hang of this. We keep our own misfortunes hidden. Other people's shame we're more than happy to trumpet out loud."

"That's possible."

"Well, what I'd like to say is that there are some details in this business about Dr. Turing that we have to be careful with."

"What exactly is it that's so sensitive?" Corell said.

"Well, sensitive and sensitive," Somerset murmured. "Let's not make this any more exciting than it really is. But let me just say one thing, and give full expression to the dramatic side in me: What I'm going to tell you now must remain between us, you understand?"

"Of course!"

"Splendid! In that case I can tell you that Alan Turing worked for the country on certain assignments, the nature of which I'm not at liberty to disclose. Because of this it's likely that he lived under some pressure. He was not allowed to whisper a word of it to anyone, not even his nearest and dearest, and we don't have any reason either to believe that he did, certainly not. We had the greatest respect for him and mourn his passing. He had an extraordinarily strong will. If he'd heard me saying all this rubbish, he'd immediately have got to his feet and started doing something more sensible . . ."

"Like the mathematical patterns in a leopard's spots," Corell said in the same light tone as before.

"Ha ha. Exactly! You're beginning to get to know him, I can tell. But to be honest, when someone dies like this you begin to wonder, don't you, did he after all do something that he shouldn't have? Not that we think he did, but part of our job is to hope for the best, and to assume the worst."

"Could you be a bit clearer?"

"Am I being cryptic again? Doesn't surprise me! 'Don't mumble into your beard,' my father used to say. I didn't understand what he meant. I didn't have a beard, after all. Never grew one either, not even during the war, ha ha, but you're not shy. That's good. Like the dutiful civil servants we are we've of course checked you out. We were actually a bit surprised that you're here, but it's to your credit, it really is. People like you are needed in the force. Isn't it pretty much every day that one reads in the papers about some police scandal? Wasn't there even something this morning?" Somerset went on in an arch sort of confusion.

"And then . . ." His voice became softer, quieter. "And then of course we heard about your parents, very sad. Must have been a terrible blow, first one and then the other. My deepest sympathies."

"It's a long time ago now," Corell said, suddenly irritated.

"How tactless of me, I'm sorry I brought it up. I was only trying . . . But where were we? You wanted me to be clearer, isn't that right? Clearer! I assume you are aware of Alan Turing's proclivities. Well, obviously you are, but you understand, we ourselves were in the dark for a long time. Once upon a time Alan was engaged to a very nice girl, Oscar knew her, and has always spoken well of the lass, but then . . . once we realised, then things appeared in a very different light, and don't think that I attach any particular importance to it on the personal level. We're all entitled to do what we feel like in our own free time, isn't that right? The way we treated Oscar Wilde was nothing short of a scandal. Or rather not so much we, the real villains in that drama seem to have been the lover, what was his name again . . . Lord Alfred Douglas, that's right, known as Bosie, thank you very much, Oscar, and then his father.

Dreadful people! By the way do you think that this Murray was in some way Turing's Bosie? Oh, all right, not . . . no, no, there are of course big differences. An artist like Wilde can take certain liberties. He maybe even should do so. But if you are working for your country, then other factors come into play. I gather that your superior . . . good Lord, I seem to have forgotten his name as well."

"Chief Superintendent Hamersley."

"That's right, that Chief Superintendent Hamersley made an impassioned speech about Burgess and Maclean, and with all due respect he probably had a bit of a nerve mentioning those jokers in the same breath as Alan Turing. But your boss was right in the sense that their defection has made people nervous. Many are asking themselves if there aren't more spies. Was it really just them? Our poor Turing was a thoroughly good chap, very gifted. Oscar is convinced that he was a genius, isn't that right?"

"Definitely," Farley said, and at least so far as Corell saw it, he showed signs of displeasure or irritation, but perhaps it was only his neck or his back that were troubling him.

"He was certainly remarkable," Somerset said. "He had the ability to think completely differently, for better or worse, mostly for the better, I think. He turned everything upside down. Didn't like authority or orders. Once I was stupid enough to say, 'In this particular matter I'm actually your superior, Alan!' Do you know what he said? 'What the hell's that got to do with it?' He was right, of course. You either have a useful contribution to make or you don't, regardless of whether you're head of the office or the emperor of China. But what was I saying? Alan Turing did possess some sensitive information, and if we're to assess the scale of the risk, to imagine our worst nightmare, so to speak, it would at least be relevant to say that he was a product of the same university environment as Burgess and Maclean. In that respect he was at least as dodgy as our friend Farley here, who knew all the wrong people."

"I did have that honour!"

"Well, I mention it now to give you an idea of the level of threat, and also to allow myself to boast about the extent of my political insight.

Ha ha. To put it in somewhat drastic terms, Cambridge in the thirties was characterised by two things: a craze for communism and a craze for homosexuality."

"Rubbish!" Farley said.

"Well, you're bound to have been busy with other things as well, like drunkenness, geometry and Shakespeare. But even you have to admit, Oscar, that those were exceptional times. There was a depression and a General Strike, and all sorts of misery. The whole system seemed to be going to the dogs, and there was much indignation—and quite rightly so, if you ask me—at all the right-wingers who hailed Hitler. The Spanish Civil War broke out . . . yes, my God . . . one can get all nostalgic over far less than this. At long last something could be done about fascism, a whole lot of students volunteered for the republican side, and they were regarded as the great heroes, weren't they? These weren't the usual cowardly intellectuals, some pathetic windbags like you and me, Oscar . . . well, Oscar seems quiet now, but you should see. Don't mention Henry James or that bloody Irishman Joyce, or he'll never stop. For God's sake don't! But as I said, the feeling in Cambridge was that the establishment couldn't give a damn about fascism, and I really understand that. I'm not the conservative old fogey that Oscar tries to make me out to be. Our government was really weak, and it doesn't take a lot of imagination to see that for many intellectuals communism was the only decent alternative. Yes, thanks to their anti-fascism those damned hooligans won glory and honour and communist cells were formed everywhere at King's and Trinity, and all of that could have been perfectly fine. Young people are meant to go off the rails politically, aren't they? And there are certainly far worse things one can do than dream about equality. The problem was just that Stalin and the Comintern were smart enough to take advantage of it. Yes, my God, just imagine . . . here they had the opportunity to get the leaders of the future over onto their side. And they really pulled their fingers out. Cambridge was flooded with communist spotters and agents, and do you know what they were known as jokingly, no, how could you possibly? The Homointern, they called them. Why? Quite simply because the Comintern focused on homosexuals. Queers were considered easier to convert to the cause of communism, partly because their sexual inclination made them more receptive to radical ideas, but also because, deliberately of course, the misconception was spread that Stalin had a more liberal attitude to homosexuality than we in the West. This was of course nonsense. Useful propaganda, nothing more. I wonder if in actual fact Stalin didn't chop the pricks off the lot of them, if you'll pardon the expression."

"You don't say," Farley spluttered.

"Well, don't tell me that sexual freedom was Stalin's lasting contribution to mankind! Sadly, however, it is true that he had a good reputation at the time with his five-year plans and all; indeed he was said to be really tolerant if you please, and many homosexuals were drawn to communism. Guy Burgess is the best-known example. Good Lord! What a dreadful story! And what an embarrassing outcome. Crazy really! God knows if he doesn't regret it today. Or what do you say, Oscar, do you think the Russians give him enough booze and little boys?"

Oscar looked down at the table with an embarrassed expression.

"Well, you never know," Somerset went on. "A spy has to be rewarded. But goodness how I'm talking! Have I made things in the least bit clearer? Good, I'm pleased. No, no, for God's sake, Alan couldn't have been more unlike Burgess. They had the same inclination, of course, but apart from that . . . Turing wasn't even much of a boozer, come on, don't look so surprised. People like that really do exist, and Alan wasn't very political either. He once signed a peace petition in 1933, but the rest of the time he stuck to his numbers and his ingenious ideas. I've never understood much of that, to be honest. Oscar is better at it . . . No, for God's sake don't start explaining it to me again."

Farley did not seem to be about to explain anything.

"Alan was very disciplined, at least when he was motivated," Somerset said. "Towards the end, Burgess was probably the least disciplined person on earth. Was liable to be rude to everybody left and right and was hardly sober even in the morning . . . but all the same, as I said, *all the same* . . . there are still a number of disturbing factors, nothing to worry about I'm sure and certainly nothing that should be passed on to anybody, not under any circumstances."

"Of course not," Corell said obligingly.

"Wouldn't it be nicer if we called each other by our first names? I'm Robert, not Bob, absolutely not Bob. Have never been able to stand it. Oscar is Oscar. A hopelessly literary person. Not at all just a boring civil servant like me. I compensate for that by being rather too zealous, which is why I'm interested in trivia like certain overseas trips. Well, how trivial is it really, it all depends on who's travelling and where they're going, doesn't it? Let's be perfectly open with each other. During his last years, Turing travelled overseas to meet men, queers basically and debauched people. He went to Norway, Greece and Paris, and to be honest, we were never particularly comfortable with that."

"The Foreign Office would surely have kicked him out long before that," Corell ventured.

"Why do you think so?" Somerset said.

"I heard something about an order to purge the public service of homosexuals."

"Purge? What a dreadful word!" Somerset burst out. "But let me say this: however much we valued and trusted Alan, towards the end he probably didn't have quite as much reason to be loyal to Queen and country. He may even have been furious—well, who wouldn't be in his shoes? Did you hear about that hormone he had to take . . . yes, you did, and as I said, it's probably nothing to worry about, not in the least. But still, guilt and anger, that's not a good cocktail, even for the best of us. That's why we need your help, your expertise, quite simply. You were first on the scene."

"It was the housekeeper who found him."

"But then . . ."

"Then I arrived . . ."

"And you went around gathering impressions, and evidence, exactly as you're meant to."

"Naturally."

Somerset was after something.

"As I'm sure you'll understand . . . against that background . . . even small things can have a major significance. Something that might seem unimportant can in the bigger picture . . ."

"Take on a completely different light. Yes, I entirely understand that." Corell was longing to get out into the sun.

"Naturally. As a criminal investigator you probably have a better understanding of the value of detail than any of us."

"I also know that flattery can get you far."

"Ha ha. You've rumbled me," Somerset chuckled. "Anyhow, I'm sure one doesn't have to flatter you. I'm sure you know what you're worth. We just wondered if you have something that you'd like to share with us?"

"You have searched the house yourselves," Corell countered, and turned to Farley who had been surprisingly quiet during the conversation, but who now waved his hands in a way which Corell immediately interpreted as a yes. They're missing something, Corell thought.

"In any case we'd heard that you picked up some notebooks and bits of paper," Somerset said.

"That's true. You're more than welcome to take them. My mathematical skills aren't what they used to be."

"So it was only mathematical notes?"

"I think so. But I haven't been through them that carefully. You'll get the whole lot," he said making an involuntary movement towards his inside pocket.

"Excellent!"

"Actually, no."

"No?"

"Alan Turing also had three books in which he had written down his dreams, at his psychoanalyst's request. I've unfortunately already sent them to his brother, John Turing."

"Oh dear."

"Sorry."

"Anything else?" Somerset said.

"No," Corell said, and suddenly realised that he wasn't going to hand over the letter, he didn't really know why, beyond the fact that he longed to read it and couldn't bear the thought of losing it before he had even found out what was in it.

"In that case we'll have to get in touch with the brother. But perhaps you can let us have the rest of it right away?" Somerset said, possibly satisfied, or possibly not.

When they got back to the criminal department Corell handed over the notebooks. "Take good care of your neck," he said to Farley. "Thank you for your political discourse. It was extremely interesting," he said to Somerset in a voice which may not have sounded entirely natural, but which he nonetheless hoped had an air of worldliness about it. He had become extremely nervous. When they had said goodbye his right hand had started to shake. He had been a bit naughty, no more than that, but still; his little prank both worried him and put him in a belligerent mood: *No, no, you don't understand. No-one tells me what to do . . . My name is Corell by the way, Leonard Corell, son of James, the author. I have a special interest in the mathematical side of my work. That's why I won't let anyone else interfere, that's all . . . My God, who did Mr. Somerset think he was? To come here and demand . . . No, I'm obviously keeping the letter for myself . . . Did I say that I was up at King's College, Cambridge . . .* Daydreaming, he sat down at his desk and now he was eager to start reading, but he felt that he was being observed. Kenny Anderson stared at him in curiosity:

"So, what was that all about?"

"Nothing special. They just wanted to inform me about certain things."

"*About certain things!* My, my, are we feeling a bit superior?"

"What . . . no . . . honestly not!"

"Well, do you want a quick one then? You did say that you wanted to get pissed today."

"Did I?"

Corell wondered if he should go outside with the letter, or if he should just ignore Anderson and read it right there, but in the same instant a name cropped up in his mind . . . *Hugh Alexander.* He had no idea why he suddenly thought of it, maybe it was just his mind straying to something he had read, but then he realised that Hugh Alexander had been a character witness at Alan Turing's trial. The name had seemed familiar, and even though the report had not said it in so many words Corell got the distinct impression that Alexander and Turing had worked together during the war. Who would know? That could perhaps be a lead. Corell got to his feet and went in to see Gladwin.

Andrew Gladwin worked in the archive room. It contained all the information on the area's suspects and convicted persons together with a small library of encyclopaedias and reference books, where Corell had been reading about the liar's paradox the day before. Gladwin was one of the best people they had at the station. He was keen on crossword puzzles and devoured historical biographies. You could ask him about most things, and because of that he was known as the Professor, or even the Oracle with the Pipe. He was good-natured and the only one at the station who had managed to become quite fat. Like Anderson he stank of alcohol, but in a nicer way, as if he only drank the better stuff or his body were better at dealing with it. He was getting on for fifty, but his hair was as thick and black as a young man's and his eyes were brown and alert well into the afternoon when his look became hazy. When Corell came in he was smoking his pipe and did not seem to be doing anything at all.

"Hello there!"

"Hello!"

"Are my services required?"

"Hugh Alexander," Corell said. "Do you know who that is?"

"The chess-player, you mean?"

"I don't know who I mean. But it's not a local thief."

"Then it might well be the chess-player."

"He was a character witness in the trial of the mathematician who died the other day."

"In that case it's definitely him. Let's see now . . ."

Gladwin rose to his feet and pulled out a copy of *Who's Who*, which seemed to have been on the shelves for a number of years, and quickly got the information he wanted.

"I've always liked chaps beginning with A," he said. "Hugh O'Donel Alexander, Irish, father a professor of engineering sciences in Cork, won the British boys' chess championship in 1928, got a scholarship in mathematics at King's College, Cambridge, studied under Professor Hardy, became a maths teacher at Winchester in 1932, head of research at something called the John Lewis Partnership in 1938, but for the most part seems to have played chess."

"At a serious level?"

"Oh yes, he was an international master, beat Botvinnik and Bronstein among other people. British champion in 1938, one of the best in the world, you'd have to say. Regarded as the best Irish player of all time. Was captain of the English team at the international Olympiad in Buenos Aires when the war broke out."

"Does it say what he did during the war?"

"Only that he worked for the Foreign Office. Seems to have got an O.B.E. in 1946."

"Him too."

"Sorry?"

"My dead chap also got one," Corell said.

"Did he, now. Did he, now . . . For my own part I hardly got a thank-you, despite being shot in the leg. How are you feeling, by the way? You look completely . . ."

"It's nothing," Corell snapped without thinking. His head was completely buzzing. "I have a thousand-pound question for you."

"Tell me!"

"If we were at war with Hitler and you were the Foreign Office, where would you put an international master in chess and a mathematician who likes riddles and logical contradictions?"

"I wouldn't use them as cannon fodder."

"Would you let them invent a new secret weapon?"

"Or think up new strategies. A game of chess is after all war in miniature. I would let them build a miniature of the war and move copies of different soldiers around in some clever way. Or think up ingenious riddles to confuse the enemy. How does that one go . . ."

"Could you please try to be serious?"

"Has this got something to do with your investigation?"

"Sort of."

Gladwin leaned back in his chair and almost lovingly stroked his own cheek.

"Leonard, my dear fellow, every war has needed more than just muscles and guns, and more often than not the intelligentsia have proved incapable of keeping out of this blood-soaked madness. Bertrand Russell was of course an exception in 1916. No, in general terms I would say that the reserves of talent have tended to be absorbed by the intelligence services or been involved in the necessary scientific industrial effort. We usually say that the First World War with its poison gases was the chemists' ghastly war, while the Second belonged to the physicists. My answer would therefore be that a person like Hugh Alexander would have been used in some form of analytical scientific work, but I suspect that's far too vague an answer for sir."

"Well, maybe. But thanks anyway."

"Don't mention it. Hello . . . you're in a bit of a hurry!"

Corell quickly returned to his desk and took the letter from his inside pocket.

16

THE LETTER WAS PALE YELLOW and surprisingly crumpled. Corell raised it to his nose and felt a slight, almost agreeable smell of bitter almonds. He looked around. No-one was watching him. Kenny Anderson, so inquisitive just before, seemed for once to be absorbed in work; and with a degree of surreptitious formality—which brought to mind a night in Southport when he had been reading the banned edition of *Lady Chatterley's Lover* by torchlight—Corell started to go through the letter, and the first thing which struck him was that it carried an hour but not a date. Perhaps it had been lying in the desk drawer for a long time— what did he know—and he read the first few words very slowly, as if to decide whether they were well written, or just to contain his eagerness. He tried to persuade himself that it was idiotic to hope for too much from the letter. He had after all only just remembered it; it was merely because he had withheld it from Farley and Somerset that it had acquired such a significance, it was still the same old letter—his little bit of cheek had not changed anything—but he couldn't help being fascinated, and with mounting excitement he read it over and over again.

Hollymeade, 02:20

Dear Robin,

I am so fed up with all the secrecy, all this damned play-acting. Is this the way my life was meant to be? One masquerade to conceal another! I am still up and wish I were miles away. Do you remember the partridges we had and the fresh eggs? It's half past two at night. The rain is beating down outside and I'm thinking about all the things

I want to talk to you about, not only what I'm not allowed to mention, but also what I have never actually got around to saying. Every day new doors slam shut. I have lost an assignment which may not have been all that exciting, but did, nonetheless, give some meaning to my life. People like me are no longer trusted and I find that hard to bear, Robin, it hurts me more than I can say. The whole of my world is shrinking. I can't even dream the way I used to. What is the point of dreams when you know that they can never come true? So much has been stolen from me and when one thing goes, other things disappear as well. Then the horizon darkens.

There is talk of promising developments on the sexual front, but I won't get to see much of that. I am being watched. The minute I set foot outside my garden all hell breaks loose and I dread to think what would happen if I were to be so bold as to travel abroad again. (Which I am planning to do, how could I resist teasing them a little bit?) They want to turn me into an old maid. One would imagine that things might have improved when I removed the implant from my leg, and perhaps they did for a while, but then came the disappointment that the relief wasn't greater. The poison disappeared from the body but not from the brain and I began to suspect that none of this was going to go away in a hurry. I am going to have to live with the trial and everything it stirred up for a long time and, actually, I shouldn't have been surprised that they went after my Norwegian boy. I might have realised that they wouldn't leave me alone. But how could I have known how painful it would be?

Just now when I tried to sleep I could feel their eyes digging into my neck and I twisted and turned until I could stand it no longer. I got up and looked down at the street through the window. The yellow lamp cast its light on the willow tree below and on my poor old brick path which I never got around to finishing (possibly because I am amused by the idea of a half-finished path somewhere), but there was no-one down there. Why would there be anyone, you might ask. Let me explain: I am being watched. At all times of the day I see this pudgy fellow in front of me or behind me, and the poor man's not even particularly good at it. He is so bad at pretending to be natural that he makes people nervous, and on his forehead he has a birthmark shaped like a sigma. Just imagine! A sigma!

One morning I had just hidden my key in the garage before going for a run when he came by as if nothing had happened. I just said out loud: what a pleasure to receive a visit from you, at which he became embarrassed and replied hm, hm, very good in a Scottish accent before shuffling off. I think he realised that I'd seen through him. He popped up again a few days later and it dawned on me that he may have been after my mail. You know, that whole crisis over my Norwegian fellow doesn't make sense unless they were reading my letters. No, no, don't dismiss me, Robin. I'm not being paranoid, I've only got that perfectly sound persecution mania one needs in order to survive. I wouldn't survive for a single day if I were perfectly healthy and really I should be laughing at that figure. He looks like a sad dog. But I can't help thinking: Is this how they thank me? By poisoning every corner of my life? Some days I have been so angry that I didn't know what to do. When you were here, did you notice the dent above the threshold, right next to the front door? Well, I did that. I kicked it in the other day with some degree of precision and I would probably have attacked the whole house if it hadn't struck me as a bit unnecessary to punish myself, of all people, when I was feeling so vengeful. Sometimes, Robin, just before daylight, I have felt such despair that I didn't have the strength to sleep or stay awake, or barely even to live. My desperate thoughts have gone round and round in circles and everything has been blown up and twisted into an evil caricature of itself, and I have asked myself if madness has now finally set in. But I haven't been able to sort it out. (Of course old W. was right in saying that we cannot observe our own thoughts since the observation immediately becomes a part of them.)

Oh dear, Robin, I am moaning on a bit. (You can get your own back by sending me a 79-page complaint lamenting the overabundance of mistresses in Leicester.) But I do, of course, apologise for not having said one word in praise of your thesis (I'll get to that) and it is true that I have found some solace. Have I told you that I have set up a workshop right at the back on the first floor? I am calling it the place of nightmares as a tribute to my mother's delicate nerves. She is convinced that I will be mixing up something lethal in there and she is right in that I am doing all kinds of silly things like trying to extract chemicals from salt. You ought to come here and join me in messing around. It's actually quite therapeutic.

For the rest I keep busy doing all sorts of things, everything but what I'm actually meant to be doing. I write down my dreams at Greenbaum's behest. Have I told you? Every morning I fill page after page in my dream books, and to be honest, I sometimes can't resist the temptation to embellish them a bit. Who wants to have uninteresting dreams? But I have also found one or two things I would like to talk about some time. Apart from that, I am thinking about going off on a dirty adventure to the Club Méditerranée at Ipsos-Corfu this summer rather than going back to Paris again. Did I tell you about the delightful young man I met in Paris? He was completely flummoxed when I suggested walking to the hotel instead of taking the Metro. I suspect he had the same relationship to Paris as we do to a Riemann surface. He was only familiar with the circles of civilisation around the underground stations and was totally incapable of working out the connections between them. Well, he did have other talents including a nice behind and I really have to say that we had a good time in the end, but afterwards he wanted us to exchange watches as a token of our trust. The fact that mine was much better than his may well have been of some significance in the circumstances, but of course I immediately agreed. After all, you have to take the offers you get. So that's the last I've seen of that watch. Hee, hee! But other than that, Robin, other than that . . . It's almost three o'clock. It's one of those nights when life has come too close. Did I tell you that I read about some lord who had been hauled up in front of the courts a second time? They had discovered another misdemeanour from his earlier life and of course that had me wondering: Is that what they're going to do with me? Dig up yet another shadow from my past? Luckily I probably haven't had as many men as I would have liked—after all, who has?—but there have been a few. Thank heavens for church à la King's. (I think there may be some gaps in your education in this area.) But I couldn't bear that. I couldn't stand the thought of them starting to dig around in my life again. The other day I saw one of the many old biddies in the neighbourhood who looked away as soon as she saw me, and don't think that I care. She can turn her head as much as she likes. But even so, isn't that unfair? I was so angry that evening that I could hardly breathe. Have you ever felt that sort of rage that doesn't even come out, but just implodes into a dark, suffocating mass?

It's true that during my bout with the judiciary I held my head up high and refused to be ashamed, but don't think I didn't feel that invisible bell on my body. I was even better than expected at thinking destructive thoughts, though maybe not quite as contrite as God the Father in his small-mindedness would have liked them to be—I am still a dissolute fellow—but very painful nonetheless, thoughts which simply turned inwards without any aim or direction, meeting nothing but a void. The place where the arguments end. Imagine if I had married Joan and somehow had children. What would my life have been then? (Both you and I have got to put an immediate stop to our childish tendency to imagine the what-ifs.) I have to pull myself together. Soon it will be day. Already I long to hear the birds. But sometimes, Robin, sometimes I wonder if what they really want isn't to see me wiped out, removed from the scene. For what have I become to those for whom I once did so very much? Nothing more than a missing link, a person whose thoughts were clear but whose wishes were wrong. Did I give the fairy the wrong answer?

The other night I dreamed of our meals at Hanslope, and then my apple at night. This afternoon I remembered the double rainbow we saw and then I thought: I wonder how you are? Sometimes I've worried that they would come after you too, you and your crazy convictions. What sort of problem do you think I suffer from? The kind that brings the machine to a standstill or that only makes it stutter on irretrievably forever? I have . . .

There followed some crossed-out words, illegible. The letter stopped in the middle of a sentence and was not always easy to understand, but without any doubt it exuded pain. It may even have been the suicide note that they were missing. No, that would be going too far. Corell had had to dig around to find it and even though it contained some dark allusions to "where the arguments stop" it felt like something too vague and messy to have a definite purpose. Instead it seemed like something which one writes at night when life appears dismal and threatening. After all, the writer felt guilty about complaining, and bearing that in mind, his attempts at humour, like the terrible "overabundance of mistresses in Leicester," had to be seen as an effort to lighten the tone. It was certainly no coincidence that it was never posted. Perhaps it had seemed completely unbalanced in the light of day. On the other hand, it hadn't been torn up. It had lain there waiting. For what? Probably nothing! We all put things away without knowing why.

He looked around. Anderson sat leaning back and smoking. Alec Block came in from the corridor and seated himself in his chair under a wall chart of wanted bank robbers in Manchester, and cast a glum glance towards Corell, as if looking for contact. Corell felt an irrepressible urge to go out. It was as if the letter needed clear air, and without a word to anyone he left his place. In the yard a flock of swallows disappeared behind the red-brick blocks of flats and he continued out towards the fields to the right and soon got to Carnival Field. More than any other place in Wilmslow, Carnival Field meant summer to him, and he stared out at the meadows, happy to see how many people were there, and with a certain theatrical force he drew air into his lungs and smiled at a horse which was cantering in circles not far away, but the whole time he was thinking about the letter. He was pleased that he had gone out. The open sky gave him a better perspective on the words and he didn't get quite so worked up. It was not really all that much to get excited about, was it?

There was much in the letter that vexed him, and it struck him that he had imagined Turing to be more awkward and lost—partly because of what his brother had told him—but these were the words of somebody cunning, who had seduced men in Paris and disappeared off on illicit trips. An incorrigible homosexual, Sergeant Rimmer had said, and that was probably true. At the same time there was more, which Corell did not understand and which made him burn with curiosity. He found the unclear sentences far more enticing than the plain ones and naturally he could see that most of it was no different from the quips and allusions that he traded with his aunt, nothing more than the small conventions and shorthand expressions used in communication between good friends, and he was realistic enough to see that his good old wishful thinking, about something big and liberating happening to him, could play tricks on him. But it did nothing to lessen his excitement.

Take the man who had been spying on Turing. Who was he? A figment of the mathematician's imagination, or someone from the Manchester police? Turing had been under observation because of his inclinations—Hamersley had confirmed that—and it surely was not impossible that some poor copper had been punished by being made to hang around outside the mathematician's house. But no, Corell did not think that the man was a policeman. Anyway, who the hell has a birthmark shaped like a sigma, a Greek letter? He decided that the man had to be rather more interesting than just an ordinary colleague. "I'm so fed up with all the secrecy." In the letter Turing used the word *they* in a vague way, and sometimes he seemed just generally to mean the court and the police or even the present times, while at others he could have meant some special people, perhaps a particular institution, maybe the same one that Somerset and Farley belonged to . . . "those for whom I once did so very much."

Corell stood still for a while and wondered what services this could be referring to. Then he shrugged his shoulders, walked back to the police station and with a burst of energy began to write his report in preparation for the court hearings the same evening.

17

OSCAR FARLEY AND ROBERT SOMERSET rested for a few minutes on a bench in Sackville Park in Manchester. Two men with bad posture walked past them and one of them said, "I think that women have never understood . . ." Further away on the lawn under a leafy tree a young woman was reading a novel with a green cover, and Farley felt a stab of longing. He always managed to find people who looked harmonious when he was feeling at his worst, as if he were looking for reminders of what he was missing.

"Shall we go on?" Somerset said.

"Just a moment."

"Is it that bad?"

"Pretty bad."

"I've got some port in my briefcase."

"I've got enough poison in my body already."

"What do you think of the policeman?"

"I don't think anything. I only hope that he survived your stupid games."

"Didn't he seem a bit funny towards the end?"

"I don't think so," Farley said, not entirely truthfully.

The young man had undoubtedly become somewhat nervous when they discussed what evidence had been found at Adlington Road. But Farley was reluctant to egg Somerset on. He had liked the policeman. While Robert had been holding forth, and some of what he had said had really annoyed him—to claim that Cambridge in the thirties had been characterised by communism and homosexuality was really too stupid even to be said as a joke—he had been reminded of his youth, and seen traits in the policeman which he recognised in himself. The way the policeman seemed sophisticated and rather grand one moment, and then almost confused and lost the next, took Farley back to those years when he himself had felt unfulfilled and unable to be himself, except in snatches or occasional moments. For a brief while he even thought back wistfully to his own old insecurity, as if something precious had gone astray as he grew into his personality and became the self-assured conversationalist he was today, but mostly he had thought about the policeman's father.

He had not known him all that well. Even so the policeman's father had occupied a special place in his consciousness. The name Corell had long been associated with the party atmosphere which surrounded Farley's early years at Cambridge. James Corell was an author who should really have been an actor. In some ways he was grandiose, the sort of person who took over every gathering he joined, and who was very quick with his repartee. But after his death Farley had inevitably cast him in the role of the melancholy clown, maybe because he started to believe that in the end James Corell had understood that his dominance on the party scene had no social value, and that every social triumph therefore left him with a bitter aftertaste, like a jester who grows sad once the applause has died down.

Nor could Farley, at the police station in Wilmslow, help but see the young man as an extension, a continuation of the drama staged by his father. The policeman would appear to have ended up far from James's circles in Cambridge and London. He seemed to have had to pay a high price, but his father was still there in his gestures and in the look, and from time to time there was an ease in his replies, an ingenuity which was reminiscent of James, and then there was something about his eyes. It was as if the policeman were always weighing up alternative courses of action. "Thank you for your political discourse," he had said to Somerset with unmistakable sarcasm, and even though that had been precisely the sort of banter Farley enjoyed, it had perhaps been a show of defiance, a fondness for heckling which reminded one of the father. But surely the policeman could not be holding something back? Why would he do that?

"Let's go," Farley said. "I'm feeling better."

"I still think that we should see him again," Somerset said.

"I think we should go home and read poetry."

"I'm sorry?"

"Poetry. It's a specially concentrated form of writing. Has been used by mankind for many thousands of years. You should take a look at it some time. There are books for beginners."

"Oh for God's sake!"

Corell could not now mention the letter in his report. But he gave the impression that there was much that had not been looked into and for once he worked with a light hand, perhaps also because it hardly mattered what he wrote. He thought that the outcome was already a given and in one sense he was only doing this for himself. He was not going to let any bureaucratic or unimaginative police eyes kill off the words. Rather he imagined other more or less imaginary readers—like his late father or even a publisher with a blurred face—who would chance on the report and who would light up. From time to time he took liberties with the form. At other times he pretended that his facts were fiction. This allowed all the peculiar details, the experimental workshop, the bubbling pan, the poisoned apple, no longer to appear as meaningless observations but rather as pieces in a puzzle that fall into place and end up fitting together to form a plain and clear picture, just like the questions in a detective story. But after a while this no longer worked and he realised that everything which appeared random or strange would remain just that, and that if after all there were to be a sequel to the story it would play out in other corridors and rooms, far away from Wilmslow and Green Lane, and then this whole inspired moment would seem a bit like masturbating: exciting while it was going on but shameful afterwards. When he wrote out a clean copy of the report he remembered something else that he had written in a distant age, when his father had called out, "Bravo, Leo, bravo," but even that did not feel like a good memory, and in irritation he hung up his hat which he had left lying on the table. At that moment the telephone rang.

"Hello," said a voice. It was a woman.

"Who am I speaking to?" he asked.

"My name is Sara Ethel Turing. I'm the mother of—"

He held the receiver away from his ear. Had an impulse to hang up. But was there not something in particular that he ought to be asking? He could not think of anything and even if he had there would hardly have been any opportunity. The mother's voice was thick with tears. Yet she did not stop talking—as if she wanted to drown out any attempt at silence.

"Alan was heading for something big, something really big," she said. "I could tell, from his whole manner. He thought of nothing else but his work. Not even of washing his hands! My God, why could he not wash them? Why didn't he do that?"

"What was the big thing he was working on?"

"If only I knew. It was impossible to understand it. But there was definitely something . . . a mother can tell things like that. Alan was so gifted, so amazingly gifted, but still like a child, you understand. He melted down his grandfather's watch. Can you imagine? Said that Granddad would have been happy to have had his watch put to scientific use, and then he was handling dangerous substances, things that were a real health hazard and I told him a thousand times. 'Don't do anything you'll regret. Wash your hands.' But he didn't wash them. Never ever!"

Corell was used to dealing with strong feelings in his job. Sometimes it made him feel more alive; it was rather like watching a powerful drama at the cinema or the theatre, but in the case of Turing's mother it was just unbearable. There was such an outpouring of grief. The words gushed out of her, and he simply could not cope. He tried to be kind.

"I'm so sorry, Mrs. Turing. Have you heard that you're one of his beneficiaries? He really loved you."

But she was not listening. She just wailed on and on and when at last he managed to stop her, he let out a loud sigh of relief, but without feeling any better as a result.

"Do stop that," Kenny Anderson snapped.

"Stop what?" he said. "I was talking to Turing's mother."

"That doesn't mean you have to hack the table to pieces!"

"No, no!"

He put down his pen, with which he appeared to have been jabbing the edge of the table. Then the telephone rang again and he reached out for the receiver. He quickly withdrew his hand and, as if that were not enough, he took his hat from the coat peg and left the room. What was he doing? He had been rushing in and out and had not had the presence of mind to ask Turing's mother some sensible questions—she could no doubt have told him one or two useful things—but he had not been able to bring himself to do it. He had thought of his own mother, his stooped and stunted mother, and the day he had left her. Would it ever stop! Was the memory going to go on hurting forever?

It was no longer so warm out in the yard, and he drew his jacket closer and tried to shake off his feeling of unease. He could not manage it. Thoughts raced through his mind and suddenly he remembered something from the letter: "Did I give the fairy the wrong answer?" Words filled with pain, he thought. As if somehow they affected him. Had he also made the wrong wishes, confusing the one friendly force who had been keeping watch over him? He reached into his inside pocket. The letter was still there. He thought about reading it again, but what was the point—he already knew it almost by heart—and for a while he wandered aimlessly through the streets.

As he emerged on Water Lane and passed the rows of restaurants and outside cafés, he had a distinct feeling of being the town's odd man out. The only people walking around are women, he thought. That was not quite true. There were men everywhere, but the feeling of stepping into a female community did not leave him, and he felt himself being observed and scrutinised. Gradually he calmed down and he may well have received some unexpected help from a radio set in doing so. A man's voice sang, "We'll have some fun when the clock strikes one" to an unusual rhythm, and it made him smile. But it was only a brief respite. Further down the street he caught a glimpse of a woman's back which immediately put him in a nervous mood, and at least it had the benefit of dispelling the discomfort of the telephone call, but that was scant consolation.

The back he had caught sight of belonged to Julie and that was hard enough, but the really worrying thing was that she was walking along with a little girl holding a green balloon. The girl had the same black hair as Julie. It could have been anybody: a niece, a cousin, one of Harrington's grandchildren, but still . . . He did not like it and was not reassured by the fact that he had never seen a ring on Julie's finger and that he had always thought of her as unmarried and solitary. He had clearly been wrong and his first instinct was to walk away. Yet he continued walking.

He quickly caught up with them and felt an unfathomable urge to grab the balloon. That damned girl was a wall between him and Julie, but when he drew level with them he gave a start. The girl had a black patch over one eye with an ugly scar underneath it. He felt uncomfortable and looked away. Just as he was about to pass them he stopped himself. *You either pretend you haven't noticed. Or else* . . . He turned around and said hello, both to Julie and the girl, and despite his excitement he saw clearly that the child automatically presented her profile, as if life had already taught her not to show strangers her disfigured side. Wasn't the face suspiciously like Julie's?

"How do you do, Mr. Corell!"

"Are you well, Miss?"

"Yes, thanks. And you?"

"Very well. It's such a lovely day."

"For once there's no rain. Are you happy with your suit?"

"Very happy, thank you. Wonderful cloth. What a lovely girl you have," he said, and wondered if he should call a child with a scar like that "lovely."

"Thank you," Julie said. She seemed to be embarrassed now. "Chanda is . . . she has . . ."

She did not finish the sentence. Nervously she pushed the hair off her face and on a better day he might have felt reassured by her lack of self-assurance and tried to strike up a conversation, but now he only felt uncomfortable. He wanted to run away. He always wanted to run away when he was around Julie, and even though he realised that he ought to let her keep talking or perhaps even better come up with some words which would show that he was different (*You see, Miss, I've found a most astonishing letter* . . .), he just said:

"How lovely to see you again! You look wonderful. Perhaps I'll come by the shop some day and take a look at something new. I hope you have a lovely day."

"You too," she answered, clearly surprised by his abruptness, and then he sped off, with a nagging feeling that he had been cheated of something.

18

JAMES FERNS, THE CORONER, betrayed not the slightest doubt during the proceedings. He was in complete agreement with Dr. Bird's line, and hardly listened to Corell's minor reservations, which were not in any case offered with a great deal of passion, although on occasion he produced an elegant turn of phrase. Ever since the conversation with Turing's mother and the subsequent meeting with Julie and the girl, Corell had felt feeble, and it had not helped that the coroner had greeted him with the words "Why isn't Sandford himself here?" In effect Corell was ignored, and many times during the proceedings he cursed to himself: "Fools! What do they really know?" All the same—and in a way he regretted this—nothing was said in court which was patently ignorant or foolish. The verdict "suicide" seemed entirely reasonable. But he still felt a stab of disappointment and hurt at how very routine the proceedings had been. Could they not at least have given the impression that the case was special?

After the deliberations, Ferns and Bird stood around chortling together as if Corell did not exist, and when they burst out laughing he imagined that it was at him and unconsciously he clenched his fists. He fantasised about various ways in which he could take his revenge. *"One day, one day . . ."* Ferns was a short man of about fifty with quite a handsome but smug face whose central point was a thin, well-clipped moustache with a military look about it. Ferns occupied a prominent position in the Rotary Club in Wilmslow and Corell had seen him a few times down at Carnival Field with two large rottweilers.

When Corell stepped out into the cool evening he longed to be miles away. He was wearing his new tweed suit for the first time, but was not at all comfortable in it. Somehow he felt *too* elegant. The suit seemed to deserve someone better than a confused detective constable from Wilmslow and he looked around, feeling rather depressed. Four or five reporters were waiting for them on the courthouse steps, not exactly a crowd, but still enough for the coroner to start primping his moustache with a vanity he did not even try to hide. Ferns loved journalists. But journalists did not exactly love him back. Ferns had a strangely convoluted way of expressing himself, but probably he did not even realise it. He drew himself up to his full conceited height. It was sickening. Yet somehow Corell could understand it. He too grew taller when journalists approached, but unlike Ferns he had the good sense not to smirk in a satisfied way. Besides, he soon had other things on his mind.

Two faces attracted his attention, the first was Oscar Farley, whose back and neck problem must have worsened. To mark the occasion he was using a walking stick, which lent him an even deeper air of melancholy and sophistication. In Corell's eyes, he made everything around him appear provincial. Yet it was not Farley who made the greatest impression. It was a man who may have been one of the reporters. His eyes were flitting about as if not wanting to miss anything, but something else in his body language suggested that he belonged to a different world. He was not expensively dressed like Farley. He wore cotton trousers and a brown corduroy jacket that was so worn that it looked more like a coat, he had no hat and did not seem much older than Corell. But the remarkable thing about him was his eyes. They were piercing, if for no other reason than because their shape was sharp and narrow and because they radiated an intensity which made the man seem unusually alert. He had a grey book sticking up out of his jacket pocket, and without really knowing why, Corell raised his hand to his hat in a collegial greeting. By then they had all gathered in a small group just above the courthouse steps, and when Ferns chose that moment to clear his throat they all fell silent. There was after all a certain sense of anticipation.

"We have established that it was suicide," the coroner said. "So to speak, an action of his own free will," he added, as if there were other forms of suicide.

"What do you base that on?" a young journalist wanted to know, which prompted Ferns into a rather long-winded discussion about the circumstances inside the house on Adlington Road.

"A man with Turing's knowledge would have been aware of the effects of potassium cyanide," Bird said. "He wouldn't be careless with something like that."

"He also had his reasons," the coroner said. "He had been through a humiliating trial."

"Why did he use an apple rather than anything else?" asked a middle-aged reporter with round spectacles, and at that point Corell wanted to say something; that was after all a question for him.

But he did not have the courage to interrupt, so he just listened in silence while Bird repeated his theory that the apple had probably been used to get rid of the bitter taste of the poison. Corell could not help imagining a cooking recipe: *Season with potassium cyanide. But use an apple to get rid of the bitter taste.* Immediately afterwards the coroner went into a convoluted explanation to the effect that the suicide had not necessarily been planned long in advance:

"It could just as well have been decided on the spur of the moment," he said. "In a man of his type, one never knows what his mental processes are going to do next."

"Why not?" said the same reporter who had asked about the apple.

"Let me put it like this. We're all different. Someone like Dr. Turing is easily unsettled, I would venture to suggest. That type of person will readily lose his composure. For him life is a bit of a roller-coaster ride, and I suspect, or rather, I have reason to believe, that Turing's mind had become unbalanced when he decided to end his days. Well, you understand what I'm driving at. Perhaps this unfortunate idea came to him all of a sudden. Maybe he was even on the point of doing something completely different when this idea came into his head." Ferns came to a halt, and there was silence.

The reporters seemed to be fully occupied in writing down his words, and really Corell should not have said anything either. But at that exact moment he caught the eye of the unknown man in the corduroy jacket and it was not just a critical glance. It was a crushing look and it gave Corell, who had wanted to make an impression on the man from the outset, a reason to protest.

"I have to say that I'm impressed by you, sir," Corell said.

"Is that so, and why?"

Ferns looked bewildered.

"Because you have managed to determine what type of person Alan Turing was with such speed and precision. But I imagine that it's based on a careful study of his life and scientific achievements."

"Well . . . in point of fact, yes," Ferns ventured.

"Although you didn't make it clear what type of person you were referring to," Corell went on. "Was it the professor type, or the passionate scientist type, or even the homosexual sort, who's driven by impulses and passions. You'll have to forgive me. I'm not even sure how many types of people there are in this particular genre; the only type that I'm really familiar with is the one who talks about things he doesn't understand and that type is standing right in front of me now."

A laugh could be heard, but Corell was not able to work out where it came from.

"What I wanted to say was . . ." Ferns began, now visibly disturbed.

"That we have no idea what motivated this man, or I hope that's what you meant. There are large gaps in our knowledge about his life. This entire investigation has been conducted with shameful haste. To pronounce at this stage on Dr. Turing's thoughts during his last day alive is nothing short of poor judgement and speculation," Corell said, and felt a moment of triumph—he thought about the laugh he had heard— but when he looked up he saw that none of the reporters was taking notes and that the eyes of both the pathologist and the coroner were bright with fury.

There was an uncomfortable silence, as if something very embarrassing had occurred, and the intoxicating sense of self-esteem which had briefly coursed through him disappeared at a stroke and he was hurled back to his feeling of inferiority. Eagerly he looked for the unknown man. But he was hidden behind a tall, gap-toothed man and for a second or two Corell had no idea what to do.

"Gentlemen, I think that's all," he said.

The words echoed with emptiness. He had no authority to bring the press conference to an end, but what was said had been said. It would have to do, and he therefore raised his hat and walked off thinking that his back must be looking pathetic, or even that his behind looked like a girl's bottom, and briefly he imagined the nasty things the crowd might be saying about him. Yet he held his head high and brought his defence mechanisms to bear. What do I care about all these bigheads?

But his embarrassment grew, and he started to wonder whether Ferns had not been right after all, or at least had not said anything that was so idiotic as to warrant a malicious attack. Is it not true that homosexuals are driven by impulses and whims? Perhaps they really do get worked up one second and are then filled with anguish and remorse the next, what did he know? In purely psychological terms Ferns probably had a point. Corell had been an idiot, nothing else. Why was everything he did always such a disaster? Besides . . . he felt empty, as if something had been taken away from him, not just a problem, a riddle with an air of the big wide world about it, but also . . . how should he put it . . . a longing. It was all over now. It had been dismissed as a dreary suicide, and he for one was not much the wiser. He had his letter but he knew as little now as he did before. Admittedly that was one of the more nostalgic aspects of his work. No sooner had he gained an insight into a life than he had to let it go, but that was usually not hard to accept. What he normally felt was more like a weariness, a sadness, as he approached the end of an investigation, but this time people had travelled up from Cheltenham, and talked of spies and major political issues.

The unfortunate thing was just that Corell could do nothing about it. He would have to go back to the usual dreary stuff, to investigations into littering in the police yard, and he started to think about other things, about Julie and the girl—all sorts of things. He was completely absorbed by melancholy thoughts and it took a while before he realised that he could hear a man calling.

"Excuse me! Have you got a moment?"

He turned around slowly and then saw the unknown man with the narrow, peering eyes and he was not only roused out of his brooding, but he also grew nervous, the way he used to at school when someone very senior unexpectedly came up and gave a friendly smile. He was pleased, but would have preferred to be left alone. Fortunately, the man began by saying exactly the right thing:

"Wonderful, the way you spoke to the coroner!"

It was so right that Corell dared to begin by being honest:

"I feel like an idiot."

"The curse of the truth-teller."

Truth-teller.

It was almost too much, and in order not to lose his composure Corell put out a hand to introduce himself. The unknown man, who despite his kind words had something very severe about him, was called Fredric Krause and was a logician at Cambridge and "a friend of Turing's, or at least an admirer." He had travelled here "to honour Alan."

"Honour?"

"If you'd known Alan you'd have realised how incredibly comical it was to hear him described as a specific type."

"In what way?"

"In every way! Or rather, if there is another person of his type, then I'd like to meet him right away!"

"Really?"

"If I understood you correctly you don't seem quite as certain as the others that it was suicide," Krause said.

"Well I suppose I'm pretty certain."

"But . . ."

"No buts. It's just that I've realised that I know far too little about Turing."

"I feel the same way."

"You do?"

The man nodded, and took a step forward, and in a fit of paranoia Corell got it into his head that the logician had come rather too close. He dismissed the thought. They were just next to Grove Street and fell in with each other. The brisk pace of the afternoon had turned into a calmer lope, and soon they began to slow down. Krause asked Corell to tell him about the death, and as he once again gave his account of the circumstances in the house, he thought that he did in fact sound quite articulate and quick-thinking.

"What's your opinion?" he asked. "Was he the kind of man who might take his own life?"

"Well you never really think that of anyone, do you. But he had had some pretty hellish things done to him, and then . . ."

Krause hesitated, and that's when Corell noticed something odd about him. When he thought something over, his eyelids quivered.

"Then what?" Corell said.

"Well, it's never easy for a mathematician to grow older, or indeed for a physicist. We're like athletes, or at least most of us are. We're at our peak in our twenties. Einstein was in fact almost old when he had his *annus mirabilis*. He was twenty-six. After that, one has far too much time to start looking in on oneself."

"And that's not good?"

"If you look inside yourself with the same energy as you would devote to investigating a mathematical problem, then it all goes terribly wrong," Krause said, with a strange lightness given what he had just said, and then he added that Alan had been an idiot to have moved here, "to this puritanical stronghold. Well, not that I want to say bad things about Wilmslow," he elaborated, as if Corell could have been offended, but, "nothing could have been more different from King's than Manchester."

"Yes, here he had to go to Oxford Road," Corell said.

"To what?"

"To the street where men pick up men."

"I see."

"May I ask you something completely different?" Corell said.

"You're a policeman. I suppose you can ask whatever you like."

"This is no police question."

"So much the better."

"I used to be good at maths," continued Corell, and immediately felt embarrassed at what he'd said.

"Congratulations," Krause said, and it could easily have sounded sarcastic, but Corell chose not to interpret it like that.

"And I'm fascinated by the liar's paradox."

"Oh, I see!"

Krause looked curious.

"And for a long time I thought that it was just an amusing little word game, but then I read . . ." in the minutes of the police interview, he meant to say, but he realised that would sound idiotic.

"Read what?"

"That in fact the paradox was a fundamental and important problem and that it had given rise to a new . . ."

Once again he paused.

"I would love you to explain it to me," he said.

"My God! You both surprise and delight me," Krause answered and broke into a smile. "The liar's paradox? Jesus! Do you really want to hear? You may never get rid of me."

They stopped.

"I'll take the risk."

"Where shall I begin?"

"Why not try the beginning."

"Then I'll have to go back to the Greeks. I suppose I could skip the Romans. They didn't have a clue. The Roman who had the greatest influence on mathematics was probably the chap who killed Archimedes. Ha, ha! But the liar's paradox, in its original version it was called . . ."

"I know about Epimenides."

They kept on walking.

"Good, then we can continue. Epimenides was first. But afterwards the paradox has cropped up in all sorts of variations. In the fifteenth century a French philosopher wrote down on a piece of paper: 'All sentences on this page are false.' Brilliant, isn't it? Simple, clear, but eternally contradictory. If all the sentences on that page are false then even that sentence must be, but then it's true because it specifically says that it is false, but on the other hand it appears on the page where all sentences are false . . . Alan once said that the liar's paradox should be used to explode robots."

"What did he mean by that?"

"When a thing is made entirely of logical systems, it should blow itself up when it tackles sentences like that. The thoughts would just go round and round until they short-circuit."

"But is it of fundamental importance?"

"Absolutely! It is totally central. It has changed our way of looking at logic, and at the world too for that matter. Well, I should say, it depends on who you ask. If you had spoken to Wittgenstein, he would have said that the paradox is just empty and meaningless."

"But that wasn't what . . ."

"Not Turing, not at all. He and Wittgenstein had classic debates about it at Cambridge."

"Did they know each other?"

"Not really," Krause said. "Alan had nicer friends than that. Besides which Wittgenstein didn't really have a clue about mathematics. But just before the war Turing and I took his course in the logic of mathematics, and then . . ."

Krause stopped and smiled, as though the memory were a sweet one. Wrinkles appeared in his face, which probably was not so young after all, and the look, the sharp brown look, narrowed even further and Corell, who had paused briefly, got a whiff of the big wide world. Wittgenstein was one of those distinguished names which had featured in the dinner table conversations of his childhood and he was not so much impressed by the fact that Turing had "had classic debates" with the philosopher as by the disrespectful tone in which Krause had made the remark. "Wittgenstein didn't really have a clue about mathematics." The words resounded with his father's majestic dismissals of the world's great men. Looking to the side he saw that they were passing a pub called The Zest. It was on the ground floor of an attractive white-washed stone house and although it was a typical Irish pub the façade was painted blue and yellow, and even though Corell hesitated—and immediately afterwards regretted it—he said:

"May I buy you a drink?"

It was as if Krause had not heard.

"A drink?" he repeated.

For a moment the logician seemed to lose his mocking veneer. He became pensive, but only for a brief moment. Then he lit up and gestured with his right hand.

"Absolutely," he said, and then they went in.

19

THEY SETTLED DOWN in the pub's saloon bar at a window table looking out onto the street. A number of green shields with coats of arms hung on the walls and also a photograph of a mountain with dramatic cliffs. The pub was surprisingly empty. Only two bored-looking men in light-coloured suits were talking at a table further away and then in the corner opposite them sat a solitary older man who had seen better days and who from time to time seemed to be on the point of saying something. But Corell soon forgot about him. He was absorbed by what Krause had to say and felt both relaxed and accepted, not just because they immediately agreed to call each other by their first names, Leonard and Fredric, but also because they drank a lot: he mild ale, while the logician, who had wanted lager and tried in vain to order some German or Nordic ones, ended up drinking large amounts of Carling Black Label.

"You have no idea how excited I was when I started Wittgenstein's course," Krause said. "You know, I'm from Prague and spent some time studying mathematics in Vienna. In Vienna there was a set which called itself the Vienna Circle and met in some shabby premises on Boltzmanngasse. I went there once and sat on an old wooden chair listening to people talking about Wittgenstein as if he were God Almighty. What would Wittgenstein have said, they kept asking. It was absurd. But it had its effect on me. I trembled at the thought of getting anywhere near him. Do you know the story of his life?"

Corell made a vague gesture with his hand.

"Wittgenstein was born filthy rich," Krause continued, "and as a young student he appeared at Russell's lectures and was a general nuisance. 'That man is impossible to talk to,' Russell said: 'He's an idiot,' and it may well be that that was a pretty accurate assessment. But Russell changed his mind. Rather than an idiot, he maintained that the chap was a genius, quite simply the archetypal genius, possessed, uncompromising and eccentric. He certainly got the last point right. Wittgenstein was unbelievable. He gave away his entire fortune, no, I don't really know to whom. I think he gave some of it to Rilke, the poet. But I have a feeling that most of it ended up with his sister, who was already rich. Wittgenstein then enlisted as a volunteer in the Austrian army and just like his countryman Hitler—they actually went to the same school for a while—he found the war edifying. He was quite simply utterly insane! As a prisoner of war in Italy he finished *Tractatus*, you know the book which ends with the words: 'What we cannot speak about we must pass over in silence.'"

"What we cannot speak about we must pass over in silence," Corell repeated.

"A pretentious and meaningless sentence. But it's expressed in elegant terms, and is enchanting in its rigour. If you don't have anything sensible to say, keep your mouth shut! Today I can't stand it. But at that time in 1939 I was entranced. I must have read *Tractatus* at least ten times and was convinced that I was finding all sorts of things in it. With that book, Wittgenstein claimed to have whipped down philosophy's trousers. He maintained that language and logic were not sufficient to deal with the big issues. Logic was at best good enough for discovering tautologies and contradictions. Philosophy was nonsense and, because he was the man he was, he acted on his convictions and moved up into the mountains and became an Austrian schoolteacher. It sounded wonderfully uncompromising. Later I got to hear that he didn't manage it very well. He would thrash the schoolboys, probably rather like those Jesuit priests whom Joyce writes about. He suppressed so much of his passions and normal feelings that he was prone to violent fits of rage."

"But he returned to Cambridge?"

"He allowed philosophy a second chance when he was given the chair at Trinity after G. E. Moore, and what do you think, do you think people talked about it at all?"

"I think so."

"There was no-one at Cambridge who had as much of an aura as he did. Just to see him from afar was a major experience, never mind being able to take his course! He gave it in his rooms at Whewells Court in Trinity and I was absolutely weak at the knees when I went there. It was like treading on holy ground when I stepped in."

"And Turing was there as well?"

"I didn't know who he was then. I hadn't even read 'Computable Numbers.' In fact it took a while before I noticed anyone other than Wittgenstein. He was electric, beautiful even, I have to admit that, albeit reluctantly. Have you seen a picture of him?"

"I don't think so."

"Well, he was incredibly imposing; thin, sharp-featured, and always dressed in simple clothes, in a flannel shirt and leather jacket, and we sat around him on the floor and on wooden chairs, half paralysed with reverence. It was like being in a monastery. He didn't even have a reading light, ascetic madman that he was, no pictures or paintings on the walls, no decent furniture, hardly even books, just a grey safe for his philosophical manuscripts, and the lectures themselves . . . How should I describe them? Wittgenstein obviously didn't follow a manuscript. It was more of a laboured production of words, and he could be very hard on himself. 'I'm an idiot,' he might say. But most often it was us he barked at: 'I might as well be talking to a cupboard! Haven't you understood so much as one word?' We didn't dare open our mouths, still less say that we didn't understand. Wittgenstein was so bloody unclear, you see, and we felt we were being dim. He was a damned bloodsucker. We huddled together like a flock of scared sheep. But there was one fellow who stood up to him . . ."

"Turing?"

"Quite honestly I don't know when I first noticed him. Alan wasn't exactly a Wittgenstein, after all."

"In what way?"

"He too was an original, I came to see that later, although in some ways, objectively speaking, he and Wittgenstein were very much alike; they were both loners. Both were homosexual, lived Spartan lives and were interested in fundamental issues. But in another sense they were opposites. Alan was shy. He often seemed invisible in a large group, and had a hesitant tone. Sometimes he stuttered quite badly. There was nothing grandiose about him, nothing at all, and at first I think he rather irritated Wittgenstein. Who is this fellow? But Wittgenstein changed. He started to listen and trade verbal blows with the chap and often he was scornful, of course he was, but you could tell that something had happened to him. Something had come to life in his remarkable brain. It's as if he brightened up when confronted with Alan, and in the end it seemed as if he only talked to him. It was as if the rest of us didn't exist. Once when Turing didn't turn up he looked altogether dejected. He was deflated. 'This is going to be an incidental seminar,' he said."

"How come?" Corell said.

"Alan was sharp. He challenged Wittgenstein, and the old tyrant liked that, despite everything. But Alan was also the only mathematician in the group. The course was called—did I say that?—the logic of mathematics. Strangely enough, at the same time, Alan was giving a course with the same name, but I had no idea, unfortunately, since that course would probably have suited me better. You understand, numbers were Alan's friends, his religion. He dreamed of giving them physical form. Wittgenstein was totally different. In his view mathematicians took their subject much too seriously. He made them the target of his constant polemicising and Turing the enemy's representative. 'Turing thinks that I want to introduce Bolshevism into mathematics,' he said."

"What exactly was the subject of their debates?"

"The very thing you were asking about, the liar's paradox!"

Corell leaned forward.

"In what way?" he said.

"Wittgenstein wanted to show that mathematics was like logic, a closed system, built on arbitrary premises, which said nothing about the outside world. He argued that a contradiction like the liar's paradox, which creates problems within mathematical systems, has no application in the real world. It was a word game, nothing more, a brainteaser. Something which at the most one could use to confuse the student. In normal usage it fulfilled no function. Other than possibly as a joke to be enjoyed over cocktails. 'What's the point,' he said, 'if I say I'm lying, therefore I'm telling the truth, accordingly I'm lying, therefore I'm telling the truth until I'm blue in the face. It's just nonsense.'"

"But Turing didn't agree?"

"No, and that infuriated Wittgenstein. He tried his damnedest to convince him."

"But he didn't succeed."

"Not in the slightest. Alan saw the liar's paradox as something deeply serious, something which had consequences far beyond logic and mathematics. He even said that a bridge could collapse."

"Because of the liar's paradox?"

"Or because of some other flaw in the foundations of mathematics. He and Wittgenstein kept going on about that bridge all the time. They built it up and tore it down, and painted into life all sorts of strange images. But neither of them gave way and in the end Turing grew tired of it. He dropped the course, and Wittgenstein was left sitting there with his tail between his legs."

"And who was right?"

"Turing, of course. He couldn't have been more right."

"You really think so?" Corell said excitedly.

"If anyone could see that the paradox was special it was Alan," Krause said. "Usually when we come up against a contradiction it's a sign that we've made a mistake, isn't it? But there's no mistake here. The phrase 'I'm lying' is correct, and grammatically faultless. But still there's no way of proving it, and that's no small matter. It's a fundamental blow against . . ."

"Our very understanding of truth," Corell said.

"Yes, and Alan had spent a lot of time on the paradox. He even used a variant of it in his argumentation in 'Computable Numbers.'"

"In what?"

"His paper about the machine. Well now, how should I explain that?"

Fredric Krause drank his beer with an eagerness which Corell would probably have put down to alcoholism if it were not so obviously a reflection of his passion for the topic.

"You know the difference between discovering and inventing," he continued. "Someone who makes a discovery finds something which was concealed, such as America or the electrons in the atomic nucleus. Someone who invents is creating new things, something which did not exist until we thought of it, like the telephone."

"Obviously!"

"For a long time mathematicians saw themselves as explorers. They imagined that numbers and the secret connections between them were given by nature, independently of man. Mathematicians only needed to draw back the veil to reveal the whole ingenious system. But eventually some began to wonder: Is that really how it is? People saw that the foundations of mathematics were not so solid after all. They seemed instead to be full of holes. The liar's paradox was just one of them. Certain absolute truths, even some in Euclid's geometry, had turned out to be relative. They could just as easily have looked different. People tried to find the square root of minus one and discovered the unit imaginary number, which according to Leibniz was an amphibian somewhere between being and non-being. More and more people began to regard mathematics as an invention, almost like chess."

Corell remembered Rimmer's words.

"Mathematics underwent a crisis."

"Some wondered whether it was even logical," Krause said.

"And was it?"

"Certainly some ambitious attempts were made to cure the patient. Gottlob Frege wanted to show that mathematics was at least consistent— despite its imperfections. It seemed as if he had succeeded. His magnum opus *Basic Laws of Arithmetic* appeared to put mathematics back on firm logical ground. But then he received a letter from an extremely friendly young man in Cambridge. The letter praised his book. The book was quite fantastic, and so on. One can just imagine the scene. Frege, the anti-Semitic old goat, leaning back, fit to burst with self-righteousness . . . well, perhaps I exaggerate, not that he wasn't an anti-Semite—his diary from later years reveals the most appalling opinions—but maybe he wasn't all that self-righteous. His work had been ignored, and he had never risen higher than assistant professor in Jena. But still . . . he sees himself as the saviour of mathematics and in this letter he appears to be receiving a well-deserved tribute. Then he reads on. The author of the letter—a certain Bertrand Russell—has, after all, spotted a small problem in the book, a contradiction along the lines of the liar's paradox. It's probably nothing important. What can a young whippersnapper from Cambridge teach Frege? The whippersnapper even apologises for bringing up the question at all. Still, Frege decides that he's going to ponder it further, and indeed becomes a little worried, and what do you think happens next? His entire world falls apart. Everything he's worked on collapses like a house of cards."

"Why?"

"Russell had found inconsistencies in Frege's way of dividing objects into different groups. The problem lay in the category of all categories which were members of themselves."

"I beg your pardon?"

"When I attended Russell's lectures at Cambridge, he tried to explain what he had seen by telling us about a barber in, let's say, Venice. The barber shaves everybody in his part of town who does not shave himself, and no-one else. Who then shaves the barber?"

"You tell me!"

"If he doesn't shave himself then he's shaved by the barber, that's to say by himself, but if he shaves himself then he must be one of those who shave themselves and then clearly he shouldn't be shaved by the barber. There's a problem whichever way we answer the question."

"It would appear so," Corell said, confused, and took a deep gulp of his ale.

"And if you convert the question into numbers, you get an expression which seems correct, but leads you up a blind alley," Krause went on, untroubled.

"So . . ."

"And again one might think this is just splitting hairs. But it isn't like that. You see, mathematicians have had a huge advantage over other scientists: they've only had to do their sums to see whether something is right or wrong. They haven't even had to roll up the blinds and look out. All they had to do was check the numbers. But now it appeared that certain expressions contradicted themselves. If that were really the case, it meant that the world was an irrational place, an Alice-in-Wonderland world."

"That sounds serious."

"I'm exaggerating again, of course. As a logician I need to inject a bit of drama every now and then. Otherwise no-one would ever listen. But it is true to say that mathematics was perceived as a discipline with increasingly blurred contours. Right wasn't always right. Wrong not always wrong. There were optimists. Russell was one. He tried to sort out the contradictions. In his and Whitehead's major work, *Principia Mathematica*, they broke mathematics down into small, small parts and tried to show that everything was connected in accordance with sound logic, in spite of it all, and that created a certain confidence. David Hilbert, one of the great contemporary mathematicians, was convinced that mathematics would be rehabilitated as a reliable science. Anything else was simply inconceivable. 'Where else would certainty and truth be found if even mathematical thinking fails,' he wrote. 'No-one should expel us from the paradise which Cantor has created.'"

"Paradise?"

Corell knocked back the last drops of his ale.

"Hilbert was alluding to the paradise of pure and clear mathematics. He called himself a formalist. There may not be an exact reality out there which corresponds to mathematics. But so long as one decides what the rules are going to be it should be possible to derive a watertight system from them—provided that three conditions are met: that the system is consistent, complete and decidable."

"And what does that mean?"

"Consistent means that no contradiction should be able to crop up within the system. Complete means that it should be possible to prove the truth of every true mathematical proposition by using the rules of the system. For it to be decidable there has to be some algorithm which determines if it is possible for a mathematical proposition—whichever one it may be—to be proved or not. Hilbert sent out an appeal to the world's mathematicians to find the answers to these questions. He believed that there must be a solution—somewhere out there. It was just a matter of finding it. Because, in mathematics, there is no *ignorabimus*," he said.

"What?"

"In mathematics one always has to be able to find an answer."

"What happened?"

"Instead of a rehabilitation he found himself with an earthquake. His paradise was lost forever."

"*Paradise Lost,*" Corell said.

"There's a chap called Kurt Gödel. Gödel is an Austrian like me, or Czech, depending on how you see things. I met him once, in Princeton, where I studied for a year, or if it's too much to say 'met,' I did at least see him. Gödel's a recluse. A strange fellow, skinny, introverted, paranoid from what I've heard and a hypochondriac. So frightened of being poisoned that he hardly dares eat. The chap's only got one friend, and it's not just any old friend. Can you guess who?"

"Buster Keaton?" Corell ventured a little joke.

"Ha, ha. It's Einstein. He and Gödel are best friends. It's really touching. In Princeton I saw them go back and forth, hour after hour, with their hands clasped behind their backs and just talk: Einstein a bit plump and good-natured, Gödel stern and sunken, the Laurel and Hardy of the intellectual world, we used to say. People wondered how Einstein—who was often quite easy-going—could spend so much time with such a misanthropist. Einstein's answer was broadly: Gödel is the whole point of this place. I understand him. When Gödel first produced his incompleteness theorem in 1931, he shook up the entire mathematical community, well at least once people started to understand it. The theorem isn't easy to master. But incredibly appealing and basically amazingly straightforward and clear. Naturally it's based on the liar's paradox."

"That too."

"The paradox is like Excalibur. It cuts through everything. In extremely elegant reasoning Gödel showed that a system which is complete can never at the same time be consistent. It's either one or the other. Take the sentence: 'This proposition can never be proved!' If it can be proved, we have a contradiction. The phrase contradicts itself. If it can't be proved then the system is incomplete. It means that there are propositions which can't be proved—even though they have been formulated entirely in accordance with the rules of the system."

"I understand." Corell thought that he really was beginning to do so, but perhaps it was just the beer.

"Gödel crushed Hilbert's dreams," Krause said. "He deprived us all of our innocence. He showed that generally speaking mathematics and logical reasoning can never be entirely free of a degree of irrationality. Nothing is as neat and perfect as we think. We cannot escape the contradictions. They seem to be a part of life itself."

"A man without contradictions has no credibility, my father used to say," Corell ventured.

"Your father was a wise man."

"Not especially."

"Oh no? But he was right. The driving force in drama and literature is our inner contrariness. That's why clichés and caricatures are so dreadful. They're too one-dimensional. But Gödel's theorem dealt Hilbert a stunning blow, since he had believed that at least the tenets of mathematics were cast in stone. For Alan on the other hand, who came to Cambridge at about this time, the theorem became a trigger, a carrot. If the foundations of mathematics were in a state of flux, it was all the more exciting to walk there. These were very exciting times and in that respect Alan was lucky. Einstein had picked holes in Newton's view of the world; Niels Bohr and his colleagues had discovered quantum physics. It was as difficult to predict the movements of an individual particle within the nucleus of an atom as the behaviour of a drunk at a party. The whole world had become less predictable, and Alan loved that. Turning conventions on their head was the very air that he breathed. When he started at King's all the talk was of Gödel. Gödel this and Gödel that. And indeed, Gödel was the hero. He was the main man. But he didn't have the solution to everything. He hadn't answered all of Hilbert's questions. One important point remained. The one about decidability. Hilbert had after all challenged the geniuses of the future to find a method which could determine whether a mathematical proposition, whichever one it might be, could be proved or not. Many were still hoping that something like that could be found, which would at least to some extent save the honour of mathematics. It was often referred to as the decision problem. Or in German, the *Entscheidungsproblem*. Max Newman, the same Newman who is now working on the digital machine in Manchester, gave a lecture on the problem. I suspect he was hoping to inspire someone to come to grips with it, not that he can have had particularly high expectations. It must have seemed insoluble. How was one supposed to find a method which could run through all mathematical propositions, past and future, and decide which could be proved and which could not? It must have sounded monumental. It seemed like the dream of a *perpetuum mobile*. But Newman . . . he came right out and speculated that there might perhaps be a mechanical way of tackling the problem."

"A mechanical way?"

"Newman meant it figuratively. A mechanical method in a purely intellectual sense where there are certain simple rules which allow you to calculate an answer. But among the audience sat a young man who had a life-long habit of taking things literally."

"Turing."

"Alan always liked to try out the literal interpretation. Once he was criticised for not having signed his identity card. 'I was told not to write on it,' he said. That's the way he was. He took everything literally and of course usually that's a sign of being a bit slow on the uptake. A lack of imagination. With him it was quite the opposite. By interpreting things literally he got a step further than the rest of us. Mechanical to him meant mechanical as in a machine."

Corell leant over the table eagerly.

"Tell me!" he said. "Tell me!"

20

IT WAS NOT EASY TO UNDERSTAND, and not just because it was so abstract. They were also beginning to get drunk. But apparently Alan Turing had been young when he heard the word mechanical being mentioned in a context where it did not belong. He was barely twenty, as young as Gödel, as young as all mathematicians were when their thoughts were innovative and great, but unlike most of the others he did not seem to be especially interested in the history of mathematics either or even in learning from others' mistakes.

He had often managed, even as a child, to find the answer on his own to mathematical problems which others before him had already solved, sometimes a hundred years earlier, and he did not seem particularly inclined to discuss his ideas. He went his own way. He was already something of an outsider because of the way he was and his tricky character, and he had his own view of the world. To others at Cambridge the word *mechanical* was not just dreary, Krause said. Now that Newton's mechanical view of the world had been revised, it was also out of date, a word from the old order before Einstein, but for Turing there was poetry in it.

"Alan had a pretty stellar career at Cambridge, and it was a new experience for him," Krause said. "He hadn't exactly shone at school. But at King's he quickly became a Fellow and was paid three hundred pounds a year and had his own room and the right to dine with the more distinguished academics, not that he cared about that, but he became free to do as he wanted."

"And what was that?"

"First he wanted to do something in quantum physics and then something in the field of probability theory, but he got nowhere and then he couldn't forget what Max Newman had said."

"About finding a mechanical method . . ."

"Which could determine if mathematical propositions could be proved or not."

"Sounds difficult!"

"It was crazy. Mathematics wasn't short of problems which could neither be proved nor dismissed, just take Fermat's Last Theorem or Goldbach's Conjecture that every even integer greater than two can be expressed as the sum of two primes. How could a mechanical method be expected to crack something which had proved too much for the foremost mathematicians over the centuries? And could something as soulless and stupid as a machine possibly make any sort of contribution to the problem? Other mathematicians had laughed at the thought. Hardy, the great God, wrote something to the effect that only the most stupid idiots believe that mathematicians can make their discoveries by switching on some sort of miracle machine. No, high-level mathematics was regarded as being the very opposite of that. It was the realm of free and beautiful thinking. Even to dream of a machine . . ."

"But Turing did . . ."

"He dreamed. But then he was not a serious mathematician, not in that sense. He kept himself apart, he didn't care to think in the same way as the fancy set, people like Hardy. He remained naive, and to be naive and brilliant, that is a happy combination."

"But a machine?"

"God knows where that came from. But we collect impressions, don't we? We gradually find ourselves running along certain tracks. An idea can appear suddenly, but it often has a long history. I said that the word mechanical had a positive or even poetic connotation for him. It may have something to do with the fact that when he was a boy someone gave him a book in which an enthusiastic scientist described in simple words how the world and the human being function—among other things the author compared our body with an advanced machine. It was clearly only a metaphor, a way to demonstrate how our insides work away rhythmically and mechanically to keep us alive. But it made an impression on Alan. He had his fondness for literal interpretations and I believe he liked the idea of the brain as a machine. It made a change from the usual bowing before the miraculous aspects of the human soul."

"He spoke of electronic brains."

"Later, yes . . . but at that time, during the thirties, he was not thinking either electrical or electronic. It was purely theoretical. Possibly he already knew then that the brain is driven by electrical impulses and electricity can't really do much more than go from one place to another. It can be here or there. On or off. It's a primitive force. Single-track and dumb and yet, our brain has written *Hamlet*, Beethoven's *Appassionata* and the theory of relativity. It seems that with just two settings, two logical constants, even complexities can be expressed, Alan understood that early on. He wasn't going to be disheartened or hampered just because machines are dumb and clumsy things. He saw greatness in simplicity."

"I'm not sure that I really understand."

"In a way it's very simple. Already Plato in his *Sophist* realised that you only needed two words, yes or no, to arrive at a solution. Have you ever played 'Twenty Questions'?"

"I think so."

"Then you'll know how much one can find out and exclude about a person just by posing yes and no questions."

"Yes, perhaps!"

"Well, imagine accelerating the questioning process or stringing together all the positives and negatives to form long combinations, then do you see just how much can be expressed with just two words, two settings?"

"I think so."

Corell was feeling more and more confused, but he pretended that it was all perfectly clear to him.

"And Alan's thought wasn't new. The idea of being able to break thinking down into a few building blocks is an old one. In the seventeenth century Leibniz had grandiose ideas about it. But before Alan, nobody—not with the same wild ambition—had set his mind on building a machine which could embrace every mathematical equation which has existed or will exist. I think he grasped a number of fundamental things early on, for example that a machine like this must be able to read these different settings, and have the capacity to memorise and store them, and above all be receptive to instructions, but I don't know how the different pieces of the puzzle came to him. No-one knows. He didn't discuss the project with anybody. But at this time he was running like a madman. He wasn't a very elegant runner, but he was a tenacious devil, he could keep going for as long as you liked and often he would run along the river, sometimes all the way up to Ely. One late afternoon in the early summer of 1935 he lay down on his back in a meadow in Grantchester after having been for a run, at least that's what he told people. Are you a sportsman? No? But I'm sure you know how there's a rush of blood when you slow down after a major exertion. Sometimes I think it's a bit like escaping from a lethal hazard. After the fear, after the excitement, you feel a strangely purifying clarity. Like climbing out of an ice-cold bath. Pieces which have been hopelessly mixed up fall into place as if by magic, and Alan, he had buried himself in these questions. They had been nagging and buzzing inside him, but he had come no closer to finding a solution. But in that meadow something happened . . . let's say that a small gap opened in the clouds and the sun broke through, or shall we just assume that he settled comfortably on the grass and totally forgot where he was and that he then, as if in a flash of light, although a flash of light is perhaps a terrible cliché in this context, let's say in a moment of blinding perspicacity—well, I suppose that's not much better, blinding, shimmering, all those words are ghastly, aren't they, light as air as I said. Sounds a bit like Christians trying to proclaim a divine vision. In any case Alan said that he had felt intense joy and that he wasn't sure later which had come first, the joy or the solution, or if they were simultaneous: if the answer came to him as pure joy. All he knew was that he had been suffused by a quivering live force and that he had found the solution to Hilbert's third question, the answer to the famous decision problem."

"What had he found out?"

"Not so easy to explain just like that," Krause said, and without really giving it a thought Corell took his notepad out of his inside pocket.

"Are you going to take notes?"

"If that's O.K.?"

"Of course, of course. Where was I?"

"You were going to explain Turing's solution."

"Yes, well, so . . . he started to write his paper . . ."

" 'Computable Numbers'?"

"Yes, just as Cantor once worked out the irrational numbers from the rational ones, Alan got to the incomputable numbers by studying the computable ones," Krause said, a little uncertain now. It was as if somehow the notepad bothered him.

"So he invented something which could decide whether mathematical propositions can be solved or not," Corell said.

"No. He realised that was an oxymoron. You could say that, by formulating the theoretical basis for a machine designed to tackle the problem, he grasped the inherent limitations of the question."

"We can never know in advance if there is a solution?"

"Sometimes we can't. Sometimes we have no idea if the machine which is doing the computing for us will be able to stop."

"Or if it will get stuck in its question," Corell added, recalling a line in the draft letter.

"Exactly!"

"So that was another blow to mathematics as an exact science."

"Alan put the nail in the coffin and Hilbert shed a few more tears. But the world got something else, as a consolation prize."

"What?"

"A programmable digital machine. A general-purpose machine which could replace all other machines."

Corell drained his glass and looked about him in wonder, but all he really saw were his own internal images.

"How did it go down?" he said.

"How do you think?"

"As a sensation?"

"Quite the opposite. Nobody was in the least interested in the machine. It was nothing. After all, it was no more than pure theory, an aid for solving a specific mathematical problem and nothing more. No-one thought of building it, presumably not even he, not then. Besides . . ."

Corell remembered his aunt's words:

"Machines were seen as being a bit vulgar."

"Anyway, no-one asked if the contraption could be used for anything other than resolving Hilbert's question," Krause said. "Mathematicians don't like to think about trivialities like the usefulness of their equations. It's considered too common. Haven't you heard the story of the boy who was one of Euclid's pupils? No? The boy asked the great mathematician what benefit he got from his equations. Euclid answered that someone should give the boy a coin so that he might make some use of the sums he'd learned. Then he kicked him out. No, one shouldn't think about such foolish things as usefulness. Mathematics is considered beautiful precisely because it is sufficient unto itself. It need only serve itself."

"But it surely can't do any harm . . ."

"To make some use of it, you mean. Don't say such a thing. You'll make the purists weep up there in their heaven. In any case few people at the time, least of all Hardy, thought that higher mathematics could be used for anything outside its own sphere, even if one wanted to."

"But Hardy was wrong?"

"As wrong as hell. As wrong as Wittgenstein. Alan was to understand better than anyone else that paradoxes and contradictions can mean the difference between life and death. But that's another story."

"What story?"

"None at all really," Krause answered, again unsettled. He even bit his lip and glared suspiciously at the notepad. "Just as you suggested," he continued, "machines were regarded as something lower-class, something for simple engineers. Definitely nothing for a grand mathematician. But Turing wasn't grand, as I said."

"How do you mean that?"

"I mean that he didn't care about that sort of thing, or rather that he didn't understand it. Do you imagine that he followed the whims of fashion, started to use expressions which were all the rage? No, he dressed appallingly. He didn't give a damn what others thought. I'm not saying that he couldn't take offence. He was already pretty lonely by then. But that's the way it was. He wasn't part of any smart societies and never understood what he needed to do to get into them. Alan wasn't good at that sort of thing. He never learned to promote himself, or see to it that he got to know the right people. He remained a loner, someone apart. He was definitely not grand."

"Didn't he get any recognition at all for his paper?"

"He was quite unhappy for a long time because nobody read it, and that's understandable. You have this overwhelming experience in the meadow, and then nothing, just an embarrassing silence. And yet . . ."

"What?"

". . . it's such an extraordinary text. Alan writes about his machines as if they were his colleagues. He talks about their state, their consciousness, their behaviour, and then he realised—and this in itself is an amazing insight—that everything which is capable of being counted, can be counted by an automatic machine, and that opens up entirely new fields for research."

"But no-one read the paper?"

"Not many! The world of mathematical logic is a ludicrously small one, and to cap it all he got some alarming news from America. Alonzo Church, a dreary old man in Princeton, who both Alan and I had as a teacher later on, had at the same time come up with another, but duller answer to Hilbert's third question. Alan had to throw together an appendix to take care of it."

"So there were no choruses of praise?"

"Little by little, Alan gained a reputation. He became known as the man who solved the decision problem, the *Entscheidungsproblem*. He was admired for it; for my own part I saw him almost on a level with Gödel, but . . ."

"Yes?"

"When all was said and done, he didn't care much about the *Entscheidungsproblem*. Unlike everybody else, what interested him was the means and not the end."

"The machine, you mean?"

"Or his efforts to gain a full understanding of the building blocks of intelligence."

"So he started to build his machine."

"At least he sketched at it. But the world probably wasn't really ready for it. I don't know. What eventually materialised in Manchester was far less exciting than what he'd had in mind."

"But do you think anything can come of it?"

"Well now . . ."

Krause looked pensive and glanced down at his white beer mat.

"When I first heard about this, I didn't really believe in it," he continued. "I thought that it seemed much too complicated to assemble the machines. But now I wonder . . ."

"Wonder what?"

"If something couldn't come of it."

21

IN THE DREAM, Alan Turing rose from the bed and there was something ceremonious about his movement, as if he had been roused by a distant summons, and far away a remote requiem Mass could be heard with church bells and drums. The air was stifling and still, as though just before a thunderstorm, and Turing wiped the froth from his mouth, but his hands were too stiff, and now, now he wanted to speak. Not one word could be heard, and yet he was trying so hard. His lips were trembling and Corell leaned forward. He cupped his ear, and yes he did catch a word or two, about something quite remarkable, something which was to become significant, and Corell dug out a notebook with an oilcloth cover into which he wrote what he heard, but however hard he tried the text was unclear and he gripped the pencil even harder. He carved in the words. He pressed them in, but the letters floated off as if on water, and now he was transported away to a railway track and to a solitary chair by the sea, and everything turned vague and white, but he had such a strong feeling of having written something down that when Corell woke up he fumbled for his notes.

For a moment he thought that he had found them. One of his note-pads from work lay on the bedside table. The first page was creased and covered in rapidly scribbled sentences, but they were just some quick notes which he had jotted down of his conversation with Krause and no mysterious messages from beyond the grave. What time was it? It must be early. He could tell by the birds and the silence and by the feeling in his body, and the headache and the extent of his hangover. He pulled the sheet and the blanket over his head.

Memories from the previous day penetrated his consciousness. He tried to keep them away, and to remain in his bubble. For as long as he could remember he had had fantasy worlds all ready for him to step into, some of which rarely changed, others which were new and shaped from things that he had recently heard or experienced. Some consisted of nothing more than things he should have said and done in real life. Others were idealised developments of minor triumphs in his everyday life and at work, but most were crazy and unlikely, yet thought out in detail. They were worlds to flee to. Sanctuaries where sorrow could be kept at bay. But on this morning, fantasy provided no refuge. Reality weighed, but not as heavily as it usually did. The day felt light. Last night had been pretty successful, hadn't it? He and the logician had had a good conversation, the kind he had been longing to have for years, although admittedly there were still some signs of his anxiety. He was not free from torment. He never was. But he had not drowned his life in drink last night. If anything, his tipsiness had restored some of his old self and towards the end they had talked about all sorts of things. He had asked . . .

He sat up.

He reached for his notepad. It was not easy to see what he had written and he did not like what he could make out. What had seemed big just now suddenly felt so paltry: *it's not the machine as such that matters but rather the instructions to it,* it just sounded dreary, it had had a different ring to it yesterday, but now . . . some words and a question mark, the same question that he had asked Gladwin in the archive room: *What does one do with a mathematics genius and a chess master in wartime?* And underneath that something which Krause had said at some other point in the conversation: *Alan was to understand better than anyone else that paradoxes and contradictions can mean the difference between life and death.*

What did Krause mean when he said that? Corell had no idea. He only remembered that afterwards the logician had been evasive or even dismissive. He was clearly holding something back. He had looked nervously at Corell's notepad, and *life and death* . . . Could it be that whatever Alan Turing had been doing during the war, Krause had been doing the same thing? Like the idiot that he was, Corell had never put pressure on him to elaborate. He had not wanted to spoil the genial atmosphere, and had been just as anxious to learn about logic and mathematics as to discover secrets about the war. Besides, he could not quite come to terms with the fact that a Cambridge academic would want to drink away an entire weekday evening with a simple policeman like him without some reason. Was the logician in fact trying to get something out of him? No, Corell dismissed the thought, and now . . . now he stretched out in bed and tried to remember more. Strangely enough he could not visualise Krause's face. Only the narrow eyes stood out in his memory, and then the eager shine of his pupils. But it had been a good meeting, hadn't it? God knows how long they had sat there for! The last part was a blur. He only had a decent recollection of when they had said goodbye. They had embraced, and that had made him nervous. The chap had after all been a friend of Turing's, and none of all the possible explanations for the long time they had spent together would have been worse, but it was probably nothing to worry about, he persuaded himself. The embrace was short and Corell had been given a telephone number and an address in Cambridge and wandered home in the rain without even having the energy to worry about his suit.

He looked around the flat. God, the place was a mess. Clothes and rubbish everywhere. When he got out of bed he could hear a crunch of gravel and breadcrumbs, and that would not have been so bad if beneath it all, beyond the disorder, there had been something congenial, but the flat was devoid of charm. The Queen Anne chair seemed to have ended up in the wrong place, the radio looked too good for the room and nothing matched, but usually he hardly noticed his home. It was only there to protect him from the world around him, an extension of his body's protective armour, and it had only once occurred to him how absurd the situation was, when he had dreamed about seducing Julie. Then he had realised that it could hardly happen here. At the most, he could have pointed at the house and said, that's where I live.

From the outside, the house had nice brown brickwork and a small garden with peonies and apple trees. But it was none of his doing. The landlady, Mrs. Harrison, poked about down there every morning in the spring and the summer. She was kind and chatty, but he never felt comfortable with her—he was afraid that she would complain about the mess in his flat—and now that he managed to leave the house before her he saw it as a small victory.

It looked like a nice day and the people he met were in no hurry at all. When he got into town he bought the *Manchester Guardian*. He was a keen reader of the papers, but this morning he did not even look at the front-page news. He turned over the pages eagerly and in the left-hand column on page eight he found it. It was about as much as the day before. It began: "Yesterday evening it was established that Alan Mathison Turing of Hollymeade, Adlington Road, Wilmslow, took his own life with poison while the balance of his mind was disturbed."

While the balance of his mind was disturbed. Those were the words of the coroner. There was no mention of Corell's intervention, obviously not, and why should there have been? This was not an article about a difference of opinion in the investigation. But he was nonetheless disappointed. He felt deflated. He had hoped for something along the lines of *Detective Constable Corell queried the statement of the coroner . . .* He had to be content with being quoted in two places, admittedly in sentences which did not feel as if they were his, but he spoke about the half apple and the bubbling pan and the smell of bitter almonds. What he said represented the facts, that was at least some consolation. Ferns on the other hand uttered his nonsense as if nothing had happened. "It was a deliberate act since you never know what a man of this type will do next."

The words seemed even more peculiar in print. The article almost seemed to say that the act was deliberate because it was impulsive. It was a complete non sequitur. Idiots, he thought. But still he felt a little better. *According to Detective Constable Corell . . . Detective Constable Corell says.* There was nothing, it was even an insult since his important contribution, which had taken some courage, had not even been mentioned, but he was nonetheless content and slowly recovered some of his good mood from the morning. Daydreaming, he turned into Green Lane and passed the playground and the fire station. On the other side of the street there was a young woman walking along and reading a book while she pushed a pram—Corell had always liked people who read while walking—but when he spotted her he checked himself. The wheels of the pram reminded him of Fredric Krause.

Krause had said that Turing's machine before the war was no more than a sketch, an idea for an endless strip which one fed backwards and forwards to read symbols, nothing complete, nothing at all, just a tool in a logical discussion, but still: already by 1945 Alan Turing had drawn up the guidelines for a full-scale electric monstrosity. Something must have happened during the war, something which took the machine to another level. It must have had some purpose during the war. The only question was what.

What do you use a logical machine for in wartime?

Corell was yelled at when he got to the police station. It was Richard Ross, who seemed to feel the need to pick a fight with him, but his intention was apparently not just to stir up trouble, although that was of course the main objective. The inspector had a purpose in mind. Scarlet with rage and his hands on his hips he stomped into the criminal department and stood wide-legged in front of Corell's desk. His lips smacked as if he were getting ready to sink his teeth into his prey:

"May I ask just what the hell you think you're doing?"

"I just got here . . ."

"I mean yesterday. After the hearing!"

"Don't know what you're talking about."

"Of course you do," which Corell of course did. "James Ferns has been in touch and said that you tried to make complete fools of him and the pathologist in front of a whole mass of journalists."

"There weren't that many," Corell said.

"It makes no bloody difference how many there were. You were apparently arrogant and insolent, and let me tell you, this is something which I will not tolerate. You represent—"

"I know," Corell interrupted. "But you should have heard that fool! It was complete and utter rubbish."

"I tell you, I don't give a shit about that. And anyway I don't believe it. I'm sure you were the one who was talking rubbish and no-one else. I've had my eye on you, Corell, and I've noticed that you've been giving yourself airs. You and your snobbish ways from Marlborough College. Well, bollocks to that. I won't accept it. Not under any circumstances. You have no business telling respectable people what they should be doing. We expect you to report on the facts and otherwise keep your mouth shut. Is that clear?"

"Yes!"

"What's the matter with you? I just don't understand! There must be something wrong."

"What do you mean?"

"Don't be cocky. Just shut up. Because it's your lucky day. You're being given a chance to make amends. Yes, however strange it may seem, you've got a friend in these parts. Hamersley, that slimy bastard, says that your report was well-written. Don't be too pleased about it. Public school tricks like that don't impress me. But now you're to be sent out into the field—on the orders of the Chief Superintendent."

"What's it about?"

"A delicate assignment!"

Delicate usually meant sordid, and it was certainly appropriate in this case too. It was a couple of years old. The suspect was a forty-five-year-old man called David Rowan who had been a dancer and choreographer, but who now owned some tailoring businesses in Manchester. Rowan lived on Pinewood Road in Dean Row with a wife from Glasgow and two daughters, eight and six years old. The wife, who was described as "that unfortunate woman" even before the circumstances of the case had become clear, used to travel home to Scotland with the children from time to time for the weekends.

During these weekends the husband often received visits from a young man "with a feminine appearance" and "an effeminate manner," and naturally he had the right to mix with "whichever pansies he liked," as Ross put it, but a neighbour, a Mrs. Joan Duffy, had one day strayed into Rowan's garden and through a gap in the curtains had seen "the most dreadful filth. You can just imagine what." The only problem was that Mrs. Duffy was a school cook while David Rowan was quite a respectable gentleman, and "quite honestly we thought that it would be awkward to get involved. There was the wife and also the children. We didn't want to cause them any unnecessary distress."

"But now we're going to open it up again?"

"Hamersley thinks it's time to give it another try. After all, the times are what they are and guidelines have been issued. Then there's also the success in the Turing case."

"Hardly a success."

"Stop being so bloody cocky! I'm obviously talking about the conviction that we got, not the suicide. If we could nail Turing, we should be able to get anybody, shouldn't we? Did you know the man was a member of the Royal Society? Did you really? And I bet you're impressed by that too. Well, let me tell you that I don't give a shit about that sort of thing when I hear that the person concerned travels all over Europe chasing bum boys."

"Surely one should only be looking at the actual offence," Corell said.

"Indeed one should. And not get all excited about a load of titles and medals! But that's not what we were talking about, is it? All that's history now. No, no, I don't want to hear anything more about it."

"I was just wondering why—"

"Shut up, will you!"

"But there's more to this than meets the eye."

"Rubbish," Ross cut him off. "You shouldn't be asking so many questions. You've got a new assignment, and if I were you I'd get started on it right away. God knows, you're going to have to bring home the bacon on this one."

All Corell felt he needed was a quiet day's work in which to nurse his hangover. The last thing he wanted was to set out on some impossible and degrading assignment. He had his pride, after all. Had he not had a profound conversation with a Cambridge academic only yesterday? I'm sorry, Commissioner, he should be saying, you have no right to talk to me like that. But still . . . even if Ross himself was an idiot—and one fine day Corell would tell him as much—he had passed on a message from a senior source: "Hamersley said that your report was well-written." Just imagine that! Had Corell himself not thought as much? He'd managed to produce something a bit special. Quite simply a bit of a brainwave. For all he knew, at this very moment the Chief Superintendent was perhaps speaking to the police chief himself: "In Wilmslow, you understand, we have an extremely talented young man I've had my eye on for some time, a writer of absolutely superb reports, I'd even say he has a literary talent, you really ought to read his . . ." He was shaken out of his thoughts by Ross growling: "Well?"

"I'll do my best," he managed.

"A confession is what we need, nothing less. The old file is in with Gladwin."

It was not much of an assignment, he thought, and he really did not see how he could make any progress with it, but he still got to grips with it right away, and asked to be put through to Mr. Rowan. A woman told him that Mr. Rowan would be home after five and without even asking if it would be convenient he told her that he would come by at that time and ask a few questions.

"What's it about?"

"I shall be informing Mr. Rowan in no uncertain terms!" he advised her, and felt resolute and decisive.

At half past one the witness Mrs. Duffy appeared at the police station. Corell had been expecting to see a little old lady with sharp features, but this was something different, not that Mrs. Duffy was any beauty but she was only about thirty, with a buxom figure and such a provocative look in her eyes that he instinctively looked down. Mrs. Duffy had a vulgar sort of appeal, and who knows, she might be able to make an impression on a court.

"Thank you for coming," he said.

"It's an honour to be of service."

"Would you tell me what you saw that day, and for God's sake don't leave out any details."

He should not have said that last bit. He got far more detail than he could ever have wished for. He even got a little lecture about gardening. Mrs. Duffy's husband was a gardener. Very good at his job. "Almost an artist in that line, and to be honest I've learned a thing or two myself."

"How useful!"

"Yes, isn't it! You see, we and the Rowans have a hedge in common. It separates our properties, and I look after it, for which Mrs. Rowan is very grateful. Poor, poor Mrs. Rowan."

"Perhaps we can leave her out of this for the time being."

"Absolutely, Sergeant, absolutely."

"I'm a Detective Constable."

"An exciting job, isn't it?"

"Well, yes, every now and then. Would you please be so kind as to continue."

"I will, I will. But all this happened two years ago you understand. I came to see you then too."

"I'm aware of that."

"And don't think that it all stopped then. Not by a long chalk!"

"Let's hear it then!"

The whole story revolved around the garden hedge, she said. That day she had been trimming it with the clippers and been obliged to step over to the Rowan family's side. Otherwise she could not have made the hedge look "nice and even," and that may well have been true but could also have been nonsense. Joan Duffy had reason to be curious. "I've had my eyes open," she said, and then she was worried for her own children. In any case she had heard a sound. She did not want to be more specific than that. She had been "properly brought up," after all. But nevertheless: "May God forgive me," she looked in "very discreetly," and of course she looked away as soon as she realised.

"Of course," he added.

"It embarrasses me to be sitting here telling you all this."

"Don't be. It was the right thing to do to come here."

"I prefer you to the man I spoke to the last time."

"We're going to try to get to the bottom of it this time."

"Do you think I should be worried?"

"No, I don't think so."

"What if he becomes aggressive, can you arrange protection?"

Protection? He'd never heard anything like it.

"Let's take one thing at a time," he said. "Could there be other witnesses?"

"I'll ask around."

"Very discreetly, I hope."

"Discretion has always been a point of honour for me."

"Do you know the name of this man who came to visit?"

She thought it was Klaus. Something foreign. Something pretty shady.

"Thank you so much for coming," he brought the interview to a close and shook her hand, and afterwards he thought that she had made an inviting movement with her hair, but he must have been mistaken.

22

THERE HAD BEEN a voraciousness about Mrs. Duffy which stayed with him, a vulgarity which got under his skin and set his nerves jangling. However hard he tried, he could not help fantasising about her body and the way in which she would thank him: "You're more of a police-man than all of the rest of them put together," or whatever it was she would say. In any case her dress would be straining over her body, and her look would draw him towards her, and actually, why should he not succeed? Not long ago he had fancied himself to be a good interrogator who could easily identify people's weak points, and sense the worry in their eyes. Did he not usually know exactly when it was time to stick the knife in? That was one of the advantages of being a sensitive soul. He saw the signs in others.

Where was he now? That was Pinewood Road over there. He was close, and he started to think of Abbott and Pickens, those bloody arses, which never cheered him up, but now it strengthened his resolve. In Corell's imagination, Mr. Rowan's face took on some of Pickens's fea-tures and he straightened his back. Imagined that he was a senior intelli-gence officer on his way to an important mission. Yet he was not exactly bursting with confidence. He debated whether to turn back. No, no! If that muddle-headed Rimmer had managed to topple Turing, it should not be beyond him to bring down an old dancer. He looked at the names of the houses. A car, a Morris Minor, drove by and now he heard a child's voice.

"Daddy, Daddy!"

He stepped into the garden. A little girl with long dark hair and small, serious eyes was splashing in a tub of rainwater. She had got completely soaked. Behind her a newly painted swing hung in a frame.

"Hello," Corell said to her.

"Hello," she answered tersely.

"You should change your clothes."

"I'm not going to."

"Don't then," he muttered and looked towards the house, a fine white stone house with a black roof and a conservatory next to the front door.

The door handle was gilded and to the right of the building was a slightly unkempt hedge and a far plainer next-door house made of green wood with well-tended flower beds but with a worn tile roof and small windows. Was that where Mrs. Duffy went around in her garish dresses? He rang the doorbell. A shiver ran through his body and all sorts of thoughts flickered in his mind. But when the door flew open he instantly became fully concentrated, as if a curtain had gone up, and he smiled his most trustworthy smile.

"Good afternoon."

"How do you do," the man said, in the same surly reserved tone as his daughter, and Corell could tell right away that Mrs. Duffy was right.

That man was a queer. Admittedly a handsome one, to be generous, fine-limbed and upright, a clear blue look in his eyes, but with something unmistakably graceful about his movements. Even the way he put out his hand gave him away. It was as if Mr. Rowan were asking him to dance, or wanted to sketch a sign in the air.

"I rang earlier. My name is Corell and I work in the police in Wilmslow. May I come in?" Corell asked in a friendly voice.

"Actually I . . ."

"I understand if you're busy. I'd heard that you own some fine gentlemen's outfitters in Manchester. Very nice. I've always been interested in clothes, even if with my salary I can't really afford to buy very much. In any case I think it would be best not to postpone it."

"Postpone what?"

"Our little chat," he said, and was not happy with the word little in that particular context, but he tried to put on an air of authority and he may well have been successful.

"Of course, of course, come in."

The man was obviously rattled and perhaps that was a good sign. There was sweat on his upper lip and as he went into his living room on the ground floor he seemed to be making an effort to walk with greater resolve than he usually did. A crystal chandelier hung from the ceiling, there was fine old furniture in the room and a whole wall full of books. It was a different home from what Corell had been expecting and he sat down in a bright yellow chair opposite Rowan. Rowan lit a cigarette.

"Nice house!" Corell said.

"Not bad."

"Nice girl out there. I gather you have one more."

"One more."

"Terrible rain we've been having lately," Corell said.

"Indeed."

The man was comically taciturn.

"But now we should have a nice summer!"

"Let's hope so."

"Isn't that how it works?"

"What do you mean?"

"That it's all rained out. That a period of bad weather paves the way for a period of good weather. It could just as well be the opposite of course. That bad things generate even more bad things. That's often the way it is with our own lives after all," Corell said.

"Sometimes, yes."

"I was here in the area the other day. A very sorry story. You may have read about it. I found the mathematician Alan Turing dead in his bed. He'd eaten a poisoned apple. Quite simply dreadful. Perhaps you knew him? Or had run into him in the neighbourhood."

Rowan shook his head, almost too emphatically.

"An extraordinarily talented man," Corell said.

"I heard him on the radio," Rowan said.

It was the first time he had taken the initiative to say something.

"What was he talking about?"

"I think it was to do with Norbert Wiener."

"Remind me who that is."

"An author who has written about robots and machines that can think."

"So Turing spoke about intelligent machines?"

"Yes."

"Did it sound strange?"

"Very strange."

"Did you know that it all began as a small mathematical argument about some problems to do with logic?" Corell said.

"No." Rowan looked confused.

"But I'm sure you appreciate how amazing it is that a tiny subtle point which only exercised a few minds and was probably seen by most as the archetypal pointless academic problem should have given rise to a new machine. But perhaps you're not interested in logic?"

"Not at all."

"You're more of an aesthete."

"I'm not sure about that."

"You usually have visitors at weekends."

"Of course, don't you?"

"No," Corell said, being perfectly honest, but nonetheless managing not to make himself sound pathetic. "Who is it that usually comes?"

"Friends."

"Anyone special?"

"That's none of your business."

The words were not really aggressive and Rowan's upper lip, which was already flecked with sweat, trembled imperceptibly.

"I'm sure you realise that we know everything," said Corell, well aware that he'd stolen this line from Sergeant Rimmer.

"What do you mean?"

"You have illegal sexual relations."

"I don't have—"

"We have witnesses."

"If you mean Mrs. Duffy you should know that she's sweet enough to go around spreading lies about her neighbours. It's the very air that she breathes, so to speak."

"We've got more than just Mrs. Duffy," Corell said with self-assurance, and he really believed it.

He'd had such a clear impression of David Rowan as a homosexual when he saw him at the front door that for a moment this felt like some sort of proof, and he suddenly sounded as if he held victory in his hands.

"What?" Rowan stammered.

"We've got a lot."

"Could you be more precise?"

"Do you want me to go through the whole lot? Look at every detail? Is that what you want, just say so, because I've got all the time in the world. For God's sake, do you really think that I would be here if we hadn't received several reports," Corell said, well aware that he was taking his bluff too far.

"No, of course not, I understand that. But I still don't think . . ."

"What?"

"That you've entirely understood . . . this is after all nothing . . . not in that sense . . ."

"Tell me all about it now!"

But David Rowan did not get any further; it was as if his lips were trying to form an impossible sentence and as he twisted in the chair his face shone with sweat. He seemed to be on the verge of a breakdown and Corell felt a foretaste of triumph, and therefore—consistent with his whole strategy—his voice became softer, more ingratiating.

"I don't want to put any strain on you."

"It's not what you think."

"Well, how is it then? Tell me! I'm sure we're wrong on several points."

"It's . . ."

With a sudden movement David Rowan covered his face with his hands.

"Now then," Corell said, "this really isn't so bad. We just need to clear up the worst of the misunderstandings. If you tell me exactly what's happened, I promise to view the information sympathetically. Perhaps we can even forget all about it. It just depends on whether you want to be open and honest."

"Would you be able to forget . . . ?"

"Provided you are prepared to co-operate, we do have that possibility," Corell said, wondering what the hell he was promising, but he was only following his instincts, and his conviction that in this situation an outstretched hand would be more effective than a threat, and so he smiled, not, as he believed, in a triumphant way but warmly and with empathy, and that seemed to have an effect.

The man collapsed. I've got him, Corell thought, and just had time to imagine Hamersley's praise—*Exemplary, young man, brilliant*—when something happened. Small, light footsteps could be heard in the corridor and a shrill voice called out:

"Daddy, Daddy, Mary has got completely and utterly soaked. She's bound to catch a cold."

At that an eight- or nine-year-old girl stepped through the door, dressed in white clothes, like a fairy. At first she did not notice that her father had a visitor but seemed wholly absorbed by the drama over the tub of rainwater outside. But then she changed. She looked at her father, and pulled up her shoulders. The big, serious eyes were drawn to the ground. She seemed afraid.

"I'm sorry, I didn't realise," she said, and disappeared outside.

David Rowan's thoughts were in an uproar. For more than two years he had thought that this ghastly story was dead and buried. Recently, he had not given it a single thought. He had even been able to contemplate his inclinations without too much shame. But this morning—it was strange—several hours before he learned that the police had rung, he had already been struck by a rising tide of fear. He had read about the mathematician who had died. He hated the newspapers. There was always something in them which hurt him. This particular article pained him for two reasons, not just because it reminded him of his father's words long ago: "I thought that people like that took their own lives," but because he had actually met Turing.

They had exchanged a quick glance once on Oxford Road in Manchester, and known afterwards that they shared a secret, a cross. Later on, when they had bumped into each other on Brown's Lane in Manchester, they had stopped, said hello and tentatively engaged in conversation. David, who had his daughters with him, said something about the weather and the neighbourhood, a few platitudes just to get the conversation going, but the mathematician answered enigmatically that he had seen two rainbows side by side, "as if nature were being overly explicit."

What was he trying to say? During the entire conversation they seemed to be tiptoeing nervously around the unmentionable question of whether they could meet again more privately, but they were both much too embarrassed and before anything could happen and before a single sensible word could be uttered, the mathematician walked off in the middle of a sentence. It could have been seen as very rude but David did not take offence. His impression was that Turing was fed up with the whole social pantomime. Hadn't he himself often just wanted to scream out loud at the whole bloody charade?

But more than anything else, the look in those eyes . . . so different, both dull and intense. There was something inaccessible about them, but they also seemed to invite. They could probably be unsettling, but David was also curious to know what they concealed, and when he got home he tried to find Turing in the telephone book. Not really with the intention of calling him, more toying with the idea, but the name had not been there and instead he heard him on the radio one day saying some strange things about machines. Had he not said that he hoped that one day they would be able to think like us? It sounded so crazy, so unconventional. At first David thought that the mathematician was just using machines as a metaphor for homosexuals. Turing had mentioned some sort of game between a man, a woman and a machine. They were supposed to pretend to be each other—my God, what was David's own life if not precisely that sort of a game of pretence?—but the discussion on the radio soon became too scientific to have been really symbolic, and David lost the thread. What he mostly remembered afterwards was Turing's stammering voice and eager tone, and for several weeks David had thought about him both morning and night. But then one day Turing disappeared from his dreams. God sent him Klaus instead.

Already the first time as they lay entwined it had seemed like a gift which he did not deserve. Not only was Klaus younger and more beautiful. He was shameless. He felt he was entitled to pleasure. He just lived life and that was a magnificent and wild feeling, even though it was not quite strong enough to transform David himself. David was unable to escape the usual burden of shame and fear, and when the nightmare with Mrs. Duffy broke out it almost felt like some sort of justice. Of course he deserved to be punished! His mind was in such a mess that he felt guilty when the police investigation did not go any further. But then time had passed and he had thought, maybe, after all, *maybe even people like me are allowed to be happy*—because the strange thing was that with Klaus in his life David became more loving even towards his wife and daughters. Everything became lighter and brighter. It was as if love in general grew.

But then today—this black day in the calendar—they had rung again and he had met this dreadful person at the door, and for one brief moment he had been foolish enough to take him for somebody good, probably only because he had seen a sort of light in his eyes, an ambiguous melancholy reflection. It turned out to be no more than the duplicity of deceit, the mendacity of the polished policeman glittering like a treacherous mosaic, and he could not understand why he was so ill equipped to deal with it. It was not long before he felt an irresistible urge to capitulate and shorten the agony. He was drained of any will to fight back, he could not think of any better explanation for it. He wanted to assume the burden of his guilt. Anything at all rather than having to hear how yet another hyena had peered through their window and seen what no-one should have seen. The mere thought was unbearable, and he noticed only vaguely, as if in a dream, that his daughter came in and then disappeared at once. *What had she wanted?*

"I would advise you . . ." the policeman said.

"Well . . . yes," he muttered, and felt helplessly lost.

But then he noticed something; yet another change in the policeman's eyes, and it confused him. The man suddenly had a pleading look, as if he rather than David were in need of help.

The daughter's steps could be heard far away, and Corell looked down at his hand. The blue veins bulged like small banked-up rivers, and without realising it he ran his fingers over them and remembered being in the kitchen in Southport a long time ago. He had looked down at his mother's brown shoes. What's wrong with Daddy? he had asked. Nothing, Leonard, nothing! It was never anything.

"Where were we?" he said.

"You were going to give me some advice."

"I advise you . . ."

For some reason Corell saw his aunt before him. Nor could he stop thinking about the girl.

"I advise you not to admit to anything at all," he said, surprised at his own words.

"I'm sorry?" Rowan said.

Corell felt an urge to get to his feet. Yet he remained where he was.

"As I said," he continued, angry with himself. "We have a lot, really quite a lot."

"New evidence or what?"

What the hell should he say?

"Really rather a lot, as I said. But so long as you deny everything no court can convict you."

He could not believe it. He was blowing his chances, but he could not bear to hurt the girl. He could not bear to do it.

"Mrs. Duffy isn't a particularly credible witness either," he went on. "For a start she was trespassing. Then it also seems to be a case of envy. You have a nicer house. As I see things, nothing at all has happened."

"I don't understand . . . !"

Rowan's voice sounded shrill, broken.

"I will see to it that you don't have to worry," Corell said. "I shall be recommending that the case is dropped."

Just as before he had stolen Rimmer's words, he now stole Vicky's:

"We should be allowed to do what we want, so long as we don't harm anyone else," he said, and felt like a bad actor, putting on a pompous air, but the words seemed to have their effect.

Rowan got to his feet with an uncertain smile.

"Do you really mean that?"

"I do."

"And I was thinking . . . what can I say . . . you can't imagine . . ."

It seemed that Rowan was going to hug him and Corell took a step back. He was not prepared to go that far, certainly not, and yet he was filled with something, he did not think it was joy, but it fizzed in him.

He was a bloody hypocrite. But he had made one person happy and his body felt lighter.

"May I offer you something, something strong? I'm soaked in sweat. I could certainly do with something . . ." Rowan started.

"No, no," Corell said. "I don't drink . . ."

It could not have been less true. He had been drinking like an idiot yesterday and his whole body yearned for a drink to settle him, but he wanted to get out and far away and he moved towards the door. He remembered, again, only vaguely that he said hello to the younger of the two daughters, but then he had a thought, and it was at least as strange as the previous one.

"There's one thing you may be able to help me with," he said.

"Anything you like! Just tell me!" Rowan smiled, once again nervous. One could tell that he had been completely beside himself.

"You're in the tailoring business," he said.

"I am."

"You don't happen to know Harrington & Sons on Alderley Road, do you?"

"I certainly do. Richard Harrington and I are quite close friends."

"There's a shop assistant there, Julie something."

"Julie Masih, a delightful girl, but it's a bit difficult to get to know her. She's had a very hard time of it."

"In what way?" he asked.

"Her mother is English. The father an Indian Muslim. Julie grew up not far from here in Middlewich, but she was married away to a cousin in Karachi who was said to be very pious, but in the end turned out to be nothing more than self-righteous and evil. Because of some supposed transgression on her part, I can't even remember what now, he threw a scoop of boiling water at her, but the idiot missed and hit the daughter instead. Poor girl! You should see . . ."

"I've seen her."

"Julie and her daughter managed to run away. I think they were helped by the embassy and an English nurse. They've been living here in Wilmslow for about a year now, but Julie is still afraid. The man has apparently made some kind of threat."

"So she's no longer married?"

Rowan's face, so frightened and serious a moment ago, now broke into a broad smile, which expressed not only the relief of a man who realises that he is no longer going to be dragged in front of the courts, but also something close to tenderness.

"Formally speaking I suppose she is, but not in the way you mean. She could probably do with a real friend."

"Well, thank you, then," Corell said, suddenly clumsy—he banged his nose against the door frame—and for a moment he could not find the door handle.

"I'd be happy to put in a good word for you if you'd like," Rowan said, but by then Corell was out in the garden and did not hear.

23

OSCAR FARLEY PUT his pen down on the mahogany table in the hotel bedroom. What he had written was nothing to boast about, just another fruitless attempt at understanding what had happened, but as usual writing things down solved nothing when the facts were missing. Once more he read through the papers he had found at Adlington Road. But as with everything else, this material contained no clues as to what really interested them: Had Turing been careless with state secrets?

It was true that Alan had not exactly been a patriot. He had hated the suspicions of these modern times and the rummaging around in people's private lives. Already when Oscar first tried to recruit him, Turing had been furious that people were protesting against Edward VIII's marriage to Mrs. Simpson. "But it's a private matter," he snapped. "It's nobody's business, not the bishops' nor anyone else's!" He did not even think that a king's marriage was a matter for the state, so obviously he would have been indignant to see his own amorous adventures become a national security issue. Damned politics, which Alan wanted nothing to do with, took the back door in and followed him into the bedroom. No wonder that he was outraged! And yet . . . surely he had not done anything unforgiveable?

Farley knew how scrupulous Alan had been about secrecy and how indignant he had been when others were careless. It was just that . . . After all the shabby attacks on Alan following the judgement in Knutsford, Oscar had taken a different position from everyone else and always spoken of Alan in lyrical terms and praised him to the skies, and there was something in this, his own picture of the situation, which disturbed him. There was in fact something about Turing which he had never been able to make out; if indeed anyone was an unbreakable code, then it was Alan himself. As Oscar now sat with his pen in his hand, he thought about how Turing had been seeing a psychoanalyst and how he had written down his dreams in three books (which the brother said he had already destroyed), and presumably made his first ever attempt at some sort of literary work. Oscar had found a short story in Turing's house about a rocket scientist who picked up a homosexual man on the street, but the narrative stopped in mid-sentence, before anything serious or sensitive had happened . . . clearly an attempt at something auto-biographical. Why this desire to confess? Admittedly Turing had been through a crisis and felt a need to get to know himself, but at the same time it was said that he had recovered during the past year; that he had come up with some extremely interesting thoughts and been full of an appetite for life. And then suddenly . . . the poison, the wires, the apple. Farley just did not understand.

Then details kept on emerging which troubled him. There was the scene outside the courthouse in Wilmslow for example. He had noticed Fredric Krause, that logician and fine fellow from the war whom he had not seen for such a long time, in the middle of the group of journalists, and he had really wanted to speak to him but got no further than a handshake and some polite exchanges. The young policeman—dressed in a remarkably elegant manner—had vented his feelings and displayed such heckling authority that for a moment Farley got the impression that Corell had known Turing or at least had more information than the others, but then it all came to such an abrupt end when the policeman disappeared down the street with defiant steps. It was a peculiar scene, wasn't it? Not only because it seemed to have surprised everybody—clearly no-one expected the gloomy policeman to explode into such an outburst of teasing arrogance—but also because when Farley turned towards Krause to say something along the lines of "That much at least was true," the logician had gone.

He had simply vanished, and there was something about the fact that one of the main people to have worked in Alan's hut during the war had suddenly popped up in Wilmslow, and then just as quickly disappeared, which Farley did not like at all. Then again in his job one always did run the risk of getting engrossed in details which have no significance and as he waited to go out for a meal with Robert Somerset, Farley returned to *The Ballad of Reading Gaol*, which made him feel better. As if there were something soothing about the pain of another man who had been punished for the same crime as Turing.

She's not married. She's not married. Corell felt a quiver run through him, and for a long time he wandered aimlessly, just to burn up the energy in his body, and for a moment he thought that he was on his way to Harrington & Sons to make an immediate play for Julie, but slowly his courage subsided. He was pathetic, wasn't he, a person who though full of good intentions fails at the decisive moment, so why should he do any better with Julie? No, no, he did not want to go either to the shop or to the police station.

So he decided instead to go to the library. Ever since the morning, he had been longing to do some more research. But it was not easy to find anything. A young man with round spectacles whom Corell had not seen before looked at him enquiringly in the reception and did not even seem to understand his question. "What do you mean?" he said, as if somehow it were an impertinent request, or as if Corell had actually meant something altogether different, even something improper.

"They are also known as digital machines," the policeman said. "Or data machines. I don't know. They are working on a major project at Manchester University. Isn't it called M.U.C.?"

"Oh I see . . . that does ring a bell," the man said, and he at once became a bit more enthusiastic. "Just wait a bit!"

He consulted a colleague and after a short while he came back carrying a black booklet, possibly an advertising brochure, or something for use in schools. The prose was simple, almost childish. Corell sat down at his usual place by the window and leafed through the booklet. In the middle of it was a section with boring photographs of a large and incomprehensible machine. Even so, one of the pictures sent a shiver down his spine, and for a brief moment, until he realised how trivial the discovery was, it felt as if he had found something of great importance. The photograph represented two older men who were sitting in front of something that looked like a television set, but the interesting part was the third person: a younger, dark-haired man standing to the right, bent over the machine. This man was without a doubt Alan Turing. The picture was taken from a distance, but Corell recognised the mathematician's profile.

There was nothing else about Turing in the captions or in any other part of the book. But Corell did read about other things, some of which caught his attention at least in part. As if to provide further evidence that the text was meant for schoolchildren it said that the machine was called the Blue Pig, why was not clear. It did not look blue. It looked nothing like a pig. Possibly it sounded like a pig. It had sung "Baa Baa Black Sheep" and the jazz tune "In the Mood" on a radio programme. It could play tunes, and produce silly love letters:

Dear Sweetiepie,

You are my friend feelings. My warmth is drawn with curiosity to your impassioned desire. My approval yearns for your heart. You are my pining sympathy; my tender love.

Your beautiful M. U. C.

That was the amusing aspect. The other was that the machine performed high-level mathematical calculations and was being used for important industrial and state projects. This machine was the future. It was going to allow Great Britain to regain its rightful place in the world. There was a lot of sales pitch. Corell did not like the tone, there was too much of the older brother about it, and actually the traces leading back in time were far more interesting than the promises of a glittering future. Corell read about a Charles Babbage, also a Cambridge mathematician. He had been active a hundred years before, in the early years of industrialism, a time with which Corell was reasonably familiar, perhaps because both his father and Vicky had told him so much about Marx and Engels. He knew that it had been a hellish time. Now he learned more. There were more deaths in the factories than there were new births in the cities, the publication said, and one important reason was poor mathematics. Enormous collections of data were needed—about railway traffic, population growth, employment figures, maritime navigation, about all sorts of rubbish, and mistakes were being made all the time. Errors in compiling tables and errors in making calculations. Trains collided. Ships foundered. People died on the factory floor, and it was a problem that the "venerable Charles Babbage" wrestled with. "He was a Renaissance man," the article said, a person who tried his hand at all sorts of things, for one thing he deciphered the "Vigenère cipher," which was regarded as one of the greatest breakthroughs ever in cryptanalysis, and he was also interested in steam engines. He once said, jokingly, just imagine if the steam engines could do my calculating for me. Soon after that it occurred to him that that was not impossible. Although he did give up on the idea of steam. But the dream of a machine which could even carry out intellectual tasks captivated him more and more and eventually he got to work. There was one idea above all that propelled him forward: the recognition that a mechanical device can assimilate information if only the relevant knowledge is converted into machine settings and positions. But he was clearly too ambitious. His machines never materialised. They remained dreams.

Corell read on, about another person who had won a competition which the authorities in North America had organised at the end of the nineteenth century, to see who could come up with the best way to catalogue the enormous stream of immigrants. That man was called Herman Hollerith.

Hollerith had invented a machine with punch cards, which registered information using binary numbers. The binary system was another way of counting, or speaking. Instead of many numbers and letters, it used only two—a one and a zero—and even if it sounded primitive and cumbersome it was a language which suited machines. The simple can be used to express the complex, as Krause had put it: the finite contains the infinite. Hollerith's devices were sold to authorities and to industry and formed the basis of the company which was set up in 1923 and came to be called I.B.M. And yet Hollerith's designs were relatively simple; these were not general purpose machines which could do all sorts of things, like sing "Baa Baa Black Sheep," or find new large prime numbers like the machine in Manchester. The more Corell read, the more certain he became that the development of these machines must have taken a leap forward during the thirties and forties, but the booklet did not really describe it well.

That could of course have been due to all sorts of things, but Corell—not one to go in for trivial explanations—became convinced that whatever had happened during the war was far too sensitive and secret to be discussed in what was in essence an advertising booklet. That still left the question of what it was those damned machines had done. Perhaps something more purely mathematical than one might imagine. Hardy had been "wrong as hell, as wrong as Wittgenstein," when he had said that real mathematics had not had any implications for the war. What had Krause meant by that? Surely not that you will win any battles by solving Fermat's riddle or Goldbach's Conjecture. But there must have been something . . . what? Corell had no clue. His thoughts went round in his head. He tried to be rational in his thinking, but was not even sure that reason was a particularly helpful guiding star. Perhaps he ought to be looking in the direction of the improbable, as in the new physics . . . Nonsense! Why even try? It was beyond his capabilities. It was meaningless, and yet; the answer seemed to be before his very eyes, although concealed, and for a brief moment he was naive enough to think that he might be able to find it. In no time at all he went from a reasonably sober reflection on the potential uses for paradoxes in war to fantasising about the sort of reward he might get for solving the mystery and what effect that reward would have on Julie. Then he ran out of steam. What a fool he was. No-one had asked him to find the answer. And in any case it could be almost anything. These machines were general purpose machines, after all. They did what they were instructed to do. It could be something to do with weapons or orbits, anything at all. He could not care less, so why bother? The investigation was closed. It was over. He ought to put it behind him, but still . . . those machines and the contradictions and problems out of which they had evolved revived his old dreams from the years in Southport; in some ways they restored a distant and forgotten hope, and he saw that he enjoyed thinking about it. He even flattered himself that he was good at it and he would happily have spent hours sitting in the library reasoning away, but he had to get back to the station and he was really exhausted.

As he sat for a moment with his head in his hands he had the impression that his fingers and face were merging into one, and possibly he nodded off. He was overcome by a surreal feeling, rather like a waking trance, when he handed the booklet back to a young woman behind the counter. She said something which he misheard as "razor and a girl," strange words, which almost seemed to be a continuation of his dream, and he stood there hesitating over whether he should ask her to repeat what she had said. Then he went down the curved staircase out into the sun.

The gravel path crunched under him like something which might break at any moment, and he grew more and more worried. What was the matter with him? He was thinking one thing and doing another. Not only had he allowed David Rowan to get off. He had promised that the investigation would be dropped, and he had no authority to do that. Sandford himself could be taking over the case when he got back from his holiday. Corell did not want to think about that, not for one second. Should he sneak into a pub and have a beer to restore his peace of mind? No, he had already wasted a lot of time and now he had to . . . he cast his mind back to a little of what he had just been reading, and in that moment he had a thought which was crystal clear and plain and swept away the rest of his reverie. Although it did seem to have appeared out of nowhere, it had in fact come by a roundabout way and had its roots in Corell's childhood when he had enjoyed inventing secret languages and sometimes scrambled the letters in his own name, to ellorc eolarnd, something which made him sound like an Arab magician. But the train of thought had also touched on Charles Babbage, the father of the general purpose mechanical machine, partly because of his name, which had an amusing ring to it, but partly also because of the cipher starting with the letter V which Charles Babbage had unravelled.

Yes, Charles Babbage had broken a cipher. He had done all sorts of things, but he had tried to build a universal machine and then had cracked a special code, which in itself did not necessarily mean that Turing had done the same. But codes are used for secret communication, and where would there be a greater need for secret talk than during a war? Huge efforts must have been made to develop ciphers and even greater ones to crack the enemy's ciphers. What use could England have made of a mathematics genius and a chess master?

In all likelihood for the very purpose of encryption and decipher-ing; and the machine, this materialisation of logic, must have been used for that purpose, indeed it was probably still being used, in fact it was probably more important than ever. There was a new war going on, he thought, a cold war which could flare up into the hottest one ever and obviously plans were being made all the time, and naturally there must be no leaks, there had already been enough damage done. Spies were unmasked, homosexual traitors had fled by boat and car to the Soviet Union. Too damned right people wanted to keep things secret, and of course it was either disastrous or fantastic, depending on which side you were on, if something secret did slip out.

It therefore occurred to him that any expert in cryptology must have been a valuable person, not just because of his skills but also because of what he had heard or read in the course of his work. Perhaps Tur-ing had known some state secrets? Maybe he knew the names of Soviet spies and informants and in any event he had been to Oxford Road. The highest secrecy had got mixed up with criminals and gossips, and he could have had the truth extorted from him. Or it could have slipped out when he was bragging. Had he not told Arnold Murray about his electronic brain?

Corell wondered if he himself might not have been capable of betraying secrets, if ever he had any, just to seduce a pretty girl like Julie, or simply to impress the right person. But no, he liked to think not. It wasn't that he saw himself as being excessively reliable, but he had kept quiet about everything of importance in his life for so long that he would probably have kept his mouth shut as a matter of course. Or would he? The more he worried about it, the faster he walked.

He did not slow down until he got to the police station. It was already evening. Most people had gone home by now, and dusk was spreading across the horizon. But in the yard, right by the entrance, were two young boys in grey overalls, sweeping up rubbish and broken glass.

They looked browbeaten. One of them had flushed cheeks, as if he had just been slapped in the face.

"Just look at that. Just look at that."

Corell could see why the boys were unhappy. Above them, at the top of the police station steps, stood Richard Ross with his hands on his hips, looking unusually tall and authoritarian, partly because the stairs seemed to increase his height, but also because the cowed look on the boys' faces emphasised the domineering side of his character. He had quite simply grown at their expense and would have looked really frightening if he had not twisted his mouth into some sort of negative half-smile, an upside-down smirk, rather like a caricature in a newspaper. He seemed to be engaged in a crusade against something which warranted neither crusade nor that level of seriousness.

"Well?" Ross said.

"What happened?"

"That bloody idiot's been at it again."

"He must have a good supply of bottles."

"Don't try to be funny. How did things go with the bum boy? Did you break him?"

Corell shook his head.

"Was he a tough one?"

"Not particularly!"

"But he wasn't going to confess?"

"He had a different story."

"Which you believed?"

"I couldn't pick holes in it."

Ross glared at him.

"So what was his story?"

When Corell was a boy he used to lie with such extraordinary ease, he could improvise a long made-up story with no great difficulty, but in recent years he had lost that effrontery. He was therefore surprised by how quickly he manage to cobble together a lie.

"That he had been practising dance steps with a younger colleague."

"And?" Ross snorted.

"He thought that Mrs. Duffy had mistaken the dancing for . . . ."

"Buggery? Don't be daft."

"Unfortunately her testimony isn't particularly good either. I reckon it's all gossip."

"You don't have to be Einstein to realise that that pansy is a queer. Just look at how he moves!"

"There are many men who are a bit effeminate, which doesn't necessarily . . ."

As if emboldened by his lie he became even more daring:

"Just look at Hamersley," he said. "The way he moves is a bit effete, after all. But that doesn't have to mean that . . ."

For a moment, Ross looked puzzled. Then something happened to his face. It broke into a smile.

"You're damned right. It does make you wonder," he said, and really seemed to perk up. There was something close to kindness in the look he gave Corell, who instinctively thought he should make the most of the situation.

"We could of course send someone else along. It's just that after the Turing case every queer will be sure to keep mum."

"No, I can't be bothered. It's Hamersley's thing. He keeps talking about a purge. A preacher is what he sounds like. But in fact he doesn't understand the first thing about police work, does he? Little pansy that he is. Ha, ha. You've got a cheek! And here I was, thinking that you were the big boss's little helper. No, I'm more worried about this littering. Boys, boys, over here by the steps as well . . ."

"In that case . . ." Corell said.

He did not finish the sentence. He just nodded at Ross, cast a sympathetic glance in the direction of the cleaners and got a timid, complicit look in return. Back at his place in the criminal department he sat nervously tapping on the desk with his pen. Good old Gladwin was smoking his pipe in the archive room and waved at him. He waved back. Then he took out the letter again and read through it once more, line by line, as if looking for some hidden meaning, or even as if he were reading it like a code, an encrypted message. Although it did not make him much the wiser he felt as if the letter had changed—as if it had become more dramatic, following the conversation with Krause. *But sometimes, Robin, sometimes I wonder if what they really want isn't to see me wiped out, removed from the scene.* Robin . . . Robin Gandy, wasn't it? There was something about Leicester in the letter, about Leicester . . . Corell picked up the receiver and asked the operator to put him through to the university in the city and when he was connected he asked if there was a Robin Gandy working there.

"Would you like to speak to him?"

"No, no," he said, "I was just wondering."

Then he thought about the liar's paradox and the new machine. He became absorbed by the topic, not like a detective or even like an academic who is trying to analyse the questions, but rather like a man who wants to understand something about himself—*why am I so fascinated?*—and suddenly he got an urge to travel, to let himself be carried off by the riddle he sensed was there, and then he realised that in some way the letter was a ticket away from Wilmslow and Richard Ross. He decided to use it.

24

A FEW WEEKS LATER Leonard Corell was walking down King's Parade in Cambridge wearing his new grey and red tweed suit and even though he made every effort to look worldly he still found himself catching his breath, like a farm boy out in the big wide world for the first time. The city seemed stunningly beautiful. It was like walking inside a painting. Everything was neat and tidy and he hoped that people saw him as some kind of academic, perhaps a young professor in the humanities, why not history of literature, and he tried to make his eyes sparkle, like someone who has read a great deal, and he thought, probably without any justification, that he seemed well-travelled, like a respected southerner on a visit. When he saw the reflection of a rather elegant man in a mirror in a shop window it struck him that he had failed to live up to that look, and that it did not deliver what it promised. He was just a façade, he thought, someone pretending to be more than he really is.

Although he did make an effort to hold his head up high, when he saw King's College he inevitably felt small and that was not only due to the meeting which awaited him. The entrance was really superb. Not even as a child, when he had been here with his father, had he realised how magnificent it was. The grass next to the gate shone in different shades of green and had been mown so perfectly that it seemed like soft velvet. Beside it stood a tall chestnut tree and behind rose the mighty chapel with its spires and towers. Bicycles lay in an untidy heap by the side of the gate and above them were the bell tower and the ornate stone frontispiece. Corell went in, happy that a blond fellow who must have mistaken him for someone else greeted him, but also struck by a vague fear that he might be seized for trespassing. That was absurd, of course, and not just because he was a policeman. King's College was a tourist attraction. No-one was forbidden to go in, but the chapel and the fountain and the sheltered world within still gave him the uncomfortable feeling of not belonging, and he thought if only, if only, without really knowing what he meant. Where was he supposed to go now?

The directions he had been given over the telephone did not help him at all and he noticed that he was beginning to miss his aunt which was of course pathetic, but he could not help wishing that she were there to guide him. It was thanks to Vicky that he had got time off. It was her cheek which had made everything go so smoothly. Tell them I'm on my deathbed, she had said. "Surely I can't do that," he had replied. "Yes, you can. Afterwards we'll say that I've made a miraculous recovery," and so she wrote a letter in a particularly shaky handwriting, in which she gave the cause of her impending death: cancer of the lymph glands. "When you tell a lie you should always provide some precise and slightly unexpected details," and it did the job so well that Ross was quite sympathetic: "I know that your aunt means a lot to you."

Now he looked around and wondered if he should ask for help. He did not have time. Two young men appeared out of the building immediately to his right. "What are you looking for," they asked while looking at him with a respect he did not feel he deserved, and he was so concerned about the impression he was giving that he hardly listened. Yet he caught enough of it to find his way. Bodley's Court was an old brownish-red stone house nearby with ivy growing along the windows and three chimneys on the tile roof. There was a well-kept lawn in front of the house and some wooden benches. A man with dark curly hair wearing a black leather jacket and black trousers sat on one of them, clearly a biker, a hard man—he had small metal plates on his shoulders—but this tough guy was writing in a booklet and smoking a pipe with a gentleness which was at odds with the first impression. This had to be Robin Gandy, and the whole of Corell's body stiffened. He had been extremely enthusiastic about this trip. But when faced with the moment of truth he was appalled by his own audacity. It was like being pushed onto a stage he had no wish to be on, and he realised that he had to put an immediate stop to the more or less involuntary charade that he had set in motion with his telephone call, in which his saying that he worked for the police had been interpreted to mean that he was calling as a policeman.

"Dr. Gandy, I presume."

"Detective Constable Corell?"

"Indeed . . ."

He got no further. He was feeling too nervous for explanations—that at least was his excuse to himself—and instead he engaged in small talk about the weather and his journey. It was somewhat odd that they were meeting here in Cambridge. Only last year Gandy had defended his doctoral thesis on a topic related to the logical foundations of physics, and he was now working at the University of Leicester, *with its lamentable overabundance of mistresses*, but when they had discussed a suitable meeting place over the telephone Corell had accepted without delay when Robin said that he was coming here. Without Cambridge the meeting would have been something else entirely and yet, as they strolled down to the river below King's College, Corell wished they could have met in less grand surroundings. Everything seemed so alarmingly solemn. Gandy was soft-spoken and diffident, and above them shone the grey speckled sky. A group of choirboys could be seen walking in the distance, a glimpse from another time. *I should tell him right away that I'm only here as a private individual* . . . Once again it did not happen and perhaps he really wanted to take advantage of the authority which his job implied.

"You had something for me."

The bridge over the river creaked under them and Gandy's face shrank and looked bird-like.

"I do," Corell said and gestured towards his inside pocket.

For over a week he had been wondering how to ask about the letter. And yet he felt unprepared now and slowed his movements. God knows what he hoped to gain, but it was only with some hesitation that he put his hand into his inside pocket. A chill ran through him. The letter was gone. He searched feverishly but there was nothing there, nothing except an envelope with spare buttons for the suit and some receipts and a coin. He pulled it all out and almost dropped it all into the river, but there . . . thank goodness. The letter was in his hands, even more crumpled now, and he handed it over to Gandy.

Gandy thanked him and crossed the bridge past some rhododendron bushes to a dirty bench covered with birds' droppings and scribbles, and there he sat down and read. It went on forever. Corell had time to run through the letter twice and think about his father and the birds and all sorts of things before Gandy took his eyes from the letter and looked up. It shook in his hands, he had a distant or pensive look in his eyes, but he said nothing. His lips trembled.

"Well?" Corell said.

"Well, what?"

There was irritation in his voice.

Ever since the policeman had rung him, the letter had assumed all sorts of different shapes in his mind and even appeared in his dreams. Now that he was walking along the path beside the policeman wearing that far too expensive suit—surely they were paid a pittance in the force?—he felt a burning eagerness which was only mitigated by his growing discomfort at the situation. He assumed that the investigators must have turned every word in the letter inside out, and that there was obviously something sensitive in there! Why else take the trouble to come here? The worst would of course be if Alan had breached his wartime secrecy obligations in an outburst of bitterness or out of carelessness. No, no, Robin refused to believe that he would have done that. The only person to have come here was a mere local policeman, or someone who claimed to be that. This did not appear to be a major operation. Alan had been careful. If anyone knew that, Robin did. However close they had been, Alan had never once mentioned his secret work, but Robin was clever enough to be able more or less to work out what had been going on above the railway station at Bletchley Park in Buckinghamshire. But he never let on; he did not want to embarrass Alan. It remained one of the taboos in their conversations.

In any case there were sides to Alan which Robin had never been able to reach, and this had caused him tremendous grief in recent weeks. There were so many things he would have liked to have done differently! He should have questioned him very seriously, and not given up until he got an answer: "How are you? How are you sleeping? How do you feel about your life?" But always there had been too much logic and science and too much joking. With Alan it was difficult not to follow suit. When you saw how uncompromising he could be you immediately wanted to be the same. Robin had not admired any of his friends as much as he had Alan. Nor had any of them been so hard to read.

A whole series of memories had flickered through Robin's mind in the run-up to the meeting with the policeman. There was he and Alan at the chess board in Hanslope, there was a heated political discussion at Patrick Wilkinson's place in Cambridge, there was some serious mucking about with the buckets in Wilmslow, and there were long walks in different parts of the countryside, there were all sorts of things which did not fit together. Had he really known Alan at all? Had anyone?

When Robin heard that Alan was presumed to have committed suicide he just wanted to shout: *No, no. I was there just the other day. He was fine! It's impossible.* So much anger welled up in him that he got it into his head that Alan had been murdered by the British secret service, or even the American one. Robin had read about Lavender Scare, that dreadful project which was supposed to clear out all homosexuals from key positions, and had not the official line against dissidents and non-conformists become ever more hostile lately? But once he had calmed down he could see that things like that do not happen here, not in England. Alan was an asset. However much he might chase after young men, he was not the sort that you would purge. The authorities had to put up with people like him if they wanted results. Then—however painful it might be to think about it—there were other things; not least the darkness which had come and gone in Alan's blue eyes. No, what really hurt was that Robin had not realised before it was too late and that he would never know the reason, unless . . .

"You had something for me," he said, and then the policeman too became tense.

He was such a young man, with dark piercing eyes, and he sometimes looked away and sometimes scrutinised him, but he now became rather clumsy. What was he doing? With his long, slender hands he gave Robin the papers, and goodness they were crumpled! Robin hardly wanted to look at them. He recognised the round flourishes in the capital letters, which were such a contrast to the compressed style of the remainder, and for a moment he thought that he could see Alan's hand movement as he wrote. The letter burned in his hands and it was with reluctance that he steered his steps to a bench on the other side of the river and started to read.

The gloomy tone of the introduction surprised him. It felt unlike Alan. He tended to put any personal or very private comments further down. But perhaps this was not an ordinary letter. Robin skimmed through it to see if it ended with some dramatic decision . . . no, nothing of that sort, not at all. It seemed more as if Alan had just given up, tired of his words, and it was clearly a letter addressed to Robin and no-one else, only more personal and naked than usual.

But there was something else as well . . . he read it again, with greater care this time, and then he understood. He had been expecting something that had only just been written, maybe even on the day Alan died, but this was no recent document. It spoke of praising his thesis and of travelling to Greece. The letter must have been a year old, without question it was older than the postcards which Robin had received from Alan in March this year, those headed "Message from the unseen world" and which he had not been able to make out for a long time, except that they spoke in cryptic and beautiful terms about Big Bang and light cones and ended with the witty words, using Pauli's observation about elementary particles: *"The exclusion principle is laid down purely for the benefit of the electrons themselves, who might be corrupted (and become dragons or demons) if allowed to associate too freely."*

That sentence had brought an amused half-smile to Robin's face. He had taken it as a joke, but maybe that was not how it was meant. Maybe the electrons were a proxy for Alan himself. There was obviously much that Robin had not understood. Looking back, Turing's whole life seemed to be full of ambiguous signs, and Robin understood more clearly than ever that he had not interpreted them correctly. He had had no idea how much Alan was suffering before it was too late and even then it had taken a letter handed over by the authorities, which was utterly crazy. What sort of document was this?

Some of it was old. Some was new. Robin had already heard the story about the French lover. But he had no idea that Alan had had some secret assignment even after the war, for the Foreign Office, he supposed, which he had lost because of his inclinations. What could it have been? Presumably something along the lines of what Alan had been doing at Bletchley? *The exclusion principle is laid down purely for the benefit of the electrons themselves.* Those idiots, thought Robin. The letter shook in his hands. Flies were buzzing around him. His anger grew, but he also began to worry. Had it been careless of Alan even to mention that assignment and had he really been watched by a man with a birthmark like a sigma? *Dear, dear Alan!* For a few minutes Robin could not bring himself to do anything. He just sat there with the letter in his hand and was only vaguely aware that the policeman was saying something:

"Well?"

A sort of pained reluctance had come over Robin Gandy, and Corell found himself at a loss. Although he had prepared himself carefully for this moment he now had no idea how to begin. It felt as if whatever he might say would be wrong.

"What do you think?" he said.

"I really don't know."

"I understand that it's hard."

"And I'm not all that keen either to interpret the letter for you. I suspect that this was written in a particular frame of mind, which wasn't necessarily very typical of him."

"*One life as a masquerade to conceal another.* What can he have meant by that?" Corell said.

"What do you think?"

That was a bloody awful answer. How would Corell know?

"No idea," he said. "Life may well be play-acting, but it's not necessarily one performance concealing another."

"Not necessarily, no."

"He may have had a great deal to conceal."

"I don't know," Gandy said, terser now.

"I'm not suggesting that he had any skeletons in his cupboard. More that he'd maybe been told to conceal certain things, to play-act, so to speak."

"Alan was a hopeless actor."

"Why do you say that?"

"Because it's true," Gandy said.

"How so?"

"What can I say? Alan found it hard to blend in. He couldn't play along, to be blunt. He was an outsider."

"He attracted attention in other ways."

Robin smiled and sighed. He struggled somewhat to get to his feet, which momentarily made him seem old, and then he started to walk.

"I think it's more a question that Alan never managed to make himself visible," he said.

"Things seemed to go well enough though."

"Did they?"

"In intellectual terms, at least," Corell tried.

"Yes, since he couldn't be pushy he had something else."

"What?"

"Self-sufficiency. But that doesn't make life any easier."

"What do you mean?"

"Perhaps that a little more play-acting and adaptation might have done him good, who knows? Alan was much too frank."

"That does him credit."

"Not in society's eyes."

"No?"

"For a homosexual there is no worse crime than honesty, isn't that right? So long as he remains a hypocrite, he's safe. But Alan was no actor, as I've said. Sadly not."

Gandy folded the letter, which he had held in his hand, and was about to slip it into his pocket.

Corell stopped him.

"I'm afraid that's police property," he said, and wondered what the hell he was doing. Instead of laying his cards on the table he was sinking deeper into his charade, and that was the last thing he wanted, but the prospect of losing the letter troubled him.

"I see . . . well . . . I thought . . ." Gandy looked disappointed.

"Thank you very much. We appreciate it. It's because Turing writes about secrets," Corell continued, more formal now as if the new circumstances called for it.

"And the thing that's so remarkable about secrets is that you don't know what they're hiding!" Gandy said, equally reserved.

He deserved that comment, Corell thought. He did not think that he would be able to extract any more useful information. He would have to count himself lucky to get away without having embarrassed himself even further and, so as not to appear indecisive, he asked half-heartedly about a few things in the letter, but it did not bring any greater clarity, apart from the information that Hanslope was a place, but Corell already knew that, he had looked it up earlier. He considered taking his leave and going home, but nevertheless tried to lighten things up by making some small talk. Gandy was polite enough in return, despite everything, and listened intently to Corell's description of the scene at Adlington Road, and at last there really came a point when the conversation turned, or at least settled into a calmer, more intimate rhythm. They were on their way back into the city and a trumpet could be heard in the distance.

"You were there, just before, weren't you?"

"Yes . . . I was."

Gandy started to tell him about it, not at all as if he were speaking to a policeman.

Alan had been the same as usual, he said, joking, laughing his staccato laugh, talking logic and mathematics, and together they had tried to concoct a non-poisonous weedkiller which they had put in buckets in the workshop on the upper floor, probably the same buckets that Corell had seen. Gandy had received no hints of a crisis nor of an impending suicide, he explained, not then, but later he had put two and two together, some looks, a few lines on a postcard, and then the apple.

The apple? Corell started.

"What was that all about?" he said.

"Alan had an apple every evening while we were working together during the war. That's what he's referring to in the letter," Robin replied, not the type of revelation that Corell had been hoping for, and clearly not what Robin wanted to say either; it was just his lead-in, his absent-minded opening.

"And then I thought about Snow White," Robin said.

"Snow White?"

"Yes."

"Snow White in the sense of innocence?"

"No, the one with the dwarves. Or more specifically the one in the Disney film, the one that came out just before the war."

Corell had not seen it. Just before the war was not a time when they treated themselves to cinema visits in Southport and in any case he was not too sure about the story, perhaps he was confusing it with *Sleeping Beauty. Mirror, mirror, on the wall . . .* who says that?

"What made you think of that?"

"Alan loved it. He saw it over and over again."

"A children's film?"

"Alan was quite childish. But it's an amusing children's film," said Gandy. "And it does have some darker scenes, and one of them, I don't know. I don't want to make too much of it, I just came to think of it. It's probably nothing, but at one point in the film the witch brings out an apple, and dips it into a cauldron of poison while she mutters a rhyme."

"A rhyme," Corell repeated, and remembered something.

"Yes, and it goes, let me see now: *Dip the apple in the brew. Let the sleeping death seep through.*"

Corell looked at Gandy in surprise.

"And then in the cauldron the apple turns into a skull," he went on, "and the witch hisses to her raven—she has a small sycophantic raven—*Look! On the skin! The symbol of what lies within. Now, turn red, to tempt Snow White, to make her hunger for a bite.*"

"You know it by heart!"

"Alan recited it many times. He liked the music in the words. He whispered it like a spell."

"And you think . . . ?"

"I don't really think anything. I have no idea what happened and what he might have been thinking. I'm only saying that I was reminded of that scene, that's all, and then . . ."

Gandy's face showed signs of concern or of sorrow.

"And then I got a letter," he continued.

"From whom?"

"From an old acquaintance of Alan's, and he said that Alan had talked about a way of taking his own life with an apple and some electric wires, I really don't know how. Admittedly this was some time ago, but still . . ."

Corell remembered the wires in the ceiling at Adlington Road and also the pan with poison and his feeling of having walked in on something sick and unhealthy.

"Was there anything specific, something apart from all the other difficulties, which could have pushed him over the line?"

"Not that I know of."

"If one is to believe the letter he seems to have felt surrounded, hobbled in some way."

"Maybe."

Gandy lapsed back into silence, as if he regretted having said anything at all.

"Turing wrote that he was afraid *they* would come after you too," Corell countered, and it struck him that he sounded intrusive and that felt like a mistake.

But to his surprise the logician smiled, not a particularly warm smile, but not too sarcastic either. Rather, it was a smile with both pride and defiance in it:

"Isn't it obvious?"

"What?"

"That I'm a fellow traveller. That I've been a member of the Communist Party."

Corell could not see why on earth this should have been obvious.

"So you . . ." he started.

"Have drunk gin and tonic with Guy Burgess. Absolutely. I am quite simply a great big bloody security risk. Our right-thinking friends should also have a go at me, Alan was totally right about that," Gandy continued, with such sarcasm that Corell instinctively tried to put on an air of worldliness.

"Now, don't look so shocked. I haven't done anything," Gandy grinned.

"Are you still a communist?" Corell asked, not liking his tone of voice now either—it sounded too naive.

"Yes," said Gandy, "I suppose I still am, or maybe not, it all depends, but you understand, when I went up to Cambridge in 1936 communist cells were being formed everywhere. Lecturers, students, professors, everyone was part of it. Where were you at the end of the thirties?"

Corell started. At the end of the thirties he was not very old, and if Gandy's question was about his level of political commitment then he had very little to boast about, so he gave only a vague answer. Fortunately Gandy did not seem to be listening.

"If you wanted to achieve anything in the thirties then communism was the only alternative. That's what I felt," he said. "The reds were the only ones who were prepared to put something on the line, and you know, we didn't just want to talk. We wanted to do something. I had a friend, John Cornford, who disappeared off to Spain and died in Cordoba a few days before his twenty-first birthday. Can you imagine how much we talked about him?"

Corell said that he could.

"I was reading physics at the time," Gandy went on. "And physics taught us that the world could not be viewed in the same way as before. Time wasn't absolute, neither was space. So much of what had been regarded as self-evident turned out to be false or only a part of the truth, and it seemed natural that the same also applied to politics."

"Did you want things to be as they were in the Soviet Union?"

"Some may have wanted that," Gandy said. "But most of us saw communism as something independent of Moscow—a force sweeping across the world which was to make it freer and more egalitarian. Some people probably even saw something fundamentally religious in it."

Corell remembered what Robert Somerset had said to him.

"And the Russians took advantage of that."

"I expect so."

They passed a small angular church and then a sign: TO MADINGLEY. They seemed to be on their way out of the city. Yellow fields stretched before them, and for a little while they walked in silence.

"Did you ever come across any Soviet agents?" Corell said.

"Not that I know," Gandy said, and he seemed not to want to say anything more on the subject, but then he changed tack again and said that of course there was some whispering that this person or that was a party member or a Russian agent and sometimes it so happened, he said, that some convinced Marxist became a reactionary overnight and then the rumours grew even louder.

"Why's that?"

"Because it was said that that's how it worked. If you were recruited then you were meant to distance yourself from communism and get closer to the government's line so that you could make a career and gain access to sensitive material. You won't after all find a successful spy with the word communist stamped across his forehead. That's what's so odd about Burgess."

"How do you mean?" Corell said.

"He was so obvious about everything. Red, drunk and scandalous. Ought to have been completely wrong as a spy. Can't think why the Russians wanted to have anything to do with him."

"He had his B.B.C. programme, Westminster something. Didn't he even interview Churchill?"

"He was certainly no fool. But he was so hopelessly obvious."

"And he was a homosexual," Corell said.

"You can say that again!"

"Were there many?"

"Many what?"

"Many homosexuals who became communists," Corell said.

"I don't know," Gandy said grimly.

"I've heard that many of them were drawn to the ideology."

"That's rubbish!"

"Yes, but . . ."

"That's just prejudice and nonsense. But maybe you're right," Gandy continued, friendlier again, "in the sense that many homosexuals felt excluded and on the margins of society. Christopher Isherwood wrote somewhere that he was so furious about all the rubbish that convention and his parents demanded from him that he wanted to get his own back, and turn everything upside down. Politics, love, literature. Perhaps there were more who felt the same way."

"And Turing?"

"He was definitely a homo."

"But a communist?"

"Not in the least bit. Not one jot. My God, where did you get that from?"

"People have suggested . . ."

"Who? What a load of rubbish. Alan was disturbingly apolitical. He was a total outsider. He was not at all someone to fall for some political fad. He was completely his own man."

"I'm beginning to see that!"

"Are you? Because to be honest that's the part I find the hardest to understand. How could his mind have been so fundamentally different to everyone else's? How could he for example come up with such an unconventional idea that the brain is computable and that it should be possible to replicate it? What do you think, shall we turn back?"

"I'm sorry?"

"Shall we head back to the city?"

"Yes, let's," Corell said pensively. "But what did you say? Did Turing think that the brain was computable and that it would be possible . . . ?"

The last thing Robin Gandy wanted to do was to cast himself in the role of teacher. He had far more troubling thoughts on his mind and therefore said nothing. He kept quiet, hoping the question would go away, but seeing that the policeman was not about to give up he reluctantly began to speak, and pitched it at the simplest level possible. But he got a surprise. The young man—who annoyed him one moment and then awakened his fatherly instincts the next—had already grasped "Computable Numbers" and many other things in the field of logic. He seemed to absorb everything with such amazing ease, and in the end Robin started to say things that surprised even him:

"In a way Alan was predestined to think that. Sometimes I even wonder if it didn't grow out of his old broken heart. You know, when Alan was seventeen he fell in love with a boy called Christopher. He said that he worshipped the ground that Christopher walked on."

"Christopher," the policeman muttered, as if deep in thought.

"That's right, Christopher Morcom. Christopher was an incredibly gifted student and persuaded Alan to pull himself together and stop being so hopeless at school. They applied to Cambridge at the same time. Not long afterwards Christopher died of some kind of milk-borne tuberculosis. It was a terrible blow. Alan was beside himself. He couldn't bear the thought that Christopher was dead. He wanted his friend to go on living at all costs, but since he disliked Christianity's wishy-washy talk of the eternal soul he came up with his own solution. He wrote a scientific paper. Maybe you're familiar with the conflict between determinism and free will: How can man, living in a universe governed by physical laws, still be independent and free? When the discoveries in quantum physics were made at the beginning of the twentieth century, some people thought they had found the answer. The particles inside the nucleus of an atom, at least each one by itself, didn't seem to have any predetermined pattern of movement. Each individual one appeared to be as unpredictable as we human beings. That's why Einstein, incurable determinist that he was, had such difficulties with quantum physics. He couldn't stand the disorder. He wanted to see the same beautiful order in the microcosm as in the universe of his theory of relativity. But for the young Alan, it became a source of inspiration. The soul, he wrote, was no more than a particular arrangement of atoms in our brain which, thanks to their independence, govern the other particles in our body. After death they leave us and find a new home. There was a little bit of hocus-pocus about it. As a grown man, Alan was inevitably embarrassed by the paper. But the remarkable thing about it was that the paper examined the way in which the atoms in our brain are connected to each other and that led him further."

"How?"

"It gave him a materialistic view of biology. Or perhaps I should say mechanical or simply mathematical. When he wrote 'Computable Numbers' he began by deciding which numbers were computable, which could be computed using a simple algorithm, and even if he recognised the limitations of such a method he was primarily interested . . ."

"In its potential."

"Precisely! He understood that something which is computable, and which we can feed into a machine, is capable of so vastly much more. I'm not saying that he came straightaway to the strange conclusion that even the brain is mechanical. At Princeton he was in fact more onto the idea that there were intuitive elements in our thinking which were totally different. But he changed his views and I think that was because he learned more about electronics. He realised how much would be gained if the process could be made to work at the speed of light."

"Then making simple connections between poles would rapidly get you to something complex and meaningful," the policeman said.

"Yes, the soulless ticking of a machine might even be able to convey the soulful. Straight after the war, when Alan started to work out the basis for what we today call the digital data machine, he was hardly interested in the practical consequences, such as the potential for calculating how to make new and monstrous bombs. From the very first he was after something altogether different."

"Like what?"

"Like trying to replicate thinking."

"Sounds insane."

"It was. But you understand, as he learned more about our brain—how millions and millions of neurons are connected to each other—he saw the similarities to his machine, not that he made too much of the comparison, definitely not, but he thought that all these connections could hardly function if they weren't supported by a logical structure. And anything that is logical is by nature divisible and replicable, which makes it computable. There may have been some aspects of quantum physics here to complicate matters, and I believe that towards the end of his life he was more and more inclined to think along those lines, but then he became more and more convinced that everything in our thinking is mechanical in some respect—even our intuition and our moments of artistic inspiration."

"How the hell . . ." Corell said.

"I think he equated creative moments with hidden mechanisms. He talked about machines with hidden functions. Take a switch. You press the button and have the impression that the light comes on immediately—as if by magic, don't you? But in actual fact there's been a process. Electrons have transported themselves along a wire. A lot has happened which we don't notice. Alan imagined that the brain functions in a similar way. An idea appears in our head and we think that it's come from nowhere. But underneath it all there's been a sequence of events, a pattern, which it should be possible to describe. Just because it's happened fast doesn't mean that it isn't mechanical."

"Surely he wasn't serious."

"He certainly was. He said that within fifty or one hundred years—he mentioned two different time periods—we should be able to create a machine which is intelligent in the same sense as you or I, or which at least behaves as if it were, and this annoyed many people, as you can imagine. Some said that while it is possible that the brain has some logical sequences which can be copied, its innermost essence is something different and greater. Alan replied by talking about onions. He said that perhaps the brain is like an onion. Imagine someone who has never seen an onion before. He peels away layer after layer of the onion and thinks, soon I'll get to the core, to what's really important in the vegetable, but at last the man has removed everything and there's nothing left. The onion was nothing more than its layers, and by the same token Alan thought that the brain has no core either, no innermost secret, but that it is only made up of its individual parts and their connections to each other. Alan refused to believe that intelligence was something unique to humans, something which can only occur in what looks remarkably like a large helping of porridge."

"Porridge?"

"He thought that that's what our brain looks like, grey and unappetising. He thought that intelligence could just as well grow out of other structures, out of other matter, for example out of the binary logic in an electronic machine and he refused to define intelligence too narrowly. He more than anyone knew that what is normal in human terms isn't necessarily the only yardstick."

"How do you mean?"

"He was used to being the outsider. Strange as it may sound, he had no trouble siding with the machine."

The policeman looked puzzled and Robin made an effort to find the right words to express himself:

"He felt that it would be wrong to discriminate against machines in the context of intelligence, and sometimes—but perhaps I am being unfair to him—I did wonder if he had this dream of thinking machines because he knew that he would never have a family. His dream of an intelligent machine was his dream of a child, not that there was anything dream-like about his theories, quite the contrary. He was extremely rational, but his vulnerable position, his feeling of always being marginalised, made him rather well-suited to seeing things from the perspective of a machine. After the publication of Norman Wiener's book *Cybernetics* a debate started—somewhat sensationalist if you ask me—as to whether it's even possible to speak of a thinking machine. A neurologist by the name of Geoffrey Jefferson, specialising in brain research, leapt to the defence of human beings. In his opinion, as long as a machine is unable to blush or write a sonnet or a symphony or enjoy the caresses of a woman or feel remorse and joy, we cannot say it is intelligent in the way that a human being is intelligent. Alan thought that was deeply unfair."

"How?"

"To start with, Alan couldn't enjoy a woman's caresses either. And write a symphony? Who can do that? Can you? He said that intelligence mustn't be given such a narrow definition. He even thought that Jefferson was being unfair in his taste for sonnets because a sonnet written by a machine would best be understood by another machine."

"I'm sorry?"

"If machines can indeed learn to think they will in all likelihood have different preferences to ours. Alan wanted to show that we are not necessarily the only benchmark. A machine can think without having to be like you and me. It doesn't even have to like strawberries and cream. Besides, he wasn't after an especially gifted machine. It only had to be as quick-witted as an American businessman, he said. In any case he devised a test."

"A test?"

"A test to see when a machine could be regarded as intelligent. Alan wrote about it in the magazine *Mind*. If you're interested, I can arrange for you to read the article, it's good fun," Robin said, showing a benevolence he did not quite understand, but there was something about the young man that inspired trust.

Robin even stopped worrying that he might be in for an unpleasant surprise. It felt more as if the man were just curious about Turing, indeed more like a student with an enquiring mind than a policeman, and Robin was therefore astonished when the conversation took a quite different turn.

It's not possible, he thought, during a dizzying few seconds.

25

THE STREET LIFE AROUND THEM grew busier and they wandered through the cobbled streets, along the beautiful houses and towers. Every now and then people said hello to Gandy, and Corell was once again intoxicated by the situation and wondered how much the suit and the company he was keeping were fooling those around him. Were the women not looking at him in a new way? He thought so, but also felt like an actor, secure only so long as he keeps playing his role. Dr. Gandy was talking about a test which would determine whether a machine could think.

"I'd love to read it," he said.

"Excellent! In that case, I'll make sure you get it."

"I'm especially interested in what Dr. Turing did during the war."

"Is that so?" Gandy said.

"I know, of course, that he cracked the Nazi codes with his machines," he continued, as if that were obvious, and it was in fact some time before he himself realised how bold his words had been.

After all, he knew nothing, absolutely nothing. It was pure speculation that Turing had worked on cryptanalysis, a loose assumption. No, it simply could not be right, Corell was just shooting from the hip and expected Gandy to react by being sceptical or perhaps even superior, and sure enough he thought that he saw an indulgent smile and bit his lip. He blushed a little. But then he noticed something else: a look of misgiving, a shadow which crossed the logician's face. Maybe Gandy was not so sure of himself, after all.

"Who?" he said, nothing more, not one word, but Corell understood that the full sentence would have been: "Who told you?" and he was filled by a sense of triumph, and replied, careful not to appear confident or pleased with himself:

"I can't tell you."

But he still managed to make it sound as if he had excellent contacts.

Gandy did not know if Alan Turing had cracked any Nazi codes. He just knew that his friend had worked on cryptanalysis at Bletchley Park or Station X, as it was also called. Gandy had no further details, except of course that he realised that Turing had been successful. When they met at Hanslope in 1944, Turing had acquired a new status. You could tell from the looks of his colleagues and the gossip and nicknames. He was called "the Professor" and was said to have been in the U.S.A., to have been shipped over as a priceless contribution to the war effort, and somehow it showed in his eyes. Not that he was conceited or pompous, but his self-esteem was higher. It was as if he had decided to stop feeling ashamed.

Hanslope Park was an old manor house which had been run by the security services since 1941 and was used as an experimental workshop for all sorts of electronic machines and constructions. Gandy had been doing research into radio communications and radar earlier during the war. At Hanslope he became an assistant on Turing's project to develop a voice encryption device for Churchill and Roosevelt's telephone conversations. Gandy liked the job. The war was about to end and it looked as if he would survive—when he had been called up he had regarded it as a death sentence—but above all he was stimulated. Turing was so quick on the uptake. There was the work but there were also jokes and often it felt as if it were all a game, albeit an extremely serious game which would result in something first-rate, and sometimes in the evenings Turing would give them talks on mathematics. Every now and then they would drink together at parties in the officers' mess. It was a good life. But one day it all nearly fell apart.

It was summer, at the start of their project. They had been out picking mushrooms the evening before. Turing had tried in vain to find a death cap, *Amanita phalloides*, and in the morning as usual they had worked on Delilah. Delilah was the name Gandy had given the voice encryption machine, after the woman in the Bible who betrayed Samson. Donald Bayley was also there. Bayley was the other assistant on the project. He had gone to a state school and studied electrical engineering at Birmingham University, and had lived far away from the world of King's College. He knew homosexuals only as the subject of unkind jokes at school and inept euphemisms in the newspapers, but now he was to make closer acquaintance with one of them. Out of nowhere Turing said:

"I'm homosexual, by the way."

Gandy never quite discovered what the point of this was. Maybe Turing was hoping that it might make for a more intimate atmosphere or he just wanted to lay his cards on the table. Bayley reacted with immediate disgust:

"What the hell are you saying? Have you gone mad?"

Later Bayley explained that he did not know what was worse, the information itself or the way in which Alan presented it: "He wasn't even ashamed." Bayley was so upset that he wanted to leave the whole project. Even Turing was unhappy about it. That was the last reaction in the world that he wanted. "Try and imagine what it's like for us," he said. "If we reveal our inclinations, then with a bit of luck things will be fine for a while, but most likely we get thrown out." Gandy said that he could understand. It's true that there had been a most unpleasant experience with an older man when he was fifteen years old (Turing admitted that fifteen-year-olds should be left alone) but then he had after all been at King's and been elected a member of the Apostles.

It had taken a great deal of effort from Gandy to keep Bayley in the project, and after some difficulty he succeeded. The fact that Turing was so noticeably different and so obviously brilliant did help. Eventually his homosexuality came to be seen as a part of his general eccentricity and in many ways Bayley had to admit that they had some good times together.

Turing moved from the Crown Inn at Shenley Brook to Hanslope Park and he, Gandy and a large fat cat called Timothy came to share a small cottage below the officers' mess. One of the men working at the mess was Bernard Walsh. He was the owner of Wheelers, a fish restaurant in Soho in London, and he was something of a magician at

Hanslope. While the rest of England lived on wretched fare, he saw to it that Gandy and Turing got fresh eggs, and sometimes partridges, and also a regular supply of fruit.

Turing worked hard, not just on the voice encryption project. He also thought a lot about the building blocks of intelligence and life, and asked himself questions such as: How is the brain formed? How does it grow to be what it is? He believed that it followed mathematical models, some sort of organisational system. The brain itself was too complicated to tackle first. It was easier to begin with the leaf of a plant or of a tree and soon they started to collect pine cones in the forest. The scales of a cone grow in conformity with the Fibonacci numbers and Alan wanted to demonstrate how that happened. Genetics, he said, gave no guide since each cell has the same genes and enzymes. Genetics did not explain how each and every cell knows how to form its pattern and how they all relate to each other. Turing wanted to explain that. He wanted to discover the mathematics of life, and he and Gandy discussed the possibilities for hours on end and scribbled sums on their notepads.

They also talked about the dream of building a thinking machine, and even though Gandy was not allowed to ask about it, or in any case would not have got an answer if he had asked, he had suspected that earlier during the war Turing had already been thinking about what that sort of machine might look like. His descriptions were detailed and full of vision and consequently Gandy too had thought that Turing must have used some sort of logical contraption to break the Nazi's communications, and that is why he flinched so when the policeman wearing the far-too-good suit suddenly claimed that Turing had cracked the German codes with the help of his machine! Not that it upset him. It was none of his business to see to it that war secrets remained secure but, along with his curiosity, he also began to worry. Was he getting himself into trouble?

"You seem to know more than I do," he said, trying to strike a casual note.

Corell did not answer and he noticed that Gandy was lost in thought. What should he say now? He could not think of anything, and felt a stab of unease.

"I don't think so," he managed to say.

"Or else you aren't who you say you are."

"To be honest, it's mostly guesswork."

Gandy looked puzzled.

"What do you mean?" he said.

"As I was reading through the report of the investigation, I put two and two together," Corell continued, glad to be able to stick to the truth. "I gathered that Turing had been working on something secret during the war and I also read that he'd got an O.B.E., so I tried to work out what a man like him might have done to deserve it."

"Surely it could have been all sorts of things."

"Perhaps. But I got the impression that he'd been working on logic during the war as well, and then I heard and read some other things. And after that this idea popped up, and somehow it seemed to fit. What do you know about it?"

"Nothing, as I said."

"I thought the two of you worked together during the war?"

"Only during the last part and then on something entirely different, which we didn't even manage to finish. Alan never said a word to me about what he had done earlier during the war."

"Not even afterwards?"

"No."

"Was it really so sensitive?"

Gandy nodded. "Presumably so."

"But we won the war. It's over."

"It most definitely isn't," Gandy said, irritated again or even angry, but then he calmed down once more and became pensive.

Gandy felt tired, and looked out over the city. They passed Trinity College and among all the people streaming out of the gate he noticed Julius Pippard, the linguist. Later on he would wonder about the coincidence. Julius Pippard was a small man. But since he held himself so well he gave the impression of being tall. Robin did not know much more about him than that he had worked with Turing at Bletchley Park.

He knew that because one day Pippard had appeared at Hanslope Park to discuss something with Turing. Gandy never got to know what they had talked about, but it was apparent that Alan was not overly keen on Pippard and perhaps that was why Gandy decided to stir things up a bit.

"Do you see that man over there?" he said, pointing.

The policeman nodded.

"That's Julius Pippard. If you want to talk about Alan's background, you could have a word with him," he said, but at the same moment it struck him as a crazy piece of advice. It could get Corell into trouble and Robin corrected himself at once: "No, on second thoughts, don't do that," but the policeman did not seem to be listening anymore.

He appeared to be lost in thought, and after a moment of silence said something strange: "I probably won't be in the police force for very much longer," and when Gandy asked what he was planning to do instead, the policeman answered: "I'm thinking of taking up my studies again."

Gandy had a feeling that there were no such plans, but he could not be sure. Although the worst of his worry had passed, he still felt nervous. What had he just experienced—an interrogation, a conversation or something quite different? When they said goodbye shortly afterwards and the policeman disappeared down Trumpington Street, it was as if he had left behind a question.

26

THE FIRST TIME CORELL had been in Cambridge was in the mid thirties, in the company of his father, and although he did not remember much about it, it had been at the same time of year as now, in late June, and it felt as if people had time on their hands and were relaxed. There was expectation in the air, and his father was happy and noisy as he always was in those days.

"Hello, hello, how nice to see you," he greeted people right and left. "Elegant as always. Brilliant book, Peter. Thanks for your letter. Oh, what an unexpected honour! Let me bow down before you."

There was a brightness about him, he was the very centre of life and of course he jangled his keys, and every now and then he turned to Leonard who was holding his hand.

"You clever boy, I'm sure that one day you'll be studying here."

With those words the cobbled streets seemed to stretch out before him like a string of promises, and they bought chocolate and books and looked at the oarsmen on the river and talked about what he should read at Cambridge. "Is mathematics exciting, Daddy?" It is exciting, but his father said that he would prefer him to study this or that. A mathematician has no-one to talk to, nobody outside his circle. Someone in the humanities on the other hand can always entertain others with his knowledge. "Like you, Daddy?" "Like me," his father answered, and Corell fantasised that one day he would walk there along the beautiful houses, full of stories, and when people made some remark or other, maybe even something quite humdrum, he would reply: "Well yes, a bit like Odysseus approaching Ithaca . . ." But it was not to be. His father let him down. He let himself down.

It was as if the city made him understand. Things he had not thought about for many years came back to him, and he remembered how he had been forced to leave Marlborough, or should he say had forced himself to leave? What an idiot he had been . . . my God, he had not even answered Vicky's letters at Marlborough. He had tried. He had. But he never actually managed to write.

His paralysis had been far too deep. Even the teachers who before had been so fond of him sensed a growing distance in him, and therefore no-one tried hard enough to keep him at the school. He had known for some time that his mother was not paying the school fees, and if only she had told him that was the problem then perhaps he might have fought to arrange the funds. But his mother appealed to his conscience. She did not even insist that he come home. Instead she said: "Naturally, Leonard, of course you must stay at school."

It was just that she could not manage on her own and that the house was falling into disrepair and no-one looked after the garden, and not one person came to visit. There was this problem and that. There was the war, there were the neighbours and the long walk to the shops, and above all the loneliness. "It's hard," she wrote, "hard."

Between the lines the letters were a plea for help bordering on blackmail, and he gave in, not just out of a sense of guilt. Marlborough was on the point of suffocating him, and when Vicky wrote: "You mustn't under any circumstances leave. I'll pay the fees," he never answered. He just emptied his lockers. He took his leave of Marlborough and ever since then he had been miles away from anything to do with the school, and it was not until now in Cambridge that he realised how much it had hurt him. He had so desperately wanted to be a part of the city, and it was not unthinkable that this whole trip was an attempt to compensate for what he had never had.

Thanks to Gandy, he gained access to the archive room at King's College, where he was studying Alan Turing's writings, and even though he was delighted to be there, he was aware that he was only imitating the academics. The pretence itself amused him—*they probably think I spend all my time here reading the most abstract essays*—but over time he felt more like a thief who has sneaked in without permission and is likely to be thrown out at any moment. Curiously enough he found a certain comfort in what the mathematician had written.

It was not only in his letter that Turing had written about theatre and drama. He seemed indeed to be fascinated by imitation, by the mimicking of human behaviour. When Corell tackled the article which Robin had spoken about, "Computing Machinery and Intelligence," he had just finished painstakingly working his way through "Computable Numbers," and was therefore expecting more calculations and symbols, but he skipped through the article, although he did also find it peculiar. Not only did Turing appear to believe that machines would be able to think, he genuinely hoped that they would become as intelligent as us, which Corell found very odd. If machines can become the equals of humans, then they might well also do better than us, and that must be just as frightening a prospect as an attack from outer space. But exactly as Gandy had said he would, Turing sided with the machines. They must not be discriminated against just because they are different, he wrote. When deciding whether or not a person was intelligent, neither appearance nor gender should be taken into account, nor in the case of a machine the material from which it was made, only the capacity to act should be considered. To put on a performance, Turing imagined a game of impersonation, where a machine had to pretend to be a human being. An examiner would be allowed to ask any questions he wanted to and read the answers on a paper print-out, and if this did not allow the examiner to determine if he was communicating with a human or a machine, then the machine would have to be considered intelligent, Turing wrote, his view being that anyone who is able to imitate us is thinking.

God knows what Corell thought about this, but Turing had no trouble in countering all sorts of objections, for example from those who said that what marks us out as thinking beings is that we are conscious, that we enjoy things and suffer and are alive. Those arguments were unconvincing, he wrote, because we only know those things about ourselves, not about our fellow humans. Those we only judge on the basis of how they appear to think and feel, and it would be unfair to demand more of a machine.

The only way in which we could prove that a machine is conscious is by being one ourselves. We will never know whether it experiences things, has feelings, and so he believed that the game of impersonation was the only solution, and therefore instead of asking ourselves whether a machine can think we should ask ourselves: Can a machine do well in the game of impersonation? Turing thought that it could, not now but in the next century, and certainly he realised that it sounded strange, or even absurd, that after a long conversation—in which we would be allowed to ask whatever we wanted—we might mistake a machine for a human being. But we are never prepared for the unexpected, he wrote, and listing the shortcomings of machines today is a poor argument on which to base a projection of what they will be capable of tomorrow. Things change. What a baby can do today tells us nothing about what it can achieve in twenty years' time.

Corell read with great fervour, and it took a little while before he noticed that someone was staring at him. People had come and gone throughout the morning, written out requests for books and documents on small white slips of paper and sat down to read for an hour or two and then disappeared—he supposed that many of them were on summer courses at King's—and while Corell had been more attentive than most to the people streaming in, he had not noticed the fellow sitting at the table diagonally across from him. It was a young fellow, not even twenty, who looked as if he might be Indian, with sparkling, amused eyes, and this boy pointed to Corell's papers:

"Pretty amazing, isn't it?" he whispered.

"What?"

"Alan Turing. I've been looking at the Gödel-Church Theorem myself."

"Have you," Corell said, feeling uncomfortable.

He was determined to avoid a discussion and saw no other way out than to pretend to have been disturbed and point to the sign asking for silence in the room. The boy nodded, looking crestfallen, which pained Corell. He was keen to make a good impression, and even though he had the time to continue reading, he took the exchange as a pretext to leave. He returned the papers and went down the stone steps out into the forecourt looking very apprehensive. He was so different from his father! In the good old days James had looked on other people—even strangers—as if it were a privilege for them to meet a person like him. But all he had left his son was insecurity and low self-esteem.

Corell, who looked nothing like how he felt—he sometimes exuded tremendous determination—started to dream about how he would walk here and look up at King's Chapel as if he had come up with something revolutionary, perhaps some new sort of machine. Wouldn't he hold his head up high then? He would give a little smile to the right and to the left and wear a brooding, slightly stern expression. Didn't all great thinkers have a stern look about them?

It started to rain. A drizzle at first. Then the heavens opened and he took shelter under the archway. After which he quickened his steps. A trumpet could be heard wailing far away, he thought the same trumpet which had been playing when he met Robin Gandy, the same woeful tones which now blended with the sound of water in the gutters and which gave colour to the city like the music in a film, and he thought about the rain which had been falling over Adlington Road that day and about a number of other things while a number 109 double-decker bus drove by with an advertisement for DULUX in the space between the windows. The engine noise drowned out the sound of the trumpet, but it soon returned and he walked towards it, past the yellow and brown stone houses and the leafy trees, and he began to feel nervous. The meeting which he was going to would not be a pleasant one. He was on his way to see Julius Pippard, the man Robin Gandy had pointed out to him, and he could not quite believe that he had had the courage to get in touch with him. It was not exactly in keeping with the image of the frightened boy who did not dare look people in the eyes. But still . . . drunk on sherry and a desire to make further progress he had looked through the telephone book last night and found the number. Not that he thought he would dial it, but then he did so after all, and only once he had got himself tangled up in lies did he realise what a mistake it had been. Here he was now, walking along, when he should really be going back to the hotel and forgetting about everything. Yet he kept walking.

Beyond the bus stop he saw the trumpet, and though he had not thought about it before, he had perceived its tones as being masculine, and imagined that they came from some poor wretch, a deserted man trumpeting out his loneliness. But leaning against a brick wall stood a young woman in a light-blue suit with her hair cropped short like a boy's. Although it cannot have been easy to play for money in the rain she seemed content, almost mocking, and that gave her an aura of pride. Corell dropped a coin into her beret on the pavement, but it bounced away and, as he retrieved it, their eyes met. For just a fraction of a moment. Yet he still felt a pang and thought of Julie. One day he would have the courage to ask her out. As he walked off the music rang in his ears like a promise. Even the rain seemed different and as the tones died away behind him he mourned them, as if a door had briefly opened and let in the sounds of a party.

He turned into Emmanuel Street and passed Emmanuel College. It was five minutes past four. There were twenty-five minutes to go before his meeting with Julius Pippard, and he realised even now that the encounter could hardly result in anything other than problems. While the lie to Gandy had in a way been involuntary, the result of a misunderstanding, he was now so tangled up in his muddle-headedness or general embarrassment that he had said he would like to ask some questions, as the police officer investigating Alan Turing's death. He must have been mad . . . All day long Corell had been convinced that he should follow his gut instinct and forget about the visit, but it was as if an irresistible force were driving him forward and he looked at his map almost in anger. He could not be far away and now found himself in Burleigh Street.

Burleigh Street was for the most part a shopping street, and Corell could well have taken the opportunity to buy an umbrella, or get a cup of tea. Better still he could have changed his mind and turned back, but he felt impatient, as if the meeting were a sore tooth which had to be pulled out soon, and he walked quickly. At the address which he had been given he found a red-brick house, beautiful except for the white-painted Roman entrance which seemed out of place, and also the dark entrance hall inside. In his imagination it felt threatening. He heard the sound of his own footsteps all too clearly and shivered. He found the door on the second floor, exactly where the directions had said, with the name Pippard over the letterbox. The name struck him as being both insubstantial and tough, and he considered going back out into the street and returning in a quarter of an hour, on the stroke of half past, but no, it felt inevitable now, and in the next moment he rang the bell. He pressed it with his finger, and then waited. Nothing happened, nothing except that a door opened on the top floor, as if the doorbell were in fact connected to it, and Corell may have nodded off for a moment in a sort of nervous drowsiness because he was startled when at long last brisk footsteps could be heard inside. The letterbox cast a faint ghostly light, there was a rattle from the lock, and Julius Pippard stood in front of him, dressed in a red checked shirt, and there was little doubt that he was annoyed.

"You're early," he said, and Corell could not think of anything better to say than, "It was raining," as if the rain had something to do with it.

27

JULIUS PIPPARD LOOKED at himself in the bathroom mirror and smiled. He was getting no less attractive with age! Just look at those eyes! Surely they revealed how intelligent he was, how strong his character? Of course, he had his faults. He became easily irritated, he got himself worked up, but he could control his emotions. That was one of the keys to his success, wasn't it? Although he still had his rooms at Cambridge and kept ties with Trinity, his position at G.C.H.Q., Government Communications Headquarters in Cheltenham, was absolutely vital to him, and he often enjoyed the feeling that his work was important, not just in the way that an academic paper is important, or that a company or university is important, but important in the sense that it *safeguards England.*

Pippard's connections to the Government Code and Cypher School, what used to be Room 40, went back as far as just before the war, and he had been stationed at Bletchley Park in Buckinghamshire. He may not exactly have been an Alan Turing, but his translations and analysis of decrypted material in Hut 4 had still been of great importance and he soon became a part of the important security vetting, and that suited him well. With his eye for human weakness he detected dangers and risks where others saw nothing at all, and before anyone was seriously worried about character weaknesses such as tendencies to sexual perversion, he understood their significance. He became the uncrowned master of that discipline.

After 1945 he continued to screen his fellow workers for reliability—

which became an even more central function in the context of the Cold War—and soon he found himself responsible for top-secret work on double-encrypted Soviet messages. It was a project called Venona, which had started in 1943 because Carter W. Clarke, head of military intelligence for the U.S.A., quite rightly did not trust Stalin—however much of a wartime ally the Russians had become. The code was broken for the first time in December 1946, and shortly afterwards the Americans realised that the Russians had been spying on them when they were developing the atom bomb at Los Alamos. Pippard and his colleagues were not yet involved at that stage, so the first time he happened to read an obscure reference to Venona was in *The Times*—not exactly the place where he usually found new intelligence, but even though Pippard was somewhat taken aback neither he nor anyone else in authority took it as seriously as they might have done. Yet it was a significant matter, perhaps the most important thing they had come across, as he realised soon afterwards when G.C.H.Q. became involved in the work. Pippard came to be one of an exclusive circle of pundits and decision-makers responsible for agreeing who was to be let in on the secret, and God knows that put him under pressure. It was crucial that no security risks be given access to this of all areas.

A series of code names featured in Soviet communications, which seemed to be covers for American and British spies who had leaked information about the atom bomb among other things. For example, the code names ANTENNA and LIBERAL appeared eventually to refer to the same person, whose identity was revealed when it transpired that a careless K.G.B. officer had mentioned that the name of this person's wife was Ethel, Ethel as in Ethel Rosenberg, which led to her and her husband Julius's arrest. Then there were CHARLES and REST—who turned out to be the spy Klaus Fuchs—and many others, like PERS whom they still had not identified, but above all HOMER, or GOMER, depending on how one transcribed the Cyrillic alphabet. That signature had sent six telegrams from the British Embassy in Washington to the K.G.B. during the war, and Pippard was closely involved in the hunt for who it might be. He and his colleagues laid the puzzle piece by piece. They sat with their lists of names and racked their brains: Could it be this person or that? And step by step—would he ever forget it?—they began to close in on the culprit, who turned out to be no less a person than Donald Maclean, the prominent diplomat and son of the famous liberal politician of the same name.

Unfortunately they passed the information on to their colleagues in M.I.6, not that they had any choice in the matter, but those idiots . . . Pippard did not even want to think about it. M.I.6. made a mess of it. Maclean and Guy Burgess managed to escape to Soviet Russia by car and ferry, and ever since then Pippard had been convinced that they in Cheltenham were the only truly competent people in the security services. Who had unravelled the mystery and who had then ruined everything?

That bloody upper-class crowd at M.I.6. must be teeming with spies, or if it was going too far to say teeming then there were irrefutably more than just Burgess and Maclean; it was impossible to imagine anything else in view of all the leaks, and they were not doing much about it either. They were an idle bunch who thought someone was trustworthy just because he had been to Eton and Oxford, and Pippard was proud, nothing less, that he'd often failed to report to M.I.6. Granted, they too had made a few mistakes at G.C.H.Q., but through no fault of his. For example, they had wanted to use the machine in Manchester for their cryptological work and had therefore contacted Turing. Pippard had been against it. He realised early on that Turing was both homosexual and promiscuous. A male slut, to be blunt.

"We can't have him back on board. We know how the Russians operate!" he argued.

But he was outvoted. Turing was still regarded as an oracle pure and simple, and he had certainly been an important resource during the war. Of course, his skills were no longer indispensable; besides which he had scant respect for his superiors and for established routines, and he hurt people with his frankness—and however brilliant he might be, it was only if he found the work stimulating. All of this was pointed out by Pippard, but nobody had listened, not then. Now at last he had been vindicated. That was how it was. Turing got caught, and there was of course a lot of fuss at the office. But even then they did not all agree to throw him out. Old Oscar Farley—that bloody weakling—defended him stubbornly:

"Are we really going to kick Alan out after everything he's done for us?"

As if Turing had not shown enough lack of judgement, and as if there were not clear instructions to rid the organisation of homosexuals. Most people of course agreed with Pippard, as a matter of principle. But it was argued that Turing was a special case. There was plenty of talk and people told a lot of romanticised stories from Bletchley Park, and it was not until Pippard shouted: "Do you want him to drag us all to ruin?" that they at last agreed to cut all ties with him. Pippard, who never shirked any unpleasant tasks, offered to talk to him, but it was agreed that Farley should do it. Not surprisingly he was treated with kid gloves until the very end and God only knows what Farley said to Turing, but clearly it was not plain enough. Turing continued to go off to Europe on dirty adventures. Why in the name of God was he not forbidden to travel, and why did someone not look into his old love affairs? No, nothing was done in the proper manner, and nobody should have been surprised when concerns continued to accumulate even after the mathematician's death. Who on earth was this policeman, for example?

He had no right whatsoever to come snooping around here. A quick telephone call to the police station in Wilmslow had informed Pippard that the man was off work because his aunt was dying in Knutsford. And now he was on his way here. Had the aunt recovered? A detective constable from the middle of nowhere could hardly cause much damage. But then you never knew. Pippard had discussed the situation with Robert Somerset in Cheltenham. Somerset had met the man already and thought that he was a bit strange, "shifty in a way, as if he were hiding something."

"I'll put the fear of God into him," Pippard had said. "Get him to understand that he's treading on thin ice!"

Yes, he would get serious with the fool. Show him who was in charge, and find out what was going on. It could even become interesting. It was just that . . . how had the policeman even got hold of Pippard's name, and how could he know that he and Turing had worked together? That worried him a bit. What time was it? The man was due in twenty minutes, and in the meantime Pippard started to write a letter in which he made some cautious advances to a young lady with a very prominent bosom whom he had met at a conference in Arlington, but he did not get very far. The doorbell rang.

Corell did not like the look that met him. He did not like the rooms either. Not just because they were impersonal and cold. There were signs of pedantry here which really made him nervous. The pencils on the mahogany-coloured desk were lined up in neat rows and the furniture, lacking both polish and character, felt as if it had been set out too symmetrically. Yes, even the cigarette butts in the ashtray on the window ledge seemed to have been arranged with care. Right in front of him hung a singularly uninteresting painting of a fox hunt in a wood which might have worked if it had been smaller, but because of its size—was it really over two metres long?—it looked grotesque.

"How nice to have a visitor all the way from Wilmslow!" Pippard said, suddenly amiable.

"Wilmslow isn't exactly the end of the world."

"Nice place, isn't it?"

"We're famous for having many hairdressing salons and pubs."

"How convenient! So you can become both drunk and handsome!"

Apart from swiftly removing a piece of paper from the coffee table, Pippard's movements were calm. The irritation which had shown when he opened the door appeared to have vanished, but that did not leave Corell feeling any less uncertain. It was as if he were standing beside someone who knew precisely what he was doing, down to the very blink of his eyes, and so, very carefully, as if wanting to make sure that it was permitted, Corell sat down on the greyish-brown wooden chair while Pippard went out to fetch some tea.

"So you have been sent here by your superiors," Pippard said as he came back with a tray.

Corell nodded.

"May I ask why?"

"To get as much information as possible."

"Hasn't the case been closed?"

"Well, yes . . . but there are still some loose ends. We don't want to leave anything to chance."

"Why don't you tell me more, so I have a better understanding? I'm not too well versed in police work. Explain to me how you operate."

In various small ways—as if he had put himself in a slightly higher chair or shown an almost imperceptible disdain in his eyes and in his tone—Pippard gave himself a crushing advantage. By a sort of invisible artistic device. Without Corell understanding how, Pippard took control of the conversation, and the more politely, the more ingratiatingly he spoke, the more he established his superiority, and Corell soon found it hard to look Pippard in the eye. When he spoke, his words sounded like empty phrases.

"In order to understand why a person has died, one has to learn about his life," he said.

"So why come to me?"

"We're talking to many people with whom Dr. Turing had contact."

"And I'm one of them?"

"Didn't you work together during the war?"

"What's given you that impression?"

Corell wanted to get away, away.

"Normal police work," he said.

"Excuse me?"

He repeated what he had said, and felt physically—like a wave of nausea—how Pippard's arrogance grew.

"How very interesting! You appear to know more than I do. Since you're so well informed, perhaps you can tell me what we worked on?"

"Sensitive information and that's why . . ."

"And what sort of sensitive information might that have been?"

"Cryptological work. You deciphered the Nazi codes with the help of machines developed by Alan Turing," Corell said, looking down at his hands in embarrassment. As he raised his eyes he expected to meet the same overbearing look as before, but he was confronted by something very different. Pippard's eyes shone with the concentration of one who senses grave danger.

What the hell was going on? Here was someone Pippard had taken to be a simple, uneducated policeman talking openly about the most closely guarded secrets from the war, and strangest of all, this person—whom he had expected to be able to put in his place with no trouble at all—was now exuding, if not assurance, then certainly cheek, and he was not only proving extremely articulate, but he appeared also to be frighteningly well informed, as if he knew all about the work at Bletchley and perhaps Venona as well. Pippard was not even reassured by the fact that the man was being so unbelievably rash. Instead he was beginning to worry that the policeman had an objective, an ulterior motive, which might close like a trap around him, and it did not even occur to him to play his trump card about the aunt who was supposed to be at death's door.

Corell did not have even a fraction of the information that Pippard thought he had, but his concentration was heightened, as if Pippard's uncertainty had restored his strength and voice, and although at first he had talked in a sort of nervous prattle, just to keep his head above water, he soon regained his confidence. He felt liberated because he had not let himself be trampled on as he had with Ross at the station. He had given as good as he got and although he was angry he never let it get out of hand.

"You're looking a bit worried," he said. "There's no reason for that. I'm very much aware of the importance of discretion. I would never discuss this with anyone who wasn't already in the know. But you understand . . . no, how could you? . . . well, it would be a breach of duty on my part if I didn't ask if Alan Turing's work during the war could have had something to do with his death. I've come to realise that he made a significant contribution. The very way he thought was different."

"You're way out of your depth, I can assure you."

"Maybe so. But the funny thing is that I've spent all day reading his papers at King's College, and I noted that he himself wrote—"

"What?" Pippard interrupted.

"—that it's a well-known fact that the most reliable people rarely discover new ways of doing things."

"What's that supposed to mean?"

"When Alan Turing wrote it, he was reflecting on the extent to which machines could be made intelligent," Corell went on. "It struck him that one prerequisite for discovering new things is the ability to make mistakes, to venture outside the recognised limits. Someone who always thinks according to the rules will never create anything. Someone who only follows received opinions, or the usual programme settings to speak the language of machines, will never come up with anything truly innovative, and can't even be regarded as intelligent in the true sense. That's why Turing wanted to add an element of chance to his machines, they shouldn't always follow strict logic, sometimes a random generator should determine what they were to do. This is how he intended to replicate free will, not that he thought that a random element would be sufficient to achieve that, but the very possibility of something unexpected and irrational occurring would at least be a start."

"I really don't see what you're driving at."

"I'm only trying to say that Alan Turing thought that, in a similar fashion, our brains have a random element. Like Russian roulette. From time to time we do crazy things. Go off the rails. But some of that is necessary for us to make progress."

"Get to the point!"

"The thing is that I'm not implying that your sense of order or your exaggerated fear of making a mistake right now is having any effect on your ability to think freely. I'm only trying to say that Turing seems to have been a different sort of person, don't you agree? He stepped outside the usual boundaries. He was creative. His thinking seems to have been fundamentally different from the conventional, and he took risks. Consequently, he made mistakes. There may even have been a sort of Russian roulette spinning inside him towards the end, for all I know."

"For God's sake, what are you trying to say?"

"Nothing, no more than that it would seem important to try to find out whether he was doing something unexpected or even risky in the time leading up to his death or if someone else was doing so, something which upset him and prompted his decision. He described in a letter . . ."

"In a letter?"

"Well, the rough copy of a letter, a draft," Corell replied, and in an instant lost his self-assurance. *Why the hell had he mentioned the letter?*

"And you've got this letter?"

"Not personally, of course."

"Who's got it then?"

"It's at the police station."

"As I understand it you've met Mr. Farley and Mr. Somerset," Pippard said, suddenly back on the offensive.

"Indeed . . . yes . . . how do you know that?"

"I'm pretty well informed, you should know," Pippard said.

"I've never doubted that."

"I even know that Somerset expressly asked you to hand over to him all the papers you found in the house."

"And I did."

"Clearly not!"

"This draft really isn't anything to . . ."

"To what?"

"To get excited about."

"Isn't it? While we're on the subject of well-informed, how's your aunt?"

Corell was overcome by an acute feeling of unease.

"My aunt?"

"Has she got better?"

"She hasn't . . ." *been ill*, he was about to say, but then he froze and realised that he had acted with a complete lack of judgement. To seek out this man and ask him about state secrets was perhaps the most stupid thing he had ever done. Maybe he was trying to say something more, but he could not utter a single word. He felt paralysed and because of that he did not notice that Pippard too was behaving strangely.

Pippard had been struck by a sense of urgency, and in his frantic mind this draft letter became a lethal document which had fallen into the hands of a chancer and a crook, and he thought feverishly about what needed to be done.

"Thank you very much for giving me some of your time. But this was clearly a mistake and now I must leave," the policeman said, which jolted Pippard back to life.

Should he force him to stay?

"You do realise that you have to tell me who else knows about the contents of this letter."

"Of course we have tried to limit the number of people in the know. But as I said . . . I must go now."

Corell felt defeated and therefore he smiled. This fixed smile had always been one of his defence mechanisms, and it was not at all a bad trick to use in the critical phase of a power struggle. Pippard seemed to interpret it as a sign of strength: "You seem satisfied."

What should he say? He resorted to a slight trick. "You wouldn't happen to have an umbrella you could lend me?" and in any other situation he would have been proud of what he had said. It was astonishingly cheeky. It was a piece of gallows humour, and it worked. Pippard just muttered and Corell saw his chance. He made for the door.

"A very pleasant evening to you in that case," he said, feeling curiously detached, and he did get some sort of reply.

He did not hear what it was. He opened the door and fled out onto the stairs, where the darkness seemed to snatch at him. But once he was out in the street he felt refreshed by the rain and started walking in the direction of the trumpet player. He thought he could hear her tunes from far away, but it must have been his imagination because, when he got there, there was no-one blowing a trumpet, just an empty, damp pavement and then the rain beating in from the side.

28

THE MORNING AFTER his visit to Pippard, Corell lay in bed in the hotel on Drummer Street, his eyes tracing the stripes on the yellow wallpaper, as if they had got lost in the labyrinth on the walls, and he could not bring himself to get out of bed until lunchtime, but he never checked out as he had meant to. He left the luggage where it was and went out into the crowd. The weather was beautiful. It was the day before the big solar eclipse and he saw kites soaring in the sky and loving couples in the streets, but that did not cheer him up. He felt excluded from the life around him, and he was thinking about Alan Turing. He must surely have reached the end of his journey. He was not going to get much further and the most sensible thing would be just to return home, and yet . . .

As if driven by forces beyond himself, he went to King's College and the library archive, where he once again read "Computable Numbers" and a paper entitled "Systems of Logic Based on Ordinals," of which he understood very little. He enjoyed the sounds of rasping pens and pages being turned and the embarrassed coughing, but the feeling of unease never left him. Not even his daydreams, however enticing he made them, could dispel the misgivings which had been pursuing him since the meeting with Pippard. He imagined Ross or Hamersley's conversation with Pippard and the talk of dismissal and sanctions, but he also saw himself as a vagrant drunk in Wilmslow, who dumped rubbish and bottles in the yard at the police station, and he thought of death, death as a poisoned apple, a bubbling saucepan and a train racing through the night. On his way back to the hotel he bought eight bottles of Mackeson's milk stout and drank them in his room, so that instead of worrying he now felt sorry for himself. It all became very sad!

He had not only chosen to forgo love. He had turned his back on friendship. The few friends he had, had vanished, not all at once, not even one by one, but so slowly that he had hardly noticed it. The decline had been so gradual as to be almost imperceptible and, he thought, he had barely even been living, he had just been plodding on joylessly, and now that for once he had launched himself into something, it had all gone wrong.

He turned on the radio in the room. A voice was talking about a coup in Guatemala. He turned it off and for a while just stood motionless in the middle of the room, swaying a little and a touch drunk, and then he started to walk, back and forth, past the bed, the wash basin, the coat stand. He got into such a state that he started to fantasise that people could see him from the street and that they thought he was someone about to take a crucial decision, or make a major discovery . . . So you know about Alan Turing? I handled the investigation into his death. You could even say that it got my career off to a flying start. A very sad story, of course, he was homosexual, you know, but very clever, he laid the foundations for the programmable data machine, a machine which . . . I see, you know all about it. Well, there's been a lot of talk about it. In that case you may also know that I myself have contributed some improvements. They occurred to me as I was reading his paper at King's College. It was in June 1954, a dreadfully wet summer—do you remember it? Roger Bannister set that fantastic record in the mile. There was a solar eclipse at the end of June . . . you saw it, then, how interesting. For my own part I had just met Julius Pippard, I'm sure you won't have heard the name, he was completely insignificant, his scientific efforts were a total failure, he was also very unpleasant, a boor . . . that probably sounds a bit harsh. I certainly wouldn't want to kick a man when he's down. But you understand, Mr. Pippard caused me rather a lot of trouble. He rang my boss. There was a frightful to-do—although perhaps I should be grateful to him. It was thanks to him that I left the police . . . oh yes, I agree with you, it's honest, good work, but I didn't find it stimulating enough. Yes of course, things are different now, now I hardly have time for anything. Thank you, thank you . . . it was nice to hear that you value my contributions. Good luck to you too . . . and remember, you get nothing for free in this world, there was a time, you see, when I was completely desperate, I paced up and down in a hotel room, I dreamed that . . .

He interrupted his thoughts and went out again without knowing where he was going. From the pub with a blue awning across the street he could hear the jukebox playing David Whitfield's "*Cara mia*, why must we say goodbye?," and he looked up at the sky. It was overcast and chilly and the day was drawing to a close, but he felt better and for a moment he even forgot his paranoia, which was an irony of fate because if he had taken a closer look, inside the pub, he would have seen a hefty man with a birthmark on his forehead, and this gentleman, Arthur Mulland, a low-ranking official at G.C.H.Q., now got to his feet and followed Corell into St. Andrews Street, where the Roman Catholic church rose in the background.

Corell would not even have needed to be especially observant because, just as Turing had written in his letter, Mulland was not good at blending into a crowd. With his coarse build and waddling walk he was far too conspicuous and often he did not even bother to keep out of sight. The years had made him tired and careless. His instructions were also unclear: "See what he's up to," and he himself did not really think there was much point in it. But times were now such that everything had to be checked out and Arthur Mulland was only doing his job, to a certain extent as a form of protest because in some ways he was like Corell. They both wandered on, full of mutinous thoughts, and neither of them had slept well, or was particularly sober. Although Mulland was married and had three children, he felt as lonely as Corell, and did not understand why he had become so moody and edgy of late. He realised that his drinking must have something to do with it. Periods of abstinence came and went. Sometimes he was cured and it was a painful process, with his nerves alternately laid bare or soothed. He was an expert in the subject. He would hold forth in learned terms about what particular type of alcohol was needed for this or that spiritual ailment. But he knew nothing about other aspects of the convolutions of his brain, and these surveillance tasks did not make things any better. All this waiting outside doors and windows gnawed away at him, and often he felt a rage against those he was meant to be watching. He would never forget the supercilious looks he got from the homosexual in Wilmslow, and he was not happy about the policeman digging around in the case, or whatever it was that he was doing. Mulland looked at his watch. It was half past six, and whether the person he was following was dodgy or not, he was definitely wearing far too expensive a suit and now the man went into a pub, the Regal it was called, and Mulland waited outside, taking sips from his silver-coloured hip-flask.

Corell ordered a lager of the same foreign brand that Krause had asked for in Wilmslow, and the images from Adlington Road, not just the external ones, came back to him as he was drinking. He remembered his inappropriate thoughts on the staircase and the memories of his father, and the fantasies about the evil night train, and he saw the mathematician before him, dead in his narrow bed with froth around his mouth, and suddenly he found it so strange. Turing had been thinking, and then he had not thought anymore. A world had vanished, a questioning intellect . . . In his article in *Mind*, Turing said that our consciousness was situated somewhere in our brain, but how are we supposed to find it? How is anything meant to be able to locate itself? How does a riddle solve itself? How can the liar's paradox escape its own contradiction?

Corell closed his eyes and tried to feel with which part of his brain he was thinking—it seemed to him to be in a place far back in his head—but he pushed the thought aside, it was nonsense, and before he had even finished his drink he paid and hurried out. It was raining again. Where was he to go? He decided just to stroll along, but after a few metres he stopped. Was there someone standing behind him? No, he must have been mistaken. There was no-one there and nowhere to go, no alley, no door to slip into. I'm imagining things, he thought, and he was. Arthur Mulland was twenty metres away, hidden by a group of tourists near St. Andrew's church, but of course Corell was also right, and now he quickened his pace. Over by King's Parade he greeted some students, just as an experiment, and they nodded back, and he tried to think a positive thought or two—such as *Here I am, Leonard Corell, walking along and pondering the paradox of consciousness*—but it wasn't very successful and then he turned around again, gripped by a new feeling of unease. It was the first time that he caught sight of Mulland. The official was close to him now, and Corell wondered something like: That's a big fellow, and aren't his trousers too short? But the thought disappeared and even though he noticed the birthmark on the forehead he did not connect it to the description in the letter, and why should he? He had not given a thought to the man in the letter for a long time. Besides, the birthmark looked nothing like a sigma. It was just an ordinary red birthmark which the man had been ashamed of when he was a boy.

Not until he was well into his thirties had Mulland stopped wearing a long conspicuous fringe, and even then it wasn't voluntary. Because he was beginning to go bald, it was no longer possible to wear his hair like that, and over the years he had developed something of an aversion to people with thick hair. The policeman had thick hair. He was young and well dressed. Women cast curious glances at him, and Mulland, who didn't get any friendly looks, decided to take a quick sip. But his hip-flask was empty and the rain was falling. It was always raining when he was out on assignment, and he glared with some anger at the policeman standing by the entrance to King's Chapel. The policeman was looking thoughtful.

Organ music could be heard, and the singing of a choir. Corell was drawn to the warmth and the glow and the smell of incense inside there, but like a steadfast atheist resisting a religious impulse he turned down towards the river, and crossed over a bridge, and that was more or less where he started to shake. It could have been the rain, or the alcohol or even a premonition, and he made for the more deserted footpaths. It would have been useful for him to have had people around him because it was in no way inevitable that he would be beaten up. In England they don't even assault convicted spies, so why beat to a pulp an ordinary policeman who had simply managed to put two and two together? There was no reason at all for it, except that Mulland was annoyed with the policeman and life in general and that he felt insulted: once again he was having to keep an eye on one of these unreliable people who had no respect for the nation's secrets, and he remembered all the excitement at Cheltenham over suspected leaks, and that excitement in some way gave legitimacy to his anger.

A bushy orange cat ran past and prompted very different reactions in

Corell and Mulland. Mulland wanted to kick it whilst the policeman not only longed to stroke its back, he also wanted to press it against his face, like a comforting teddy bear, and just as he was passing a bench and a large tree a twig snapped behind him. A shiver ran through his body. He became frightened. Yet he did not turn around, not then. He kept walking. What did he hear? The rain, of course, the wind in the leaves, and then the steps. They were just behind him now and considering how slowly Corell was walking, they should have passed him. It was probably nothing to worry about. And yet . . . the weight of the footsteps and the breathing, which seemed too heavy for someone moving at such a slow pace, increased his fear. Should he turn around? He did not have time. The steps behind him speeded up, and now Corell spun around and saw the man for the second time, still oblivious to the fact that the birthmark was a clue, a link to another context, and his only clear thought was that he was in trouble.

Yet Mulland had no intention whatsoever of hurting anyone. He had made sure that they were alone and wondered if he should strike up a conversation, and even that would have been against his instructions, but violence? Never! That would put him in a very difficult position, but still, something in Corell's face, his frightened look, his fine features, his youth accentuated by the fear, and then the words, "I don't have any money!" provoked Mulland. *Did that idiot think he was going to rob him?*

"I'm a policeman," the man said.

"Some policeman."

"What do you mean?"

"Well, running around leaking like a sieve."

"What are you talking about?"

Corell did not understand. The meeting with Pippard came to his mind, but something in him refused to link that to this lunatic standing in front of him. He seemed much too brutal for mathematics and riddles, he gave the appearance of being a real thug, and that in itself made the danger seem greater. Mulland felt belittled. He could see the fear in Corell's eyes, and as he stepped forward, emitting a whiff of stale breath, the policeman screwed up his face in disgust and terror and that is when it happened. Mulland saw red. He shoved the policeman in the chest and, as Corell reeled, he shoved him a second time, harder than before.

Corell only just managed to keep his balance. And yet, as he was teetering, he managed to register a number of details; one of the man's eyes seemed larger than the other, his teeth were yellow, and he had a double chin, but more than anything Corell noticed the birthmark, and that gave him a feeling of déjà vu, not that he yet made the connection to the letter. But it put him on his guard.

Like a feinting football player Corell skipped from side to side and, when he spotted an opening, he ran past the man but, right by a stone which was to become stained with his blood, Mulland caught up, to some extent conscious of the insane or even ludicrous way he was behaving. Yet there was no hope now that he would leave Corell alone. In his over-excited state Mulland had started to see a threat, even an actual security risk, and briefly it was as if Turing and the policeman merged into one in his mind and that perhaps exacerbated his rage. He grabbed hold of Corell and pulled him down onto the grass, feeling increasingly humiliated in his anger and his clumsiness.

It was clear even then that the absurdity of the situation was part of its danger. Not far from the Eucharist being celebrated in King's College's venerable chapel, Arthur Mulland, father of three, was crawling around in the shrubbery like a brawling schoolboy, and when he discovered, while struggling to get Corell onto his back, that his knees had become filthy he became even more furious, not because he cared about his trousers, but because the grass stains reminded him of how vulnerable he had been as a child. He had admittedly become more and more moody with the years, but that was why he was obsessed with maintaining his dignity and when he failed to do that his outbursts were even more extreme. He became senseless with rage.

All his disappointments, all the inadequacies he saw in himself, all his competing urges and duties, came together in a pure destructive burst of energy, and he struck again and again, first with his open hand while he still had some sense in him, then with his fists and at last, when Corell spat in his face, he pounded the policeman's head against the stone, somehow fully accepting that he was beating to pieces not only Corell but also his own life, and actually it was strange that he could keep going for so long. They were not far from the river and the footpath, but Mulland was certainly helped by the rain. Few people were out. The city lay quiet. The crowns of the trees hung over the river and thunder was rumbling in the distance. The only surprising part of the soundscape came from two young girls singing Schubert's "Ave Maria" far away. To Corell they sounded like heavenly voices from a dying world, while for Mulland it was just a distant irritation, and it's true that the girls' voices were not trained or even serious. There was irony in the song, but when Mulland woke up out of his fury, and with increasing surprise looked at his coarse hands and the blood which trickled out of the policeman's dark curly hair, the singing voices became an alarm clock, a siren song from a better world.

What had he done?

The blood also seemed to be draining from his own body, and he resisted an impulse to lie down on the ground next to the policeman, and he wanted to pray or to hit himself, but he did nothing, nothing other than pant heavily. Hitting so hard and frenziedly had deprived him of all strength and, without thinking, he listened for the song. It was gone and, even though it had irritated him just then, he missed it now. He was of course afraid that someone would find them; at the same time he had a desperate longing for company and he thought—he did not know why—of a pretty little ebony box which he had found in a small back street in Ankara, and which he sometimes used to stroke with his fingertips, but he could not find comfort anywhere.

He got to his feet and walked away in the darkness.

29

THE NEXT DAY THERE WAS an air of heightened expectation not only in Great Britain but in many parts of the world. A total eclipse of the sun was to reach its totality at 1:29 p.m. local time in England, and millions of people were getting ready with glass blackened with soot and strips of exposed film. People said that no less a person than Galileo had ruined his eyes by staring at a solar eclipse without protecting them. Sunglasses were not enough, the newspapers wrote, and many wondered—as if these warnings triggered some sort of compulsive urge—if they really would be able to resist the temptation to gaze directly at the darkening sun.

Many experienced a heightened feeling for life. There was a sense of occasion about Cambridge, and a number of people found it hard to concentrate on their studies. Others were not at all affected by the excitement. Certain of them were fortunate enough to be so absorbed by their intellectual pursuits that they paid no attention at all to the celestial attractions. Some had missed it all, which was an achievement in itself. There was continuous coverage of events in the newspapers and on the radio and the increasingly popular television. There was gossip and chatter on the streets and in the squares. But one should never underestimate how selective the human mind can be. People often miss what is right in front of their eyes. They only see what they are used to seeing. Generally speaking, we are unprepared for major change, and even in Cambridge more than one person was surprised by the darkness.

Others who were more snobbish or who had an inclination to be contrary, of the sort which the finer university cities produce in especially large numbers, saw it as their duty to ignore what everybody else was interested in. According to them—even if there were variations in the argument—an independent human being ought to shun such hysteria. After all, a solar eclipse is no more than a shadow, and should concern no-one besides astronomers and poets. When everyone else is looking up, one is better off looking down or to one side. What matters is to stand out, not just so as to make oneself interesting, although that was of course an important part of the attitude, but because these people thought that only those who stand to one side discover what their contemporaries overlook. Great talents have no time for mass psychosis.

Some were too gloomy or ill to bother, while others were just so irritated that they ignored the whole spectacle. Oscar Farley was one of them. He sat on his ergonomic chair—which had lately been installed— at his desk in Cheltenham, and put down the receiver with a theatrical gesture designed to show an invisible audience how displeased he was. Farley had from the very first been opposed to having the young policeman followed. He had said that it was a lot of nonsense. But he had been outvoted, and had reluctantly conceded. If they were to be able to prevent and discover new leaks they really had to focus on what was essential. Of course, of course, the policeman might well have been a chancer, a crook, but to send Mulland after him, no. Mulland was not stable . . . Farley could not understand why he enjoyed so much support in the firm. Just the state he got himself into over Turing's leanings had struck him as unhealthy—moral indignation was the last thing Farley wanted to see in a surveillance report, but more than anything it was the telephone call. It was not just the failure. Blunders were part of the job. It was the tone and the details, or rather their absence, and with a grim expression Farley rose to his feet and went out into the corridor. It was still early and he was not sure that Robert Somerset had arrived. Since his divorce, Robert had been in the habit of arriving late and leaving late, but yes, Robert was sitting in his room with a cup of coffee. His face lit up when Farley came in.

"Hello Oscar. Look at these." Somerset put on a funny pair of spectacles, which made him look like some sort of a parody of a secret agent. "Specially made for the eclipse."

"Mulland rang from Cambridge."

"Could you give me a moment to myself? I'm having a cup of coffee."

"He's lost the policeman," Farley said.

"Clumsy of him. Was he drunk?"

"I don't know. But he claims that Pippard was right, and that there's something fishy about the policeman."

"Strange how Pippard and Mulland seem to have become great pals all of a sudden."

"Yes, handy, isn't it?"

"Your back seems better. Did you try that exercise I showed you?"

"Mulland says that the policeman deliberately shook him off; that he realised he was being followed."

"And you don't believe that?"

"He said other things as well. He said that there was someone else following the policeman, a younger man with Slav features and something brutal about his face. Mulland gave a description of him."

"Sounds strange."

"It did sound strange."

"So he was making it up?"

"Either that or he was making too much of what he saw."

"What are you going to do?"

"I'm going there. Corell doesn't appear to have checked out from his hotel, so he should turn up there sooner or later."

"I assume you'll take along something decent to read."

"I'll take your specs. They look better on me," Farley said in a light tone, and put them on.

Somerset did not seem to be amused.

"So it's not that someone is trying to make contact with the policeman?"

"It could be just about anything. But I don't feel very comfortable letting Mulland and Pippard handle it."

"Pippard has been incredibly zealous."

"Zealous," Farley snorted, and took off the spectacles.

"And focused."

"We've all been so bloody focused and zealous that we've gone crazy as a result," he sneered, and walked out of the room to go back and sit down at his desk again.

Zealous and crazy . . . Ever since Burgess and Maclean disappeared, the mood had become increasingly hysterical, and that was quite understandable. There could be a third, a fourth and a fifth spy out there—possibly that bloody man Philby who had after all known about Bletchley and who had had Burgess living with him in Washington—and it was, no question, of paramount importance that they be caught, and that no more unreliable characters should be admitted into the inner sanctum. But it was just as clear that the suspicions had poisoned people and got them to chase after everybody who was different and unconventional: Was there not a lynch-mob mentality in all this smouldering unease? Farley had seen a rage at the firm which scared him and more than ever he wanted to get away from it all. Yet he packed a small bag into which he slipped a book of Yeats's poems and a freshly ironed white shirt which had been hanging in his room for a few days.

Then he asked Claire to book him a train ticket to Cambridge.

"I won't be away for long," he said.

Mulland was sitting in his hotel room, drinking from his hip-flask. It was just as well that Farley could not see him. Not even the drinking stopped his hands from shaking and he reeked of alcohol and sweat. He was pale and shrunken. Yet he was not about to give up. "These are dangerous times," he muttered, as if the assault had been no more than a necessary battle, part of a crusade, and all the time he was trying to find a way out of the mess he had got himself into. During the course of the night he had worked out the lies that he had told Farley. He knew that they had their shortcomings and that the description of the fictitious follower—*Slav features and brutal*—was a bit too obvious, not just because of the reference to the Russian menace. It also laid him open to other accusations, but he thought that it was good enough, or maybe even quite clever. He thought about Pippard. Pippard became a lifeline, a hope. *Julius will sort this out.* Mulland was not seeing very clearly at all, and when images from the evening before welled up, he contemplated them as if from a distance, as if they did not concern him.

After the assault he had felt a short period of relief, as if all the pent-up rage inside him had at last found an outlet, but it was a deceptive feeling, an illusion of calm. Panic had set its claws into him, and so far as he could recall he had barely looked at the policeman. He had just understood that things were bad and had looked away, and therefore his clearest memory was not of Corell but of his own bloodied hands and the rain falling on them and then the realisation that he had to get away. He had staggered off and roamed around the city until at last he had recovered his senses and returned to the hotel, where he washed his entire body and fell into a deep but short sleep.

God Almighty, what had he done? He stood up. He sat down again. He drank mouthful after mouthful, sometimes water, sometimes whisky, and thought that he ought to ring Irene, his wife, to tell her that all was well, but that was idiotic. Nothing was well and for the last few years their relationship had been lousy. Something like this obviously had to happen for him to be overcome by such sentimentality, and he let his thoughts stray to his sons—especially to Bill, who had begun to study medicine—and he tried to recall their faces, but it was all hopeless. He kept seeing the policeman with his slanting eyes instead. *Could he still be lying there? Could he . . . ?* Mulland picked up the telephone and asked the operator to put him through to Hotel Hamlet in Drummer Street. When a man's voice answered he hung up, feeling ill at ease. *No, no, he can't be there, he must . . .* He flew up and looked at himself in the mirror; at first he was horrified—*Christ, I look awful!*—then not altogether dissatisfied. He wiped the sweat off his upper lip, tidied up his thinning hair and smiled artlessly as if trying to fool himself as well. Then he rushed out into the city and made for King's College. But he slowed down. *What's the hurry?* and when he saw a sign in Market Street for the Regency Café, and realised that it was a simple place, a working-class café of the sort that he had not expected to find here in this elegant city, he stopped and ordered a pot of tea and an egg sandwich. *I must calm down first!*

Oscar Farley sat on the train and even though he tried to read his Yeats—Yeats was the reassuring landscape that he kept returning to—his thoughts were alive, and the longer the train journey went on, the more they dwelt on Turing. It was not so long ago that the mathematician had been sitting opposite him in Cheltenham and said in his stuttering, resigned voice:

"So you don't trust me anymore."

"Of course we do. It's just that . . ."

It's just that . . . what? Farley did not remember what his answer was—presumably he had got tangled up in some lengthy excuse—but it had been painful. He and Alan went back a long way. Farley had been one of the people who had recruited him to Bletchley. Already back then they were looking for mathematicians and scientists rather than linguists and classicists, and a number of independent tips had come in from the old network in Cambridge about Alan, the young man who had solved the *Entscheidungsproblem*, and who had studied at Princeton and of his own volition taken an interest in cryptology. They knew that he was a good recruit to have. But no-one could have imagined . . . Farley remembered the first time he had noticed Alan at Bletchley. It was in the ballroom of the mansion which at the time was already being used as a hub and command centre. There was a group sitting on the sofas and drinking. It must have been during the autumn of 1939, but they were in high spirits in spite of how the war was going. He himself was almost happy. Bridget was there too. They had just become a couple, but since they were both married they were playing their charade, pretending that they did not know each other, and that just heightened the passion between them. Ever since he was a young man Farley had been the life and soul of any social gathering. He always saw to it that no-one was left out or ignored. He assumed a sort of fatherly responsibility for every conversation, and therefore soon discovered that Alan Turing grew quiet and sat uncomfortably in his chair whenever the discussion took a lighthearted turn. People laughed, and so did Alan, but just a little bit late, like a boy who hadn't got the joke, but wanted to pretend that he had. He seemed lost and embarrassed, and Bridget—who must have been thinking along the same lines—asked politely:

"Forgive me, Dr. Turing, but what were you working on at Cambridge?"

"I . . ." he started. "I was looking into some simple questions about . . ."

Then he locked up. Not one word passed his lips. He just got to his feet and disappeared out, and at the time no-one understood why. But soon they would all come to realise that when Alan did not think that people understood what he was working on he could not say a word, and that could of course be taken for snobbishness, for arrogance, but he probably just could not cope with people who were too far removed from his world. He had no understanding of women whatsoever. His eyes would look down when they went past. He would chain his tea mug to a radiator so as not to lose it, he kept on mislaying things and he dressed eccentrically. But at the time, the things that were different about him were considered a part of his talents. That was before . . . Farley looked out of the train window and as he saw Cambridge approaching, he felt a stab of longing. Cambridge was his real home. How wonderful it would be if he were not here for work! As he rose from his seat his back started to hurt. He swore and stepped down onto the platform. It was getting close to one in the afternoon. There was not much time until the eclipse and the city was already coming to a halt.

Mulland was in a state of high excitement and heading in the same direction as Farley. His whole body exuded tension, but there was a clearer look in his eyes now. So much had happened to him. After his breakfast on Market Street he had rushed into King's College—utterly unaware of how out of place he looked—and continued down to the place where he had assaulted Corell. As he approached it, he had slowed his steps, and caught his breath. He was expecting it to be painful, and some part of him realised that he was a culprit returning to the scene of his crime, but he was unprepared for the physical discomfort that he felt, and if it had not been for the fact that he had become obsessed with this idea during the early hours he would doubtless have turned around. Instead he kept going. He found it odd that he remembered the surroundings so vividly. Every bush and tree seemed strangely familiar, as if the fury and madness had in fact sharpened his senses, and he remembered the trumpet he had heard and the girls' "Ave Maria" and the thoughts that had gone through his mind. He understood at that moment that he would not find anything. The place looked shockingly innocent. There was no body there. Nor had anything been left behind. Not until he looked closer did he see blood on the stone and the loosened earth. A cat could be heard—was it the same one as yesterday?—but there . . . In the grass by the side of the path lay a simple small notepad without covers. He picked it up and flinched when he noticed a stain on the front page which he thought was blood. Shamefaced and glancing furtively from side to side, he put it away in his inside pocket and then turned back towards the fountain and the chapel. In the end he could contain himself no longer.

He sat down on a bench opposite the entrance to King's College and leafed through the notepad. One of the first things he saw was the name *Fredric Krause* which was underlined twice. There was something about the name that got him worked up. *The most important thing isn't the machines but the instructions to them.* What did that mean? *How can contradictions be a weapon for life and death? How can the liar's paradox be a sword in a war?* Further on in the notepad he saw the words *code breaking* and *Bletchley* and then an argument about how the ability to make mistakes was a precondition for intelligence. *Is that why Turing lets the machine make mistakes in its test?*

It would be an exaggeration to say that Mulland understood what he had found, but in his excitement he became convinced that this was a crucial document, something which might even justify his assault and for a long time he wandered back and forth until he found a telephone box. Nervously he dug a few pennies out of his pocket and gave the operator Pippard's direct number.

"It's Mulland."

"What's going on?" Pippard said.

"You were right about the policeman. I have proof. I've got his secret notepad."

He knew that it sounded contrived and that the word *secret* was far-fetched in the context.

"What are you talking about?" Pippard said. "Somerset said that you had lost him. Farley's on his way to Cambridge."

"Is he? Where's he going?"

"Where? I have no idea. I imagine he's going to the hotel where Mr. Corell is staying. Surely the policeman will turn up there sooner or later."

Mulland said that was possible. He did not like the fact that Farley was coming here, and tried rather casually to say something convincing about the man with the Slav features who was supposed to have followed the policeman. He seemed not to be succeeding and so he blurted out the name Fredric Krause as a way of luring Pippard into changing the subject.

"Does that ring any bells with you?" he asked.

"Oh yes, very much so."

"Who is it?"

"An acquaintance from the war," Pippard said.

"Krause seems to have been the policeman's contact. He's underlined his name on the notepad."

"What are you saying?"

"I'll tell you more later. I've got to go now."

"No, no . . . you must explain. Don't you see?"

"I don't have the time."

"But for God's sake, man! What's the hurry?"

"I have to find the policeman."

"I thought he'd disappeared?"

"Well . . . yes, but I think I know where I can find him," Mulland lied.

"O.K., O.K. Track him down then and make sure he stays in Cambridge! It's essential that we get to speak to him! Not that I have any idea what you're drivelling on about. But Fredric Krause, Jesus . . . if it's as you say, that really does worry me."

"Krause doesn't sound English."

"Precisely."

I knew it, raced through Mulland's mind.

"I'll be in touch," he said, and although he could hear Pippard saying something more, he hung up and hurried away. After ten metres he stopped, and stood still for a second or two, swaying backwards and forwards. Then he went back to the telephone box. He took out a new coin and asked the operator to put him through to the Hotel Hamlet. It took a long time. For God's sake . . . it was only a local call. Surely that couldn't be so difficult? He had to put in another fourpence and when at last he was connected he asked to speak to Mr. Corell and even though apprehension flickered in his mind he did not for one second imagine that the policeman would be there. He just thought that making the call would be therapeutic for him. But the man's voice on the telephone hesitated and sounded strange. *Did he know . . . ?*

"I don't know."

"What?"

"He's asked not to be disturbed."

"Just put me through. It's important."

"Has something happened?"

"Let me talk to him," Mulland said, and he heard the ringtone echo again and again, and in the end he could stand it no longer.

Excitedly he rushed out of the telephone box and raced off at great speed, in contrast to everything else in the city—the people around him were standing surprisingly still—but he did not dwell too much on that. Pippard's words rang in his ears, *if it's as you say, that really does worry me,* and Mulland muttered to himself: "I was right, wasn't I?"

30

THE TELEPHONE RANG. Corell wanted to answer but did not have the strength, and all he could do was open his hand pathetically as if expecting someone to put the receiver in it. Then he sank back into his daze again. There was blood and earth on the pillowcase. A checked shirt was wound around his head. His eyes and cheeks looked black and bruised and swollen out of shape. If someone had asked him at that moment what had happened, he would have said that he did not know, that he had perhaps just fallen out of bed and hurt himself, and maybe that it was good that it was getting dark because he wanted to sleep. He needed to curl up and nurse the pain in his ribcage and forehead, and he might have succeeded in doing that if he hadn't noticed something: a stillness, a silence which spread over the city, and for some reason he thought of his mother. She used to try to tell her fortune by dropping molten tin into water over the fireplace in Southport, a surprisingly pleasant memory not just because of what had happened but also given how he used to think of her, but the recollection faded away.

The shadow outside swept all too quickly across the sky and he became frightened and confused, he even sniffed as if to make sure that the stench of bitter almonds had not crept in here too, and he felt a closeness in the air, but he could not work out what it was. Then he realised that the cars, birds and people had fallen silent, not gradually as in the evening but as if at a given signal, and then he understood: it was the eclipse, and bit by bit it all started to come back to him. He remembered the rain.

He recalled being assaulted and lying in the grass and thinking that his life was draining out of him. Later in the night he had got up and been sick over a bush. He had hawked and coughed up blood and been conscious, as if it were a matter of life and death, that he must not move his head. But he kept on walking, driven by an instinctive need to get home—home to the hotel. At one point he ran into some late-night revellers who insisted on helping him, but he turned them down firmly. Like a wounded animal he wanted to be left alone with his injuries, and when he got back—how on earth did he manage to find his way?—there was no-one at the reception. He opened the door to his room with the key which was still in his pocket and fell into bed, or to be more accurate, he drank some water first and wrapped the shirt around his head, but then . . . Most of it was as if shrouded in mist. He felt dreadfully sick, and there were moments when he must have been hallucinating. When the cleaning lady knocked on his door he hissed that he did not want to be disturbed—why had he done that?—and so she muttered something and disappeared. He had a feeling that she would be back. He wanted her to come back. He needed help. Now that his thoughts were clearer he felt tremendously sorry for himself, and he ran his hand over the shirt on his head, he could feel the scab under it and he thought: It's bad, isn't it? He was in pain. He was stiff and with squinting eyes he looked out of the window . . . *The whole world is united in experiencing this great event together, and I'm lying here. So unfortunate, I who have read* . . . He saw himself sitting at King's College, and imagined some admirer coming up to him . . . *Not so loud, sir. I see, I see, thank you for the compliment, mathematics is like music to me* . . . he had not entirely recovered his senses, but slowly the events came back to him and he remembered Pippard and the letter; my God, the letter. His hand went to his inside pocket, and he dug around nervously, but yes indeed, it was there, all the pages seemed to be intact, and he was tempted to read it again. But his notepad? Where was that? His hands searched all over his body, but no, no pad. He glanced towards the bedside table and his suitcase. The pad was nowhere to be seen and that dismayed him. He recalled the man who had beaten him. What sort of person was he, and why had he attacked him of all people? He'd had a birthmark on his forehead, and his trousers were too short . . . it must be the man from Turing's letter . . . all at once that much was clear to Corell. But his thoughts were interrupted.

He heard steps in the corridor. It must be the cleaning lady. Maybe she has a doctor with her, he thought. That would be good. There was a knock on the door. It was louder than he had expected.

Farley was in a terrible mood, and his back hurt. Shafts of pain radiated from the small of his back to his neck, and he surprised people on the streets not just with his height, but with his head which was leaning to the left because his body was so stiff, making him look as if he were struggling to see some remote point way up high. In actual fact he was hardly even looking at the sky. He was engrossed in his pain and when he did look up at the eclipse it was with the impatience of someone irritated by a change in the weather. As he walked into Drummer Street he saw the entrails of a dead animal, and even though he quickly looked away, it upset him. The carcass made him feel uneasier still, even the brightening light and the waking world failed to improve his mood. He thought about Pippard. He was sure Pippard could not be right! Pippard was an idiot. Could the policeman really have found out so much, and was it even conceivable that he was passing information on to mysterious people? And then Mulland: *a man with Slav features was following Corell!* No, no!

It was true that Farley had been puzzled by Corell from the outset, because he was so full of contradictions and because of his astounding show of cheek and authority outside the courthouse in Wilmslow. He might also have been a bit unpredictable, and felt that he had some scores to settle. To some extent it ran in the family, they had talked about that at the office yesterday. Both his father and his aunt were said to be subversive elements, yes indeed Farley had thought, rather nice people in other words. If only you knew how much rubbish I think you talk. But of course, if you added it all together, you could not help feeling a bit worried. What was that letter, for example, and why had the policeman kept it to himself? He started to walk faster, and at one stage he thought that he saw Mulland some way off, but he was probably mistaken, and in any case he was deep in his thoughts.

Rumour had it that Mulland had gone off the rails once at a race meeting at York. It was said that he had been seen crying when the horse he had backed fell at the last bend, and that he had later laid into some poor devil who had asked what was the matter with him. No-one had bothered to investigate what had happened—it was said to have been very much exaggerated—and that was obviously a mistake. Sentimentality and violence were not a good combination. Besides, Mulland drank too much. Why did he of all people get away without an internal investigation? Was it because he had Pippard's blessing and because he parroted all the accepted views?

Farley looked at the street number and found the hotel, a simple place he had never heard of and which did not even have an awning. From the outside it looked like a residence, and inside the décor was shabby and rather uninviting. On the walls were photographs of actors who had played the role of Hamlet, including Laurence Olivier who was pressing a grey skull almost lovingly against his cheek, and immediately to the right of the entrance was a large pot plant which looked in need of water, but there was nobody in the lobby. Farley rang a silver-coloured bell on the front desk.

"For God's sake!"

Nobody came, not even at that, and he rang again and had the absurd feeling that the place had long since been abandoned. It took a few minutes for a young man in a white shirt and black waistcoat, and with a large gap between his teeth, to come running in from the street. There was something touching about him, something gawky and awkward.

"Sorry, sorry. I was looking at the eclipse. Fantastic, isn't it?"

"I suppose it is."

"What can I do for you, sir?" he said.

"I would like to see Mr. Corell."

"You too?"

"What do you mean?"

"I just met a man on the street who absolutely wanted to speak to him."

"So Mr. Corell is in?"

"I believe so. He wasn't answering his telephone, but he spoke to the cleaning lady. He asked . . ."

"Which room is he in?"

It was 26, and although there was an old lift and his back was sore, Farley took the stairs. He thought it would be quicker. The information that someone else wanted to speak to the policeman made him nervous. He did not know what exactly it was that was worrying him, but he was beginning to fear that the policeman really had done something unforgivable. That would be such a setback, wouldn't it? He hated it when people like Pippard were proved right for the wrong reasons—or perhaps, he should say, when unsound attitudes yielded the right results, and for some reason he thought of Alan, Alan stroking his silver ingot in the forest.

It was surprisingly dark up on the second floor. Had a light broken? The wall-to-wall carpet was brown and frayed. He got the feeling that he was walking along a prison corridor, but then he stopped, and he probably tensed, or he made a careless movement. There was a stab of pain in his shoulder blade, and he groaned: "God!" Yet his attention was caught by something else. He heard a sound like a sigh, and although it was not loud or even dramatic it made him feel uncomfortable, he did not know why—perhaps it was just his nerves—but now something else could be heard; an agitated whispering, and a thud and as Farley speeded up his steps he became convinced that something serious was happening, and he started to jangle the keys in his pocket nervously and loudly.

31

CORELL HAD LOCKED the door when he staggered into the hotel room that night. So it was no good shouting "Come in!"; he had to open the door himself. But he barely had the strength to get up. He was feeling sick, and it was as if his body were crying out: Lie still! And yet he needed to get up. He had to take a drink and go to the toilet. He might as well try. But God, it was hard. Everything was swimming before his eyes and his head felt heavy.

"I'm coming. I'm coming!"

With an immense effort he stood up and kept his balance. He saw it as a minor triumph and moved forward in a crouch. The street was waking up again to its hustle and bustle. Birds and people were coming back to life, and he tried to take pleasure in that, but the light was hurting him.

"Who is it?" he said.

He did not catch any answer. He had to focus his full attention on walking and to the extent that he wondered at all who was knocking, he thought it was the cleaning lady or the porter, or a doctor who had been called. It did not occur to him that the cleaning lady had never seen him. If he was worried about anything, then it was whether he would manage to get as far as the door. That alone struck him as a risky undertaking. His head spun even more and he thought: *I'm not going to make it,* but he battled on and discovered to his relief that the key was in the door. But the lock was stubborn and he had no strength in his hands. Give it another go! And then it worked. He opened the door and prepared to stage a dramatic little collapse—he wanted to show what a sorry state he was in—but there was no cleaning lady or anyone else from the hotel out there. Someone very different was standing in front of him, smelling of sweat and alcohol.

Mulland had his orders: he was to see to it that the policeman stayed in Cambridge. Besides, he wanted to get to him before Oscar Farley and give his version of events first. He was obsessed with the need to sort the situation out and turn it to his advantage. Over and over again he looked at the notepad in his hand as if it were a fantastic trump card. But as the sky darkened and the people around him watched in rapt attention, his spirits sank and he saw the policeman before him in various different guises, even one which appeared to be Corell as ghost, and he started to feel hunted. Time seemed to be running away and he rushed on, as if there were no turning back. For a long time he did not notice what was going on around him. A young man was standing outside Hotel Hamlet, holding a piece of soot-blackened glass in front of his eyes. He said something incomprehensible about madness.

"Excuse me."

Surely the man can't have been talking about him?

"Sir! Be careful! Don't you have anything to look through?"

"I'm not looking. But what did you say? Didn't I hear you say something about madness?"

"What . . . yes . . . I just said that I now understand how people became religious and went mad in the old days when they saw this sort of thing."

"Possibly. Do you work at the hotel?"

The man did, and yes, there was a guest called Mr. Corell, and then he gave out the room number, with some reluctance, it seemed, and soon after that Mulland was walking down the dark corridor. As he knocked he muttered to himself, "Calm down, calm down!," but when nothing happened—when no footsteps could be heard from inside—he knocked again. He almost could not bear to wait, but at last he heard a voice and a movement, and he felt his body grow tense, and almost as a reflex he began to count down, *six, five, four,* as if waiting for an explosion, and now the door was opened.

The policeman was the most pitiful sight imaginable. Corell shook and was bent and beaten to a pulp.

"No, please, no," he hissed, and raised his hands to his head, where a blood-stained rag or rather a shirt hung down over his shoulders like some bizarre hairstyle. Mulland closed the door and took a step forward, perhaps just to say something or to extend a helping hand, but his steps were too swift and forceful and the policeman staggered. He grabbed at the wall, and slowly, like someone who has decided to lie down, he fell to the floor. It was heart-rending. He drew his legs up to his chest, with his hands still holding his head and the shirt. Mulland felt that he ought to do something now, right away. He remained standing and in a voice which he realised sounded unnatural he said:

"I'm not going to hurt you. I'm going to help you. But you must understand . . ." He was about to say something about how serious it was to conspire with people like Fredric Krause, but saw that it would be pointless and instead looked around the room. There was a red Bible on the table, and an open suitcase on the floor. Mulland tried to gather his thoughts and decided, among other things, that he needed to get the policeman into bed and that he himself ought to sit on the chair in the corner and read through the notepad. He wanted to prepare thoroughly before speaking to him, but then footsteps could be heard in the corridor. Or could they? Yes, they came closer. There was something familiar about them. Isn't it amazing how much one can read into just a few sounds from a floor? He was immediately sure that it was Farley—maybe because he had been in his thoughts all along, and because Farley had always occupied a special place in his life. Mulland had long admired Oscar Farley's dignity and independence. But lately these very qualities had come to irritate him. Farley made Mulland feel uneducated and dense, and these days Mulland preferred to turn to bosses like Pippard who thought and reasoned more like he himself did. Perhaps he even bore a latent resentment against Farley. When there was a knock at the door he looked desperately towards the window.

"Good afternoon, Dr. Farley!"

There was nothing warm about the greeting. It was not just that the tone was cool. The words were spoken before the door was completely open and before they had even seen each other. But still Farley was reassured; he recognised the voice and saw it as a good sign that Mulland was there, despite everything, but the feeling of confidence only lasted a second. Mulland's face in the doorway gave him a fright. There was a look of panic about him but . . . how could Farley describe it . . . he also seemed sad and lost, impossible to read. Not only did his breath stink, he reeked of alcohol, he was also waving around a pad of paper as if it were something incredibly important.

"Look at this. I've got proof. Clear proof. He's leaking, and this has to be taken seriously . . . it's our biggest secret, the Ultra secret, isn't it? Not even I know much about it, I really don't, but he . . . he's been in contact with foreigners," Mulland went on, completely beside himself, and at first Farley listened intently—he got the impression that it was the notepad that had got Mulland all worked up—but then he stiffened.

There was a man lying on the floor with a battered face and a blood-stained shirt wrapped around his head.

When Corell realised who had come tramping into his room he was so terrified that he could hardly breathe, and although it was the last thing he wanted he had collapsed in a heap on the floor. He was convinced that he was going to be beaten up again, and held his hands over his head to protect himself and just waited. *Now . . . is he going to kick me now?* But when nothing happened he began to hope, or even to dream, and gradually sank into oblivion, or rather into that borderland between the waking and the unconscious world. At first all he felt was his nausea. But then, as if from far away, he became aware of something, a presence and a sound, which he took no notice of at first, but which began to give him a sensation of his childhood in Southport. He even imagined that he could hear the creaking floorboards of the house, but no, that could not be right. He recalled the danger and the man with the birthmark. But that did not help. He lost his sense of orientation and allowed himself to be carried away. He let the hallucinations take over and now, it was very clear, he could hear the jangling of keys, his father really was here, and he thought: about time too, and then he tried to say something.

Farley could hardly take it in. And he certainly failed to understand why Mulland had not told him at once about the man on the floor instead of raving on about the bloody notepad. *That idiot . . .* Farley bent down and put his hand on the man's back, and then he realised: it was the policeman. He seemed to be in a bad way and Farley cast a furious look at Mulland. But he just threw up his arms so Farley turned to Corell instead.

"How are you? Can you speak?"

"I found the glove!"

"What's that?"

"It was lying by the rails. I've still got it. I think I've still got it," said the policeman, and it was obvious that he was delirious, not only because what he was saying lacked any context.

His tone was muffled and distant, and Farley thought that he must get Corell into bed and call a doctor. But his back, *God damn his back!* He hissed at Mulland, "Come and help me!" and when Mulland did not immediately obey he stiffened, again alarmed, but he pushed that aside and now Mulland finally came. They lifted, or rather dragged, the policeman to the bed, and gave him a glass of water, and Farley removed the shirt from the policeman's head and tried to examine the wound, but all he could see was a tangle of locks of hair, dried blood and earth.

"There, there. We'll look after you now."

"I've . . ." Corell began.

"Can you ring reception and get a doctor here," Farley said, turning to Mulland.

Mulland did not move.

"Hurry up!"

Mulland went to the telephone, but checked himself almost at once, and stood for a few seconds, bent and apparently lost in the middle of the room, with those agitated eyes looking down at the street, and Farley just wanted to shout: *What the hell have you done?* But he realised that he had to reach through to Mulland, and he tried a gentler note.

"I understand that something dreadful has happened. We'll have to talk about it in peace and quiet, and I promise to examine your notepad. I'm sure there's a lot of interesting stuff in there. But first we have to get the situation under control, don't we?"

Mulland nodded reluctantly, but still made no attempt to lift the receiver, and Farley turned towards Corell, who looked alarmingly pale. His eyes appeared like thin slits above the swollen cheeks.

"Do you want more water?"

"Who are you?"

"I'm Oscar Farley. We met at the police station in Wilmslow," and then the policeman's face lit up.

He smiled as if he had run into a long-lost friend and that could of course be seen as another sign that he was incoherent—after all they hardly knew each other—but for the first time Farley felt some relief. Perhaps he is not in such a bad way after all, he thought. *Now I'll fix this. Now I can sort it out.* But now was not the time to feel triumphant. He turned around and saw that Mulland still seemed to be extremely agitated. What was the matter with the man?

Farley had said that the way Mulland and the others had been watching Alan Turing was disgraceful—"Have you any idea what Alan's done for us?"—and those words now echoed in Mulland's frantic mind. It was as if all his old admiration for Farley had turned to disappointment and anger, and as Farley now not only looked at him with distaste but also gave the policeman a warm smile, something more snapped in Mulland. He felt excluded and rejected, and he wanted to say something, something serious and memorable which would have Farley recognise that he was dealing with a dangerous man, a traitor even, but all he managed to utter was:

"You must understand—"

"What are you talking about? What on earth have you done?"

"There were . . . there were certain circumstances—"

"I'm sure there were. I don't doubt that for one second," Farley interrupted. "But quite frankly I don't feel like hearing it all now. Still I'm dumb enough—so utterly stupid—that I'm going to try my best to save your skin."

"You are?"

"Yes, because we're sitting in the same boat. Because we're both up to our necks in this bloody mess. It's this paranoia that's in the process of consuming us all. But first I want you to get out of here, now, at once. Are you listening? Calmly and quietly, you're going to walk away from here, right now."

"But the notepad? Don't you want to hear what's in it?"

"Give it to me, I'll read it."

"But . . ."

"No buts, give it to me!"

He probably ought to hear that lunatic out. Understand what happened. But it felt impossible to think clearly when Mulland was around. Mulland's nervous presence made him shiver and he repeated his words "Give it to me!" and, believe it or not, that deranged drunkard hesitated. Then he nodded sullenly and handed Farley the pad.

"Good. Very good. Now go!"

"You promise."

"I'll do what I can. But in return you have to . . ."

"Pippard wants me to stay. He said that the policeman has to be questioned."

"In that case you call Pippard and tell him that I've got everything under control. I'll question the policeman. But now you must . . ."

"Go?"

"Yes!"

Mulland stood there, swaying back and forth as if he were being pulled in different directions, and seemed to want to say something more, but then he grabbed his hat and slouched off. He walked out of the room with hesitant steps, and Farley breathed a sigh of relief. His whole body sagged together and he felt that he needed a drink. He felt that he needed three, four drinks, and a long holiday, and a good back doctor, but he would have to grit his teeth. He glanced at Corell. The policeman looked really terrible. But his eyes were clearer now, and Farley pulled up a chair, and looked through the notepad. As far as he could tell—but he was not looking especially carefully—it was filled with casual notes about Turing, nothing secret, just comments on the mathematician's writings.

"Never promise a lunatic anything," he muttered.

"No!"

"Was it he who attacked you?"

"It was him."

"I'm sorry. I'm really sorry. Can you bear to tell me about it?"

The policeman tried. He drank some more water and talked about his meetings with Gandy and Pippard, and then he described the assault—already at this stage a tendency to dramatise the account became apparent—but he was obviously suffering, and Farley suggested that he should take a break. Did he want to see a doctor? "No, no!" Corell only wanted to rest for a while and when he closed his eyes Farley wondered if he should contact Somerset, but he decided to get some more information first—if only to find out how on earth the policeman had learned about the code-breaking. He brought out his Yeats book, but he could not concentrate and the time ran slowly away. He looked at the policeman often. Wasn't it strange the way sleeping faces, even as battered and bruised as this one, took on something appealing and, almost embarrassed, Farley had to suppress an impulse to stroke the young man's forehead. A woman shouted outside. There was something inviting in her voice, as if it were addressed to him personally, and he had to concentrate to gather his thoughts. When at last the policeman woke up, Farley smiled with real joy and gave him more water.

"Are you feeling better now?"

"Yes, I think so."

"Shall I get you something to eat?"

"I'd rather keep going. I want to tell you what I have."

"Are you sure?"

"Yes I am."

"Forgive me then if I get straight to the point. You must—and this is very important—let me know who told you that Dr. Turing worked on cryptology."

"Nobody! No-one has even hinted at any such thing."

"In that case how can you . . . ?" Farley broke off and put his question differently. "Where did you get that idea from?"

"You could say that it started with a question."

"A question?"

"Yes," Corell said, and he described how he had been sitting in the library in Wilmslow and wondering what use the government might have had for a chess master and a mathematics genius.

At first he sounded weak and hesitant, but then he came alive. It was really astonishing. The words seemed to come so easily and quite soon it began to appear somewhat unreal to Farley. It all just poured out. His sentences really crackled and, however hard Farley tried to remain sceptical, he was stimulated, really exhilarated. He said to himself: *No, no, this sounds too good to be true, too simple and at the same time too intelligent.* But still he was drawn into it and did not say much. He just listened in fascination as the policeman explained how he had become bolder and bolder, as if driven forward by his own questions.

"I realised that Turing must have developed his logical machine during the war. In 'Computable Numbers' the device is just an intellectual construct, nothing more—isn't that right—an instrument of higher logic, but afterwards . . . you understand, at King's College I read a bit about his A.C.E. Do you know about that? Yes, of course you do, he sketched it out for the National Physical Laboratory in 1945 or 1946, and I understood enough to realise that the machine was very much more complex than the one in 'Computable Numbers.' It struck me that the man must have learned more during the war and I began to wonder why. Could his machine have had some use in the war? There was no doubt that Turing had been doing something highly secret—that was something that you were all very clear about—and the fact is that it helped me. I asked myself: What is more secret than anything else in wartime? Planning, I thought: all those strategies, subterfuges and shadowy agreements! Oddly enough, my aunt had given me a new radio just then and I started to imagine how different military leaders send important messages out into the ether: "Assemble the troops there and there." "Bomb this or that city." Now, I'm no engineer. I can't even cope with the telephone exchange at the police station. But I understood enough to know that whatever goes out on the radio, in a way goes out to everybody. Extraordinary efforts must have been made for the communications to be secure, and equally vast resources must have been put into cracking the enemy's messages. I had no idea how it was done. But I read Turing's articles, and there were some sentences that stuck in my mind. Alan writes that a sonnet created by a machine is best understood by another machine and at first that sounded weird. Machines neither understand nor appreciate anything, and I thought that Turing was just talking about a distant future when his machines would be able to think. But then it occurred to me that in many respects already today machines understand each other better than we understand them. We aren't the ones who find the people who we want to telephone. It's the electronic signals. When we listen to the radio it's the radio waves that locate the aerials; and then I started to think that, for a machine, poems or music could take almost any form, for example something that would be complete gibberish to us, such as a coded language, and that a machine based on logic—of the sort that Turing was working with—would of course be capable of distorting language, if I understand it right. In his article in *Mind*, Turing himself writes that the field of cryptology would appear to be a particularly appropriate application for machines, and slowly I became more and more certain that Turing built machines which designed or cracked codes. Machines which could understand incomprehensible music."

Farley held his forehead. *Machines which understand incomprehensible music.* It was incredible. It was as if he could hear Alan speaking, and obviously it was unsurprising that the policeman sounded like Turing. Corell had after all spent the last few days reading the mathematician's writings, but it still felt as if a ghost were there. It restored to Farley something which he had been missing, and with surprising clarity he remembered the mansion, the ugly huts and the clattering machines.

32

Bletchley Park

IN THE AFTERNOON OF February 23, 1941, Oscar Farley came walking along the grey brick wall towards Hut 8. It was cold and misty and the hut looked dull and plain with its ugly pitch roof in the light fog, and, as so often before, he cursed at the sight of the bicycles by the entrance. He had to clamber over them as he stepped into the long corridor. It was one of those days when his limbs and head ached with the hopelessness of the war. Ever since Paris had fallen in the early summer of the previous year he had suffered from nightmares and misgivings. Often he imagined the Germans teeming across the countryside like locusts and naturally he drank too much and slept badly, not just because the bed was too short for his six feet five, but because the worry never left him. Hut 8 smelled of chalk and creosote. One could hear the noise of telephones, telegraph machines and the creaking sound of feet on the wooden floor. The head of the hut had his own room, or to be more accurate cubby-hole, and for some reason Farley took a deep breath before he knocked. In those days, Alan made him nervous. That was of course ridiculous. Alan stammered and found it hard to look people in the eye and Farley was not only older and his boss, he was vastly more worldly-wise and self-confident. It was just that . . . how could he explain it? Alan's eyes seemed to look inwards into a parallel world, and Farley felt lightweight in his company, even as if Alan could see straight through him, and often he wondered: What's he thinking about? What's going on behind those blue eyes?

Alan was not in. But Farley bumped into Joan Clark, who told him that Alan was down by the lake, playing chess with Jack Good. "Playing chess?" Farley repeated, almost indignant, although he knew that was not fair. Alan was no shirker, but the words sounded so carefree that Farley felt envious. Even if he had the time, he would not have had the peace of mind to devote himself to a game, and Joan must have noticed that he was displeased because she answered that Alan was not so much playing chess as thinking about whether there was some definitive method for doing so.

"He wants to mechanise the process. I think he dreams of being able to teach a machine to play."

"That's a bright fellow you've found for yourself," he answered.

"Seems like it."

"Why don't you try and tidy him up a bit?"

"I'm working on it."

Farley did not find Alan down by the lake, and that was hardly surprising. It was no weather for playing chess outdoors. Ice still covered the water and Farley looked out over the surrounding area, surprised at everything that had happened during the last two years. When they had first come here, in the spring of 1939, Bletchley Park had been a peaceful place with its elms and yews, not that Farley had liked the place even then. The early Victorian lack of style of the mansion irritated him, and he had often been gripped by the feeling that life was ebbing away from them, that the house had enjoyed its moment of glory in another, better era. But in 1939 he had not had to make an effort to hear birds sing, or even the sound of fish jumping in the lake. Not only had the trees been cut down but the place had become an industry. Everywhere new houses and huts were being put up, and instead of nature one could hear machines. How he longed to get away from the place! He knew that he had been extraordinarily lucky. He did not have to shoot or be shot at, or even salute, and sometimes it felt as if his Cambridge life had simply moved here. Intellectual curiosity and hedonism were in the air. People played rounders and cricket on the lawn, and then there were women: masses of young beautiful women, not least his Bridget, his tall wonderful Bridget, only he with his height and stature could make her seem small in comparison, not to mention all these talented people from the universities. The level of conversation was nothing to be despaired at.

Nonetheless, life at Bletchley had developed into a heavy burden, and he would have been surprised to learn that many years later he would long to be back there again. Never before had he been so exhausted, so spent. His temples pounded with tiredness, and of late he had noticed that he was not understanding abstract reasoning as well as he used to. He had lost his sharpness, which was of course reason enough to feel nervous in Alan's presence and, for the first time in his life, Farley was beginning to feel that he wanted to be alone. It felt like his worst time ever and so it truly was from an objective, national point of view. Hitler controlled the continent and had his pact with Stalin. The Yanks did not seem to have any interest in getting involved in the war, and England was losing the Battle of the Atlantic. Karl Dönitz—who was still only a Vice Admiral—led the German U-boat war with increasing success, and each week more and more British ships were sunk. Some sixty or seventy were now being lost every month. Having the world's largest fleet was no help if you did not know where the enemy was. Old England was being cut off from the world, and if anyone understood what it would mean if the gang in Hut 8 could crack the Germans' naval Enigma code, it was Farley. Then England's ships would no longer be fumbling in the dark. Then they would be able to defend themselves and strike back, and he ought to be able to feel a certain cautious optimism, or at least to see some light in his despair. Today he was carrying with him one of the most promising pieces of information for a long time, but he didn't want to believe it. From the very first he had been convinced that it was impossible to break the naval system of codes, and that they would never experience the privilege of being able to read what the Nazis were planning or to know where they were to be found at sea. For a long time they were not even able to distinguish which messages came from the U-boats and which were sent from land. It was all incomprehensible, and although they might eventually crack the Luftwaffe codes, the naval system was by a long way more complex. It provided no openings. Pessimism was no virtue during a war but it could be justified, and Farley knew that most people agreed with him. Even the head of Bletchley, Commander Alastair Denniston, had declared it openly:

"It can't be done. We'll have to find other ways."

But not everybody had listened. Alan Turing had not. He never seemed to listen. That was one of the strange things about him. He set himself apart. There was something indefinable in his character, a degree of independence which sometimes went so far that it seemed like a mental block. Even when obeying orders, he only seemed to be following his own personal agenda, and this faculty, this quiet autonomy, which also meant that he was incapable of taking anything for granted, left many feeling uncomfortable. Some, like Julius Pippard, maintained early on that Turing was "unreliable" and that he only produced anything useful if he was sufficiently stimulated. That was unfair, but not altogether untrue. He would only bother with an assignment if it was challenging, and from that point of view it was a linguistic stroke of genius to describe the Germans' naval codes as "unbreakable." That was just the sort of description that Turing needed. He only really got going if he was free to think along innovative lines and question the obvious, but it would take some time before Farley really got to understand him. To begin with, no-one could fathom Alan, least of all the women. His Bridget used to say that she could not tell if Alan was afraid of her or just uninterested.

"Whenever I go by, he starts to mutter to himself."

That's what made the whole business with Joan Clarke seem so peculiar. Alan was the last person in the world Oscar would have expected to get engaged, but he had been happy to record the news in Turing's personnel file and hoped that the information would put an end to the gossip which was already doing the rounds. Turing probably had no idea that Farley was also involved in the security screening of his colleagues at Bletchley. Turing probably saw Farley only as a liaison officer who maintained contact with the naval intelligence services O.I.C. and N.I.D., which may have been a reason why they gradually grew close. They both lodged at the Crown Inn at Shenley Brook, a few miles north of Bletchley, a rather simple red-brick place with a butcher's shop and a pub on the ground floor. The landlady, Mrs. Ramshaw, was the size of a house and had a laugh which could be both hearty and heartless. Sometimes she complained about all these young men who had turned up in the area and didn't seem to be doing their duty for England. This bothered Farley. Alan Turing could not have cared less. He lived in his own universe, and unlike Farley he was not always trying to make himself popular.

Farley's weapon in life was charm, but neither charm, authority nor charisma worked on the mathematician, at least not when serious matters were involved. In Alan's world, nothing important could be decided by vote or imposed from on high. Only someone who knew what he was talking about could influence him and that often made Turing inflexible. But Farley slowly found the code to him. So long as he put aside the small talk and went straight to the heart of a matter and spoke with concentration and passion, it was entirely possible to use serious topics to tease out a lighthearted, bantering Alan and to hear his staccato laughter which so quickly cleared the air of tension. But he entirely neglected his outward appearance. Alan always looked unbelievably shabby, dressed any old way, with a bit of rope holding up his trousers instead of a belt, and with his shirt unbuttoned and left hanging outside his trousers. Some days he did not dress at all but just put his overcoat on over his pyjamas, and hurtled away on his bicycle, absorbed in his own world. He was unconcerned by everyday things, and there were ugly bulges above his cuticles. In his nervousness he bit his fingers, which were red and sore and covered with ink stains, and anyone judging him by the look of his fingers alone would pronounce his neurosis incurable. Yet Alan seemed happy, as happy as a young mathematician who is consumed by what he loves most of all on this earth: his numbers and logical structures. In any case he was a godsend to Bletchley and to England.

The Nazi encryption machines were called Enigma and had been constructed by the inventor Arthur Scherbius. They consisted of scramblers, reflectors, entry rotors, a keyboard and a readout board with display lamps. They were not just incomprehensibly intricate, they were flexible. Their complexity could easily be enhanced. Since the Poles had decrypted the system—that alone had been regarded as a miracle—the Germans had increased the number of leads on the plugboards from six to ten, and the number of different settings had become 159 million trillion, or whatever it was. Farley only remembered that it was 159 followed by twenty-one noughts. He had said to Bridget that it sounded like a whisper from the infinity of hell.

"How on earth are we going to do this?"

Alan had an idea. "Only a machine can defeat another machine," he said one day as he crossed the lawn to the red shed which the former owner of the mansion had used to store his apples and plums, but which was now used as a place for major strategic discussions.

"What?" Farley said.

"Or let me put it in a different way. If a machine creates music, who then is best able to appreciate its tones?"

"No idea," Farley said. "Some poor wretch with a tin ear?"

"Another machine, Oscar. A machine with similar preferences," Turing continued, and made it sound as if he were talking about preferences which were completely different from those of machines, and then he smiled his strange smile, which was both contemplative and challenging at the same time.

With that, he disappeared over to the labyrinth of yews which was soon to be chopped down. Looking back, Farley understood that this was the beginning of the breakthrough. By that time of course he already knew that the Poles, led by Marian Rejewski, had built electro-mechanical devices which methodically worked their way through the Enigma settings. They were called bombes, probably because of their ticking noise, or according to another version because Marian Rejewski had had the brainwave while eating a so-called ice cream bombe in a café in Warsaw. These machines had been the major contributing factor to the Poles' success. But they were no longer of any help, not since the Nazis had increased the number of leads in the plugboards. At Bletchley they needed a much more advanced device, a machine which could cope with the Enigma's modernistic cacophony, and it was evident that this was the sort of apparatus that Alan was thinking about. God knows that his help was needed.

During the autumn and winter of 1939, all they managed to pick up from Nazi communications was pure gibberish, a string of combinations of letters with no pattern or meaning. The earlier gold rush atmosphere at Bletchley was replaced by a creeping despair, and it often felt as if they were all surrounded by an indecipherable buzz of malevolent plans. Farley succumbed to his pessimism and every now and then drank himself into oblivion. He worked hard during the days but could not manage to keep the unpleasant thoughts at bay, and somehow he knew that his romance with Bridget was doing him as much harm as good, and more and more he thought of his wife in London with such pain that he could not take pleasure in anything at Bletchley.

Alan on the other hand seemed totally and utterly spellbound. Normally a star from Cambridge who had become a fellow at the age of twenty-one would hardly be likely to contemplate building a machine, but Farley soon understood that it was as if Alan had been made for the task. His great dream was to mechanise thinking, to materialise logic, so to speak. Farley had read mathematics for a while before a brief sojourn in economics and had then moved on to English literary history and his studies of Yeats and Henry James, and even though he had forgotten most of it, he knew enough of mathematics to realise that Turing had a special affinity for his subject. It was as if the numbers in his thoughts were crying out to become flesh and blood. Farley knew that, some years before the war, Alan had written a paper setting out the idea of a machine which could receive instructions from a paper strip, rather like a pianola, and tick its way through all sorts of mathematical problems. The machine was just a theoretical construct, designed to answer a specific question in logic, and so far as Farley knew, no-one had taken the trouble to build it. But Alan had long been dreaming of building something similar and now he had his chance, not of course to put together something quite so advanced and versatile, not at all, but at least a simple cousin in logic which could see through another machine or, so to speak, understand its music.

Alan sat for hours bent over captured Enigma machines, with no sense of time or place, scrawling his illegible scribbles into a notebook. He became still more unkempt and dirty, which of course shocked some. *Should he not at least wash?* But there were plenty of people too, like Farley himself, who were used to this kind of bohemianism from Cambridge and for the most part Alan was left to his own devices. He became the free artist at Bletchley. He was known as the Professor; in some ways he became a living legend.

Yet Alan was not as peculiar as many later tried to suggest. People at Bletchley had a tendency to romanticise things, and to caricature their colleagues, in part to make life at the mansion seem more exciting and remarkable; but the anecdotes about Alan also had another purpose: to make him easier to deal with. Reducing him to an eccentric, a misfit with strange habits, made it easier to accept his incredible talent, because it really was quite extraordinary. The speed with which he grasped the labyrinthine complexity of the code system, for example.

Already in January 1940 he presented his drawings. Farley would never forget it. There were such high expectations, so many rumours doing the rounds. Alan has made a reverse Enigma machine, an "antithesis," it was said; "something which can understand their tones," Farley added, and got a few surprised looks.

Others were sceptical. "To be quite honest, I'm not expecting very much," Julius Pippard said, and things did not get any better when Alan stepped into the red shed which still smelled of fruit. He looked crazy. He was wearing a long flannel shirt which was rather like a dress and you could hardly see the difference between the stubble and the dirt on his face. He placed a large notebook on the reddish-brown table and pointed to the pages, as if that made things any clearer. Everything seemed such a hopeless mess. There were about a hundred handwritten, illegible pages of text which were full of alterations and ink blots. As designs go it must have been close to impossible to work from, and whispers could be heard here and there in the shed: "What on earth is this?" Before Alan could say a word Frank Birch, the head of the naval intelligence section in Hut 4, stepped forward and touched the notebook with his finger, as if trying to see how much dust had gathered on it. Birch had left King's College, Cambridge, before the war and tried his luck in the theatre. He knew how to make an impression on a gathering of people.

"So this is the solution to our problems?" he said, and while you could not exactly say that he sounded mocking, he was definitely being sarcastic, which hardly contributed to the feeling of confidence in the shed.

"It quite likely is," Turing said.

"Quite likely?" Birch repeated theatrically, and even though he was trying to amuse rather than criticise, a feeling of impatience spread throughout the shed, which could have developed in any number of directions, and Farley remembered that he had glared at Turing's infected hands, those fingers which feverishly leafed through the notebook as if he had discovered at the last moment that he had forgotten something crucial.

The meeting in the old fruit store was the culmination of a long period of hard work for them all, so it was not surprising that there was tension in the air. A couple of people who were present had publicly declared that it was a scandal that Alan had been allowed to work on the project so much on his own, bearing in mind how much was at stake, and even Alan himself may have sensed a certain hostility, though he did not normally care much about moods. At the start he spoke entirely without his boyish enthusiasm. He stuttered, and there cannot have been many who understood what he was talking about. The engineers kept asking him to be more precise.

"As I was saying," he replied, time after time, biting himself in the back of the hand with a preoccupied air.

But then something happened. One of the engineers said, "Bloody hell, of course, yes," and at that Alan's assurance began to return. He even laughed. "Exactly, exactly, isn't it hilarious?" he said, and a certain confidence spread throughout the room, because although Alan's design was complex, it had a seductive simplicity which little by little sank in among those who were there. Three Enigma machines would be connected in such a way that they could rule out alternative settings for the scramblers and plugboards by finding logical contradictions in the code system. The fact that contradictions could betray themselves was something that Alan spoke about with particular enthusiasm and for a brief moment he disappeared off on a tangent. Farley remembered that Turing mentioned the philosopher Wittgenstein without it really being clear why, but he soon found the thread again. When the right settings were found for all the machines, then the circuit would be complete and a lamp would light up. The only problem was that the whole contraption could not be used unless they could get hold of cribs. Cribs were pieces of encrypted text whose content they could guess at, words or phrases whose meaning was apparent from the context. In other words, they had to decipher a small piece of text in order to decipher a larger piece, with the help of the machine, which might seem paradoxical; they had to crack the code in order to be able to crack it. But more than anyone else, Alan had understood the value of the old decrypted texts which the Poles had given them. Not that the messages taught him anything at all about the code system or the Enigma machines. On the other hand they did say a lot about the Germans' routines, for example that the word *Wetter*, weather, appeared in the same place in the weather reports just after six in the morning, and that certain messages from ports and fortified positions where nothing much happened often began with the words: "I have nothing to report."

All these patterns and repeated phrases provided them with the necessary cribs, and Farley sometimes thought how beautifully fitting it was that a chaotic person like Alan should find his entry point in something that was too regulated and orderly. In the Germans' tendency to formalise things—and express themselves in too similar ways—he found their Achilles heel. With a logical machine, and the knowledge that we all have a tendency to act like machines and develop habits and repetitive patterns, he went onto the attack, and in this Farley had to hand it to the engineers: it progressed with great speed. The construction was finished by March 1940 and, my God, Alan's drawings had turned into a bronze-coloured monster two metres wide and two metres high, which sounded like two hundred little old ladies clicking away with their knitting needles, and which evidently needed to be handled with a certain care. Ruth, poor thing, one of the female operators who was meant to learn to use the machine, kept getting electrical shocks and at least two of her blouses were ruined by oil stains.

The machine did of course have its flaws and Farley was not especially surprised when it did not seem to work particularly well.

"Did you think it would work just like that?" he snapped one evening when a heated discussion broke out over not just the machine but also Alan's belief in his own abilities.

All it needed was for Gordon Welchman, the Cambridge mathematician who had become the head of Hut 6, to increase the capacity substantially with some simple steps, among other things by adding an electrical circuit, something which came to be called the diagonal board, and already by early that same spring the code-breakers in Hut 6 managed to crack the codes of the German air force and artillery. For a while the secret communications were read like an open book, and that was beyond reason. It was wild and beautiful, and it gave the Air Ministry and the War Office critical knowledge not just of the Nazi invasion of Norway and Denmark but also of the Germans' air raids over England. Often the military command got information about both the time and place for attacks and it was not unusual for them also to learn exactly how many planes the Nazis had lost and at what speed they were being replaced. Alan Turing's monster machines were a godsend to Great Britain and new ones were being built all the time and they were all given names like Agnes, Eureka and Otto, and soon Farley came to love their whip-like sounds—the heartbeat of logic, as Welchman said—and he was by no means alone. The contraptions were called the oracles, and a stream of congratulations came from London, and sometimes Farley wondered how Alan himself took it. Alan was not an open book. It was impossible to tell why on some days he could not look anyone in the eye while on others he smiled his Mona Lisa smile. He did not exude any sense of triumph, but to be fair he also had a lot to do. The Enigma settings changed every day at midnight, and he and his colleagues had to map out the habits of the German operators, and guess what form their laziness or whimsy might take, for example that they could not always be bothered to be creative when they decided the key settings for the day, and that instead of something random they would choose letters which lay in a row or on the diagonal on the instrument panel. Probability calculations based on human idleness were always a part of the job.

Alan was eventually moved to Hut 8 to try to break the much more difficult naval Enigma code and sometimes those in charge worried that he was wearing himself out. People said to Farley: "You live with Alan, keep an eye on him!"

But Farley could never get to grips with Alan's habits. Unlike the German operators, Alan lacked regularity. Sometimes he slept until late in the morning, sometimes he disappeared off to the mansion already at dawn. One morning—one of the last days that Farley was still living at the Crown Inn—Alan was sitting down at the breakfast table reading the *New Statesman*. Even at a distance you could see that something had happened to him. His eyes were red and swollen. He seemed to have been crying all night long and Farley decided not to disturb him. That was probably stupid. If Alan was in a crisis, he ought to reach out a hand to him. But there was something about those tears which so inspired respect. It reminded Farley of when he was little and saw his father cry. It felt like prying, and it was of course also the last thing in the world that the commanders at Bletchley wanted to hear. Alan was the golden calf. If he was out of kilter, so was the rest of Bletchley. There were admittedly one or two things about the mathematician's body language which were at odds with the tear-stained eyes: he seemed for example to be solving a crossword puzzle in the newspaper, and so Farley said in the most gentle tone he could muster:

"Hello, Alan, is there anything I can do for you?"

"Hello, Oscar. I didn't see you. Did you say something?"

"Can I help you with anything?"

"How kind of you. But I'm afraid my wish list is far too long. I'd like a new bicycle and also better food and then peace, of course, and harder crossword puzzles. Did you have anything particular in mind?"

Farley said he did not, and he took himself off, puzzled. Fifteen minutes later he was wandering along the gravel path towards Bletchley, and as he recalled it he was thinking about his wife to whom he was being unfaithful and her great sadness at the fact that they had never had any children. Then he heard a noise behind him, a ticking which merged together with the crunching of the gravel path. It was a sound which he had learned to recognise. It was Alan and his old bicycle with the hopeless chain. But when Farley turned around he saw something very peculiar. Alan was wearing headgear with a sort of elephant's trunk, looking like a gas mask, and Farley just had time to sniff the air nervously and experience a moment's panic before Alan waved cheerfully, and it took a while before Farley understood that the gas mask was Alan's protection against allergy and that the tears at breakfast had been caused by nothing more than hay fever.

It became increasingly important to break the naval signals as well, and the pressure from London grew more and more desperate:

"Crack that bloody code."

But the Germans devoted vastly greater care to the naval system. They understood better than anyone what it meant to have an edge in the Battle of the Atlantic and it seemed as if the system were unbreakable. Alan was able to increase the capacity of the bombes and he went ever deeper into his probability theories, into the complex weighing of proof and chance, and this allowed him to improve the extent to which conclusions could be drawn from the contradictions using the *reductio ad absurdum* principle. "I use the liar's paradox as a skeleton key," he explained, and it proved to be one step along the way, but it was not enough. It seemed as if they would also have to get hold of the German U-boats' codebooks in order to have any chance of success. But how were they going to do that?

Farley was constantly discussing the question with M.I.6 and O.I.C. but got nowhere, and the mood grew worse and worse. More and more often Frank Birch blamed everything and everybody in his theatrical outbursts, and perhaps that was no more than the usual moaning which they all needed to be able to get by, and which Birch had developed into his special art form: "We have to crack the bloody code because we have to!" he roared on one occasion. But one day things became unpleasant. Pippard from the internal security department was there. Pippard had an unwavering ability to fall in line and to believe without any reservation in the official version of things. Not that he was unintelligent or even that he lacked humour or independence, but he was incredibly receptive not just to orders and decisions but also to the unexpressed wishes of his leaders. Any opinions he voiced were as often as not those which were on their way into the organisation, and on this particular day, while Birch was going on about how impractical Alan was and sloppy, how he lost things and never bloody well did as he was told and just banged on about his theories on geometrical relativities and Uncle Tom Cobley and all, Pippard blurted out:

"Besides, he's a queer."

"What the hell are you talking about?" Farley hissed.

He had heard the rumours, of course, and just like Pippard he was aware that it used to say "probably homosexual" in Turing's personnel file, but he himself had crossed out that information when the engagement to Joan Clarke had been announced, and in any case Farley could not care less, he himself had been at King's. Homosexuality did not bother him any more than someone drinking beer straight from the bottle, and he tried to change the subject, but Pippard stood his ground and said that he had spoken to a chap who had heard that Alan had tried to seduce Jack Grover down by the lake and that Alan had perhaps let himself be ruled too much by his lust and had therefore lost focus. My God, thought Farley, who doesn't let himself be ruled by lust?

"Go to hell," he said, and that hardly improved his relationship with Pippard.

But the mere thought that Pippard and other backbiters could have Alan declared a security risk started to worry Farley a great deal, and to be honest, it ought to have worried them all. Homosexuality was still not regarded as such a big thing, but these were desperate weeks and hysteria grew by the day. Hitler's power on the Continent and at sea increased and the naval Enigma system remained impossible to break. They had just one hope, an idiotic thing, a daredevil plan which had been worked out within N.I.D., the Naval Intelligence Division in London, by Ian Fleming, the young assistant to the division's head, John Godfrey. Farley knew Fleming only a little. He had been friends with his brother Peter, who had written the rather brilliant travel book *News from Tartary*. Ian Fleming did not really make as robust an impression, but he and Oscar found it easy to talk to each other. They were both book lovers and prone to similar neuroses, a touch of hypochondria and a constant desire to play the man of the world. Fleming got terrible headaches, which he always blamed on a piece of copper which had lodged in his nose after some sporting accident at Eton, but the chap was full of ideas and initiative, Farley could not deny him that, even though he had a tendency to brag and to tell rather tasteless stories. According to Fleming's plan—which was given the code name Operation Ruthless—they would get hold of the codebooks from a Nazi vessel by arranging for the Air Ministry to give them an airworthy German bomber. The plan was for them to hand-pick a group of five tough men, including a pilot and a fluent German speaker. The team would be dressed in German air force uniforms, made up with blood and wounds and then head off to crash the plane in the middle of the English Channel. The idea was for them to send out an S.O.S. signal in German and then await a German rescue ship. It has to be said that Farley took a sceptical view of the plan right from the beginning. So much could go wrong, most of all when the crew was to play its charade and board the ship and at a suitable moment shoot the Germans and get hold of the cipher equipment.

But Farley, Turing and their colleague Peter Twinn from Hut 8 allowed themselves to be persuaded—perhaps in part because there was not much else to hope for and because they had not yet made the connection between Fleming's tendency to exaggerate—the chap should start writing novels or something—and his ability to make plans. In September 1940 he went down to Dover to begin preparations. A German Heinkel bomber had been made available, and a crew recruited, a good team according to Fleming, "an absolutely phenomenal force. I haven't decided yet if I'm going to take part myself in the plan," and Farley came to believe in the plan, even though he did wonder how many English elite troops there were who could speak German without an accent.

At this time security was being tightened at Bletchley. Nobody was allowed to know a single word more than was necessary. Ideally people should have no idea what their colleagues in the other huts and houses were working on, and just the knowledge that someone like Turing was on top of all of the vital knowledge became an increasing source of worry, and behind the scenes Pippard was working away with his smear campaign. What was driving him? Farley did not understand, but he noticed how Pippard carried along more and more people with him and how the atmosphere was being poisoned. He suffered along with Turing! The absurdity was that Turing had to succeed with something which had been considered impossible in order to silence his critics. But the naval Enigma remained impenetrable and there was no good news from Fleming either. "Tomorrow," he wrote. "Or the day after tomorrow. Just relax. I'll sort this out." But like hell he did. The days passed. People wanted to wait for the month end, when the German ships would get fresh codebooks. But when the end of the month came, nothing happened, and Fleming's telegrams sounded ever more evasive and vague, and soon Farley and Turing did not even need to say anything. Just by exchanging a look they understood the situation: "Not today either!"

In the evening of October 16, 1940, Farley was standing in his room next to the mansion library and looking out over the lake and the huts when a young man brought him a telegram from John Godfrey in London: OPERATION RUTHLESS POSTPONED INDEFINITELY, it said, but it might just as well have said "dead and buried." It was the death blow, Farley understood that at once, and he kicked his tin waste-paper basket and felt a stab of disappointment and shame. He should have realised right from the start. The plan was a lot of nonsense and nothing more, and he became seriously worried when he gave Turing the news just afterwards.

"We'll never pull this off," Alan said with a pessimism which was utterly unlike him.

33

THE SHARP TENSION Corell had felt in his chest had subsided and, even though he still ached, the pain felt less unpleasant now, like the after-effects of a successful long-distance run or a worthy fist fight. Every now and then he even enjoyed himself; it was ages since he had last met a person who stimulated him as much as this and now the words flowed again, all the old, clever phrases, the abstractions, the mental leaps, the dramatic points and the effort to keep a grip on them, returned with a new energy. *The more exciting it is, the more detail the audience wants to have.*

All the maxims he had heard when he was a boy now guided him onward and as much as Ross or Kenny at the police station killed off his words, Oscar Farley made them come alive and Corell told his tale honestly, or rather, it felt honest. But soon he had the same sensation that he had as a child: his account took on a life of its own. It provided a frame that had not been there from the start, and he ended up inventing some details and observations, not lies, as such, more like embellishments, links which the story seemed to need, and slowly he discovered what he had perhaps always known: life becomes different when it is recounted, it changes and takes on new marker flags and turning points. He did not mention the conversation with Krause in his description, and he gave new significance to events which had not long ago seemed unimportant, and often the situation seemed so strangely familiar, as if he had travelled back in time to those evenings in Southport, or as if he were even being turned into another, better person. But that was nonsense of course. This was not a time to be enjoyed. This was an investigation involving state secrets, and he knew better than most that it was a standard interrogation tactic to create an illusion of well-being, and the suspicion flared up in him that all this warmth he thought he saw in Farley's eyes was just a trick, a way to get him to say the wrong thing. But all the same . . . he let himself be intoxicated by the conversation. Insincere or not, it healed him and, bit by bit, overconfidence seeped back into his veins. He babbled on and made new associations and mental leaps. Some were stolen from Krause and Gandy. Others were direct quotations from Turing's writings, and while he knew that he was going too far, he was still surprised when Farley's facial expression abruptly froze.

Machines which could understand incomprehensible music.

Corell's words not only reminded Farley of Alan and Bletchley. They put him back on his guard. One could say that he sobered up step by step, and remembered the whole background and everything that he had heard from Pippard. He was still stimulated, and he continued to feel affection for the policeman, but as time went by his suspicions grew, and he worried that he had let himself be affected by the vulnerable look in Corell's eyes and by his own feelings of guilt, but perhaps most of all by the policeman's talent. He had been cheered up, in the same way as when one of his students turned out to be a pleasant surprise, and he had even thought that the policeman might be a resource to be recruited. But as he went on he came to focus more on the performance itself; on the storyteller's joy and the feeling of how he was trying to make his tale match up to some literary model, and without wanting to—he hated to burden sons with the sins of their fathers—the policeman's father surfaced in his thoughts again: James Corell, the spellbinding jester with his wild and fantastical, but not necessarily true, yarns. Was this the same phenomenon appearing in the next generation? He did not know. He just had an uncertain feeling that something was not quite right, although he continued to defend the policeman in his mind. He did not for example think that Corell knew anything like as much as Pippard imagined, and he refused to believe that the policeman had sold on his information; he could not even picture how that might have happened. That bloody suit which Pippard had gone on about and which now looked so hopelessly filthy, had been paid for by his aunt Vicky and, as for Mulland's talk of a man with a Slav and brutal appearance having followed the policeman, Farley did not believe one word of it. He remained convinced that most of what Corell had said was true. And yet . . . the feeling that something was not quite right, that it all seemed somehow too straightforward, grew inside him, and then it struck him: *the letter.* How could he have forgotten that? It was the letter more than anything which Pippard had got so worked up about.

"Pippard said that you've read one of Turing's letters?"

"Yes . . . that's true."

"What sort of letter is it?"

"It's right here," Corell said, pointing at his inside pocket.

"In Wilmslow you said that you didn't have anything more?"

"Hasn't my entire story demonstrated what an idiot I've been? I should have given you the letter and I shouldn't have come here and more than anything I shouldn't have gone to see Pippard."

"But you did."

"This whole saga has driven me to do things which I shouldn't have done."

"You realised there were important things there which you knew nothing about."

"It wasn't just that, unfortunately. It was more about myself. About silly old dreams. I wanted . . ."

"May I see the letter now?"

Corell let him. He handed over the crumpled pieces of paper and before Farley began to read he became nervous. His hands even shook; he could not have explained why, but he was afraid of all sorts of things, afraid that he would be identified as the shit who had kicked Alan out of G.C.H.Q., but above all afraid that Alan had given away state secrets after all, and that high priests like Pippard should be proved right. So he hurried through the letter. Such sad reading! It pained him. Yet it also calmed him. A more orthodox civil servant, a Pippard, would probably have had much to say. It had certainly been careless of Alan even to mention that there were secrets and above all that he had lost an assignment, however obscurely it was described, but apart from that the letter was no flagrant breach of the security regulations and if there was anyone who should have felt ashamed it was Mulland and those who had sent him out. *He is so bad at pretending to be natural that he makes people nervous. Where have they found him?*

Yes, where?

Farley should not have promised him anything. No, no, Mulland should be thrown out of G.C.H.Q. at once—and maybe he too should be.

With tired eyes he looked around the room. A couple of beer bottles stood on the windowsill and there was a suitcase with a few clothes and some books on the floor, and then two glasses and the notepad on the bedside table, the pad which Mulland had been making such a fuss over.

"What do you think?" the policeman said.

"About the letter? It makes me sad. Turing was a good person. We've treated him badly."

"Was he a great thinker?"

"Without any doubt," Farley said, without really being present.

He had picked up the notepad and started flicking through it again, and only vaguely, out of the corner of his eye, he noticed that Corell lit up, as if Farley had said something to make him very happy.

"What makes him that?"

"Makes him what?"

"A great thinker."

"He . . ."

Farley caught sight of the same name that Mulland saw in the notepad. *Fredric Krause.*

"It was very unwise of you to keep that letter," he said, rather than get involved in talking about Turing's greatness.

"Are you going to report this to my bosses?"

"No. Are you?" he answered in a flippant tone which he regretted at once.

He had to stop being so mild and weak. He had to stop letting himself be blinded by his sympathy for the policeman, above all now that he had discovered Fredric Krause's name in Corell's notepad. *Fredric Krause.* Farley had a worrying feeling in his stomach, not that he had ever thought that Krause was unreliable. But he had popped up at the courthouse in Wilmslow, and afterwards just vanished. Could he have . . . ? Farley refused to believe it. No, no, and yet; he could not get Krause out of his mind. He remembered the logician one late evening under the naked lightbulb in Hut 8, but above all—he remembered this with strange clarity—he recalled how Krause had been standing on the lawn outside the mansion at Bletchley talking to Alan Turing about razor blades and men's socks. There had been such a light and teasing tone between them, as if they really were very close. This must have been just before the silver ingots arrived at Bletchley.

34

Bletchley Park, II

ON ONE LEVEL, the setbacks in the war did not seem to affect Alan Turing. He had an extraordinary ability to lose himself in his concentration, and it was well known that he had little interest in outside circumstances. But afterwards, when his envious enemies had taken their spiteful revenge, Farley wondered if the sense of hopelessness had not also seeped into Alan. He did of course hide it behind quips and practical jokes. He was not someone to complain directly. On the other hand, he did come out with a number of strange things:

"If the Germans come I'm going to start selling razor blades in the streets. I'm going to buy a whole stock of them!"

"Stupid idea. You'll be arrested for flogging murder weapons. You should put your money on ladies' stockings instead," Krause said, standing next to him.

"In that case I'd rather sell men's socks!"

"Why not sell ladies' stockings to men. Could become all the rage. Göring would probably buy a pair himself."

Turing's eyes lit up and he and Krause started to make nonsensical plans for what they would do in a Nazi England. It was not easy to work out what was serious and what was just fooling around. Farley did not understand either of them very well.

At this time, Turing had bought two silver ingots for £250. The silver was transported to Bletchley by train and received with much ceremony, and at first it was all rather hard to understand but soon it transpired that Alan was hoping to live off those ingots.

"What do you need the silver for?" Farley said.

"The same as any other capitalist. To get rich."

In fact money was the last thing that Turing was interested in. But he was capable of developing theories about all sorts of things, and he must have had heard from somewhere that silver and gold had appreciated the most during the last war, and therefore he was now planning to bury the ingots in the forest. They could lie there, increasing in value, like seeds in the earth. He could not deposit them in a bank. The Nazis would be bound to empty all bank accounts.

"Do you want to come along?" Turing said.

Farley did not. He did not have the time. But still he said yes. He had orders to keep an eye on how their star was feeling, and therefore one day they went off to the forests in Shenley with the silver loaded onto an old milk cart. They passed Shenley Park, a pretty teahouse and two orchards before they came to a clearing next to an old pagoda tree. There was not much to be said for it as a place. The ground was uneven and stony and not much light shone through. Still, the pagoda tree gave the spot a certain austere solemnity and, since they did not have the strength to drag the milk cart any further, Turing decided that this would have to do. Farley objected that it would be hard to find the place again. There were few distinguishing features, apart from the pagoda tree, and that was unlikely to be standing there forever. The trunk was already damaged. But Turing thought that the place was good enough. He did not want to make it too easy for himself, he said, and pointed out that the tree would probably outlive them all. It was about one in the afternoon. The day was beautiful but somewhat chilly and a black and unusually large beetle was crawling on the ground. "Look at it," Alan said, with honest fascination, and did not seem to be in any hurry to start digging. He sat down on the milk cart.

"You don't seem to want to make it easy for yourself," Farley said.

"I don't?"

"You said . . ."

"Oh yes . . . I only meant that there's not much point in a treasure if you don't have a treasure hunt. I have no wish to bury the silver at the bottom of my garden. I need a bit of a challenge. That's something that you should understand, Oscar, you're always talking about the story . . . the importance of the story. What would the treasure of Monte Cristo be without Dantès's adventures? Empty and vulgar, don't you think?"

"I might well still enjoy what I could do with the treasure."

"Ha, ha. But you must agree that the real charm lies in the treasure map. The mystery is always greater than its solution."

"Just so long as we're not talking about the naval codes."

"No, no!"

"I'm relieved to hear that!"

"Don't turn this against me now, you clown. I'm only trying to say that the riddle has an appeal which the solution deprives it of, however clever it may be. The answer sort of removes the yearning from the question."

"I agree with you, Alan, of course. Yeats thinks the same. If there's anything divine then you'll find it in the question, not the answer. That was incidentally a charming way of putting it: *The mystery is always greater than its solution.* Maybe that's why I always think detective novels are fun to start with, but always so dreary and predictable towards the end."

"That's absolutely right! It always ends in such a terrible anticlimax. I can't understand why Wittgenstein is so mad about them."

"About crime thrillers?"

"He devours them. He even subscribes to Street & Smith's *Detective Story Magazine.* His whole apartment is full of them. It's completely mad. He can't stand Gödel, but . . . his favourite book is *Rendezvous with Fear,* by the way. It's written by someone called Norbert Davis. I bought it to see what it's like, and I can't exactly say that I enjoyed it, but I saw immediately that the hero is just like Wittgenstein."

"In what way?"

"Neither of them is much of a believer in logic. They'd rather wait for the right moment and shoot their way to a solution. You could say that both of them go by intuition and aim for the weak spot."

"But you're not like that."

"I believe more in logic," Turing laughed.

Farley did not understand what was so funny.

"For me logic is pure magic, as Welchman said. Pure magic! Ha, ha. In any case, I don't think that it's as cumbersome as Wittgenstein makes out. I'm rather more convinced that we'll get far with it, maybe even all the way to this clearing."

"But it's the reasoning, the search itself, which fascinates you most of all?"

"I want answers just as much as anyone else, and I hate it when people, like religious people, capitulate as soon as things are difficult to understand, but I think that the harder it is to find something, the more value it has once you get there. It's obvious, really. Not even Wittgenstein wanted to find the solution to the mystery in his crime novels on page nineteen. He wanted to wait and sweat. The difficulty of the hunt is after all part of it and gives the treasure its value. I might not get any more for my ingots on the silver market just because I've buried them, or even because I'm making an encrypted treasure map. But something happens to the silver when I hide it, doesn't it, Oscar? It acquires an additional intangible value."

"It gets a history."

"Precisely. Both you and I become a part of it. Besides . . ."

"What?"

"There's a beginning which is part of what sets the value. I mean, someone who's had a certain type of experience early in life maybe has a better ability to appreciate certain treasures than others. One might for example assume that a person had once lost something immensely valuable . . ." he said, and got himself all caught up.

His stutter returned, but after a while it was clear that he was talking about himself, at least to an extent. It was he who had once lost something. He had lost a friend called Christopher Morcom who had been to Sherborne School with him. Alan said that he worshipped the ground that Christopher walked on:

"In his company everything became richer and better. Before I met Christopher, I was hopeless at school. My housemaster wrote that my prep was the most careless and ignorant he had ever seen."

"You were the boy who was good at numbers."

"But I wasn't even particularly good at mathematics. The headmaster wrote to my parents to say that I was antisocial, and that it was doubtful whether I would be moved up a year. I was alone. I didn't get on with anyone. Have you noticed how hard I find it to look people in the eye? In those days it was even worse. But then I caught sight of Christopher, and couldn't take my eyes off him. He was a year older, and so beautiful and slender that my whole body ached. Just his hands . . . you understand, Oscar, while I was clumsy and shy, Christopher was the school's shining light. He got scholarships and prizes, and I would never have dared to approach him if it hadn't turned out that he had a talent for numbers too. He loved mathematics and science, and he also had the most extraordinary eyes—I don't just mean that they were beautiful. He saw fantastically well with them. He could point out Venus in the middle of the day without a telescope. I wanted to become like him. Christopher had a telescope, and I wanted one too. On my seventeenth birthday, I was given one, and also Eddington's book about the constellations. It was as if Christopher and I had been bewitched by the heavens. We visited an observatory and bought a star globe. At that time, a comet was going to become visible in the skies and we often sat up in the evenings looking for it, and I felt such excitement that there must have been more to it than just the comet. We knew precisely where it was meant to appear, somewhere between Equuleus and Delphinus. We were full of expectation and sat still for hours. But we never got to see it together. We saw it separately, but never together. One winter's day, a boys' choir visited our school. I wasn't too taken by the music, it was nothing special, not at all, but as I stood there and listened and looked at Christopher, it shot through me, and I thought You and I, Christopher, we'll be seeing a lot of each other but . . . I can't explain it . . . I was afraid of the opposite. I became frightened. I found it hard to sleep that night. I lay and twisted and turned and looked up at the sky. The moon was full. It felt as if I were going to lie awake for a long time. And yet I must have dropped off. I woke up at three and heard the monastery bell ring. After a while I got up and walked over to the window. I'd stood there on many other nights and looked for the comet. But this time I remained standing and stared at the house where Christopher lived and then I was struck by a feeling of pure horror. I'll never be able to explain it. The next day Christopher wasn't in school, and not the following day either, and I asked my housemaster about it. I got evasive answers. A few days later a master came to see me in the morning, and I realised at once that something had happened. "Prepare yourself for the worst," he said. "Christopher is dead."

"What had happened?" Farley asked.

"Some time when he was small he had drunk contaminated milk which had caused internal lesions. Christopher never said anything about his illness. In fact he never said anything which would either worry or embarrass me. But that night as I stared at the moon in the dormitory he fell ill again and this time he didn't make it. He died in a hospital in London. One moment he was there and then the next . . . It hurt so much. I started to think that Christopher continued to live on in some sense. Religion wasn't my thing. It couldn't give me any comfort, no, all I had was my science, and like the bewildered boy I was I started to cook up a theory all of my own. I simply took some thoughts from quantum physics, which I used to create a dream in which Christopher lived on somewhere else. I wasn't just being silly, it was part of a trend at the time. I'm sure you know, Oscar, that ever since the discoveries in quantum physics, about the unpredictability of particles, all sorts of earnest drones have been using them to explain life and free will. These days I can't stand those scientific fads in which people throw themselves over the latest ideas and try to apply them to their own everyday experience. But one thing did stay with me. It was the thought that what we call the soul can't be something separate from the body, or from the universe either for that matter. We're all a part of the same exploding star, and just as lifeless things are governed by laws, so living things must be as well. There must be some structure, some logic."

"And that's what you're looking for?"

"Sort of. I have at least made a small start."

"And everything began with Christopher Morcom's death?"

"Who knows when different things begin?"

"I can certainly tell you when the weather is about to turn. We should set off."

Alan took a black shovel from the milk cart and dug a hole in the stony ground. With a sort of mocking solemnity he lowered the silver down into it and then looked up at the crowns of the trees and the sky. He patted the grass down over the hole, as if he were tending a grave.

"May you rest in peace," Farley said.

"Until I resurrect you," Alan said.

After Ian Fleming's plans had been scrapped there was no good news at all, and often it felt as if the war had been lost. Europe was in the hands of the Nazis, and as yet no-one suspected that Hitler would soon be turning his troops eastwards towards the Soviet Union, his own ally, and launch himself into a fight on two fronts, and that instead of getting support from the Japanese on the eastern front he would let them indulge in their own madness by drawing the U.S.A. into the war. People knew only that the Nazis dominated the Continent and the seas, and that it would be impossible to crack the naval Enigma, and thereby win the Battle of the Atlantic, without new codebooks.

It was a cold winter and nothing was happening. But then came the news that Operation Claymore appeared to have been successful. Claymore involved five British destroyers on the Norwegian coast with the secret assignment to obtain German coding equipment. Just after six in the morning of March 4 one of the ships, H.M.S. *Somali*, had sighted an armed German trawler called *Krebs* in foggy weather not far from Svolvær, and opened fire. The report did not say precisely what had happened, but the Englishmen had soon disabled the trawler, and in normal warfare that would have been more than adequate, but in this case it was nowhere near enough. Farley knew all too well that in these situations most commanders would choose to sink the vessel rather than board it, and that was also one of the reasons why so little code material had got through to Bletchley. From what Farley understood, this captain too had not wanted to storm the trawler. But a signals officer, Lieutenant Warmington, was adamant, and in the end the captain gave way and the crew clambered on board with weapons drawn. Exactly what then took place was not clear, except that Lieutenant Warmington had seized a document in the German captain's cabin which contained headings such as *Innere Einstellung, Äussere Einstellung* and *Steckerverbindung*, and that had an undeniably promising ring to it. It sounded as if it contained key settings, even though the report did hedge its bets. The German captain seemed to have had time to destroy some of the material.

The papers were expected to reach Bletchley within a few days and that could mean a breakthrough. Or yet another disappointment. Farley remembered coming up from the lake to the mansion and asking after Turing. "Try the dining room," Peter Twinn said. Farley did not feel like going there. He avoided the dining room if he was not going to eat. But he did go there of course and was engulfed in a dreadful smell of cabbage, boiled fish and something which reminded him of custard. Alan was indeed sitting there, poking at a pale potato which lay smothered in yellow congealed grease and from a distance he seemed to be asleep with his eyes open. A glassy look radiated from his eyes. His cheeks were grey. He seemed exhausted, and with weak hand movements he waved away some of the cigarette smoke which was blowing towards him from two directions and Farley reluctantly thought that there might be something to the rumour that Alan was in the process of wearing himself out.

But when Farley called across and explained that they might have found their key settings, something remarkable happened to this face. Not only did it gain colour. It became younger. It started to shine, the way it had out in the forest in Shenley, and Farley felt that he had to dampen his words by adding a note of gloomy sobriety:

"But I'm afraid I suspect that most of the document is missing."

He did not want to raise Alan's hopes too much. He thought that the mathematician seemed to be in one of those states of nervous excitement which quickly and in the face of the slightest disappointment could easily turn into apathy or collapse. But afterwards, when Farley thought back, he could see that this was the moment when Alan set off towards his great triumph, which would help them to end this miserable war.

35

FARLEY HATED THE PARANOIA of these new times. But somehow he knew that he could not do his job without at least some of that affliction, and as often as he took exception to what he thought was his colleagues' excessive suspicion, he was also afraid that he was not managing to push himself to be as sceptical as he should. He was analytical and could read people well. He had no difficulty in spotting holes and inconsistencies in the stories he was told. As a man with extensive literary knowledge, he could easily identify all the little signs of untruth, and he noticed quickly when someone simply did not know something. But perhaps in spite of everything, Farley was not so good at unmasking the really serious liars, those who lied as easily as they told the truth. It was like when he was a boy and read a good novel and did not want to believe that it was a made-up story. How could something which painted such clear images in his mind be pretence?

Farley had to see a cloud before he worried that it was going to rain, and he was perhaps too quick to take a liking to people, especially if they were young, gifted and beaten black and blue. It really was true that he had for a moment considered whether G.C.H.Q. should recruit Corell, and not only because it would be a simple way of keeping the policeman's knowledge about Bletchley Park in the firm. He thought that Corell could be useful. His judgement had let him down, it was true—there was something quixotic about his Cambridge adventure—and he took too many risks, but his powers of deduction seemed impressive. The recruitment criteria for the security services had been under discussion ever since Burgess and Maclean's defection. It was no longer good enough simply to assume that respectable membership of the upper class and a background at Eton and Oxford was sufficient, as M.I.6. used to do in earlier years. Being a product of the higher social strata was no longer regarded as a guarantee of loyalty, in fact rather the opposite. The upper class seemed to breed arrogant libertines, so the services had started to bring in people from other classes and to be much clearer about recruiting on the basis of talent and dependability. So why not try Corell?

First and foremost because he did not seem to be all that depend-able and also because there would have been wild protests from Pippard and others. No, Farley reasoned, instead of impressive, the policeman's powers of deduction could just as easily be regarded as *too* good—a sign that something was not quite right. Corell's account may have sounded convincing when presented in bits, but when you put it all together and looked at it as a whole, did you not then get a different feel from it? The policeman's reasoning, which had got him all the way to Bletchley Park and Turing's bombes, was supposed to have been based almost wholly on logical deduction, and yes of course, the conclusions were not in the least bit unreasonable. They were entirely logical, it was true. But per-haps when he had accepted them Farley was reacting rather like some-one who is reading about old discoveries and inventions: when all is said and done, the solutions do not seem so spectacular, because you already know the answer. When you have all the discoveries and inventions, you do not understand how difficult it actually was to arrive at them. Could it in fact have been Krause who leaked? Is that where the policeman's deductions came from?

Farley could not understand what the motive might have been. Krause had had a good reputation at Bletchley and Farley knew that there had been an extensive security vetting before the logician became a British citizen at the start of the war, above all due to the fact that he had been most warmly recommended by Turing, and it was thought that he would be a significant addition to the cryptological effort. There was perhaps one occasion when Pippard, with his ever suspicious eye, mentioned Krause's former citizenship as a risk factor—was Austria not Hitler's home country after all?—but apart from that, Farley could not remember that anyone had ever questioned Krause's loyalty. But was there nevertheless something to it?

Farley remembered that Krause had said something to the effect that too much patriotism blinds one and that what a country really needs is people who view it without the preconceived notions of love, but that was the sort of remark they all came out with at that time. It was before the Cold War poisoned people's minds. No, no, if there was anything there at all then Farley thought it lay in Krause's admiration for Turing and his fury when he heard Alan's backbiters talk about him when he was not there.

Had the logician leaked secrets to avenge the injustices suffered by Turing? Was he no longer willing to show loyalty to a country which treated its heroes so badly? And in that case who else other than Corell had received his leaked information? Farley looked at the policeman, at his eyes which seemed so small under the black and blue swellings, and he gave him some more water. "There, there," he said. "Have some more to drink!" He got up and soaked a towel and very carefully washed the policeman's wounds. It felt good to have something to do. It eased his worry, and made him feel less miserable himself.

"Thank you," Corell said.

"Shouldn't we use first names? Please call me Oscar."

"And please call me Leonard."

"Leonard it is. It's strange, you're so very like your father. You're so young, but you remind me of the old days."

"Did you like him?"

"I did. I never heard anyone tell a story like he could, not until I met you, that is . . ."

"Now you're exaggerating."

"Not all that much."

"My father always used to say that I told a good story. But since then I have never heard anyone else say it."

"You'll be hearing it again. You can be sure of that. Sometimes you even tell things a little too well."

"What do you mean?"

"You leave some things out."

"I don't."

"Is this your notepad?"

"It is."

"In the pad you've underlined the name Fredric Krause, and that honestly makes me nervous."

"Krause was part of it all during the war, wasn't he?"

"I really think that it's my turn to ask the questions."

"Yes, of course . . ."

Corell was happy that they were on first-name terms, and he loved to hear that he told stories well. He took it as a sign that the danger was over, and that he and Farley could now devote themselves to getting to know each other. He wanted to ask about his career and about literary research at Cambridge, and what he most of all liked to read. But then from out of the blue came the attack and an entirely different truth sank in: the friendliness had only been intended to soften him up, and in an instant he had dropped his guard. He felt crushed. It had been so incredibly stupid not to have said anything about the evening in the pub in Wilmslow.

"What did Krause tell you?"

"Nothing."

"Nothing?"

"Or rather, a lot. He told me about the crisis in mathematics and about the liar's paradox, and about Gödel and Hilbert. He gave me all the background to 'Computable Numbers.'"

"But nothing about the war."

"Not one word. I even noticed that he changed the subject and became nervous as soon as we touched on it."

"Where did you meet?"

Corell told him. He gave as detailed an account of the meeting as he could and said—which he thought was true—that he had avoided mentioning Krause so as to appear more sharp-witted himself. He had wanted to make Krause's reasoning over the liar's paradox his own. It had been pathetic and silly, he admitted, but the logician had not leaked any secrets, not in any way, so no suspicion should fall on him, no, no: "Don't drag him into this."

"You've dragged him in yourself by trying to keep him out of it."

"I was an idiot."

"Make up for it, then. Give me one good reason why you would suddenly want to spend an entire evening together."

Corell answered something along the lines of, "we were just having a nice time," but he felt so dejected that he really did wonder why anyone would bother to spend an evening with someone like him.

Farley saw the policeman's face fall. He saw the eyelids blink and his hand pass over his forehead and he was reminded of Turing that last time at Cheltenham. It was so sad to drive a wedge into someone's self-esteem; it always hurt him to dent someone's enthusiasm, and he looked down at his own hands, his strangely old hands, which had been transformed into something so aged and fragile without him noticing. When had that happened? He looked out at the city, and tried to straighten his back.

"Krause seemed to like being a teacher," Corell said. "I think he quite simply wanted to educate me." Farley let the words sink in. Was that a plausible explanation? A disciple thirsting for knowledge who goes out for a beer with someone who likes to teach? It was true that Krause was fond of talking and of popularising his subject. He was said to be a good lecturer and Farley remembered one time in Hut 4 when Krause had brilliantly vented his spleen about old Hegel, and Krause was certainly full of curiosity whenever the topic was Turing. Corell's story could be true. It could also be rubbish. Dear God, how tired Farley was of all this. In a voice which sounded stern only because he put a huge effort into it he said:

"I'm sure you realise that we will be interrogating Fredric Krause in depth. It would look very bad if you were hiding something."

"I'm not hiding anything."

"In that case confirm to me one more time that Krause didn't say anything about what he was working on during the war."

"He said nothing . . . or, yes . . . he did say one thing . . ."

Is it going to come out now?

". . . we were talking about the fact that Wittgenstein didn't think the liar's paradox had any significance outside strict logic and then Krause said that 'Wittgenstein was as wrong as hell. Alan Turing if anyone knew . . .'"

"What?" Farley said impatiently.

"'. . . that paradoxes can mean the difference between life and death.'"

"Didn't he say anything more than that?"

"No, he then changed the subject. He never even mentioned the war. But it started me thinking. How can paradoxes mean the difference between life and death?"

"How indeed," Farley said, and felt an involuntary smile again.

36

Bletchley Park, III

AFTERWARDS, WHEN FARLEY had reason to look back and wonder how things could have gone so wrong, he tried to remember if there was a specific moment, a single point in time, when the breakthrough came at Bletchley. He could not think of anything. The triumph did not come as a goal does in football. It happened step by step, and each one brought such new problems as to deprive it of any sense of joy, certainly there was no clash of cymbals to mark its arrival, and in any case they seldom had time to celebrate. They worked hard and most of all Farley remembered the worry and the waiting, first for the documents from the German trawler, then over the work with the analyses and the bombe machines. He could very well recall the complaints and the irritation: "Why the hell isn't anything happening? What's Alan doing?" But it was not easy. Rather, it was a minor miracle that they had already come so far.

When the material arrived on March 12, 1941, Turing realised at once that they could have done with more. The German captain on the trawler really had destroyed most of the codebook, and Admiral Tovey was probably right to have hauled the commanders of Operation Claymore over the coals for not having taken greater risks and also searched other ships. But hindsight was no help to them in Hut 8 and all Farley could do was pray to the God he did not believe in and try to reassure the Admiralty that Turing and his colleagues were doing all that they could.

"They say that he's careless."

"Maybe in everyday life, but not when it matters. If anyone can manage this, it's Turing."

"But we've heard . . ."

"I promise you. We'll get there," he interrupted, and the words left a stale taste in his mouth.

But he wanted to give them hope. Gloomy reports could only trigger idiotic changes and what they needed in Hut 8 was peace and quiet in which to work. These were desperate times. Behind each breath and between every line in the conversations with London one could sense the longing for a breakthrough, and it was not hard to understand why. That spring, the Nazi U-boat fleet grew faster than ever before, and matters were not helped by the fact that the Germans could now also use the ports on the north coast of France. Farley remembered a brief conversation at Bletchley with a Commander Glyver.

"How is it out there?"

"Like swimming among sharks."

People were convinced that the heavy bombardment of the larger cities in England and the constant attacks against British shipping were merely a preparation for the Nazi invasion, and from time to time people yelled at Farley:

"For God's sake, haven't they cracked the bloody system yet?"

But you could not crack the system once and for all. Since the settings on the Enigma machines were changed every night, they had to start again every morning, and progress was slow. It took forever, and although they deciphered messages every now and then, it was always too late, and the worry and irritation grew: *People are dying out there while they mess about with their bloody mathematics. Why isn't anything happening?* As it happened, a great deal was happening. Alan Turing's methods for mechanising their guesswork and weighing probabilities grew more effective by the day. Ever since he had built his bombe machines, he understood that there was a geometric relationship between the cribs and the encrypted text, and he became more and more adept at testing it by feeding his machines with contradictions, with paradoxes. He and his colleagues also managed to reconstruct the Enigma machines' so-called bigram tables. More and more telegrams were also decoded, soon with only three days' delay, for example one from Admiral Dönitz himself, the architect behind the Nazi U-boat offensive:

ORDER FROM THE ADMIRAL TO ALL U-BOATS:
THE ESCORTS FOR U69 AND U107 MUST BE AT LOCATION 2
AT 8:00 A.M. ON MARCH 1.

The sad thing was that it was deciphered too late and that no-one knew what was meant by Location 2. Countless problems remained. But it was a start. It gave reassurance. It increased the pool of knowledge about the system, and if there was after all a point when Farley thought "we'll get there," then it was one evening just before the blackout. He was sitting in the tracking room in Hut 4 on one of the terrible wooden folding chairs and discussing the security profiles of the newly arrived mathematicians with Pippard. At that time, new recruits were streaming in to Bletchley Park. They all solemnly had to sign the Official Secrets Act and were threatened with imprisonment if they leaked a single word. But compared with what would follow after the war, security was rather light, above all because they had no choice. They needed all the competent people they could find. This was also a time when one trusted people.

There had, however, been one change in the thinking behind security. Just as they investigated people with left-leaning sympathies, they now had to look just as much for those who were drawn to extreme right-wing movements: Were there any new recruits who might be likely to collaborate with the Nazis during an invasion? Like many from the right, Pippard did not find this change of course easy. He remained more interested in keeping an eye on those who diverged sexually and "other unreliable elements," those who could become victims of blackmail or sell out their country for their own profit.

"The cynics worry me more than those with ideological convictions," he said, and Farley explained very calmly that Pippard was talking rubbish, but without being too vehement about it, and he was pretty glad when Birch stepped into the room and interrupted them.

Frank Birch had sounded off about Turing and Peter Twinn and complained about their extravagant mathematics, saying all sorts of idiotic things in his impatience, but he was never one who could not change his opinion, and say what you would about him: grumpy and contrary though he was, he was more entertaining than most. He was someone you noticed, and as he now stepped into the room, dressed in a raincoat and a crumpled felt hat, he immediately drew attention to himself.

"Look at this," he said, eagerly waving a deciphered and translated message from Hut 8, which Farley immediately snatched and quickly scanned through to satisfy himself that it contained nothing untoward.

At once he smiled. His face broke into a huge grin, as if he had just heard an uncommonly good joke. The telegram read:

FROM: COMMANDER IN CHIEF OF THE NAVY.

THE U-BOAT CAMPAIGN MAKES IT NECESSARY TO LIMIT STRICTLY THE NUMBER OF THOSE WHO ARE AUTHORISED TO READ NAVAL SIGNALS. ONCE AGAIN I FORBID ALL THOSE, WHO DO NOT HAVE EXPRESS ORDERS FROM NAVAL HIGH COMMAND, TO CONNECT TO THE U-BOAT ENIGMA FREQUENCIES. I WILL REGARD ANY ATTEMPT TO CONTRAVENE THIS ORDER AS A CRIMINAL ACT DESIGNED TO COMPROMISE GERMAN NATIONAL SECURITY.

"What do you think," Birch asked with a note of triumph in his voice. "Have we made ourselves guilty of a contravention?"

"Seems like it!"

"So the Germans might get cross with us?"

"There is that risk."

Farley laughed, and it seemed like the first time for some while. Not many days later he got word that a message from the Führer himself had been cracked, ending with the words: CONQUER ENGLAND! Not exactly a reassuring phrase, but the mere fact that they had read it made it less likely to happen. They also became quicker and quicker at deciphering communications, and soon that began to make a real difference. A key development was the discovery by Turing and his colleagues that some old and boring reports from the German weather ships stationed off northern Iceland had not been despatched with the naval codes, but with a simpler system. This discovery led not only to yet another cryptological advance but also to plans being made to launch a live physical operation in the real war. The British Navy understood the value of getting hold of the codebooks from those ships. In this new action, the weather ships *München* and *Lauenburg* were stormed, gifting Bletchley new material, and by some time in May the naval intelligence officers could read the Nazis' navy communications like an open book.

One could hardly overstate the significance of this. The British fleet now had the ability to strike back. Convoys with essential supplies for England could dodge the German U-boats. During July, British shipping losses sank below 100,000 tons for the first time since 1940. Life seemed brighter and of course it helped that the Germans had ordered a large part of their fleet down into the Mediterranean, not to mention the unexpected news that Hitler had broken the Molotov–Ribbentrop pact and launched an attack against the Soviet Union. The invasion of England no longer seemed so likely, and Farley guessed that even all of those at Bletchley who knew nothing of the successes in Hut 8 still understood that something had happened. The mood became lighter and the daily newspapers carried fewer and fewer announcements of Englishmen who had drowned or frozen to death.

The problems did not of course all disappear. Cracking the naval Enigma was like starting a new game of poker every morning. There was a constant need for new guesses and bluffing, and new questions had to be asked all the time, such as how they were to use the information. Of course the deciphered material had to be used. It could save lives every day. But if it was used too diligently, the Germans might suspect that their naval codes had been cracked, and once more add complications to the Enigma system, so that the code-breakers would be back at square one again overnight, with everything unreadable and black. Those in charge at Bletchley were aware of the problem. There was a risk that every cryptological step forward would itself prepare the ground for a fresh setback and on many earlier occasions decisions had been taken to sacrifice both lives and equipment so as not to reveal that the communications were being read. Nor was it the first time that misleading manoeuvres were staged, to make it seem as if they had won the information through more traditional forms of espionage. But never before had the situation been so sensitive, and never before had such care been taken, and it frustrated many. Late one evening Farley was walking down the long, creaking corridor in Hut 8, letting himself be enveloped by the noise from in there, which could be heard through the thin partition walls.

"Hello, Oscar!"

Behind him, and only barely lit by the brown glow from the naked lightbulbs in the ceiling, Fredric Krause looked out from one of the side doors, he who thirteen years later was to cause Farley so much anxiety. Krause was a strange combination of sociable and shy. He was more open and accessible than his friend Turing, but Krause too had an evasive way about him. It was said that he had synesthesia, that he saw colours when he thought of numbers, and that figures formed kaleidoscopic images in his mind.

"Hello, Fredric," he said. "How are things?"

"Not too bad!"

"Worn out?"

"Not really. May I ask you something?"

"Of course."

"Did we attack the U-boats at Bishop Rock?"

Farley knew the answer to the question. But should he give it? The truth was not always edifying, especially not for those who slaved day and night and who were still young and enthusiastic, and he therefore meant to mumble something along the lines of: "Of course we did." But Krause seemed to see through him.

"We didn't," he said.

"What happened to our convoy?"

"We had to sacrifice it. I'm sorry, Fredric."

"What kind of bloody idea is that . . ." the Austrian began, but he did not continue, and neither was it necessary.

It was obvious how disappointed he was, and Farley considered laying his hand on Krause's shoulder. He just said: "It's a hell of a war," and he really meant it. Obviously they had warned the commander of the cargo ships in the area, but that had not been enough because the Admiralty had refused to send any destroyers out to attack the German U-boats. They were afraid that too much use had already been made of the deciphered information; the convoy had therefore been sacrificed.

A lesser evil had been accepted in place of a greater one. This was the constant cynicism of war.

Even so, it was long a question of whether this was enough. Many at Bletchley were convinced that summer that it was only a matter of time before the enemy became aware of their success, and there were also signs that the German High Command had started to become suspicious. How could it have been otherwise? There had to be a reason why the English had suddenly become so much better at escaping the German U-boats. Luckily—as was apparent later—the Nazis' paranoia was misdirected. They seemed to believe that their naval Enigma was unbreakable, and that was not an unreasonable conclusion. How could the Nazis understand that England had people like Alan Turing? Instead of making their Enigma machines more advanced, they shot their own officers, and O.I.C. and M.I.6 tried as hard as they could to contribute to that delusion. False information was spread about spies in the Nazi ranks and for a long time this seemed to be successful. Bletchley retained an astonishing degree of insight into German naval planning. The Admiralty knew almost as well as the Germans where the U-boats were located and with each day Alan Turing's star status increased, at least among the few who were in the know.

Running on the principles laid down by him, the systematised work flowed so well that his presence was not needed as much as before, and he had more and more time to devote to his pastimes, to his efforts to mechanise the playing of chess and his theories about the mathematics of the plant kingdom. He lived in a world of his own. If he only had what he needed, it seemed that he could exist anywhere, whether on a desert island or in a castle, and from what Farley could recall Alan was one of the few who never complained about the food or how little leave there was. He even seemed to be happy, although with the benefit of hindsight it was not hard to see that the worries were even then piling up like clouds. Someone as different as Alan was unlikely to win Churchill's confidence without there being consequences.

That episode was a drama in itself. Only a few of the inner circle at the mansion knew that the prime minister was due to come to Bletchley Park to boost the morale of the members of staff and to congratulate them on the progress achieved with the naval Enigma. Normally, a tour like this would generate nothing but enthusiasm. But the visit coincided with a row about resources in Hut 8. Farley could not see what the fuss was about. Why did they not immediately get what they wanted? After all, those in positions of responsibility knew how vitally important the work in Hut 8 was. Yet nothing happened. Turing and his colleagues needed more people, and more machines, but everything moved so curiously slowly, without it really being possible to work out whose fault that was. Inertia was just ingrained in the organisation and, in all honesty, Alan was not much of a negotiator. He understood neither bureaucrats nor hierarchies nor the fact that some people always cause difficulties and do not get things done, and it was almost a pleasure for him to relinquish the leadership of the hut to Hugh Alexander.

This did not entirely let Alan off the hook. He was the hero at Bletchley and few things in politics were said to fascinate Churchill more than intelligence work and cryptological analysis; the prime minister therefore had a full overview of the work at Bletchley. During the first phase of the war, he wanted to read every word which was deciphered there, but when the material started to arrive in boxes and crates he gave up and contented himself with daily summaries.

Farley remembered the waiting on that day, September 6, 1941; how the few who were in the know waited around at the sentry box and the barriers, and how the cars then rolled in, and a door flew open. There's something strange about fame and power, isn't there? Farley felt a stab of humiliation. It seemed to him undignified that he was affected so much. It was as though the ground were pulling him down, as if gravity were trying to force him to bow, and for a moment he imagined himself hearing the soundtrack from a newsreel. *With determined step the prime minister inspects* . . . Something unreal came over Bletchley generally as Churchill climbed out of the car with his large stomach and tightly fitting waistcoat. He was a caricature of himself. He even had his cigar and he glanced around, looking both grim and amused, and said something that Farley could not hear but everyone laughed at, even Farley himself. He grinned, although he had not understood a single word, and around him people had trouble standing still. They crowded around the prime minister, greeting him nervously, and then started to move off in a group over the lawn, past the streams of Wrens, secretaries, W.A.A.F.s, Royal Engineers and academics. Everywhere, people gave a start: *Isn't that . . .?* A solemn mood began to spread and like a fire it consumed what until then had been the everyday atmosphere pervading the estate. People stopped in mid-step and became conscious of their own bodies. Farley on the other hand began to relax and managed to take a more sober view of the situation. It was one of the first days of autumn, with traces of yellow in the foliage and rooks soaring in the air. Robins pecked at breadcrumbs up by the stable yard, and to the right and left of him a strange game was being played out. On the one hand everybody wanted to be the one to answer the prime minister's questions, and have the privilege of looking him in the eye (so as not to give as ridiculous an impression as the others, Farley stayed in the background), while on the other hand there was a general sense of embarrassment, which grew and grew. It was as if they had received smart visitors but had not had the time to tidy up properly first.

Since so few on the premises had been told about the visit in advance, because of the security risks, no-one had had the chance to dress up for the occasion, not that Farley thought that Churchill cared about that sort of thing anyway. He just puffed on his cigar and reeked of his alcohol, and exuded a careless determination. But the chaos in Hut 8 clearly pained Captain Edmund Travis, the acting director of Bletchley. The prime minister could not even open the front door. He pressed his heavy body against it, but someone was sitting in there, leaning against the doorframe, and since they all made for another door instead, Churchill tumbled in on top of Hugh Alexander. Hugh was sitting on the floor, sorting out transcripts, though goodness knows why he could not do it while sitting in a chair. Hugh of course flew up, when he saw who was coming in, but he had absolutely no chance to hide the mess of paper in the room or the overflowing waste-paper baskets marked with the solemn words *Confidential Waste Paper.* Churchill, however, quickly mastered the situation and grinned in recognition when he realised who it was.

"Are you finding any time to play chess?"

"Unfortunately not, sir."

"No, this isn't exactly a time to enjoy ourselves. Bloody Hitler. Where can I meet the young man with the machines?"

"Do you mean Dr. Turing, Prime Minister?"

There must have been some who wished that Churchill had not asked, or who even hoped that Alan was not around. But of course the whole entourage trooped off towards Turing's room, some of them probably silently praying that he was in a reasonable state, but in his eagerness Travis forgot to knock. He immediately regretted it. Alan was sitting in his chair, leaning back and knitting. This strange man, who had not shaved for a week and clearly had not had much use for a comb, was busy with something that looked like a long blue scarf and not even Churchill could immediately grasp the situation.

"Oh, that looks nice," he said, while Alan flew up, half scared out of his wits.

"What, no . . . not at all . . . actually not . . . I do . . . I do apologise, Prime Minister. It . . . it helps me to thi— to think," Turing stammered.

"Really, is that so? Unfortunately, knitting isn't one of the art forms that I've mastered. But of course I still understand. Good ideas can come when your mind is on something completely different, isn't that right? And your thoughts, Mr. Turing, we all need them. I've understood that. So by all means, keep at it . . . and the scarf is also bound to come in handy."

Everybody laughed, but some could barely hide their embarrassment: knitting . . . can one imagine anything more ridiculous? Such a woman's thing, as someone whispered, and on top of everything else Alan did not manage to look Churchill in the eye. He just rambled on about probability theories while his eyes darted along the walls, and perhaps it really had not been much of a meeting, as Pippard maintained so emphatically afterwards. But Farley would probably still say that there had been a warmth there, or at least a new level of attentiveness on the part of the prime minister which suggested genuine interest. Yes, Churchill was probably just amused. So long as the geniuses are successful, it's probably only good fun if they're also eccentric, and Farley was in any case convinced that Churchill was just joking when he later said to Travis: "I know that I told you to leave no stone unturned in finding good people, but I hadn't expected you to take it quite so literally."

All the same this worried some of the less imaginative people at Bletchley, and the important visit also had unexpected consequences.

In Hut 8 the shortage of staff and resources became increasingly acute. Yet precious little was done about it, why was still not clear, but somewhere there must have been direct opposition to the team in the hut, perhaps out of pure envy. Otherwise the absence of any action would be inexplicable. Things became so bad that the deciphering of the naval Enigma was under serious threat, and in the middle of October Turing and Hugh Alexander and a few others went behind the backs of their leaders and turned directly to the man who had visited them. They wrote to Churchill that they were in desperate need of reinforcements and more machines, and in no time at all an investigation had taken place and orders came from on high. Churchill wrote to General Ismay under the heading Urgent: *Action this day! See to it that they have everything they need with extreme priority and report to me when it is done!*

After that the work went better, but the opposition did not go away, and new problems awaited.

On February 2, 1942, the Germans put a fourth rotor into the naval Enigma machines. The codes became twenty-six times more complex and Hut 8 was transformed yet again into an industry of its own with several hundred employees who were in fact dependent more on new and more powerful machines than their own brains. Turing was moved over to the mansion and became a general strategist who was only called on if something really difficult came up. But he still had his enemies, not least Pippard, who could not get over the fact that Turing had gone behind his back.

One day Farley saw Colonel Fillingham standing and yelling at Turing by the barbed wire fence not far from the entrance to the drive. It must have been in the spring of 1942, and Farley was immediately worried. He saw it as a matter of national importance to keep Turing out of trouble. But soon he calmed down a bit. Fillingham was well known for always shouting at people and Turing did not seem to be particularly troubled. Perhaps the row was just about Turing's shambolic appearance and it was probably something to do with the Home Guard. That was Colonel Fillingham's area of responsibility and Turing had surprisingly enough become one of his recruits because he wanted, as he said, to be able to defend himself if the Nazis came after him.

"What's the matter?" Farley wondered.

Colonel Fillingham was a large, red-faced man, who was hardly able to compose himself. In an agitated voice he said that "young Dr. Turing thinks that he can do exactly as he pleases," and when Farley asked in what way, the colonel pointed out that Turing had not turned up for any of the Home Guard's parades, even though he was "obliged to do so under military law."

"I've tried to tell the colonel that I'm not subject to any military laws," Turing said.

"I'm sorry, Alan, but if you've joined the Home Guard then I'm afraid you probably are. The colonel is fully within his rights to give you orders. Am I right, colonel, in assuming that all that parade business can't be too burdensome?" Farley continued in a conciliatory tone.

"I'm not so sure about that," the colonel said angrily.

"But I'm being serious, Oscar," Turing continued. "I've protected myself against these sorts of situations. You've just got to take a look at my application form!"

"Your what?"

But they did as he suggested, and Colonel Fillingham had to admit that Turing was right. One of the questions in the form was: *Do you understand that you are subject to military law?* and Alan, who had given the question very careful thought, had come to the conclusion that the best answer was to say no. There was no reason to say yes to anything which in all likelihood would bring him no advantages, he explained, and even though Colonel Fillingham did not seem to be entirely satisfied he completely ignored Turing after that. Thanks to his keen grasp of game theory, Turing was excused from parade duty, and the story became a part of the mythology surrounding him, but obviously the story also spread to Pippard and the likes of him, and although they too laughed at it, it was becoming ever clearer that the snare was being drawn tighter around Turing.

The situation was difficult for all of them. Bletchley was without doubt the most important source of information for the military leadership. It was the place on which a large part of the war strategy rested. But it was not only what was happening there that was secret: the fact that there was anything at all going on there was in itself a secret. Officially, Bletchley Park did not exist. Not even generals and Churchill's close collaborators had any idea that there was such a place, and to hide its existence a whole world of lies and smoke screens was created, which resulted in the rest of the British security services getting far more credit than they deserved. The secrecy weighed on all of their shoulders. But few were as exposed as Turing. His fingerprints were everywhere, and when the U.S.A. was dragged into the war and built up its own cryptology industry, Turing was shipped across the Atlantic, and soon his bombe machines appeared there by the hundred. This gave him unique insight into the world of secrecy in America too, and the pressure on him grew by the day. He continued to be the all-too-fragile spider in the web, and watchful eyes were always directed at him.

When a message from Heinrich Himmler was decoded in which he mocked the English for allowing homosexuals to work in the security services, it is true that many at Bletchley wore a satisfied smile: "If only that gangster knew!" But the same attitude was spreading to them too, and it did not help that Turing had broken off his engagement to Joan Clarke.

Farley would never forget the day when he saw him sitting outside the mansion with one of his black notepads, apparently unconcerned by the excavators and workers out in the courtyard. He wore a hostile look, but Farley knew that might not mean anything. Whenever Alan was writing or calculating something, he always radiated rage. Like a beast of prey, he seemed prepared to sink his teeth into anything that might disturb him. Yet, oddly enough, he did not appear to mind being interrupted, and therefore Farley was so bold as to say hello and for once they did not start talking about cryptology. They spoke about Joan and, when Farley asked why the relationship had ended, Turing quoted Oscar Wilde's words from *The Ballad of Reading Gaol*:

"Yet each man kills the thing he loves."

A man kills the thing he loves. For someone like Farley, those were not just known and hackneyed words. He saw in them the Wildean affectation which not even his time in prison had managed to eradicate, and even though there was certainly truth in the words in many a situation outside the poem too, in this case it just seemed to be an excuse. A man kills the thing he loves? Of course! But most of all he kills the thing he must. Farley sensed the real reason for the break-up, but said in his most sympathetic voice:

"I understand. I'm so sorry!"

Nor was there any reason to pry. There were so many others doing it already. Pippard put the old notation back into Turing's personnel file and even underlined the word homosexual with two black lines. The big star at Bletchley came to be seen more and more as a risk. The government, Farley thought, did not even dare to reward him properly. All he got was a miserable O.B.E.

37

THE TELEPHONE GAVE an unexpectedly loud ring and Corell started as if he had been hit. The sound seemed to carry a new threat with it and since neither of them moved, Corell just had time to hope that they could simply let it ring, but then Farley got to his feet.

"I'll get it!"

There was something solemn about the way he gripped the receiver.

"Yes, yes, of course. He's here. I've spoken to him."

To Corell it sounded like a conversation between two prison guards. He heard a stern and unpleasant voice at the other end of the line and felt his stomach knot. Yet the rest of the conversation did not sound as worrying as he had feared. Farley's yes turned into a series of nos.

"No, no, you've got this out of all proportion. There's no danger, that's absolutely clear. He's only been unwise, no it doesn't appear as if any damaging information has got out, and honestly he doesn't know very much. Calm down, Julius . . . don't you hear what I'm saying? I have the situation under control."

The prison guards appeared to be at odds with each other. Farley even seemed to be defending him, and in the end Corell began to see the conversation as a struggle between a friend and an enemy.

"Well, yes of course we need to go on investigating this, but you really worry me . . . No for God's sake don't listen to Mulland. He's got the wrong end of the stick. He's out of his mind . . . he's assaulted . . . he's quite simply mad . . . for God's sake Julius, you're not even listening to me. I'm telling you no. No! Now I have to go and deal with this! Goodbye!"

Farley hung up and Corell suppressed an urge to ask about the call. He fixed his eyes on a crumpled part of the blanket just below his chest, which he thought looked like a face, and then he closed his eyes and pretended to try to sleep. Julie surfaced in his thoughts; Julie who was lovingly dressing the tailor's dummy in the shop window.

"Am I free to go?" he said.

Farley appeared to hesitate. He seemed agitated after the telephone conversation.

"You are. But I don't think it's advisable from a purely medical point of view. We should get a doctor here after all."

"No, no. I just want to get away from here."

Corell felt a sudden impatience.

"Where to?"

"I don't know. Just away. To my aunt in Knutsford."

"O.K., I'll see to it that you get there!"

Farley did not know what had got into him. He was not at all as convinced about the policeman's innocence as he had pretended to Pippard. But after all that had happened he thought that Corell deserved to be accompanied by somebody and he was also curious to meet the aunt, who according to their records was an old lesbian suffragette with a keen interest in literature. Somerset had thought that she might be the key to the policeman's behaviour, and even though Farley did not altogether agree—keys were seldom so simple—he had the impression that there might be something interesting there. He also wanted to get away from the hotel before Pippard or anyone else started poking their noses in even further, and so he pulled out his telephone book.

There were many he could call. Looking back later, it would surprise him that he had chosen just Jamie Ingram. It was as if he were looking for a companion, an accomplice, more than a friend or a colleague. Ingram was the black sheep of the Ingram banking family. Not that Jamie was a criminal or even particularly dishonest, but he was a scandal waiting to happen who drank too much and liked to provoke. He had turned up drunk to Farley's lectures and it was said that he had thrown the dean's bicycle into the Cam after a stupid row about a game of bridge. On the other hand, he was not quick to judge when someone else's life went off the rails—probably because he knew how easily it could happen. He also owed Farley a favour or two and seemed more than happy to be able to help.

"My dear professor, are you in a fix? I sincerely hope that there's a woman involved!"

"No, and unfortunately I'm not even drunk. Can you come?"

Ingram turned up in a new white Aston Martin, which he had borrowed from his father, a slightly vulgar car Farley thought, especially since it was to be used for transporting a beaten-up policeman to an aunt in Knutsford, but Farley was nevertheless touched by the gesture. "We should do things in style," Ingram explained, looking a bit too extravagant himself, like the car.

He was wearing a red scarf and a linen jacket and his blond hair had a studiedly dishevelled look to it, but from the first moment he acted naturally and professionally. For example, he had the good taste not to enquire what had happened. He helped Corell to his feet with the greatest care and offered him a shot from his hip flask, bourbon he said it was, and took the opportunity to compliment Corell on his hopelessly filthy suit.

"Some dry cleaning and a bath and you'll be all set for the reception rooms again."

Since Farley's back was more or less out of action, Ingram had to help the policeman down on his own, and while Farley paid Corell's bill, Ingram was so charming and easygoing that for a little while life seemed somewhat less complicated. After Ingram had given Farley some brief instructions about driving the Aston and had handed over the keys with the words "My father wouldn't mind at all if you dented it a bit," he took his nonchalant elegance off without even having told Farley when and how to return the car. These carefree, rich young rascals are good in that way, Farley thought. They demand as little of others as they do of themselves.

"Thank you very much indeed. I'll be in touch," he called out, but the young man was already too far away, and Farley turned instead to Corell.

The policeman sat in the passenger seat, pale and shrunken as if nothing surprised him any longer, neither the car nor anything else. Farley told him to wait. He crossed the street and bought chocolate, orange juice, fresh bread and ham. Before driving off they ate, and some colour returned to Corell's cheeks. He said that his neck and head were hurting less. He did not say much else. His flow of words had dried up and he most certainly did not want to see any doctor. He wanted to get to Vicky's. "There's something I want to say to her," he explained, and for a long while they drove northwards in silence.

Darkness fell. The traffic thinned and the roads stretched out before them like long restless arms. Farley held the steering wheel tightly and longed for a book, or something that could anchor his thoughts, and he tried to recite "Michael Robartes and the Dancer," but was not able to. He was much too unfocused, and although he wanted to chat, he was reluctant to disturb the policeman. Corell slept or dozed on and off, but even when he was awake he sat deep in his thoughts, and only once they had passed Corby did he begin to liven up somewhat, and only then because Farley had prised him open a bit by asking questions about his life and family.

"My mother is dead," Corell said.

"My colleague told me. How did she die?"

"Shrivelled and mad in a home in Blackpool. But we didn't have much contact during the last years. I was there quite often towards the end, but she spoke to me as if I were someone else."

"I'm sorry. Of course I know what happened to your father."

"He stepped in front of a train."

"Must have been hard for you."

"I suppose it was."

Farley tried to talk about something else, but the policeman stayed with the subject of suicide.

"I've thought about Alan Turing's last steps in life," he said.

The thought ran through Farley: Who hasn't thought about them?

"Is there anything in particular you've fastened on?" he asked.

"There seemed to be so much going on in the house: experiments, calculations, a meal with lamb chops. Does one really eat a good dinner knowing one is going to die?"

"No idea. People on death row do it."

"Or he made up his mind later, after the dinner."

"Maybe he did."

"Sometimes I've wondered what it would have taken for him to have second thoughts. Would it have been enough for a friend to have knocked on the door and said a few nice words, or for a dog to have barked outside and led his thoughts off in a new direction? Or was the decision irrevocable?"

"You do wonder," Farley said, not entirely sure if it was Turing's or his father's suicide the policeman was talking about.

"And then he ate a poisoned apple," the policeman said.

"The fruit of sin. The fruit of knowledge."

"Strange in a way, don't you think?"

"Why?"

"Sometimes I've wondered whether he deliberately laid out riddles for us."

"At any rate he knew that the mystery is always greater than its solution."

"Did Dr. Turing really think that we would be able to build an intelligent machine?"

Farley was about to answer, "No idea. What do you think?" when it struck him that he might just as well take the question seriously. He had after all spoken to Alan about it.

"I think so," he said. "You know, one day I surprised him when he was sitting reading Dorothy Sayers's *The Mind of the Maker.*"

"What's that?"

"A more or less theological book in which Sayers tries to interpret God's creation of the world through her own experiences as a writer of fiction. The author as God, you understand. It's often said that an author has absolute power over her characters, but that isn't true, not if you're a good writer like Sayers. If the characters are to come to life, they have to free themselves from their maker and acquire traits of unpredictability. A writer who takes her work seriously knows that it's the characters' demand for a life and an existence that drives a book, rather than its original plot."

"And for there to be life, there must be contradictions!"

"It takes an element of unpredictability and irrationality. I know that Alan was especially interested in Sayers's thoughts on Laplace. Do you know about him? Laplace was a French mathematician and astronomer whose work was influenced by Newton. His universe was strictly governed by the laws of gravity and his most famous idea was that an intelligent being who knew the position and movement of every particle in the world would be able to work out exactly what was going to happen in the future. Everything was predetermined in a precise pattern of causation, which God had set in motion before he took himself off the scene. It was determinism taken to its extreme, and Alan didn't have much time for it. But he was fascinated by the thought of a creator who, as Sayers put it, has put his pen down and his feet up and left the work to get on with itself. I know that Alan thought about it a lot. He started to look around in the pool of light cast by that idea, as it were. This was 1941 or possibly 1942 and I'm sure you'll understand that I can't tell you anything about our work, except that what we were doing was a little bit like Laplace's universe—well, I probably shouldn't really tell you that either. But we had found a working method which ticked along more or less by itself and we no longer had the same need for geniuses like Alan. There were thousands of us working together, and most of us were doing incredibly simple things, even just routine operations, but together we formed a highly sophisticated organism. Seen as an entity, we must have appeared to be the oracle, no more nor less, and for someone like Alan, it wasn't hard to see parallels with the human brain. Each tiny cell on its own is not necessarily all that special, is it? But there's no denying that the totality is, so what counts is not the parts themselves, but the way they are assembled, and that prompted him to ask himself: Is there some other way in which something intelligent can grow out of parts which aren't in themselves intelligent? Can a purely mechanical and routine process give rise to something which has talent and originality?"

"And Turing's answer was yes," Corell said.

"Absolutely. In the same way that Newton and Laplace saw no contradiction between a mechanical view of the world and a belief in God,

Alan saw no contradiction between the mechanical and the intelligent, or for that matter between the mediocre and the inspired."

"Now you've lost me."

"Have you heard people talk about the wisdom of the crowd?"

"Only about the idiocy of the crowd."

Farley gave a laugh.

"That is of course the better-known, unfortunate part," he said. "There's nothing so stupid as people who follow a crazy leader and work themselves up into a lynch mob. Or as Friedrich Nietzsche said: 'Madness is the exception in individuals but the rule in groups.'"

"True!"

"Indeed, but in another sense it would appear that a large group of people could be more intelligent than anything else."

"How so?"

"As with us during the war, for example. But also in another way. You know, some time ago I read an extract from a novel by the scientist Francis Galton. It's called *Kantsaywhere*. It describes a Utopia where a better sort of person is being bred. Pretty awful rubbish, to be honest. But the book interested me for various reasons, and I started to take a closer look at Galton's life. He was a terrible elitist, who thought that incredibly few people had the necessary genetic qualities to lead a community. He looked on normal people as hopelessly ungifted. But the funny thing is that towards the end of his life he stumbles on an entirely different truth. By that time Galton is an old man visiting a livestock market in Plymouth. He happens to walk past a competition, where anyone is allowed to guess the weight of an ox, or to be precise the weight of an ox after it's been slaughtered and skinned. Galton expects people to be useless at guessing, since people in general are such benighted arses. But do you know what he finds? Once he has collected all the suggestions, and worked out the average, treating all those who have taken part as one person, so to speak, he notices that the contestants have guessed right, almost to the gramme."

"How is that possible?"

"Because that's how a group functions. It can be incredibly intelligent and come up with better answers than all of the experts, provided the individuals who make up the group think independently, and that's the beauty of it. Crowds have a hidden wisdom. When Galton worked out the average for all the participants, their shortcomings cancelled each other out, and their knowledge accumulated. All of the tiny pieces of the group's puzzle of knowledge formed something very sophisticated. Alan loved that sort of thing. He was fascinated by ant-hills. They're made up of mindless insects, but they're extraordinarily complex and rich in intelligence, and somehow I believe that's the core of his thinking. It's not each cog in itself . . ."

"It's the way they relate to each other."

"Or how they form a whole, and I can't help thinking how exciting it sounds. In any case I know that Donald Michie, one of Alan's clever friends, believes this can become a new field of research."

"What?"

"The attempts to create an intelligent machine out of simple electronic components. From a Christian point of view, that is of course pure heresy. Alan of all people knew that."

"But that was part of his dream?"

"He dreamed."

"Why, do you think?"

"Why not? For all I know he longed to have a machine as a friend. Besides, it wouldn't surprise me at all if something valuable comes of it. Donald Michie spoke of Alan's theories as a buried treasure which will one day be unearthed."

"Just like his silver."

Farley started.

"How do you know about that?"

"His brother told me."

"Of course. We saw each other outside the morgue," Farley muttered.

"How are you feeling, by the way?"

"Better. Do we still have far to go?"

"A little bit. You're close to your aunt, aren't you?"

"I suppose I am," the policeman said.

"Haven't you always been very . . ." Farley was searching for the right word, ". . . very devoted to each other?"

"No, not always," Corell said. "There was a time when I didn't want to have anything to do with her," he started, but then stopped abruptly.

"Would you like to tell me about it?" Farley tried.

"No, I don't think so."

The policeman seemed to drift away in his thoughts. At one point it even looked as if he were smiling.

38

WHAT'S WRONG WITH GETTING SOME HELP?

Many years ago, when Corell returned home to Southport after leaving Marlborough, the next blow fell, and he should have been prepared for it. He had seen it coming. But his mother's coldness felt like a blow from which there was no recovery. Did she ever say a single word that concerned him? She was wholly preoccupied with herself and her mute suffering. Paradoxically enough, in the midst of the hardest time in her life, she seemed to have become incapable of serious conversation, and worst of all, she expected him to play along.

He was allowed to complain about the prices in the shops, the food shortages and the toil and drudgery around the house, and even the parlous state of their finances. But he had to keep quiet about everything that was important and painful. Any suggestion that he too might be suffering had her mind working overtime to change the subject: "Look at how it's blowing out there!," "Could you do the washing up today?" or "Aunt Vicky wants to come and visit us again. But we don't want that, do we?"

He rarely objected. More than ever, he dreamed at the time of someone who could deliver him and make his life more bearable, and there was probably no-one better suited for that than Vicky. But his aunt also gave out such energy and enterprise that it made him feel guilty and a failure and feeble, and instead of trying to get the only person who could have given him a sense of home to come to him, he made plans to escape. The dream of giving it all up and fleeing became his drug and his hope. I'm getting out of here, I'm taking off, he thought time after time until at last it all came to a head. It was a morning in autumn. The war was over. Labour had come to power. They had dropped atom bombs on Japan and his mother had locked herself into her bedroom. If he had only been able to see a little clearer he would probably have known that she was ill. She seemed to be suffering from a psychological block so deep that she had virtually left this world and stepped into an alternative reality where she appeared to be waiting for something great and overwhelming to happen. "We must be looking our best when the time comes," she might say, creating an atmosphere of such madness that he was convinced that it was contagious and often the anger welled up in him: *What about me, what about me?*

He was not proud about it—there was precious little he was proud of—but when he heard his mother moaning as if in passion in her bedroom he could not stand it any longer. It was purely physical; at least that is what he would claim. That he was about to suffocate, that the raw smell of madness was poisoning him. That evening he packed a few clothes, books and a bottle of sherry in one of his father's old brown suitcases. At that time he did not touch alcohol, but he wanted to mark his departure and make it seem not just like an act of desperation but as a first step out into adulthood. When he saw the red clock tower at the railway station on Lord Street it was as if a shock ran through him, and he felt a growing intoxication, not just because of the sherry. The world lay before him. He was free and independent and that feeling lasted for hours, up to the moment when he vomited on a street corner on Portland Street in Manchester and the feelings of guilt and nausea mixed with everything else. Not only was the city bombed to pieces and full of ruins. A curtain of grit and coal enclosed the streets and had he not known that England had won the war he would never have believed it. Because of the electricity rationing, there was hardly anyone out after ten and everywhere he felt a sense of apathy. It was as if he encountered his own hopelessness on every street corner.

A sense of doom came to rest over his life. He lived in lodgings and shelters and often starved. He suffered. He was ashamed—how could he just have walked out on his mother?—and it is quite possible that he found salvation in the brown poster on Newton Street or, if salvation is too strong a word, it was certainly the beginning of some semblance of order. "Excellent career prospects in the police force for men and women with courage and character," it said, and Corell was perhaps not especially drawn by the words but there was something there. In fact there was often something there. A single word about a profession or destiny, of almost any kind, could get him dreaming, and God knows this something did not feel like much.

He just applied and nothing more was needed than a few formalities, a short interview and some papers to be filled in, and a couple of days later, before he knew where he was, a bus was taking him off for thirteen weeks of training in Warrington, and for a long time he saw it mostly as a game, an escapade. But time passed and an episode that was only meant to be incidental became a life, something regular. He got himself a poky little room on Cedar Street, not far from the Salvation Army, which smelled of gas and mould, and which had neither furniture nor wallpaper.

That was where he saw Vicky again. It was a spring day in 1947—although it might just as well have been any season, seen through his grimy black windows. He was twenty-one. In a photograph from the time when Corell first put on a uniform and his silly helmet, he looks desperate and undernourished. He could be a man of thirty-five just back from the war, but on the few occasions he saw himself in the mirror he thought he saw the same boy as before. He had no idea what impression he might make on someone who only remembered him from earlier. When he heard the knock on the door he was lying fully clothed on his bed.

"Leonard, Leonard. Are you there? For God's sake open the door," a woman was shouting outside, and of course he recognised the voice but he could not place it, and even when his aunt shouted, "It's Vicky, Leonard. It's me. I've been looking for you everywhere," he did not understand.

Reluctantly and in some confusion he shuffled towards the door. As he opened it, he gave a start, as if he had seen a ghost. It probably had nothing to do with his aunt. At that time she had not aged much. She was the same short-haired, lively Vicky as before, and bearing in mind all the broken people he had met, she was something of a miracle of class and dignity. What frightened him was rather the impression he himself provoked in her face.

"Leo, Leo. Is that really you? What have you done to yourself, and why haven't you been in touch? If you only knew . . ." she muttered, so emotional that he could not imagine that it was anything to do with him, but she had been looking for him everywhere. In her frenzied state she had rung around and eventually spoken to the police in Manchester and thanks to her persistence or her desperation, as she put it, she had been told that they were not aware of any injured or dead Leonard Corell, but that there was as it happened a cadet by that name. "Police cadet," she had said. "That can't be my Leo, not a chance." But she had still gone down to the police station on Newton Street and managed to find some information about where he lived. That is why she had come. He did not like it. Why should she care about him?

"I'll manage on my own," he said, and that was when his aunt exploded.

"Stop it," she shouted. "Stop! Why on earth should you manage on your own? You have a family, Leo. You have me, and I have been looking for you everywhere. I've turned the whole of England upside down. I've been beside myself with worry and I've thought . . . Don't look at me like that. What are you thinking? That I've come here to tell you off? I just want to see that you're alive. That you're on your feet. Don't you understand?"

"Leave me alone. Go away."

"Not on your life! But God, what's the matter with you? (He must have looked terrified.) Your mother is all right. She's ill, but we've got her into a home in Blackpool. So for God's sake, Leo, don't be so angry with me, and stop punishing yourself right now."

"I'm not punishing myself."

"Have you seen what you look like?"

"Stop it!"

"What's wrong with getting some help?" she shouted. "Don't you see that I've been sitting in my bloody flat in London, wanting nothing more than to help? I'm sorry too, Leo. I am so dreadfully sorry for what happened to James and you all, that I can hardly sleep at night. Do you have any idea how many times I've tried to come to your help? Every time I was stopped and I hang my head in shame for not having come anyway, and I couldn't stand the thought, I really couldn't, if you go the same way as your father."

"I'm not planning to kill myself, if that's what you think."

"No you certainly shouldn't. Definitely not," she said, quite beside herself, and he could not remember if it was then or later that their eyes met in a look of complete understanding.

It probably took Vicky some time to work her way past his pride but, after the meeting in his digs, they started to see each other from time to time, and every now and then he accepted help from her. He got money, dinners and clothes. But he declined the support that she was really offering: a chance for him to start studying again, a new opportunity. Stubbornly, he clung on to his job, maybe just to punish himself, or because he could not bring himself to take any more risks. He was being an idiot, quite simply. It was as if that was gradually dawning on him. But now there really was going to be a change, he promised himself as he sat there in the car.

A light fog lay over the roads and fields, and they were no longer passing many cars. At one point a bird flapped in front of the windscreen and Farley braked hard and felt the pain bite into his back. But it soon passed. He and Corell had been silent again for a while, and he would have liked to go on talking, not just because he enjoyed his conversation with the policeman but because he could not get over the thought that he might have missed something, some detail which could cast new light over the whole affair.

"This whole Alan Turing business seems to have become something very personal for you," he said.

"Well, yes . . . maybe."

"Have you spoken to your aunt about the case?"

"Why do you ask?"

"She's said to be a very wise and forceful woman."

"That may be."

"And I was thinking . . . but perhaps it's too personal . . ."

"Just ask!"

"Have your efforts on behalf of Turing . . ."

"Yes?"

". . . got anything to do with the fact that your aunt's homosexual?"

"Is she . . . ?" Corell began.

Then he sank into himself, and not with a single word, not with one gesture, did he betray what he was thinking. He rather stiffened into a smile, which could have meant anything.

"I've always . . ." he said at last.

"What?"

"I've always . . ." he repeated, but got no further.

After "I've always . . ." he had been about to continue with "disliked homosexuals," but he could not bring himself to say that, or anything else for that matter. A flood of thoughts and memories streamed through him; there was Vicky's thin, stiff body leaning on the silver-tipped cane. Those brown watchful eyes looking at him and the mouth with its mocking smile, there was Vicky who tucked him up in bed at night and gave him breakfast in the mornings. How he had longed for her! He looked out of the car window, rejoicing at every yard they were putting behind them, because he knew they were bringing him closer to her, and time and again he had thought about how he was going to tell Vicky everything that had happened in Cambridge, but now . . . no. It can't be right, it must be a false accusation. He was sure of it.

Or was he? She had always weighed her words so carefully and been mindful of his fragile self-esteem and tried hard not to hurt him, except of course for the time the other week when they talked about Turing . . . The idea needled him and he fought against it, as if against some terrible threat, and rehearsed arguments against it, whatever came to mind—her femininity, her love of children—but it was no good, nothing helped. He should have realised long ago. What Farley said was true and while the fog thickened out there the pieces fell into place; the visits from Rose, the absence of men, her brusque dismissal to family and friends when told "Go and get a man yourself," and then the impassioned defence of homosexuals: "Those who are different also have a tendency to think differently."

He tried to push it all out of his mind and fantasise about wonderful machines growing out of logical structures, but all he ended up with were grotesque and hopeless thoughts. Abbott and Pickens at Marlborough came back to him, and he imagined his aunt and Rose in dreadful positions, and he thought about Alan Turing lying dead with froth around his mouth in his narrow bed and he remembered the letter: *Is this the way my life was meant to be? One masquerade to conceal another!*

It was all nothing but lies!

"Damnation!"

"I'm sorry?"

"Nothing."

It was never anything. But he felt let down and furious. How could she? The walls of the car seemed to crowd in on him and he thought that not only had he lost what he had been looking forward to all afternoon, he had also been deprived of the only person he had on earth, and he wanted to punch his fist through the windscreen, but he just sat there, trying to control his breathing.

They were driving slowly because of the fog, and night had already fallen by the time they approached Knutsford. For a long time they had not said much to each other. Farley had quickly realised why Corell had fallen silent and he tried in every conceivable way to say that he understood and was sorry if he had been clumsy, but the policeman did not seem to want to touch the subject, and so Farley had engaged in small talk instead and recounted some anecdotes. He got carried away to such an extent that he had even come close to breaching his Official Secrets Act obligations, which was certainly not like him. He was so used to covering things up and keeping quiet that he sometimes told quite unnecessary lies. He might say to his wife that he had been to Scotland, when he had in fact been in Stockholm. Others made extravagant boasts about what they did during the war. The people from Bletchley were not allowed to say a word, and that had its effect on them. Keeping all these secrets had robbed Farley of his natural openness, and only on very rare occasions, such as this one, sitting next to the young policeman who seemed to be feeling so ill again, was he in the mood to talk. He wanted to be honest for once and say that Corell's instinct to dig around in Alan's past had been entirely correct. There was a real story buried there behind all the smoke. Alan had helped to shorten the war, perhaps as much as Churchill himself, and those in positions of responsibility had watched over him like hawks. But naturally he said nothing.

"Do you think she's awake?"

"She's a night owl."

There was a light shining in the window of the top floor, where Vicky normally sat and read. Apart from that, the property seemed unusually dark and menacing. It took a while before Corell realised that the light on the lamppost in the yard was broken and that the fog, which had lent such a ghostly feeling to the main roads, also lay over Vicky's place. For the first time ever, the house looked almost deserted. It seemed as if it had had its heyday, and was now just waiting to fall into total decay. He imagined his aunt up there as a lonely ruler over a forgotten and unhealthy, dark and crumbling castle. In a bittersweet daydream, he saw himself being thrown out of the house, and wandering away at dawn. With an effort, he rose out of his seat and as he got to his feet, the ground swayed.

He staggered but kept his balance, and he and Farley walked to the door together. He was overcome by a sense of indifference but, as he got nearer, the silence began to hurt. It was the kind of silence which precedes a painful experience and contains something explosive, and he listened eagerly for some other sounds than the crunching under their feet. In the distance, the noise of a car could be heard, dying away. Some small animal rustled in the bushes. It felt hard to ring the doorbell, and he turned towards the car. Should he ask to be driven home instead? He pressed the bell angrily and soon he could hear steps from inside and also the sound of a tapping cane. Long afterwards, he would often recall the rattling in the lock, and the rather short wait which seemed so long and uncomfortable, before Vicky stood there in the doorway. There was something about her face, something frightened. The vivacious eyes appeared bird-like and afraid.

"Dear me, dear me. What's happened?"

"He's been badly beaten up," Farley said.

"My God. Why?"

"It's a long story, but I have to say that I bear some of the responsibility for it myself!"

"What are you saying? Beaten up? That's crazy. But don't just stand there, now. Come in, both of you. My dear boy! I'll look after you now," she said, and turned towards Farley in an excited state. "I'm probably quite confused. But isn't it you?"

"What do you mean?"

"Farley, the expert on literary history. I loved your lecture on Yeats last autumn. I've got your book . . . but what are you saying? Could you . . . ? My God, my God . . . I don't understand. I really don't understand anything."

"I can explain . . ."

"You'll certainly have to do that! My God, Leo, let's get you into bed right away. If this is any of your fault, Dr. Farley, then help me at once. Don't just stand there! But my God, man, what's the matter with your back, and Leo, Leo, why aren't you saying anything?"

"I think he's in shock," Farley said, and then Corell felt for the first time that he wanted to say something, but he soon gave up.

He just glared, like a sulking child, and if there was anything he agreed with his aunt about then it was that he wanted to get into his bed upstairs right away, and slowly and without condescending to give Vicky even one glance he staggered up the stairs and with his aching head lay down and closed his eyes. He wanted to get away, away, to his own inner worlds, to the sweetness he had so often found in his self-pity, but he noticed with irritation that Vicky untied his shoelaces and ran her hand over his hair.

"Is there anything you want?"

"Nothing."

"We must call a doctor."

"No," he hissed.

"Are you mad, Leo? My God, what's going on?" his aunt said, and turned towards Farley, who had followed her up the stairs, and at that moment Corell opened his eyes again.

He looked at Vicky. She was very agitated and he half wanted to shout at her. He wanted her to suffer as he was doing and to see what it felt like to be let down and know that no-one ever said a single true word, that everything was just lies and fabrication, but not even now could he bring himself to do it. His chest filled with anger and every muscle in his body was tense. Yet his feelings were not entirely straight-forward.

Wildly conflicting emotions seemed to get in each other's way and he nevertheless wondered in fairly lucid terms if it was not unfair to pick a fight with Vicky when she was putting him to bed with such care. It was like returning a caress with a slap in the face. She meant no harm. She was just . . . he closed his eyes and thought about machines which pretended their way through peculiar tests, and about all the times his aunt had done things for him and somehow he understood that while he might perhaps not like homosexuals he could not very well dislike Vicky. She might be a pervert, but she was still the most precious thing in his life, and for want of anything else he stated very clearly that he wanted a beer, preferably a mild ale, and then a large glass of sherry.

39

FIVE DAYS LATER HE was back at work and at first he did not feel worried. The events in Cambridge seemed to have made him immune and he thought: *I couldn't care less about it. I couldn't give a shit if I lose my job.* But it was only a matter of time. The all-too-familiar daily grind brought back his usual self. His armour against the world cracked, and soon he was trembling at every telephone call, and every time the door opened. He imagined Chief Superintendent Hamersley coming in and proclaiming: "A Mr. Julius Pippard called." But nothing happened, not for a long time. His colleagues were even unusually friendly and not only enquired about his bruises but also asked after his aunt.

"She's a steely old bird. She'll be all right," he said.

But he was never really fully present. The days crept forward sleepily and the most sensational development at the police station was that a fellow officer, Charlie Cummings, was arrested for littering in the yard and was thrown off the force. Nobody could really explain why he had done it. But it was said that he was fed up with all the moaning and the hypocrisy, and apart from Alec Block—who slipped a careful comment to Corell that "my God, do I understand Cummings"—the general impression was that the man had a screw loose. Corell said that he had no opinion on the case. Generally, he kept his head down. He was very casual about his job, and he took a number of liberties. He went for long aimless walks even during working hours and on one such occasion he found himself approaching Harrington & Sons. The sun was beating down. Many people were out, and it was one of those days in Wilmslow when no-one seemed to be working, and he would have preferred to turn around or to disappear into Spring Street. Yet he kept going straight ahead. To go back would have been silly, he decided. But he could not stop himself from pausing to do up his shoelaces, just as he had once done outside Alan Turing's house. After that he walked on uncertainly and when he saw the tailor's dummies in the shop window, he started to whistle, but it did not quite sound relaxed; he was not a natural at whistling, so he stopped suddenly in mid-tune. There were a few customers in the shop. That was good. It would help him to pass more unnoticed, but then he spotted Julie, and as usual he felt not only happy, but also uncomfortable.

Julie on the other hand . . . she just stood there next to Mr. Harrington, and there was an emptiness in her face, a silent waiting for instructions, like a soldier in a sentry box, but then she broke into a smile which almost shocked him with its enthusiasm. She shone. She was beautiful. But he . . . he had the absurd thought that she was smiling at someone behind him and he must have appeared stiff. Now Julie's eyes looked worried and of course he tried to make up for his awkwardness. He took off his hat and made an effort to look both lively and worldly, but somehow it didn't quite come off. His smile strained at his cheeks and he felt that he was being observed. He wanted to disappear and obviously realised that he would cut a pathetic figure, but he saw no other way out. He just gave a peremptory nod and went off. He vanished with his ridiculous stride, and all the time his anger and humiliation grew. He was so worked up that he started kicking a red tin of beans which followed him rattling along a good bit of the way.

When he got back to the police station, Detective Sergeant Sandford informed him that Chief Superintendent Hamersley wanted to see him, and Corell answered with surprising peevishness:

"That's just typical!"

He had been waiting for this meeting for a long time, and his whole body filled with foreboding, but when the chief superintendent took a while coming, Corell had the time to pass through many stages and he began to hope that things would perhaps not be so bad after all. He even fantasised a scene in which Hamersley said to his fellow bosses in Chester: "He's got talent, that Corell. Have you read his report about the Turing case?" But then immediately he was thrown back into his worst fears and thought: It's obviously Pippard who has called or, even worse, Farley who's let me down and come to the conclusion that I have no judgement and am rotten, maybe even a traitor who leaks war secrets.

Slowly, Corell started to feel a rage, a defiance, and when Hamersley came in, Corell looked at him without understanding. The chief superintendent did not look the same as last time. His modern spectacles were gone and had been replaced by a more traditional pair. Had someone told him that the old ones were ridiculous? They shook hands. With a quick glance Corell tried to work out what was going on and thought that it did not appear to be so bad after all. Hamersley was not giving off his usual faint paternal smile. But neither did he look overly stern.

"And how's young Mr. Corell, then?"

"Well . . . very well, sir."

"I see . . . I'm glad. Have you had an accident?"

"Just slipped, sir."

"Must have been really bad, then. My goodness! It looks almost as if . . . there we are . . . Inspector, that's excellent!"

Ross came into the room, which did not improve the situation, and even though Corell knew that Ross disliked Hamersley, at that moment the two of them seemed to be conspiring against him.

"Let me come straight to the point," Hamersley said. "A few weeks ago I was speaking to some very senior church dignitaries, two bishops as a matter of fact, and I can tell you, they're worried."

"Priests!" Ross snorted fractiously.

"Yes, yes, I know of course that one shouldn't mix up one thing and another. Police work is one thing and religious matters another. But sometimes, gentlemen, the issues overlap. Don't you agree?"

"Sometimes maybe," Ross said.

"That's it. Corell, you remember our conversation a few weeks ago. We touched on one or two rather important subjects. Now unfortunately we have to take this one step further. Do some cleaning out even in our own backyard. Have you got a lot going on at the moment, by the way?" Hamersley turned to Corell.

"Not particularly," Corell answered, trying hard to work out what Hamersley was referring to.

"Good. Very good. There are things which need to be dealt with here and you won't be lacking support from above, because as I said: we're in the fortunate position of having with us both the Church and modern-minded politicians. Do you mind if I sit down, by the way? Thank you. Very kind of you. What do you say, Richard, isn't Corell a suitable candidate for this assignment?"

"Possibly," Ross said, sceptical.

"Possibly? I'm convinced that he's exactly the right person. Of course, it was unfortunate that he didn't get that dancer. But you can't always succeed. And it isn't easy either to get people to confess just like that. I would even venture to say that other methods are needed. We must take a step forward. Have one foot in the future. Surveillance is the word, gentlemen. A conventional method to be sure, but far too rarely used, especially in these situations. Don't you agree?"

Neither Ross nor Corell answered.

"Homosexuals are destroying our society and sapping the strength of the nation, we're all agreed on that. You should have heard the bishops. Do you know what they said? That it isn't just a question of male perversion. Even women . . . well, one would rather not think about it."

"Female homosexuality isn't illegal," Corell ventured.

"True, true. But do you know why, gentlemen? It wasn't criminalised so as not to give women any silly ideas. A woman's heart is after all so impressionable. No, I just mentioned it to illustrate how far this has gone and to remind us that we have to strike back. Take a tougher line, quite simply. I have therefore personally—yes, this really is my own initiative—started a co-operation with Manchester, and you may well then say: What have we got to do with that degenerate city? But I can tell you: some of the traffic from Oxford Road has moved here to Wilmslow. Now, don't look so shocked"—neither Ross nor Corell had registered any change of expression—"that's the unfortunate effect of the work that's been done. When you get a grip on things in one place you drive them elsewhere, and maybe the perverts think they're safer here. They probably imagine that life will be easier in Wilmslow. Now, don't take this as criticism of the criminal investigation department, or on second thoughts do, if you feel like it. People are often more naive in small communities. Let's make no bones about this. We're here to put things right. Have you heard of a hair salon on Chapel Lane called

Man and Beauty. Yes, I know, just the name, and some hair salon it is too. The man who runs it . . ." Hamersley took out a pad and looked at it, "a Jonathan Kragh. His salon seems to have become a meeting place for queers. People say they even accost each other openly. We've had reports from many sources, among others from Mrs. Duffy, who's helped us before. A very persistent lady, I have to say."

"An old gossip," Corell heard himself say.

"I beg your pardon?" Hamersley burst out.

"She may have her problems. But, if we're going to rely on sources like that, then I don't want to have anything to do with this assignment."

"What are you saying, boy?"

It was as if Hamersley did not want to believe what he was hearing.

"That I'm not going to do her bidding ever again."

"That's outrageous!"

"I'm only speaking the truth. She talks complete rubbish," Corell said.

"You shouldn't slander a woman who has been so committed to trying to help us all. Besides which I have to tell you . . ."

Hamersley glared at Ross, as if to get support for his indignation, and when the inspector shot in, "That's the way he is, I told you so," Hamersley got even more worked up, and started talking in a loud voice about "duty and responsibility, law and order," and he might very well have been able to reduce Corell to silence. He sounded extremely unctuous, but then he made a mistake. He pointed out that the danger is all around us:

"I hate to mention it, Corell. But I have compromising information about someone who is close to you."

"Are you referring to my aunt Vicky?" Corell said in an icy calm—he had no idea where it came from—and when Hamersley said with quiet menace, "Yes, since you say so. She's the one I mean," Corell stood up very quietly and at the same moment got the feeling that he was standing on stage, and was therefore glad to see that he had an audience. Sandford, Kenny Anderson and Alec Block were not far away and stood listening in astonishment, and before Corell opened his mouth again he made sure that he smiled, an extremely proud smile, as if the row were nothing other than a major triumph.

"In that case, my dear Chief Superintendent, I can inform you," he said, with emphasis on the word "dear" because he could see that it was very insulting, "that there are certain differences between you and my aunt. To start with, she's wise and deserves full respect. Secondly, she hates hypocrisy, and you, Mr. Hamersley, are probably the worst hypocrite I've ever met. But above all . . ."

"How dare you!" Hamersley interrupted, deeply agitated, and the mere realisation that he had made a chief superintendent lose his composure oddly strengthened Corell's calm, and lent even greater assurance to his words:

"No, no, you listen carefully to me, or come to think of it, it was perhaps a good thing that you interrupted me. I was just about to say something mean about how you seem to be a pansy yourself but, to be honest, I've started to wonder whether there really is any reason to make disparaging remarks about pansies. Queer would in any case be far too generous a name for you. You're nothing but a ludicrous weathervane blown about by other people's opinions. All you're good for is to persecute people who don't fit in with your tidy principles and I despise you for it. I despise you almost as much as I revere my aunt. Besides, I now have to leave. I'm assuming that I have a new job to find," he said with the same apparent calm, and he made as if to go. Yet he remained where he was and looked around in wonder. It was as if he were expecting something like the aftermath of a grenade attack, but Ross and Hamersley appeared to be more bewildered than furious and it was a second or two before the chief superintendent came to life and took one or two threatening steps forward.

"I have to tell you . . ."

"What?"

"That you've been standing here defying the law, and that's very serious. Do you hear me? There will be consequences for you," he shouted and Corell wondered for a moment if he ought to respond to that too, but instead he took his trilby from the coat stand and nodded briefly in the direction of Alec Block, who answered with a cautious smile.

Then he went towards the stairs and once he was well out in the yard his inner turmoil blended with something else and he smiled again, not a forced and theatrical smile like the one just before but one with something genuine and sincere about it which seemed to rise from his chest to his eyes and the further he walked the wilder and more defiantly the thoughts sang in his head: *Here goes a man who's capable of absolutely anything. He may even take the road past the gentlemen's outfitters on Alderley Road, because he's thinking of getting his hands on a pretty girl. Yes, that's how cheeky he is!*

But in the end he did not have the strength. The strain had taken its toll and he thought of Oscar Farley and wondered if he ought not really to be getting in touch with him now. The sun was about to go behind a cloud. A cooler wind drew in from the north and he started to dream of his bed, not the miserable bed in Wilmslow but the one waiting at his aunt's in Knutsford, and as he did so his head sank down towards his shoulder, as if he were about to fall asleep.

EPILOGUE

Introduction to the conference on Alan Turing at
Edinburgh University on June 7, 1986.

RICHARD DOUGLAS, Professor of Computer Sciences at Stanford
University—who has taken the main responsibility for this gathering—
opens the proceedings:

"Dear colleagues. Dear friends. I won't detain you for long. I just
want to say first of all how genuinely delighted I am that so many leading representatives from so many widely differing subject areas and
institutions have come to attend this first conference on Alan Turing.
My goodness, when I see you all not only do I feel pride in the very
depth of my heart. I also realise what an influence Alan Turing has had
in so many areas. What a remarkable person he was, such a man for all
seasons! What an extraordinary thinker!

"We have a busy programme ahead of us, with many fine speakers
and interesting seminars. After our introductory address, Hugh White-
more will be telling us about his play *Breaking the Code*, which is based
on Andrew Hodges's excellent biography *Enigma*, and which has its pre-
miere this autumn at the Haymarket Theatre in London with Derek
Jacobi in the lead role, Jacobi whom we all know from the television
series *I, Claudius*. Before lunch there will be what I'm convinced will
prove a very exciting panel discussion, focusing on the Turing test. All
shades of opinion are represented—even Professor John Searle is here.
He has promised to reveal some new thoughts about his famous theory,
'The Chinese Room.' This afternoon, Donald Michie will tell us about

Turing's dream of a machine which can learn from its mistakes, and compare it with the latest developments in A.I. research. We have this and much else to look forward to.

"Of course I also want to draw your attention to today's date. It is exactly thirty-two years since Alan Turing died at his home in Wilmslow, in the middle of such a sad time in our history. It was over the Whitsun weekend in England and the weather was dreadful. One person who was there and saw Alan Turing lying dead in his bed is with us here today. Ladies and gentlemen, I'm proud to introduce to you former police detective constable Leonard Corell, among other things honorary doctor here at Edinburgh. But I would imagine that in our company he doesn't need any more of an introduction. We all admire his work. Welcome to our gathering, Leo!"

Amid loud applause Corell comes on to the rostrum, dressed in a brown corduroy suit and black polo-neck. He has curly brown hair with grey streaks and a bald patch right on top of his head. He is lean and elegant and even if his body seems to be a bit stiff and slow there is great power in his voice. He speaks without notes, and appears to enjoy being on stage:

"If you enjoy my work," he begins, "tell my critics that right away.

"I've had to put up with quite a lot these last few years, and with some justification I suppose. For one thing I'm responsible for that absurd and misleading information in *The Times* the other day: that Apple's logo is an allusion to Turing's apple, and I must now once and for all clarify that this is pure nonsense, which can probably be put down to my fixation with that apple. Alas, I should have listened to my late friend Professor Farley, who used to say that one should pay no attention to symbols. Symbols are deceptive tools. A writer ought to leave them to the reader. But, above all, I should have realised that when Wozniak and Jobs launched their Apple II, there was virtually no-one who knew anything about Alan Turing's life, at least not all of it, and the reason I got such an idea into my head is that I knew more than I should, in my capacity as a special servant of the state, and then of course also that I so badly wanted that damned logo, clad as it is in the colours of the rainbow—which are becoming the colours of the whole gay movement—to be Alan's apple. Now they say it isn't so. Now we're told that the logo is a reference to Newton's shrivelled old apple, which of course as you all know apparently never fell on the physicist's head. Yet I wonder, and I'm not going to give up so easily. I still ask myself why a bite has been taken out of the apple. In some ways I ask myself if there isn't something of Turing in this after all.

"I am deeply touched to have been asked to make this introductory speech here today, not least because my wife, Julie, and my daughter, Chanda, whom I have not seen for so long, have travelled up from Cambridge, and because you are all here, all of you whose works I have read with such passion over the years. I too will not detain you for long, or go into the subtleties of 'The Chemical Basis of Morphology' as I usually do, or even wind up the data experts with my critical views on A.I. Instead, I will confess to an old vice. I'm a daydreamer. Maybe one of the worst that you will ever have come across. The only problem is that, when you're sixty, it's difficult to dream about the future and think: when I'm seventy, then the breakthrough will come, and the Hollywood contracts will arrive. (Well, stranger things have happened.) That's why I dream back into the past. I fantasise about building a time machine and travelling to Adlington Road. But instead of arriving on June 8, 1954, as I did back then, I appear on June 7, and do you know what I've got with me? Well, some of the excellent books that we've all written, but above all a trendy-looking new laptop. Just imagine! The rain is pouring down. It's Monday, Whit Monday and all is quiet in the neighbourhood. Maybe it's already growing dark, and I ring the doorbell. Nervous footsteps are heard on the stairs, and then the door opens, and there he is with his deep-set blue eyes, and he's probably very upset. Perhaps he's already wearing his pyjamas and has already dipped the apple in the pan. He says:

" 'Who are you?'

"I assume that I'm allowed into the house only reluctantly, and it's probably just as well for me to get right to the point:

" 'Dear Alan. I know your life better than you can even imagine and believe me, I know: right now, you're feeling terrible. You've been poisoned with paranoia and prejudice, but one day . . . one day we'll hold a conference in Edinburgh with hundreds of prominent people who have been researching you and your thinking, and here Alan, look at this, here is a universal machine, a computer as we call it now. In 1986, everyone has one, or nearly everyone anyway, and look at these books. They're about you. Isn't that remarkable? You're one of the great war heroes and are regarded as the father of an entirely new academic field. You're becoming an icon for the whole homosexual movement and are considered one of the most influential thinkers of the twentieth century.' And then, my friends, when I tell Alan Turing that, he smiles. At long last, I see him smile."

A NOTE ABOUT THE AUTHOR

David Lagercrantz is an acclaimed Swedish writer and crime journalist. He is the author of *The Girl in the Spider's Web,* the fourth novel in Stieg Larsson's Millennium series, and the coauthor of the best-selling autobiography by international soccer star Zlatan Ibrahimović, *I Am Zlatan Ibrahimović,* which was short-listed for the William Hill Sports Book of the Year Award and nominated for the August Prize in Sweden, as well as the author of three other novels and numerous biographies in Swedish.

A NOTE ABOUT THE TRANSLATOR

George Goulding was born in Stockholm, educated in England, and spent his legal career working for a London-based law firm. Since his retirement in 2011, he has worked as a translator of Swedish fiction.

A NOTE ON THE TYPE

This book was set in Monotype Dante, a typeface designed by Giovanni Mardersteig (1892–1977). Modeled on the Aldine type used for Pietro Cardinal Bembo's treatise *De Aetna* in 1495, Dante is a modern interpretation of the venerable face.

Composed by North Market Street Graphics, Lancaster, Pennsylvania

Printed and bound by Berryville Graphics, Berryville, Virginia

Designed by M. Kristen Bearse